Flashman's Winter

Robert Brightwell

Published in 2021 by FeedARead.com Publishing

Copyright © Robert Brightwell.

First Edition

A CIP catalogue record for this title is available from the British
Library.

Introduction

This book fills in two gaps in Flashman's career, hitherto uncovered by his memoirs. Readers of *Flashman in the Peninsula* may recall that when he met Robert Wilson, then commanding the Loyal Lusitanian Legion, reference was made to their earlier adventures in Russia. The opening chapter of *Flashman and the Emperor* also refers to Flashman and Wilson exacting revenge on the former French Police Minister, Fouché, after the execution of Marshal Ney. This tale is also included as a separate short story at the end of the book.

The bulk of this volume is taken up with Flashman's adventures in what was then Prussia, but which now comprises Poland, Russia and the Baltic states. In 1806 Prussia declared war on France and in a disastrous campaign lost most of its territory. Russia was forced to come to its aid and Britain too sent observers to assess how to help. Flashman and Wilson join this mission in what should have been a safe diplomatic visit – but of course was anything but.

From bloody, frozen retreats to battles in blizzards, they are soon in the thick of the action as a country fights for its very survival. Diplomatic intrigues follow and, with the aid of a Russian countess, our hero uncovers the enemy's plans – and works to thwart them.

Flashman's Winter is the eleventh book in the Thomas Flashman series. Chronologically, it fits between *Flashman and the Cobra* and *Flashman in the Peninsula*. *Flashman's Christmas* sits between *Flashman's Waterloo* and *Flashman and the Emperor*. As always, if you have not already read them, the memoirs of Thomas's more famous nephew, Harry Flashman, edited by George MacDonald Fraser, are strongly recommended.

Robert Brightwell

Chapter 1

"The captain says we are sure to founder, sir." Wilson looked ashen-faced as he delivered the message. He threw himself into a chair and buried his head in his hands. As if to emphasise his words there came a grinding noise from the keel beneath us. It was a baritone accompaniment to the soprano shriek of the wind whistling through several broken panes of glass in the stern cabin window.

The recipient of this portent of calamity stared at him impassively. Covered in blankets, his long unruly hair now wet and hanging down his face, he looked more like a half-drowned vagrant than a peer of the realm and royal emissary. Lips curling in irritation, he turned his gaze to me and shouted above the noise of the storm, "What the devil did he say?"

"Captain Dunbar says there is no hope," I yelled back over the tempest and another groan of twisting timbers. "He has thrown overboard everything he can to lighten the ship, but we are still stuck fast on this wretched sandbank." I swore under my breath, feeling a surge of self-pity. Lord Hutchinson glared at me as though I were personally responsible for this debacle. Our mission was over before it had begun, and it was a miserable end. The coast of Sweden was in sight, but we would never reach it, not alive anyway. I was destined to die amongst a tangle of ropes, splintered wood, freezing water and in the company of one of the most objectionable men I had yet met.

Wilson and I had just spent the last hour with the crew desperately passing rocks from the ballast up through the ship to go over the side, but it had made little difference. The huge waves were pushing the vessel along the bottom and now she was taking on water through strained planking.

"What about the boats?" demanded his lordship, glancing across the cabin to where his brother Kit sat in the corner.

"They would be snatched away in the wind if they tried to launch one," I explained. "Even if by some miracle they got one down in the lee of the ship, it would not last two minutes before it was swamped in this storm." Like the exhausted Wilson, I felt close to despair myself.

Our best chance now seemed to be holding on to some wreckage when the vessel finally broke up. It would be a desperate business in this blow, but if it abated, it was still possible a few might survive.

Despite our alarming predicament, his lordship showed no great concern. Indeed, he continued to glare at me with distrust, as though he suspected that I was about to make my way off the ship alone in the jolly boat. Damn me, but I would if I stood the ghost of a chance in it. Then his brow cleared as he grunted, "Berkeley told me you had served time in the Navy, so I suppose you know what you are talking about." A slight smile crossed his features and he gave a snort of amusement. "Your father-in-law at least will be pleased with today's work. He also made clear that he would be delighted if you did not return from our endeavour."

"The treacherous bastard," I muttered in disgust. It was no great surprise that Berkeley wanted me dead; he had tried to have me killed before I married Louisa. I had naïvely thought he had used his influence to get me appointed to this doomed diplomatic endeavour to help me support his daughter. Now I realised that he was probably already making plans to end her brief and imminent widowhood.

A thudding noise started above my head, but I ignored it as the ship lurched once more. A large wave slammed into the stern, breaking another of the windows and sending several more streams of water gushing into the cabin. "The devil with it," muttered his lordship, hauling himself to his feet and shrugging off the now soaked blanket. His major general's uniform underneath was wet and rumpled to match its owner. There was also a soup stain down its front from an unsuccessful attempt at eating supper. He looked over to where his younger brother still sat, nervously holding on to the table edge. Looking his kin in the eye, he gave a small shrug of apology for dragging him into this mess. That slight gesture probably spoke a thousand words between them as Kit gave a wan smile in reply.

Wilson must have seen the silent exchange for he suddenly wailed, "This is all my fault. Every time I am in a bloody ship it nearly sinks."

"*Nearly* sinks," repeated Hutchinson. "Then we must keep some hope." He glanced up at the planking above our heads, "What is that thudding? Are you sure they are not trying to launch a boat?"

"I will go and see," I offered. In truth I just wanted to be away from that cabin and have a moment to myself. I fondly remembered my last farewell from Louisa. Despite everything, I could not comprehend that I would be denied her arms around me again. I lurched out into the companionway as the deck rocked beneath me. I was just contemplating going to my cabin to await our inevitable destruction, when I realised that Wilson had followed me.

"I thought I would give his lordship some time alone with his brother," he explained, before leading the way to the ladder. He was several inches taller than I and stooped low under the deck timbers. Even half drowned in soaking clothes he maintained the soldierly appearance of a cavalry officer. Reluctantly, I followed. I was drenched once again with spray before my head was through the hatch. Wilson had already been knocked off his feet by the wind. He was holding on to a stanchion on the far side of the deck, shouting something that was lost in the clamour of wind and waves. The ship shuddered from another impact and looking up I saw spray break over two men high in the mizzen top. At first, I was surprised that they had risked the climb until, wiping the seawater from my eyes, I saw what they were doing. They had lashed themselves to the top and were wielding axes on the base of the topmast. It was already swaying as now I noticed that the staying ropes had already been cut. My head whirled around to confirm the source of the thudding we had heard below. Sure enough there were more axes at work at the bases of the main and foremast.

Captain Dunbar stood nearby, a rope around his waist securing him to a rail, as he watched his crew dismast his ship. Judging a break in the waves, I rushed towards him and quickly wrapped an arm around one of the rails nearby. "What the hell are you doing?" I demanded. "We will never survive here without masts?"

He grimaced as his face caught a burst of spray and then took a deep breath to reply. Even then I only caught some of his words above the wind. "…Won't survive with them…only weight left we can lose." There was a splintering above us and the mizzen top was snatched away as though grabbed by a giant hand. One of the axemen was knocked flying, saved only by the rope around his waist.

I stared around to get my bearings. There was a lighthouse five miles off our beam, but it had ignored our signal guns of distress, as had a ship that had sped past down wind. Not that there was much that either could do. Had the ship tried to put about, it would probably have had the sticks torn out of her. Since then, the guns had gone over the side, along with pretty much everything else. We knew that there was at least fifteen feet of water all around us and our frigate, HMS *Astraea*, only drew eighteen. One good shove and we could be free, although without masts we could then easily be blown onto the rocky shore beyond.

I watched the seamen toil with their hatchets and felt a twinge of hope that we might see this day out after all. Heaven knew how much the masts and all the sails and cordage weighed, especially soaked through, but it had to be a good few ton. Dunbar was an experienced seaman and it was not his fault we had run aground. We were in the narrow channel known as the 'sleeve' between the coast of Sweden and Denmark. It was a funnel into the Baltic and the currents were strong, constantly moving the submerged sandbanks so that charts were quickly out of date. There was the sound of more splintering and first the mainmast and then the foremast came crashing down over the port side of the ship. Dunbar led the rest of us forward, armed with knives, cutlasses and boarding axes, anything to cut ropes and get the wreckage over the side before our lightened hull could capsize. We hacked and sawed at ropes with blades held by frozen fingers as though our lives depended on it – which they did – careful not to get our feet entangled in cordage as it was ripped away by wind and waves. The port rail was nearly under water, breakers rolled across the deck and at least two men were carried over the side. I thought we would never be rid of the wretched spars, but as another surge of water swept across the deck, I felt a rope end pulled from my hand.

Our success was acclaimed by a mighty fork of lightning that split the black clouds above us. As the resulting thunder crashed out louder than any broadside, I did not hear Dunbar shout, but saw his mouth open as he waved his arms wildly above his head. Yet I did not need to understand him, for at that moment the vessel moved as though balanced on a pivot. We turned ninety degrees and then joyously and unmistakably, the hull rose to meet the next wave.

We were free and I remember Wilson hugging me in relief as we cheered along with the rest of the crew. A wave washed over both of us knocking us from our feet, but I did not care. We were saved and my father-in-law would be deprived of seeing his daughter in widow's black for a while longer. The thought made me turn back to the hatch, just in time to see Hutchinson and his brother emerge. They must have tired of waiting for us to report and come to see what was happening for themselves. The moving planks beneath their shoes answered their question. I watched as his lordship stared about in surprise at the lack of masts and rigging above their heads. He looked back at the quarterdeck, presumably searching for the captain, but Dunbar had gone forward to the chains. In the storm the captain stood no chance of hearing the leadsman call out the depth unless he was beside him. As I got to my feet, I felt a jolt and knew that the anchor cable had been cut. We were now moving with the sea, rather than fighting against it. When I looked again Hutchinson was disappearing back down the hatch, apparently satisfied that all was under control, while his brother roared with laughter and relief into the wind like a madman.

The sense of salvation did not last long, however, for while we were now safe from grounding, we were taking on water faster than the pumps could push back over the side. Already three feet of it was sloshing in the hold and as it shifted its weight with every wave there was still the risk we could capsize. Wilson, Kit and I took our turn on the pumps that night, as did the other officers and men, to keep the inflow to a minimum. It was backbreaking work, and the hands changed every fifteen minutes. Despite our efforts the water level in the well crept up to five feet.

9

We had got free of the sandbank at around six in the evening, when it was already dark in those latitudes in late November. Dunbar's original plan was to anchor again in deeper water until dawn, before navigating the rest of our passage. The stove was lit and hot food provided as well as a large tot of rum for all. Meanwhile several sailors had rigged a jury sail on what was left of the mizzen mast to keep us pointed into the wind, which by then had dropped to a mere gale. Yet any thought of complacency was diminished by a glance into the hold where several lanterns illuminated the progress of our losing battle with the Baltic Sea. By midnight it was clear that we were unlikely to still be afloat by dawn. The anchor was raised and once more we were cast adrift with just a small triangle of sail to guide us in the right direction.

We used the lighthouse as our guide and then, in the early hours, we spotted another to show we were on the right track. Dawn found us near the Swedish shore and two boats put out to us to help stem the worst leaks and give some relief to those manning the pumps. The wind now took us south and by ten in the morning we dropped anchor again off Elsinore in Denmark. We had sailed twenty-five miles with a sail little bigger than a pocket handkerchief and by then had thirteen feet of water rolling below decks.

I cannot say I was sorry to leave HMS *Astraea,* which looked like she might founder yet in the harbour. Instead, as we were rowed ashore, I stared up at the imposing ramparts of Kronborg Castle, which dominated the anchorage. My thoughts turned again to our mission. Acting as a diplomatic observer did not sound like an arduous task, which was why I had jumped at the opportunity. I imagined warm, comfortable beds, royal banquets and pretty ladies-in-waiting, while we earned recognition at home from our gathering of court gossip. It certainly seemed a lot safer than my earlier roles as soldier and sailor. I really should have paid more attention to that castle, for it was the home of Prince Hamlet, immortalised by Shakespeare. If you think that play is full of treachery, madness and intrigue, well read on. The only thing this tale lacks is a ghost!

The governor of Kronborg Castle was quick to provide hospitality to envoys from the British government. The night we arrived was the first since I had left England that I was warm, well fed and able to take my ease. As well as having time to rest before we continued our journey, we also had the opportunity to catch up on the latest news. Things were moving quickly in Eastern Europe, which was the reason we were there in the first place.

Back in 1805 a coalition against Napoleon's France was formed by various allies including Britain, Austria and Russia. Despite various entreaties, the only other significant power in the region, Prussia, chose to remain neutral. The coalition enjoyed mixed fortunes; Britain had beaten the combined French and Spanish navies at Trafalgar, but a few weeks later Napoleon had crushed the Russian and Austrian armies at Austerlitz. After the battle Austria was forced to sue for peace and Russia to retreat to its own territory.

A year later and for reasons that defy understanding, Prussia decided that while it had not wanted to risk joining a coalition, it could now beat Napoleon on its own. It had the mighty Prussian army that, twenty years before, had been commanded by Frederick the Great to a series of impressive victories. Its officers were supremely confident that they could beat the man they dismissed as the 'Corsican Corporal'. Sadly, their elderly generals had failed to appreciate that military tactics had changed since their heyday. Their famed iron discipline was no match for Napoleon's flexible system of army corps. Each French marshal had a force of twenty to thirty thousand men including infantry, cavalry and artillery, capable of fighting on their own or in coordination with others. At the twin battles of Jena and Auerstedt the Prussians were roundly thrashed by a French army half its size. Ironically, it was not even the 'corporal' who beat them; most of their army was defeated by the tenacious Marshal Davout, a man I was to know well a few years later.

A dominant Napoleon was soon in Berlin, while the Russians hurried men forward to protect their western border and support the routed Prussians. The balance in Europe was shifting in favour of the French, and vital supplies that Britain needed from this region, such as tar and timber for the Navy, were in jeopardy. London decided to send an envoy who could report on this fast-changing situation and help shore up allied resistance against Paris. Their representative needed to be someone with military experience, but who also possessed immense tact and charm to deal with the humiliated Prussian king as well as defeated Prussian and Russian generals. The envoy had to persuade them to continue their resistance, while assessing what support Britain could provide. Quite how they alighted on Lord John Hely-Hutchinson for this role is beyond me, as someone less suitable is hard to imagine.

It is true that Hutchinson had military experience. He had inherited command of the British army in Egypt back in '01 and forced the French garrisons to surrender in both Cairo and Alexandria, driving them from the country. However, he had been so unpopular amongst his fellow officers due to his unsoldierly appearance and scathing demeanour, that some had tried to block him getting the command. From just a brief association with his lordship, my sympathies were entirely with these mutineers. Hutchinson had all the charm and tact of a bear with its balls caught in a trap. He was the most rude and curmudgeonly individual I had yet come across. It was absolutely no surprise to learn that he was an acquaintance of my father-in-law. The pair both took a delight in making others as despondent as them. From what I could gather, his appointment was solely due to him being a confidant of King George.

Neither his younger brother Kit nor I had any diplomatic experience, and my first impressions of Wilson were not favourable either. He had served with Hutchinson in Egypt, which was why his lordship had invited the major to join us, but I could not imagine how or why the two men would get on. They were complete opposites: Hutchinson was stooped, unkempt and wore a permanent scowl; Wilson was over six foot, usually immaculately turned out in his cavalry uniform and as energetic and cheerful as a puppy chewing on a sugar cone. As I surveyed our party, our mission looked as doomed as the sinking frigate in the harbour.

The following day we set off together in a carriage on the twenty-five-mile journey to Copenhagen. Despite Nelson attacking the Danish fleet there five years before, relations between Denmark and Britain were surprisingly good. Surrounded by more powerful neighbours, the Danes could not afford to make too many enemies. Hutchinson sat in the corner of the vehicle glumly staring out at the snow-covered countryside and spoke only to complain about the cold. To fill the silence, Wilson prattled on about how the houses reminded him of England. He had a huge bearskin to keep him warm, which, as a dutiful toady, he had offered to our chief. Hutchinson had declined, muttering something about fleas, and consequently Wilson had shared it with me. He told me that the bearskin had been recommended to him by someone who knew Russian winters well and suggested that I acquire one myself. I took his advice, which I am sure saved my life.

We reached the city just after dark and found rooms in Bowe's Hotel. We did well to get them as the city was full of Prussian refugees, often with harrowing tales of ravaging French armies. Their reports confirmed that the Prussian kingdom, which had once stretched in a wide swathe all the way down to Austria, was now reduced to just a small strip of territory to the east and a handful of fortresses, mostly along the coast. The once proud army had almost entirely melted away either in desertion or taken prisoner.

"The French will soon mop up what's left," predicted Hutchinson. "We had better not delay too long here or Prussia will cease to exist before we reach her." I confess that I thought he was right. The inexperienced armies of Russian serfs being rushed east were intended only to support the more professional Prussian soldiers. Now they would find themselves in the front line against Napoleon's marshals and, based on their performance at Austerlitz, the Russians would not put up much resistance. With luck, I thought, we would be home again in a few weeks and while our mission might have been a failure, no blame would be attached to us. I would be back to annoy my father-in-law with my very existence and warier now of any new 'opportunities' he pushed my way.

We had to wait a week for another naval vessel to take us on up the coast. If the time we were delayed was representative of the diplomatic life, then I was all for it. While his lordship only stirred himself to meet ministers and royalty, Wilson, Kit and I were invited to a range of dinners, receptions, theatres and even the palace. Most of the Danish gentry spoke English and we had a fine old time. We met a couple of Danish princesses and even saw the king once at the theatre. He was acting very oddly, pacing up and down inside his box and then peeking out from behind the curtains like a child. When I pointed this out, I was told that the king was stark raving mad. His queen had been sleeping with his doctor, while he had cavorted round every brothel in the city. A crown prince ruled the country now, which was probably just as well as the king had a habit of scrawling lewd drawings on papers presented for his signature.

As we toured the city, I was amused to see Wilson presenting copies of a book he had written as gifts. He must have had at least a dozen of them in his sea chest. The book was his account of the Egyptian campaign. It had caused a stir when first published as he had accused Napoleon of murdering some five hundred of his own wounded to avoid them falling into the hands of the Turks. The French had hotly denied the claim. I thought this unlikely as it meant that they would have murdered *all* their wounded, rather than just the ones they were unable to move. Wilson was sure that his source was reliable and was disappointed to find that his tome was not available in any Danish bookshops. With the virulent anti-French sentiment, particularly among Prussian refugees, he was sure that he could sell many copies and planned to write to his publisher.

That week in Copenhagen was the most pleasant we were to experience for many a month, for soon we would all have far more pressing matters to worry about. Ahead lay almost unbearable hardships that tested the limits of human endurance. It saw victories that felt like defeats, monumental incompetence, blind courage and ultimately a defeat that led to a victory. But all that was to come. Mercifully back then we were in ignorance of our fate, or I would never have boarded the sloop HMS *Sparrow*, which was to take us on the next stage of our journey.

Our precise destination was in some doubt. The course was set for the port of Danzig, but we feared it might not be in Prussian hands when we got there. If it had fallen to the French, we planned to proceed further up the coast until we reached the last Prussian port of Memel, assuming that had not capitulated as well.

Wilson was right that he was cursed as a seafarer, for we had barely got out of Copenhagen when this new vessel grounded on a sandbank. We had a local pilot aboard, but clearly these mounds move quickly in the current. Fortunately, there was no damage and we got off without too much difficulty…only to head into another storm. We were blown past Danzig yet somehow managed to tack our way back. Half a dozen telescopes were trained on the flag flying from a building on the shore. While I could not make out what it was with my glass, I could see that it was not the tricolour of France.

The city of Danzig is a short distance up a channel that is linked to the Vistula River, the largest river in the region, which gives good access to the interior of the country. From half a mile out to sea it looks a pretty place with towers and domes of churches appearing behind city walls and large houses visible on the edge of the surrounding forest. From a closer inspection, however, it did not bear up so well. Most of the buildings are wooden medieval affairs that lean over the dark and dirty streets. We were there for a few days as we tried to discover what was happening in the rest of the country. Rumour had it that the French were marching further inland to face an army of Russians and Prussians that were combining forces, but no one knew for sure. Some twelve thousand Prussians had been left to defend the city, but it would be no easy task. Apart from two strong bastions, the rest of the city walls were as ancient as the houses and in need of repair. We paid our respects to the garrison commander, a man near eighty years of age. He assured us that the city walls would be reinforced and stronger when 'those bastard Austrians arrived'. Lord Hutchinson gave a heavy sigh before pointing out that on this occasion his enemy was, in fact, the French.

We quickly discovered that the Prussian court had no confidence in the defence of Danzig either and had retreated further up the coast to the city of Konigsberg, halfway between Danzig and Memel. We would have to follow them. Yet the stay in Danzig was not entirely wasted, for while walking the streets I found a furrier and bought myself a thick bearskin as Wilson had suggested. None of us relished the prospect of a further sea voyage and so we decided to travel on by carriage. Hutchinson and Kit sat on the forward-facing seats while Wilson and I settled in opposite. It was another freezing morning and our breath had only just started to defrost the carriage windows when his lordship looked up and barked, "Well, gentlemen, what do you make of Danzig?"

"They have over three hundred and fifty cannon on the walls and in other defences," started Wilson. "I spoke to some of their officers who said they were sure that they would give Bonaparte a bloody nose if he tried to assault the city." He pulled his bearskin tighter around his shoulders and added, "But I doubt that the French will start a siege now. They will go into winter quarters and wait until the spring."

Hutchinson nodded to indicate that such a thing was possible and then turned his gaze to me. "And you, Mr Flashman, what is your opinion?"

I had kept quiet as I had reached an entirely different conclusion to these more experienced soldiers, but now I took a deep breath and blurted out, "I think the city will fall."

"And why is that?" probed Hutchinson, with, I thought, a touch of menace in his voice.

"The garrison commander is a senile old fool, who probably has not seen action in twenty years. Great stretches of the walls are weak, and some have already started to collapse. I saw what siege guns can do in India and I doubt that they will hold out here for long."

"The Prussians are strengthening them," interrupted Wilson, but Hutchinson held up a warning finger to allow me to continue.

"Even the Prussian king does not think the city can hold," I went on, "or he would have stayed here to lead its defence. But to leave

16

twelve thousand men in a doomed city when most of his army has already been destroyed is madness. He needs all the men he can get."

Hutchinson nodded again. "You surprise me, Mr Flashman. Berkeley told me you were a feckless fool, but I see you have some sense." Before I could take any dubious pleasure from that remark, he added, "Of course, you are both wrong." Then he rapped his cane top on the roof of the carriage to signal it to stop. A minute later and we were all standing on the icy road, staring back at the city we had just left. "Well, gentlemen, what do you see?" demanded Hutchinson.

We stared about us, puzzled at what we were missing. The city walls facing us were one of the strongest sections as they protected Danzig from any attack up the river. "The ramparts are much weaker on the other side," I muttered defensively.

"Never mind the walls," Hutchinson snapped. "Look there." He pointed to the several miles of flat land between the city and the sea. "That is where the French will go. They will surround the city and stop it getting supplies by sea, then they have only to wait. Unless they want to starve, the Prussians will have to sally out from behind their walls and clear a passage for ships to reach the city." He turned to Wilson, "You said you spoke to the officers; did you speak to the common soldiery?"

"I tried but they were hard to understand," he admitted.

"Many are Poles," explained Hutchinson. "They have seen Prussia and Russia swallow up their old kingdom and I doubt they have much of a wish to die for their conquerors. More than a few are likely to escape over the walls rather than defend them. Some might even join the French."

"Surely not," protested Wilson. "They must have heard the stories of how the French have treated Prussian civilians, not to mention the tyrant's other crimes."

"Robert," started Hutchinson, and I was to learn that his rare use of first names was usually to soften acerbic criticism. "You must not let your hatred of Bonaparte blind your judgement. There will be many Poles who will have heard of the principles of the French Revolution. They will see him as a potential liberator, however misguided that may be." His lordship's gaze turned back to me. "Flashman, you are right that the Prussian king needs all the men he can get, but he also needs time. A small garrison would see the city fall quickly to the French, who would then head on north to Konigsberg. Twelve thousand men should ensure that the city holds out at least a month or two, which should allow the Prussians to re-organise themselves and combine forces with the Russian army."

That appeared to be the end of the conversation and, as we got back into the carriage, I began to realise that I had misjudged Hutchinson. While Wilson and I had explored the city, accepted invitations to the officers' mess, been to the theatre and bought supplies, he had been making a careful assessment of the fast-changing situation we found ourselves in. I could not fault his judgement either, which meant we might be in this freezing carbuncle of a country for longer than I wished.

We rattled on through the countryside, but the roads got steadily worse and by lunchtime we found ourselves at the end of a fifty-mile-long spit of sand and shingle. It ran between the sea and a huge inland lagoon called the Fischer Gaff. This exposed strip of land with just a few clumps of bent fir trees for shelter was said to be the quickest route to Konigsberg. It may well have been on horseback, but in a carriage the progress was tortuous. The road, made from boulders taken from the sea, jolted us about until we began to feel seasick. When we weren't experiencing spine-jarring jolts from the stones, the carriage would get bogged down in dunes of sand that had blown across our path. Eventually, we all got down and walked for a while to rest our bodies. The coast there is famous for amber and we strolled along the shoreline, dodging the waves, as it is easiest to spot when the stones are wet. The coachman rushed down to tell us that the gathering of amber was illegal under penalty of transportation, but Hutchinson just laughed. "Let the king come this far south to reprimand me and I will give him his pebbles back."

It was ten o'clock at night when we finally reached the town of Pillau, which guarded a break made in the spit to allow shipping to use the lagoon. There was no hotel here, just a room we all had to share

18

with two strangers, one of whom snored loudly enough to wake the dead. Wilson and I rose early the next morning and went to explore the fortress on the edge of town. It looked strong, at least, with walls that were star shaped if you could look down from above. It would be formidable to attack as the only approaches were by sea or along the exposed strips of sand and shingle that ran north and south.

I was tired and grumpy. The sooner this miserable mission was over and I was back home the better. Even Wilson was despondent that morning. His back hurt and he was dreading our return to the carriage. A short ferry ride took us over the sea channel and then a whole day of further uncomfortable travel awaited us on the northern strip before we were to reach our destination.

Chapter 3

The new Prussian capital of Konigsberg was at least grander than Danzig. The streets were wider and well laid out with several impressive squares. In one, in the centre of the city, a gallows had been set up and at first glance it looked like two soldiers had been hanged. However, on closer inspection they turned out only to be effigies, which we later discovered were of two Prussian generals who had defected to the French. Of those that had not been captured, few Prussian generals remained in service. Some had retired in shame at their failure and several more, their units destroyed, had applied to join the Russian service.

The city itself was crowded and there was an air of desperation about the place. All hotels were full, but we managed to get some attic rooms in a lodging house. On each landing we had to squeeze past trunks of possessions as residents remained packed and ready to leave at a moment's notice. Konigsberg was heaving with refugees, many still distraught and only too keen to tell you about their escape and all they had lost. Rumours circulated the streets like blown autumn leaves. Some claimed that the French army had already stopped their advance, others were sure that they would be here in days, while yet more insisted that the rump of the Prussian army had joined the Russians, and all would now be well. Hutchinson wrote to the court to advise them of our presence, but they were not receiving visitors – the queen was said to be suffering from nervous exhaustion. Wilson, whose back now hurt him to sit, spent part of a morning prowling up and down the street outside the small mansion that now served as the palace. He swore that he saw both the king and queen staring glumly out of the windows at their much-reduced domain.

We still had no information about what was really happening in the country to send back to London. Then we learned that the Russian commander, Marshal Kamenski, had left his army to report to the Prussian king. A meeting was arranged with Kamenski and two Prussian generals to update Hutchinson. The rest of us eagerly awaited his return, hoping for some firm news rather than gossip.

His lordship's features were even grimmer than usual when he finally re-joined us. "Gentlemen," he barked at us, "we should follow the example of the Prussian civilians and remain packed and ready to move."

"It cannot be that bad," protested Wilson. "Kamenski is a very experienced commander and the Vistula will be a major obstacle for the French to cross."

Hutchinson gave him a pitying look. "The entire French army is already across the Vistula. Kamenski is a sickly fool who has made no effort to defend the eastern bank. His army is still pulling back, around a hundred and twenty miles south of here. When I asked him what his plans to defend Prussia were, he admitted that he had none. Instead, he complained that the tsar had refused to allow him to resign his commission due to ill health. The Prussian generals tell me that he is trying to persuade the king to sue for peace." He gave a snort of disgust and added, "I have seen more fight in a corpse!"

There was a stunned silence as we took this in. There were now no significant obstacles between the French and Konigsberg, or indeed the rest of Prussia. Napoleon's army would prefer winter quarters in a large comfortable city to being out in the countryside. There had been a thaw in the weather over the last few days, leaving the roads muddy rather than frozen solid. The French army could be here if they chose in five or six days.

"What are we going to do?" asked Wilson.

"Well," replied Hutchinson, "you, Kit and I are going to dinner at the palace with the king." He turned to me, "You are staying here. The palace does not provide dinners to humble captains." The snub rankled, but I was not too annoyed. I would probably have a better time without them. I had to admit that Wilson in his full fig cavalry major's uniform and medals looked far more at home in a court than I did. My captain's commission was in a highland regiment, but I was damned if I was freezing my bollocks off under a kilt in the Prussian snow. I would stick to my old plain red uniform coat with one epaulet, no medals and a pair of warm trousers.

I watched them go off in their finery. Even in the full dress kit of a British general, Hutchinson still managed to look as though he had slept in a hedge. Then I settled myself down with a bottle of schnapps and a stew that the innkeeper swore was beef, yet looked and tasted suspiciously like horse.

With the future of his country hanging by the slenderest thread, I imagined the Prussian king was pulling his allies around him and making desperate plans for the survival of his nation. Not that I could see any stratagem that would work. His best hope was to seek refuge with Tsar Alexander on Russian territory. I had seen slaughterhouse pigs with a more promising future than Prussia. Our landlord was of the same view. When I asked him what he thought would happen, he gave a sly grin and opened a drawer. Inside was a roughly sewn French flag that his wife had made in anticipation of their next guests.

I half expected Hutchinson to announce our imminent departure on his return from the palace and so foolishly stayed up waiting for news. I thought we would spend the next morning in the docks looking for passage away from the city. Instead, when the party came in, they had not a care in the world. To my astonishment, Wilson recounted that he had spent most of the evening talking about uniforms. The king was obsessed with the appearance of his army and they had discussed how he had earned the cross of a knight of the order of Maria Theresa. I stared at them in astonishment, wondering if they or I was going mad. Kit told me that his brother had presented the king with a letter from our own King George, but as this was some two months old it was hardly timely advice. When I looked to his lordship for some pithy summary of the evening, his only conclusion was that the wine was awful. And with that, he turned for his room.

"But what of the war?" I exploded. "What is the king planning to do to save his country from the French?"

"He is expecting the Russians to beat his enemies for him," called out Hutchinson over his shoulder as he left.

Alone again, I poured myself another glass and concluded that the rest of the world was insane rather than I. The idea that the Russians, who had already abandoned the best natural barrier, would now stop running, turn around and beat the French was absurd. Even their commander admitted that the war was lost. A king who was more interested in the braiding on tunics than the future of his country, deserved to lose his throne. By all accounts, it was his wife who had the backbone between the pair of them. Bonaparte had started rumours that the Prussians had only joined an alliance with Russia because she and the tsar were lovers. Now she hated the French emperor with a passion. Sadly, she was too ill to attend the dinner, but I imagined she would use what little strength she had left to box her husband's ears when she learned how he had squandered the evening.

I awoke the next morning with a sore head from too much schnapps. My mattress was the bearskin, which stopped some of the draughts and softened the hard floorboards beneath me. Hutchinson was the only one of us with a bed and straw mattress although it was, he said, thin and lumpy. I was aware of a ringing sound and for a while I was not sure if it was inside my skull or not. No, it was outside, a church bell. Then as I listened another started up. It wasn't Sunday, I was sure of that. I sat up suddenly in alarm, instantly regretting the move as my head throbbed. A third bell had started to ring: were the French here already?

I roused the others and we dressed hurriedly. By the time we got out onto the landing the stairs were hopelessly jammed with other residents shouting that the French were coming and there was not a second to spare. It took us a full five minutes to negotiate the stairs, squeezing past fat *Frauen*, and their children, men hauling heavy trunks and the landlord blocking the way, demanding people paid their accounts before they left. I noticed that his French flag was on his desk ready for use. When we finally emerged onto the street the pandemonium was in full flow, with carriages trying to force their way through crowds moving in all directions.

"Should we try for the port?" I asked. We had no horses; our best hope of escape was to get a ship out into the lagoon and then on into the open sea.

"We are not going anywhere until I know what the hell is going on," barked Hutchinson. At that moment a mounted dragoon appeared at the end of the street and seeing the panic all around him, he fired his carbine into the air. For a moment I thought he was French, but then I realised that the coat was Prussian black. He was shouting something to those about him. While we could not hear his words due to the hubbub all around us, I saw several women sink to their knees in the dirt. Fearing we were already trapped, I followed in his lordship's wake as he roughly pushed his way through the throng. As we drew close, the horseman recognised our red coats and shouted his news in English. It was the last thing we expected to hear.

"A victory?" I repeated in disbelief. "How can that possibly be?" The dragoon knew nothing more and said that even the king was waiting to hear the details.

"We should go to the palace," suggested Kit, "then we can hear the news as it comes in." Nodding in agreement, his brother led the way down the street to the royal residence where a crowd was already gathering. Not content to wait with the masses, Hutchinson pushed his way to the front and, on seeing our uniforms, the guards admitted our entry. Inside, we found most of the Prussian court milling around in similar ignorance. It transpired that a Prussian officer had been sent to Konigsberg with the news, but he had lost his hat in the battle. Knowing his monarch's obsession with uniforms, astonishingly, he had sent someone on ahead of him to get a new hat from the barracks so that he could appear before his king properly dressed. The hallway was alive with rumours as officers, brought up on the martial glory of their nation, speculated on the defeat of their nemesis. One old colonel had heard categorically that the French were now in full retreat and fleeing back to the western bank of the Vistula. "With our combined army on their tail," he assured me, "they won't stop running until they reach Paris." His wife wondered what damage they would find in their Berlin home when they returned. Another officer insisted that Napoleon had been killed in the battle and that now the French marshals were fighting among themselves to see who would take his throne. It was possible, of course, but given the facts we *knew*, it sounded more like wishful thinking to me.

Eventually, the long-awaited officer arrived and courtiers cleared a way through the throng for him. With the exception of his shiny new hat, his uniform was covered in mud and dust from his journey, and what looked like a bloodstain on his left sleeve. He stared in apprehension at the myriad of colonels and generals demanding news from him, but a man who would not appear hatless before his ruler was not going to blurt out his message before he had told his monarch. The flunkeys led him upstairs and a short while later we heard that the king and queen were going to appear on the balcony to speak to the people. We pushed our way out once more and were just in time to see the royal couple appear. It was the first time I had seen King Wilhelm Friedrich III, a stiff, awkward man, but the queen on his arm was an absolute stunner. Judging from the peons of rapture coming from Wilson at my side, I was clearly not alone in that opinion. We both began to understand how the Prussian army had been persuaded to take on the might of France alone.

The king held up his arms to still the crowd and then shouted out that there had indeed been a victory at a place called Pultusk. A Russian army had defeated the French, inflicting over seven thousand casualties. The royal couple then disappeared back inside, leaving a relieved crowd, some still holding trunks of possessions, cheering in relief at their deliverance. I glanced at Hutchinson, who was watching proceedings with a brooding suspicion, "No mention of Russian casualties," he grunted, "or what the French are doing now. We need to find out more." We turned to go back inside, but found our way blocked by palace servants. They announced that no more news would be forthcoming at that time, but one gave our chief an invitation to a royal reception that evening. We were promised that answers to all his questions would be given then.

"Perhaps they don't yet know Russian casualty numbers," I suggested as we walked back to our lodgings.

"Yet they know the French ones," sneered his lordship. "Which are easier for a general to count, his own men or the enemies? I'll wager that the Russian losses exceed those of the French."

"It is possible that the French really are in full retreat," suggested Wilson. "If they have taken many of their wounded with them, their losses could be even higher."

Hutchinson gave a snort of derision, "It is *possible* that my mistress has not been in Lord Calderdale's bed while we have been away, but I suspect that is just as likely as a full French retreat." He gave a heavy sigh and added, "This victory could be worse than a defeat."

"How can a victory be worse than a defeat?" queried his brother.

"You heard those chattering fools in the palace. It will only take a small victory to encourage them into some act of reckless stupidity. They just need to keep their heads down until the spring when more Russian reinforcements should arrive, then they will stand more of a chance."

Hutchinson departed that evening for dinner at the little temporary palace. I think we all shared a sense of trepidation about what he might discover. When he returned, though he mostly grumbled about the king's appalling wine cellar, we learned that our fears had been fully justified. During the day more messengers, both Russian and Prussian, had arrived and with their news, the picture was becoming more complete. The victory, such as it was, had been won by a General Bennigsen. He had taken over from Marshal Kamenski when the latter had lost his few remaining wits. The marshal had ridden around the army in his carriage, shrieking to his soldiers that all was lost and that they should run for their lives. In those circumstances it was a miracle that there was a battle at all. This Bennigsen, commanding the first Russian army, had stopped the retreat and drawn up his force to face the pursuing French. There was a second Russian army under a General Buxhowden, but the two generals had quarrelled. Even though the second army was close enough to hear the battle, its commander refused to get involved and retreated towards the Russian border.

"They claim to have beaten Napoleon," scoffed Hutchinson. "It is more likely that they have mauled the forces of just one French marshal." Given that there were at least half a dozen French marshals with their own armies in the vicinity, this meant that only a small part of the emperor's forces had been engaged. "It was a bloody business, though," he continued. "Fought in thick mud that slowed down the advances of both sides. They insist French casualties are at least seven thousand, but they have no idea of their own."

"But surely they can count the bodies on the battlefield?" asked Wilson.

"No, they can't," replied Hutchinson. "They retreated from the battlefield the next morning. The French are camped there now."

"Isn't the victor of a battle the general who holds the field at the end of the day?" Kit's brow creased in puzzlement. "Doesn't this mean that the French really won the battle?"

"No, it means this Bennigsen has got some bloody sense," retorted his brother. "If he had stayed there, the other French marshals would have closed in around him like sharks on a wounded whale."

I can't speak for the others, but I went to what passed as my bed that night more confused than ever. The situation was further complicated the following day when the other Russian general, Buxhowden, sent a message claiming that he too had achieved a victory, albeit on a smaller scale. This time, though, there were no great celebrations, for word had spread that despite the Russian claims of success, both of their armies were still moving backwards towards their border. For all the fighting, Prussia's future looked just as precarious as before.

Over the next few days Konigsberg was alive with rumour and speculation. Some claimed that the Russians were regrouping for another attack. A Russian nobleman insisted that Kamenski had not gone mad and was just luring the French into a trap. Cossack scouts captured prisoners with copies of the French *Bulletin* newspaper, which claimed that the battle at Pultusk had been a decisive French victory. It was normal for armies to downplay their own casualties and exaggerate those of their enemies, so it was hard to discern the truth. Not for nothing was there a common expression to 'lie like a *Bulletin*.'

News came in that both the Prussian and Russian armies were short of supplies, while some escaped Prussian prisoners reported that the French too were on the verge of starvation. Both armies had been trying to live off the land they were fighting on. The poor Polish peasants would have seen their farms raided by first Prussian and then Russian armies and finally by the French. Even though Napoleon's men were masters in the art of foraging, there would be barely enough left to support an abstemious mouse. With weather alternating between snow and heavy rain, the roads were almost impassable due to snow-covered frozen ruts or deep mud. Neither army could easily get supplies to their fighting men, even if they had them.

Hutchinson was sure that it would be impossible for either force to fight on through the depths of winter. They would need to find somewhere to feed and shelter their men. Some thought that the French would retreat across the Vistula, where it would be easier for them to source supplies. Others, like his lordship, were worried that they might find a nearer coastal city a more comfortable option... Konigsberg had far fewer defences and defenders than Danzig, making it a tempting target. I suspected he was right. We thought we were suffering hardship in our attic rooms, where the contents of our chamber pots were frozen solid each morning. Yet life must have been near unbearable living exposed in the snow and mud. A solid roof and warm hearth would have been a powerful incentive to capture the city.

A week after we had heard about the battle, I was awoken one morning by a boot knocking persistently against my ribs. Opening my eyes, I saw Hutchinson's mottled features glaring down at me. "Get up, Flashman, we are leaving."

"What? Are the French advancing?" I asked as I gathered my wits.

"No, but it is only a matter of time. I discovered last night that the king and queen are leaving tomorrow. When the people find out there will be a mass exodus north, I want to get ahead of them."

"So where are we going?"

"Memel. It is the only Prussian coastal town left."

Looking at the map I saw that our route would take us on another of those sand and shingle spits, this one even longer than the one before. I thought that there must be a better alternative route inland, but it turned out that those roads were even worse – they would add days to the journey and involved swamp and marshland. Our route would be a shingle track again, but this time we would be more prepared. Wilson and I found some sturdy horses to ride while Kit acquired a light, well-sprung carriage for him and his brother. We packed plenty of food too, for little would be available on the way; we would be sixty miles travelling between the sea and another inland lagoon.

Without a carriage seat jarring my spine, I imagined that this journey would be rather better – how wrong I was! We had barely set off before the wind began to pick up. By the time we were on that exposed strip of land it was blowing a hurricane. Sand was picked up from the beach and blasted at us with a force that stung our cheeks. Rider and beast were forced to turn their faces away from the tempest. Hutchinson and his brother fared somewhat better, for they were able to pull up the leather hood on the carriage. We found the first post house at dusk, which was fortunate as we could have easily missed it in the dark. It was a low-lying, three-room shack hidden among the dunes. A Russian general, his wife and two children were already there in one room while we were to share another.

The place was filthy, and overnight an icy wind screamed through numerous gaps in the planking. The next morning the weather was even worse as a snow blizzard hampered visibility further. We waited a while, hoping it would abate, but if anything, it got worse. Regardless, we had to press on to find the next post house before nightfall. So, wrapping our faces in scarves to protect against windblown sand and ice, we set off once more. The ground was firmest near the seashore where the receding tide had compacted it, but we had no apprehension of the other dangers it hid until we came across the Russian general's carriage. It had found a patch of quicksand and was buried up to the axles, with the tide turned and sea now returning quickly.

The occupants were all shouting for help over the roar of the waves beyond them. Judging from the disturbed sand, one had already tried to leave the carriage but had been pulled back when they had started to sink. It would be touch and go if we could get them out before the crashing waves ripped them away. We quickly dismounted and Kit brought a long spare leather rein from the carriage, which we all held on to as we gingerly tested the ground underneath us. Leaning into the wind and squinting against the sleet and salt spray we got to within ten feet of the carriage before my boots started to slip. The mother was near hysterical now, holding out one of her children to be rescued. We threw one end of the rein towards them and the general tied it around his daughter's waist. The girl had barely stepped onto the sand before she was hauled off her feet as we yanked her towards us. Lying on her side, her weight was more spread out than if she was standing. Soon the other child was with us and then the mother was being dragged over the sand. She had tried to stand but the general had shouted something to her, so she had remained prone as we pulled. He and the coachman had cut free the horses and then they too were hauled across.

We had just untied the general, who had insisted on being last, when the first wave smashed into their carriage, ripping off one of the doors and pushing it over so that it was half on its side. It was a timely reminder that we needed to retrieve our own coach and mounts. The women and children climbed into Hutchinson's carriage, while his lordship, Kit and the Russian general each rode one of the rescued horses. They were led by the coachman, who at least knew the way to the next post house. By the time we reached it my clothes were soaked through with sleet and spray and I was frozen with cold. I was fast concluding that the French were welcome to this desolate country.

There was only one small fire in the post house. We fed it with wood and sat around, nine sets of teeth chattering together, sounding like the clatter of a cotton mill. Eventually, as fingers thawed, we changed into drier clothes and helped our companions to do the same. The Russian general grinned as he found himself wearing Hutchinson's spare dress uniform jacket, while his wife and daughters wrapped themselves in our bearskins. A local man was sent back to see if he could retrieve any of the Russians' baggage, while we shared the last of the food we had brought with us. The general did not speak English, but like many wealthy Russians, he spoke French. Hutchinson was keen to understand how the Russian army was recruited and trained and how well it would stand up against the French. What we learned filled us with dismay.

Except for a few fashionable Guards regiments, filled with recruits from the nobility and the gentry, most Russian soldiers were conscripts. Some were petty criminals, but the majority were selected by landowners from among their serfs to meet quotas set by the tsar. Naturally, the landowners kept their best men for their estates, sending instead weaklings, troublemakers or simpletons to fill their allocation. Enlistment was for twenty-five years, and many viewed it as a death sentence, for hardly any would see their homes again. Training was a brutal business with soldiers beaten into submission. The general explained that it was unwise to build a training camp near a river, as many of the recruits would try to drown themselves in despair. When I asked how many musket balls they were trained to fire in a minute he looked puzzled. To our astonishment, he told us that in peacetime infantry soldiers were given two cartridges a year, which were fired in salutes for the birthday of the tsar and the regiment's colonel. The Jäger or sharpshooter regiments were given eight cartridges a year. Seeing our expressions at this, he proudly told us that the bayonet was the prime weapon of the Russian soldier.

You can imagine how well we took this information. The only good news the general could give us was that the Russians had lots of artillery, although he did not mention how often that was fired. Instead, he grumbled that it was almost impossible to move guns in this weather. After torrential rain, the heavy cannon would sink into the mud up to their axles and then when it froze overnight, the guns would be set solid in the earth, taking hours to hack out again. After this enlightenment we sat staring glumly into the fire as the futility of our task dawned on us. Even the irrepressibly optimistic Wilson looked shaken. A couple of times I heard him mutter, "It surely cannot be that bad," as he gazed into the flames.

The next morning we left the Russians to wait for their luggage and a new carriage that was being organised for them, and set off again. The wind had eased a little and as we approached the top of the shingle spit, we found the wrecks of several vessels on the shore. Most were old, their exposed wooden ribs pointing at the sky like the skeleton of a beached whale. There was a break in the embankment just south of the town of Memel to allow ships to enter the lagoon and these vessels must have foundered as they tried to reach that shelter. As we waited for the ferry another rider galloped up with news that the Prussian king and queen were on the road just a day behind us. Not only that, he also announced that the French were advancing, just as we had anticipated. A column of their troops had been seen less than thirty-five miles from Konigsberg.

"Some French marshal wants a comfortable bed for the winter," concluded Hutchinson, pulling his greatcoat collar up around his neck. "Not that I blame him. He will be more comfortable than the Prussian queen tonight, that is for sure."

There were ice floes in the channel that we had to cross to reach Memel – the larger ferries would not risk the journey. We had to pay the owner of a smaller boat to take us across, with Wilson and I brandishing long poles to ward off any small bergs that came our way. Unfortunately, we were forced to leave the horses behind in the care of the ferryman. Over the next few days, the man acquired a sizeable herd of half-frozen horses left on the shore, as we were followed by a trail of desolate refugees, including most of the Prussian court.

As one of the first arrivals, we were able to find rooms, but the city of Memel was far smaller than Konigsberg and it quickly filled up. Members of the nobility found themselves competing for boxes in the small theatre to sleep in as it had been turned into a dormitory. Those less fortunate snored among the seats in the stalls. At least two elderly aristocrats had died on the journey. When the rush of refugees had followed us, they often found the few meagre post houses full and many had been forced to sleep outside in the storm. Their families must have felt a bitter irony when they learned that, inexplicably, the French had stopped their advance. They had not reached Konigsberg and were rumoured to be retreating away from it. Happier would have been the relatives of a princess of one of the Germanic states who, about to give birth, had stayed in the city.

People were exhausted and close to despair; this was the last vestige of Prussian territory. If it fell, then the country would cease to exist. It was a bitter end for a nation that just a few months before thought it could beat the empire of the French. Their hubris had left them close to beggary. We saw the royal family trudge on foot through the street outside; the foolish king picking his way between the puddles to keep the mud off his gleaming boots, while his wife struggled on behind, half held up by her ladies in waiting.

Their new residence was even smaller than the one before. Absurdly, they tried to maintain the illusion of monarchy over their near non-existent realm as though they were still in Berlin. Weary dukes and countesses would be invited from their theatre box lodgings to attend necessarily intimate receptions. Wilson managed an invite to one and was introduced to the queen. He had always been in awe of royalty, but now he came back gushing with praise at the queen's nobility and fortitude.

"She was the damn fool who persuaded the king to go to war," grumbled Hutchinson, less than impressed. Wilson, though, was not to be put off. He still had a copy of one of his wretched books in his luggage and rushed off to have it specially bound in her honour as a gift. Quite why he thought a near destitute queen, freezing her tits off in a draughty town hall, would want to read about a British campaign in the heat of Egypt is beyond me.

Hutchinson was hoping that both armies would now settle into winter quarters and that hostilities would be suspended until the spring. Given the weather, you would think that the generals would have little choice. This would give the Russians more time to bring up reinforcements that they were gathering from across their vast nation, even if they were of dubious fighting value. We had already developed a healthy cynicism over the quality of Russian recruits. It was not helped when we learned that one of the cavalry regiments coming from the Far East did not fight with swords or carbines, but with bows and arrows.

Yet despite our expectations, a series of couriers galloped up the shingle spit with quite different news. We met one of them when Wilson and I crossed back across the channel to retrieve our horses. The little village on the far shore had doubled in size since we were last there, but closer inspection showed that the new 'houses' were in fact dozens of abandoned carriages that were now covered in snow and ice. My companion had been bemoaning the fact that exactly a year before he had been suffering from heatstroke in South Africa, when we encountered the royal messenger. A swig of brandy soon loosened his tongue and then he was all too keen to impart his news.

Bennigsen was claiming that an advance by Russian forces had prompted the French to withdraw from Konigsberg. His army had captured hundreds of French prisoners, who were starving wretches dressed in little more than rags. Others, particularly recruits from some of the German states, had deserted the French army to join the Russians and Prussians. All insisted that morale in Napoleon's *Grande Armée* was collapsing. The men were exhausted from marching in appalling weather. Supply lines had been stretched to breaking point by the French advance, while not a scrap of food could be found in the captured territory.

Hutchinson dismissed these reports as gossip and wishful thinking. He refused to credit that the French would be intimidated by the

Russians, especially after what we had learned of their rudimentary training. But then came a messenger with news that Marshal Bernadotte's headquarters had been captured. According to the exhausted rider over twelve thousand gold and silver coins had been seized along with other booty stolen during the French advance. To prove his claim, the officer presented his king with a French marshal's uniform coat and a small gold plate adorned with a Germanic family crest. It was evidence that could not be ignored.

We had begun to take the extinction of Prussia as a foregone conclusion. I for one was looking forward to this seemingly inevitable event as an excuse for us to leave this frozen wilderness and return to the comforts of London and Leicestershire. Yet now all was in doubt. Despite our expectations, every report assured us that it was the French in retreat and the Russians driving them back. That an army of conscripts barely capable of distinguishing one end of a musket from the other, could dominate perhaps the greatest general and army Europe had seen in a generation, made no sense at all. Unfortunately for me, there was only one way that we could find out for certain what was going on.

"Flashman, I want you to go to the Russian headquarters," announced Hutchinson. He had just summoned me to his room and was sitting on a trunk by the window, so that the weak wintry light shone on a letter he was holding. He clearly doubted its contents, for he held it up and added, "We need to know if they really are pushing the enemy back, or if the French are retreating of their own accord."

This was unwelcome news indeed. To the best of our knowledge Bennigsen was some one hundred miles south of us. When I thought of the struggle we had endured to come north, the thought of turning around again filled me with dismay. But not only would I be going back south, this time I would be going inland, and would be far more vulnerable to getting involved in this brutal war. It would be a damn dangerous business and I instantly recalled Hutchinson's earlier admission that my father-in-law wanted me dead. As if reading my mind his lordship gave a wry grin. "If you think I am sending you at Berkeley's request you are wrong. You are not going alone. Wilson and Kit are coming with you and of all people, I would not put my brother in undue jeopardy."

"Why do we all need to go?" I asked, puzzled, for it still seemed an unnecessary risk. Then I clamped my jaw shut, for if I talked him out of sending the others, I might find myself alone and in even more peril.

Hutchinson gave a grunt of amusement. "You all have your own particular skills that I need at the front. Wilson is an expert in cavalry but is inclined to believe the best of the Russians and the worst of the French. You, I am told, know about infantry, but..." he gave a sardonic smile. "Well, I have been watching you Flashman. You seem to believe the worst in most people regardless of nationality. Unlike Wilson, I doubt you will be disappointed. My brother knows little of military matters, but he will observe the politics between the Prussian and Russian commanders. I want you all to send me your reports, which I imagine will be quite different."

Chapter 5

Our return to Konigsberg was considerably faster than our ordeal to Memel. This time the three of us shared a lightweight barouche carriage fitted with sled runners that moved easily over the now snow-covered sand and shingle track. We reached our destination in just twenty-four hours. We had seen little of the journey, wrapped up under blankets and bearskins behind the curtains of the carriage. When we did have to stop and get out, the icy wind made us gasp. It transpired that I was the only one of our party to have misgivings about our trip. Kit welcomed the chance to escape the brooding influence of his brother, while Wilson was positively champing at the bit to see some action. To listen to him, you would think that the Russians were likely to drive the French all the way back to Paris before we caught up with them.

Wilson's enthusiasm was certainly not tempered by our first meeting with the Prussian commander of the Konigsberg garrison. The man assured us that the French were in full retreat. A recent sortie from the force at Danzig had captured over seven hundred starving French prisoners who insisted that their own army was in revolt over the lack of supplies. Napoleon himself was said to be in Warsaw, on the far side of the Vistula River. His various marshals were in front of him, but their men were spread across a strip of territory two hundred miles wide to gather what little food they could from the countryside. Meanwhile, General Bennigsen had now been confirmed as the Russian commander-in-chief to replace the deranged Kamenski.

"The tsar is on his way west to join our king and together they will assure victory," insisted the commander. Bennigsen was clearly anxious to impress his monarch with his enlarged command. He was convinced that now was the time to attack the French, while they were weak and dispersed. He had moved his headquarters to a place called Ostrolenka, some one hundred miles south-west of Konigsberg. There they had pushed back the French forces that had threatened the city and were pursuing them further out towards the west. The garrison commander assured us that all the reports he had received confirmed that the French were still falling back. He did, however, offer us a small escort, as bands of deserters from both armies were roaming the countryside, pillaging whatever food and valuables they could find.

We had seen that Russian officers rarely travelled long journeys on horseback, at least during winter. They preferred small, light carriages or sledges, called *britska*, with their saddle horse tied on behind. The speed of our return to Konigsberg had confirmed that this was the right approach and so we set off in our barouche again, this time with half a dozen Prussian lancers riding alongside. We quickly discovered that the rutted road was best avoided. The sled runners bounced off frozen ridges of earth that had been pushed up by earlier vehicles. Several of these wheeled vehicles were still embedded in the road, now hidden under humps of snow to be manoeuvred round. It was far easier to go across open country when we could, but all too often we were impeded by hedges and forest. We left all navigation to the coachman, and I was pleased that we were not speeding along as we had down the beach to Konigsberg. As far as I was concerned, there was no rush to arrive. The further we travelled from the sea and availability of ships to take us home, the more uncomfortable I felt.

When I pulled back the corner of the curtain over the carriage window, I was met by a strange alien countryside. It was completely empty and barren, just a sea of white fields, interspersed at intervals with broken fences and dark black forests. Any livestock had long since been eaten by passing armies and anything of value taken. The peasant cottages were little more than hovels and some of those had been torn down too, or thatch removed from their roofs. Whether their occupants were still around was hard to say, as we barely saw another living soul.

We found an empty stone barn to shelter in that first night. There was room for the men and horses and all were fed with supplies we had brought with us. Several of the lancers broke up a nearby hut and soon we had soon made a blazing fire from its timber in the middle of the space. As we sat keeping warm, wrapped in our bearskins, Kit and Wilson argued over whether we would all be in Berlin by the spring.

"Have you forgotten what that Russian general told us about their army?" I asked. "Do you really think that an army that only fires its guns twice a year will beat the French? Remember what happened to the Prussian army, and they were much better trained."

"My brother does not think the Prussians stand a chance," admitted Kit.

"Nonsense," protested Wilson. "The French are fighting far from home. Their supply lines are stretched. They are not used to the terrain or the weather here. Soldiers always fight better when they are protecting their own territory. Now is the time to challenge the Corsican despot, while he is exposed and weak. The Swedes hold Pomerania on the north German shore behind the French lines. If we landed British troops there, we could open up a whole new front and stretch French forces beyond breaking point. I have suggested that we recommend this to London and his lordship said he would think about it."

Kit and I exchanged a glance. I think we both knew that Hutchinson would not spend much time considering this idea before discarding it. Even if the Swedes were willing to join such a precarious alliance, any British force landed would be dangerously isolated. Our escort commander had been selected as he spoke English. I asked him whether he thought that the Russians could push the French back. At first, he was reluctant to give an opinion at all. His faith in his own much vaunted army had proved horribly misplaced as he had seen it swept away. He thought himself unqualified to give an opinion. Eventually, he concluded that the Russians "*had* to succeed, for if they failed his nation would be lost".

We saw our first Russian soldiers the next day and the encounter was certainly not an auspicious one. As the most junior in our party, I sat on the seat in the carriage facing backwards. We had the curtains drawn to keep what little warmth we generated within the coach, but on occasion we would all peer out to view the countryside we were passing through. We spent much of that morning riding on a trail through the middle of a forest. Once when I peered out, I could have sworn I had seen a horseman trailing us in the trees. I called out to the others, but by the time they had stuck their heads out of the windows on that side the fellow had gone.

"Perhaps it was a bush that looked like a man," suggested Kit. "A single rider will not bother us with half a dozen lancers as escort."

I was sure he was right and although I stared out a few more times, I did not see the rider again. We stopped mid-morning to stretch our legs and rest the horses. I remember that I was taking a piss against the trunk of a tree and marvelling at the vast quantity of acrid vapour I generated in the freezing air, when through the steam I glimpsed movement again. I barely had time to shout out an alarm, for galloping towards us, just twenty yards off, were a dozen horsemen. There was no doubt as to their intentions; they lowered their lances as they approached and I saw one nearest to me grinning darkly in anticipation of a kill. I must have looked an easy mark, mouth gaping open in astonishment and hand still holding my cock instead of a weapon. I had not completely lost my wits, though, for I had the presence of mind to tuck it back in before I drew the wickedly sharp blade of my sword. There was no thought to run – I instinctively knew that would be fatal. The only cover was the wet tree in front of me and I just had time to throw myself against its trunk. That would spare me the charging lance, but the villain was bound to stab at me with the point or a sword as he rode past.

As soon as I glimpsed the nose of his mount coming around the bark, I began moving back around the tree to avoid the inevitable thrust. As I did so I heard a pistol crack nearby and the ring of metal as blades met. My assailant reined up when he found me gone, while I whirled around looking for a better hiding place. But there was none to be found and the rider was already turning his mount looking for me. They had to be one of those bands of brigands, for they wore no uniforms. They would show us little mercy. Our only chance was to fight them off. My man still had his back to me and so I sprinted forward to take the opportunity it presented.

I was just pulling back my sword for a killing thrust when our escort commander ran towards me, holding out his hands and calling out, "*Nein, nein, Kameraden!*"

If they were comrades, that appeared to be news to the horseman. He followed the escort commander's gaze and saw me rushing up behind him. The rider and his horse were lightning quick, I will say that for them. The horse sprang forward while the lance whipped round with its steel tip set to gash my face. I slashed my own blade up to block the shaft and the Damascus steel bit deep into the wood, ripping the lance from the rider's hand. He looked furious to be disarmed and immediately gripped the hilt of his own sword, but our escort commander was up to him now and holding on to the bridle of his horse.

"*Kameraden*," he repeated, this time a little uncertainly, as he watched more of the strange horsemen appear through the trees on the other side of the track. I pulled the lance from my blade and looked about. Kit was standing ten yards off holding a smoking pistol, while Wilson, sword in hand, was turning to watch the riders warily. My assailant glared at me, anger clear on his features and in his cold blue eyes. With a grunt he moved his left hand and I saw he had a short whip tied to his wrist. There were no spurs on his boots and his horse stepped forward a few paces with the lightest of touches. He held out his hand for the return of his lance. I glanced at the escort commander, who nodded vigorously as he stared about at the other riders who had now started to circle us. "*Kameraden*," the officer repeated, holding up his hands to show he had no weapons. He pointed to us and called, "*Britische Offiziere.*"

None of the riders looked the slightest bit impressed with this news and I was not sure that they had understood a single word. They just continued to move around us, inspecting us impassively. I was reminded of wolves circling their prey. They all wore thick woollen coats of various colours, and fur hats. They were well suited for the winter weather and with lances and swords, with pistols and knives in their belts, they were armed to the teeth. Slowly, I gave back the lance, keeping my sword in my hand ready for any sudden hostile move.

I watched the rider glance down at the hilt of my weapon with interest. I had won it in India. It was coated in gold and set with several gemstones. There was a chill to his gaze, which he proceeded

41

to direct first at Kit and then Wilson. They were both wearing British officer uniforms – Wilson particularly impressive in polished boots and full cavalry rig. The man who had attacked me seemed to be in charge as I noticed the others watching him as he now turned his attention to the expensive saddle horses tethered behind our barouche sled. For all the talk of "*Kameraden,*" I got the distinct impression that he was deliberating on whether the repercussions of killing us would be outweighed by the loot they could steal. He reached a decision. He glanced down at the lance in his hand – the shaft was now half cut through. With a grunt he snapped the weapon in half and tossed it in the snow at my feet. Then shouting a command, he led his men back into the trees. Within a few seconds they had disappeared as quickly as they had arrived.

"Who the hell were they?" demanded Kit.

"They must have been those brigands we have been warned about," answered Wilson.

"No, they are Cossacks," explained our escort commander. "They are used to scout around the Russian army. They did not recognise your red coats. It is just as well you had an escort, for they know our uniforms."

"For a moment back there, I was not sure that was going to save us," I admitted. "You looked worried too."

The escort commander shrugged. "They do have a reputation for murdering, robbing and raping and then asking questions later. But Prussia must now take all the allies it can get."

"Are you sure about that?" asked Kit as he reloaded his pistol. "Those fellows look like they would do more harm to friend than foe." Before we got back in the sled we searched through the luggage for our other pistols and spare ammunition. When we set off, we each had a brace of them ready to fire should we encounter the Cossacks again. This time, despite the cold, we also kept the windows open and a wary eye out on the surrounding countryside.

About an hour later to our surprise, we came across our first column of Russian infantry. We had been heading south on a track to find their headquarters and had assumed that their army was to the west, between us and the French. Instead, here some were heading in the opposite direction to us, back towards Konigsberg.

"Do you think that the French have beaten them already?" I asked. "If they are retreating, we would do well to turn around now. We don't want to get caught up in the chaos of a rout."

"You should have more faith in our Russian allies," chided Wilson, who had nearly been killed by one of those so-called allies earlier that morning. "They are marching in good order; they do not look like they are on the run to me."

The only way we would find out what was happening was to ask. We pulled off the trail towards the edge of the trees to give them room to pass. Then we waited expectantly for a closer look at these soldiers that the Prussians were putting so much faith in. They were preceded by a group of their officers, all travelling in small, light one- or two-person *britska* sledges, with their saddle horses tied on behind. We descended from our carriage as they approached and as they drew level, Wilson called out to ask if any of them spoke English. This time our Prussian escort stood next to us to ensure that there was no doubt as to which side we were on.

The man I presumed was their colonel looked at us with disdain. Perhaps he was surprised that we had survived the encounter with his cavalry screen. Languidly, he raised his whip and with shouted commands from the sergeants, the long snake of men behind him shuffled to a stop.

"Do you speak English?" Wilson tried again. It was quieter now the sled had stopped moving and without the trampling thuds of the men behind. The column was now half obscured behind a fog produced by hundreds of lungs in the still, frozen air. The colonel looked at the officer in a sled alongside him, who shrugged dismissively, and so Kit tried another approach. *"Parlez-vous français?"* And so it was we discovered that the only language we shared was that of our common enemy.

We explained who we were and asked where they were going, wondering if the Russian headquarters had moved. The colonel told us that Bennigsen was now further west at a place called Mohrungen.

Their scouts had reported that the corps of one of the French marshals was further east than the rest. He said that Bennigsen believed it was vulnerable and could be cut off from the rest of the French army and destroyed. "That fucking sausage-maker has the whole damn army racing north and west in this filthy weather so he can trap them," the colonel complained, pulling his fur-lined cloak tighter about him. "We should be resting in our winter quarters now. The only thing we should be trapping are our Polish whores."

As several of his officers laughed in agreement, I queried, "Sausage-maker?"

"General Bennigsen is a Hanoverian," explained our escort commander before shooting the irritable colonel a glance and adding, "but he has fought in the Russian army for over thirty years."

"He is a fucking foreigner," the colonel retorted. "A Russian army should have a Russian commander. Kamenski would not have had us rushing like this."

"But Kamenski has gone mad," protested Kit. "An experienced officer like your general is better than a lunatic."

"Pah! Who says Kamenski is mad? The sausage-maker, that's who." The colonel shifted uncomfortably, probably aware that several of his officers were now staring at him. From their expressions, they had all heard the rumours about their former commander. "Anyway," he continued, "we have lots of good Russian generals who could command the army. Kutuzov is Russian; the tsar could bring him up from the Black Sea to lead us." Evidently, deciding he had dallied enough talking to strangers, the colonel raised his whip and his sled sprang forward. More commands were shouted and the column behind started to trudge forward in his wake.

"Well, my brother was certain Kamenski was a few pennies short of a shilling when he met him," announced Kit. "If he was not actually insane, he had certainly lost all appetite for fighting. He was claiming to be ill too and… My God, look at them."

The rest of us were already staring at the ranks of men coming towards us. To this day I am not sure if it was an awe-inspiring sight or a pitiable one. Probably a bit of both. While their officers were clean-shaven and warmly wrapped in furs on their sledges, these men could not have been more of a contrast. Without exception all were bearded, their faces half covered with ice and snow in their whiskers. Each had a shako hat and a woollen greatcoat, although many of these were patched or torn. It was hard to judge what state their uniforms were underneath, but the sight of their boots made us shudder in horror. They were shuffling through over a foot of settled snow and it was hard to see the feet of the front ranks as they were almost permanently submerged in the drifts. But as the ground was flattened out in front of them, we clearly saw the hardship of the ranks behind. Heaven knew how long they had been marching from their own vast country to this one, but a number no longer had boots at all. Their feet were covered in rags, and often pieces of wood or tree bark had been tied underneath to give them some protection as they stood on the frozen ground. Nearly all those that still had some form of footwear were sporting impromptu repairs to their boots by means of extra wooden soles and strips of cloth or even tree vines, which held them together. Between the rags and split leather could be glimpsed bare toes, some frozen white and a few black with frostbite.

That was shocking enough, but what really disturbed us was their expressions. In a British army, the air would have been alive with moaning and complaints. In truth, many would have refused to march at all unless their life depended on it. But these Russian peasants went past without a word of protest. Most did not even bother to look in our direction. They marched with their eyes locked on the back of the man in front, as though they had accepted that this was their lot. It looked like any sense of humanity had already been beaten out of them.

"Christ, if they can march like that in this weather, you have to wonder what will stop them in battle," said Kit, echoing the thoughts of us all. "Some of their bayonets looked rusted onto the muzzles of their muskets, many have missing flints, and look, that one has no hammer on his gun at all."

I watched as rows of the steel-tipped guns went past. In the British army bayonets were only fixed prior to a charge as they made loading the gun much more awkward. I remembered what the Russian general had told us about their ammunition and how the bayonet was their main weapon. "Let us hope that they have some cartridges left in those pouches, although you could hardly blame them for using a few to start fires to keep warm." I reflected that the last time I had seen an army fight had been in the heat of India. I very much doubted that my experience there would be a lot of help in Prussia.

Once the column had passed, we got back in our warm carriage and set off on what was now a shorter journey to meet Bennigsen. After being tramped down by over a thousand feet the snow was now compact and we were jolted around as the sledge runners bounced off the resulting humps of harder ice. Not that any of us complained, for when we looked out of the windows now, we saw a sad trail of Russian stragglers limping slowly after their comrades. Any discomfort we experienced was a mockery of the term compared to theirs.

It grew warmer that afternoon and occasional flurries of snow turned into heavy and persistent rain. By nightfall we were still out in the countryside and the horses were tired, struggling to make headway through what was now a slush of mud and ice. We pulled off the road and while we slept in the carriage, our escort cut down branches and spread out some canvas to make a bivouac. Water drummed down on the leather roof of our barouche, but just as I was about to sleep, over the din I heard a new noise.

"Is that thunder?" asked Kit, sitting up again. We pulled back the curtains, looking for any flashes of lightning.

"That was gunfire," shouted the escort commander, confirming my own suspicions. He pointed west from under their shelter and added, "It is coming from over there." We listened carefully, even briefly getting out of the carriage to try and hone down the direction, but with a forest between us and the likely source it was impossible. To my mind the sound was coming from above us, as though bouncing off the low cloud. The only thing we could be sure of was that it was some miles distant. The isolated French marshal was clearly putting up a fight.

The gunfire had stopped by next morning, but the weather was even wetter. We did not need the coachman to tell us that the road was impassable and that wheels, hooves or sled runners would certainly sink into the morass of mud. There was no alternative but to mount our saddle horses and go through the forest, where a carpet of leaves and pine needles would allow us to make progress. As we set off, we speculated on who had won the battle that had been underway the previous night.

We were now heading deeper into Prussia. If the French had won, I surmised, there was a risk that we could be cut off from the coast, but Wilson scorned this suggestion. "If the marshal has been attacked for being ahead of his fellows, then he would hardly advance further. That would just leave him more exposed. Mark my words, the frogs will be running back over the Vistula as fast as they can go."

I did not give much credence to this wild optimism. Wilson would always believe the worst of the French and the best of the allies. But then at midday we reached Mohrungen and finally met Bennigsen, who if anything made Wilson look like a pessimist!

The Hanoverian could not have been more welcoming when we reached his headquarters. He was in an ebullient mood and had every right to be. According to the pins on his map, he had pushed the French back at least fifty miles in the north of the country. He showed us the long line his army had marched to the north and then east to catch the French unawares. Then he brandished a list of reports that proved the French were retreating: Konigsberg was no longer under threat; overland contact with Danzig had been re-established; and a siege around the Prussian fortress of Graudenz on the Vistula River had been lifted by the French, who had been seen withdrawing to two other bridgeheads on this key waterway. Even the Prussian royal family had felt it safe to return to Konigsberg and Hutchinson was bound to have travelled back with them.

"The French will stay on their side of the Vistula now for the rest of winter," Bennigsen predicted. "Bonaparte is still in Warsaw and will remain there to lick his wounds and rest his army until the spring. By then we will have more reinforcements from Russia, led by Tsar Alexander himself and we will push the French out of Prussia entirely." His grin of satisfaction was only slightly broader than that of Wilson, who could not help but smirk as his predictions were vindicated. I confess I was more than a little surprised – and greatly relieved – at the news. The messages received directly from Danzig and Graudenz were clear evidence that the French had retreated. It seemed that we had greatly underestimated the Russian forces. Having reassured us that all was well, Bennigsen insisted that we stay at his headquarters and dine with him that evening.

We sat in our room all afternoon, scratching away at despatches for Hutchinson. Wilson's was doubtless triumphant, while mine was rather more apologetic. As things turned out, however, they were all to be thrown into the blazing fire in our hearth before we left.

I was starving by the time we were called down to dinner. I thought we would be eating in the officers' mess with Bennigsen's staff, but instead it was a more intimate gathering with just one of his aides, a major called Schmidt, who also came from the Germanic states. As we tucked greedily into two roast fowls, a small mountain of potatoes and several bottles of wine, Bennigsen questioned us on the British view of the conflict and whether our country was likely to commit troops to the spring campaign. We assured him that we would report very positively on his recent action, but it was far too early to predict what the British government would do. I hid a smile as I thought of Hutchinson's reaction to our reports. He had been contemptuous about the Russian army, which reminded me of the troops we had seen the previous day.

"We passed one of your regiments on the way here," I told Benningsen. "We were all impressed with their fortitude, marching in deep snow when certainly their footwear showed they had endured the rigours of a very long journey already."

"Ah, the Russian soldier is used to hardship," he replied abruptly, dismissive of their suffering. "The life they come from as peasants is harsh too. They march until they are told to stop, with little complaint."

"And are your officers as obedient?" Kit enquired politely.

Bennigsen smiled, obviously guessing at what had prompted the question. "Some do not like to be led by a foreigner," he admitted. "But few show any initiative – it was beaten out of them by the old tsar. All Paul was interested in was smart uniforms and ruler-straight ranks of men. The fool would march regiments up and down outside his palace for hours as though they were the toy soldiers he played with as a boy. Obedience was everything to him." He laughed, "At Pultusk I sent a Russian officer to a colonel on my left flank with orders for him to advance. The colonel was killed before the man arrived, but did my messenger deliver the order to the next in command? No, he brought it back to me as the note was only addressed to the colonel. Tell me, would a British courier be so stupid?"

We agreed that they wouldn't. Bennigsen rose from the table. "Now, speaking of orders, I have some to write, but please stay here, gentlemen. Enjoy your wine and cigars.

As I went to bed that evening, I was warm, dry, well fed and feeling secure. It was the last day of January and it seemed that there would be peace for at least another two or three months until the spring thaw. A shout from outside our lodging reminded me just how fortunate we were. I went to the window to see at least a score of hunched figures trying to sleep and shelter from the rain under the eaves of the house we were in. A door on the floor below had been opened, throwing light into the courtyard. Several hungry men were squabbling over a bowl of kitchen scraps. I saw what looked like a potato fall into a puddle and immediately two hollow-cheeked soldiers fell to their knees, feeling about in the muddy water to retrieve it. One grabbed the prize and, stuffing it quickly into his mouth, staggered off into the night.

The next morning I almost felt guilty as I found plates of meat, eggs and bread in the officers' mess set out for breakfast. Bennigsen was there as well, discussing a document with some of his officers. When he saw us enter, he came over to show it to us. "One of my generals captured a courier with this note yesterday," he explained. "The general suspects it is a ruse to get us to pull back. What do you think?" We looked at the note, which was short and to the point: *The emperor will commence our attack on the first of February.*

"But that is today!" I exclaimed, feeling a sudden chill of alarm. "And I thought you said that Napoleon is in Warsaw. How far away is that from here?"

"He is, or at least he was when we received the last report two days ago. That is two hundred *versts* from here." On seeing my puzzlement, he added, "Around a hundred and thirty of your miles."

"That is an impossible distance for him to cover in two days," insisted Kit, looking at a map on the table, "especially over such boggy terrain."

"Our messenger came the same route," cautioned Schmidt, "perhaps slower than Bonaparte. Remember too that his soldiers were already much closer to us than Warsaw."

"It cannot be true – they are bluffing us." Wilson dismissed the note. "They must have told the courier to allow himself to be taken.

All the reports on the French army indicate that it is lacking supplies and in no condition to go on the offensive."

While Wilson was always contemptuous about Napoleon's forces, on reflection I thought that he might have a point. It was the memory of that column of Russian troops that persuaded me; I had never seen such endurance. At that point in my career I had not fought a French soldier, but I reasoned that an army which marched to the revolutionary banners of liberty, brotherhood and equality, would not submit to such an ordeal. Even Bennigsen was doubtful, although I sensed that he was trying to get our agreement to ignoring the note as evidence to the tsar if he was proved wrong. In the end he sent out orders to his outposts and the Cossacks to capture any couriers they could and to report any signs that the enemy were about to go on the offensive.

We settled down for breakfast and while Wilson prattled on about how they had beaten the French in Egypt, the rest of us were rather more subdued. Afterwards we went outside as it had at last stopped raining. Mohrungen had been built on a rise in the ground, but we could not see far as we were surrounded by rolling hills and forest. We strained our ears for any sign of battle to the east yet the only sound we heard was birdsong. We spent the day loafing around the headquarters and by four o'clock the daylight was waning; the countryside was still silent and we were certain that Napoleon was bluffing... Then we saw the new message from a second captured courier.

The French rider had been detained the previous day, but only now had the note reached Bennigsen's headquarters. It came from Marshal Berthier, Napoleon's chief of staff, and it was addressed to Marshall Bernadotte, whose forces were fighting to block our communications with Danzig once again. In a few sentences it revealed the strategic genius of the French emperor. Until now the French army had been marching east and the Russians west to meet them. However, the recent push to stop the French advance on Konigsberg had seen the Russians move north as well as east. Mohrungen was just over thirty miles south of the Baltic coast. Bernadotte was informed that his emperor had spotted a new opportunity to destroy the Russians. The marshal was to continue fighting, drawing in as many of the Russian forces as possible, but he was not to advance to block the coast. Napoleon would bring the rest of his army from the south to hook around the Russian left flank, cutting off any escape route to Russia and then drive them north into the sea.

While Bennigsen hurriedly issued orders to recall his forces and set up a rear guard to the south, I studied the map. Directly due north was the Fischer Gaff, the huge lagoon we had ridden past between Danzig and Konigsberg. I knew that the land around it was flat and swampy, which was why we had travelled along the shingle spit instead. An army would not survive long on ground like that, especially in winter. We could not even move directly east from Mohrungen, as the Passarge River and some lakes lay in the way. We would need to travel south first, towards the approaching French.

We were all quiet now, even Wilson. I had always feared being trapped by the French in the depths of the Prussian countryside, but that stretch of coast could be even worse. The French would block any retreat to Danzig or Konigsberg. Even if we had ships to lift an army of seventy thousand out of the lagoon, which we didn't, French artillery would shell and sink many. I remembered all too well the howling winds off the sea. With no shelter, little to eat and freezing temperatures, the French had only to wait for winter to do their work for them.

"Should we try to leave the army and return to Konigsberg?" I asked hopefully when we were alone.

"We would need guides and an escort, and I doubt that Bennigsen can spare them now," reasoned Kit. "Anyway, my brother sent us here to see how well the Russians fight the French. I doubt he would be impressed if we left before the first major engagement."

"If the army is trapped then Konigsberg would fall too," added Wilson. "But the Russian soldier is far more resilient than the French – and they are used to this weather. We will be much safer in a force of seventy thousand Russians than striking out on our own."

Dinner that evening was a sombre affair. Even though I had lost my appetite with thoughts of the trials ahead, I forced myself to wolf down what was available. We did not know when the next meal would come.

We left at first light, travelling to a place called Jonkendorf, twenty miles to the south-east. It was where Bennigsen had ordered his forces to congregate. In many ways it was a pleasant morning, dry, sunny and despite all our worries, silent, apart from the mournful singing of Russian soldiers as they trudged by. By noon there was still no sign of the promised onslaught.

"Do you think that second message could have been part of a ruse too?" I wondered. "For the cost of two captured couriers Napoleon has forced the entire Russian army to withdraw, while the French rest tucked up warm in their beds." I was not sure if that was a real possibility or just wishful thinking, but barely were the words out of my mouth than we heard it.

"That's cannon fire," warned Wilson. We strained our ears and could just hear the faintest rumble on the wind.

"I think you are right," agreed Kit. "But it is a good way off. Let's hope the rest of the Russian army gets here before the French."

All that afternoon we watched as troops and artillery arrived and were ordered to form a defensive line facing south. It looked a strong and well thought out position, with a river protecting our left flank. I could not help but think of the regiment we had seen days before and particularly the stragglers that had limped after it. Many had left bloody footprints in the snow and already looked close to exhaustion. How would they feel, I wondered, when they were told to about-face and march back the way they had come?

By nightfall at least twenty thousand infantry and several batteries of guns had arrived, with many more instructed to march on through the night to join us. There was, however, the remnant of the Prussian army, some eight thousand men who couriers had not yet reached. For all we knew they were still advancing north-east in accordance with the earlier plan, while the rest of the allied army were rushing south.

Once they reached Jonkendorf, many soldiers were sent further south to support the rear guard, which would buy us more time to combine the army. We saw troops of cavalry and irregular Cossacks riding to join them. At least they did not have to worry about food and ammunition as a major supply base and the army's hospital was situated nearby in the town of Guttstadt, to the north-west.

The cloudless day meant that the night was bitterly cold. Fortunately, once again Bennigsen had found space for us in his headquarters. We shared a room with three Russian officers. There was so little fuel for the fire that one of them smashed up three chairs and fed the splintered wood to the flames. Even then I was glad of the bearskin for warmth. We got little sleep that night. I remember lying there in the darkness and listening to the sporadic fire of distant cannon, which had undoubtedly become louder since we had heard it first.

The following morning I scratched at the ice on the window to see what was happening, but it was thick on both sides of the pane of glass. Stepping outside, the cold air made us gasp as it hit our lungs. All around us were exhausted soldiers. Some had collapsed in whole ranks to sleep on the icy ground, huddled in rows for warmth. Even then yet more were re-joining the army from the road that came down from the north. With their clothes and beards covered in frost, they looked like an army of ghosts in the early morning mist. As we went up to a gun position, I saw an officer in a sled leading his men forward. Closer inspection revealed that he was fast asleep, his head lolling on the furs around his shoulders. He kept going south, past the headquarters, his phantom soldiers trudging after him until a gunner brought his horse to a stop.

It was eerily quiet now. Both the French and our rear guard must have fought to exhaustion and the firing had stopped at some point during the night. Reaching the ice-covered cannon, we found another officer who could speak English, a German, judging from his accent. He explained that the rear guard was still some six miles south. "The Cossacks are raiding what little supplies they have and killing any unprotected artillery. Our boys are proving tough for them to push back, but when they do, they will find us waiting for them. We will take some beating as it is, and there are more guns on the way."

There was already a line of some one hundred heavy cannon, protected behind a ridge across the chosen battlefield. We had heard more guns with the rear guard and there were batteries of lighter horse artillery behind us to be deployed as the engagement unfolded. The surrounding fields were now filling with bivouacs of men. A sizeable force of some thirty thousand had been amassed, plus whatever made up the rear guard, and still more were arriving from the north. If the morale of the French army was as weak as we had been told, then this latest advance and the freezing weather would bring them close to breaking point.

"We will see Napoleon beaten here," announced Wilson, who was evidently thinking along the same lines. "His reputation for invincibility will be smashed on Prussian soil."

All that morning it seemed that Wilson was right. The battle with the rear guard resumed and while we could not see the action six miles away, we could hear it and it was fierce. Wagons of powder and supplies went south and returning couriers reported that every French attack was being stopped in its tracks. This was just as well as the men at Jonkendorf needed time to recover. To this end, cauldrons of hot food were soon boiling away. Wilson wanted to ride south to see the action for himself, but Bennigsen would not allow it.

"You look too French in that cavalry helmet and my men will not know the red uniform," he cautioned. "You should all get yourselves Russian fur hats."

He was right; they were much warmer, which meant I no longer had to wrap a scarf about my ears. Suitably attired we loitered around his headquarters, watching as the last units re-joined the Russian army. I was feeling quite relaxed as things were going well and if anything, slightly disappointed. It might seem strange, but since my teens I had been brought up on tales of the 'Corsican ogre'. The young general who had pushed the British out of Toulon, captured northern Italy, conquered Egypt, made himself ruler and then emperor of France, beaten the combined armies of Austria and Russia, before annihilating Prussia. Yet here he was getting roundly thrashed by less than half of the Russian army. It was like watching a celebrated prize fighter go down to the first punch. Not that I was ungrateful, mind; an easy victory and a safe journey back to Konigsberg would suit me very well. Being present at the battle of Jonkendorf – even if I had seen none of the fighting – would be something to boast of when I got home. I really should have known better.

According to Kit's watch it started at a quarter past one in the afternoon: a new cannonade to the east. Initially, Benningsen was not unduly concerned. "I have a flank guard out there," he told us. "It is commanded by Kamenski's son, who is anxious to repair the disgrace of his father. He will not let me down and besides, the rivers there will block any French advance." But then as the afternoon progressed the news went from bad to worse.

It was now clear that as well as pinning down our rear guard, Napoleon had sent at least two of his marshals to go further around our left flank. Somehow the Cossack scouts had missed them. One marshal's forces now pinned down Kamenski, who found that the rivers offered little defence. After the recent cold weather, the ice on them was now thick enough for the French to cross over. He did his best to protect us from the south and east, fighting a desperate action, but it was not enough. The second marshal had travelled even further north before swinging west to get behind Kamenski. More importantly, this French corps had captured the near undefended town of Guttstadt in our rear, where the Russian hospital and stores were located. This depot was ten miles north-east of us and had been thought safe from the French in the south.

For over an hour a series of often bloodstained couriers reported events that transformed Bennigsen from a confident general to an ashen-faced commander, staring at his map for any kind of inspiration to save the situation. He was being attacked on two fronts, with the forces in Guttstadt threatening to cut him off from Konigsberg and escape back to Russia. By dusk he was left with little alternative: "We have to retreat," he announced to his officers. "If we stay here, we will be encircled and left to starve or driven to the sea." He drew a line on the map from our position to Konigsberg, "We will leave after nightfall. Tell the soldiers to light fires to fool the French that we are still here. Our march will take us along this line, but we must get ahead of the French if we are to break out back to Russia."

It was a sobering assessment, but no one argued against it. There was no alternative; we had been comprehensively outmanoeuvred. Napoleon *was* the master tactician rather than the prize duffer I had taken him for. Even Wilson was muted in his criticism of the French. We went away to pack our possessions and ready our horses, on whom our lives were likely to depend. It was dusk by the time we returned to headquarters. We had planned to join Bennigsen on the retreat, but to our surprise he had already left.

"He wanted to survey the route ahead," explained Schmidt as he rolled up maps and papers. He probably also wanted to get ahead of the inevitable log jam that would result when seventy thousand men, horses, cannon and wagons tried to retreat down three very narrow roads. We had discovered that local landowners made it a feudal duty for their peasants to keep the roads maintained. Consequently, to give themselves less work, the serfs would only make them wide enough for one vehicle. If a cannon lost a wheel in a forested section, then either all behind would have to wait or trees had to be cut down to make a route around.

As we tucked into some eggs, meat and sliced black bread on the table, Schmidt told us that the cannon would take the middle of the three routes so that they did not hold up the retreat, while cavalry and infantry would take the roads on either side. He wished us well as we got up to leave and then held us back. "Here," he called, throwing us an uncut loaf of the heavy dark bread from the sideboard. "Divide that between you. God knows when our next meal will come."

With our pockets full of food, we stepped out into the night and immediately pulled our bearskins around us. Pin pricks of light all around from campfires illuminated a train of artillerymen pulling their guns away from the defensive bank. Columns of weary soldiers marched in the same direction. Some would have only arrived earlier that day from their march south and yet now they were heading off again. Snow began to fall as we mounted up to join them. I think we all had a sense of foreboding, but none of us could imagine the horrors to come. We were about to embark on a brutally cold and deadly race with the French army. It would only end when two frozen armies fought themselves to a standstill in the bloodiest battle yet known.

It is hard to portray with pen and ink the full horror of that journey. My hand shivers a little at the mere memory. It lasted six days and left a thick trail of ice-gnarled corpses in its wake. By the time we reached the designated roads that first evening, the snow was coming down so thickly that we had no idea which one we had taken. All I could do was squint through the blizzard to see the man in front and follow him. At least the awful weather enabled Russian soldiers to slip away from the French. I doubt Napoleon knew the Russian army was on the move until the following dawn. We ended up walking beside our horses to save their strength; we could not go faster than the men around us anyway without risking becoming lost. The animals' bodies gave us some shelter from the howling, ice-laden wind as we stumbled over unseen rocks in the snow. I had a scarf around my face so that only my eyes were visible under my new fur cap. The blizzard was disorientating, causing occasional moments of panic when I thought I was alone. At other times I trudged forward almost in a trance.

We covered near twelve miles that night, Benningsen wanted to get past the French outpost at Guttstadt before he allowed the army to rest. It might not seem far to you, but it was the longest distance we covered in a day on that awful trek and by far the quietest night we had. Despite the hat, scarf and fur, I was shivering with cold and exhausted when we came across men shouting at us to stop and directing us towards a hillside to rest. We were so covered in snow that only Wilson's six-foot height distinguished him from Kit. There were some trees ahead of us and so we staggered over to them for what little shelter they would provide. My fingers were so numb it took me three attempts to tie the reins of my horse to one of the branches. I had not slept for over a day and so, with little ceremony, I slumped down on the leeward side of one of the trunks.

"W-we sh-should sleep t-together for warmth," muttered Wilson through chattering teeth. In a moment Kit was slumped against my left shoulder, with Wilson on his other side. Soon Kit's head was lolling against the tree and he was snoring softly, while I was distracted by the arrival of a regiment just in front of us. A score of them were pulling on ropes that I realised were attached to a cannon barrel they were dragging through the snow. Half a dozen more were rolling two large wheels over the ice and then came another group pulling what was left of the gun limber. Relieved of their burdens, they staggered off near us and fell to the ground in rows on the open snow. In little more than minutes we were all transformed from men into snow-covered humps.

"Flashman, wake up!" The voice urged from my left and an elbow hit that side of my body, but as I came reluctantly into consciousness, I felt something tugging at my bearskin from my right. I opened my eyes and squinted into the bright dawn light to see two cruel eyes looking down at me over a grinning mouth. Yet what really attracted my attention, was the wickedly sharp blade the man was waving under my nose. His left hand was pulling at the pelt around my shoulders and instinctively I pushed back against the tree to trap it where it was.

"No!" I shouted as it finally dawned on me that I was being robbed. I knew that the fur could mean life itself to me over the coming days and I was not going to give it up without a fight. My left hand grabbed the wrist holding the knife while my right took a firm grip on the now receding animal skin. It took all my strength to keep the blade away from my throat. My own weapons were tucked out of reach within my buttoned greatcoat, but I was aware of Kit struggling within his clothes and Wilson rolling away to get to his feet.

"No you don't, you villain," Kit called out as he withdrew a pistol from under his own bearskin. As he cocked the weapon I remember thinking that the powder was bound to be damp. My assailant evidently assumed the same as he gave one final heave to wrench the pelt from my grip. Kit's hand was still shaking with cold as he pulled the trigger and to my surprise there was a sharp crack as the gun fired. The thief fell back, giving a roar and rolling away in the snow, while I leaned forward and pulled the fur back from his clutches. Wilson was on his feet now, drawn sword in hand as he stood over my assailant, who was clutching the side of his head and cursing us in his own language. As he moved his hand, I saw a ragged hole in his ear lobe.

He was bloody lucky; the way Kit's hand was shaking, the ball could have gone anywhere.

The shot and commotion had woken those around us. Men were starting to sit up from where they had lain half buried in the snow, like ghouls rising from the grave. Many glared at us with resentment; whatever their dreams were, they had to be better than our current predicament. It had stopped snowing, but the weather was as cold as ever. I was just thanking Kit for his assistance when there was a roar of rage from a Russian officer across the clearing. He strode towards us looking absolutely furious. I hurriedly staggered to my feet, undoing some of my greatcoat buttons so that I could more easily reach my sword and pistols if required. The villain who had tried to rob me was also getting to his feet, whining a complaint to his officer and pointing an accusing finger at Kit. The Russian shouted angrily in our direction and more of their soldiers rose to stand. Things were starting to look ugly. I slowly slid my hand inside my coat until my cold fingers closed around the butt of my pistol. I did not draw the weapon. It would have been excessive, for the officer was only carrying a riding whip. As he reached us, I tried to explain what had happened, although I doubted he would understand.

"That man tried to steal my bearskin," I started. "He had a knife to my throat and we only shot him to defend ourselves." The thief began talking again too, which to us was just a fast babble of sound, but he held up his open hands in that international gesture of innocence. It did him no good. To our surprise, when the officer raised his riding crop it was to lash down on his own soldier rather than threaten us. The man squealed and fell to the ground, his body curling in anticipation of kicks, which it duly received. Eventually, the thief rolled away and, staggering to his feet, ran across the clearing.

"I must apologise for that vermin troubling you," the Russian spoke in perfect English. "You must be the British officers I have heard about." He stared about us and frowned, "Are you travelling alone? Do you not have an escort?"

"We were attached to General Bennigsen's headquarters, but he went to scout the route ahead and left without us," explained Kit.

The trace of a smile played around the officer's lips. "Then let me show you some *Russian* hospitality. His words clearly implied that Bennigsen's Germanic care of his guests was far from satisfactory and at that moment I would not have disagreed. But then he added, "I will attach some of my Cossack escort to protect you."

"I am not sure we would feel any safer," I countered. "A band of those same men tried to kill us a few days ago." I pointed at the retreating thief, "and isn't that man a Cossack? He is certainly dressed like one."

"That man will be flogged later," insisted the officer. "But I assure you that the Cossacks have their own code of honour. If they are assigned to your protection, they will do so with their lives." Without waiting for our acceptance, he wished us a good morning and turned on his heel. As far as he was concerned, the matter was settled.

"Cossack hospitality, that is all we darn well need. I am not going to sleep comfortably knowing that those rogues are close at hand," I muttered to the others as the officer strolled out of earshot. I half hoped that we would get back underway on our journey north before our so-called 'protectors' arrived, but the army showed no sign of wanting to resume their march. Indeed, many were only now arriving in the camp after spending the night on the trail. We were in a shallow valley. There was a frozen stream at the bottom while above us the surrounding hilltops were covered in thick forest.

We thought about setting off to look for Bennigsen, but the dense woodland could hide brigands or French hussars and we did not fancy riding off by ourselves. In the end we returned to where we had left the horses and ate breakfast, gnawing disconsolately on some of the tough black bread we had in our pockets. The valley was filling with men and various groups had managed to light fires – some form of gruel was being prepared for the ones nearest us. We watched the trails of smoke rise into the air and Wilson moaned, "It will not take the French long to see this camp."

"They will have our trail to follow in the snow," added Kit. "A blind beggar could track that. We will never be able to shake them off... Ouch, I am sure that there are stones baked into this bread.

Either that or I have lost a tooth." He spat out the offending small pebble into his hand before tossing it away. As he did so we heard the rumble of guns to the south. "It sounds like they have found us already," he added.

The gunfire sounded several miles away, though as we listened it grew in intensity. "Surely the French have not got all their artillery into the hills already," I queried. "At least some of those guns have to be Russian. Let's hope they can keep the French at bay long enough for us to get away." I was hurriedly getting to my feet, for there was a new urgency to our departure now, when a voice came from behind me.

"We leave at noon," the man announced. I turned to see a smiling Russian lieutenant holding out his hand in greeting. "Dmitry," he introduced himself. In fact, he gave a surname as well, but it was so long that none of us could remember it afterwards. "I am the commander of your new escort," he explained.

"I hope you can assure us that they will not murder us in our sleep," I retorted sharply. "I woke this morning to find a Cossack knife at my throat."

"Yes, I have been told," replied Dmitry, still smiling and ignoring any hostility. "But you need not worry. When you ride with us, you are one of us," he insisted. "No Cossack would dream of stealing from another." Given recent experiences, I was not sure whether to be insulted or reassured.

"You speak good English," said Kit, trying to be more welcoming. "Have you been to England?"

"No, but my mother is English. There are lots of English ladies' maids in St Petersburg."

"Why noon?" asked Wilson, gesturing towards the sound of the distant battle. "Shouldn't we use all the time that the rear guard are gaining for us?"

"The general does not want the army too strung out on the march. French cavalry could outflank us and break it apart. We will march from noon until dusk. The rear guard will fight during the day and use the night to pull back."

"When will they sleep?" I asked.

Dmitry shrugged, "They will have a few hours before the French catch up with them in the morning."

I could not see how the rear guard could survive such a punishing schedule for long. They had already held off the might of the French army for two days before the retreat started. Now they were expected to continue to fight for days while marching through freezing temperatures during the night. I thought that they would be in a state of exhaustion when the French attacked the next day, but I was to be proved wrong. They kept fighting day after day after day. Years later Marshal Ney boasted to me in his usual colourful manner, that the survivors of the rear guard he had commanded on the retreat from Moscow were so tough, their balls were attached with wire. Well, these Russians were just as tough and they were fortunate to be as well led too. Their commander was Pyotr Bagration, probably the best Russian general they had. He was to perform miracles over the coming days, especially given that his troops were poorly trained.

Dmitry re-joined us at midday with six Cossack troopers to form our escort. They looked exactly the same as the men who had tried to kill us previously, armed with swords and lances and mounted on strong ponies. We had fed our own horses that morning with some oats we had with us in a sack, but there was not enough for a long journey. The animals had raked the ground with their hooves looking for grass, but there was precious little to fill their bellies. They had shivered during the night alongside us. I wondered if they would make it back to Konigsberg – and if we could make the journey if they didn't.

Trumpets blew to signal the start of the march. Cold, tired men were marshalled into columns and then we set off in the vanguard of the army. A regiment of hussars was to the front and we could see bands of other Cossacks riding through the edge of the trees on either side of us. We went on foot to rest the horses and if you ignored what was happening behind us, it was a pleasant walk. The sun shone, the air was crystal clear, if cold, and the snow crisp under foot. With sturdy boots my feet were dry and I was warm enough in my greatcoat so had tied the bearskin to the saddle. We had been walking for over an hour when I looked back at the army from a rise in the ground. Already the leading regiments were half a mile back and there was a trail of suffering humanity as far as the eye could see. Never have I appreciated more the craft of my bootmaker. Even from that distance we could see that beside the blocks of men coming slowly forwards, was a crowd of limping stragglers. I shuddered at the memory of the ones we had seen days before and wondered if they were still amongst those in view, or if they now lay frozen and still on the trail behind. For once I was glad to be in the vanguard of an army, for the selfish reason that I would not have to watch their agonies.

It was not even three o'clock before we reached a group of staff officers, who ordered us to halt in another wide valley. There was still no sign of Bennigsen, but Schmidt was there and evidently the general was getting reports on the state of his men, as he had decided that they could go no further today. We had barely covered eight miles, but as the first regiments staggered into the valley, we could see that the Hanoverian was undoubtedly right. Nearly every man was limping and many were being held up by their fellows. Officers kept some of them moving, though, as parties were sent off into the nearby trees for firewood. I thought we would have to do the same, but then a Cossack rode up and spoke to Dmitry, who announced that we were leaving for some abandoned cottages. We were to learn that most Cossacks see themselves as merely attached to an army rather than members of it. They have their own leaders and live and fight to their own rules.

For the first time that day we mounted our horses and galloped up the slope away from the valley that was now filling with soldiers. There was still an hour of daylight left as we trotted along a trail through the trees before descending towards a sizeable village. There must have been at least a hundred Cossacks there already. The previous occupants were long gone and had taken what possessions they could carry with them, but some things had been left behind. I saw one of our escort chase and impale a fleeing hen on a lance with considerable skill. In no time our horses were sheltered amongst a herd of mounts in one of two barns and men were tearing thatch from the roofs of several of the smaller cottages to feed them. Fires were lit in the other properties and we were soon inside watching as the hen was plucked for the pot.

I found myself warming to the Cossacks, quite literally, as we were pressed into the parlour of the cottage shoulder to shoulder. As they laughed and chatted in their own tongue, they made sure that we all got cups of the chicken and potato broth produced on the stove. Not that there was much chicken in it; there must have been three fowls and a few pounds of potatoes between a hundred men. We didn't complain though. The broth was hot and it felt good to have something in our bellies. There were thirty men in our cottage and soon they settled down for the night. The snoring would have drowned out the noise of a steam-powered lumber mill, but I did not mind. We were fed, a fire still blazed in the hearth and with so many bodies in the room, it was comfortably warm. As one of the men relieved from sentry duty opened the door to the outside there was an icy blast, which only made me more grateful. Just a valley away thousands of men were sleeping out in the open, as we had done the night before. That had been bone-sapping cold and I was not sure how many more nights like that I could survive.

The next morning as we stepped out of that warm and stuffy cottage the first gust of wintry wind nearly took our breath away. I soon had my bearskin wrapped tight around my shoulders once more, not least because it was snowing again. We mounted our rested and fed horses and made our way back through the forest to re-join the army. It was an eerily quiet ride as the snow muffled the hooves. Once more the sound of battle to the south had ceased. The rear guard must have pulled back and when we saw the state of the Russian column, we all questioned how much longer the French would be able to continue the pursuit. I watched a sergeant walking down a line of humps in the snow, kicking each one or hitting it with a stick. Most began to stir but a few did not. As we passed another regiment we saw two soldiers dragging a corpse towards a line of bodies by the side of the trail. We had seen stragglers before, but now even the hardy Russians were dying of this winter. The ground was far too hard to bury them; they would just be abandoned where they lay. They had already been stripped of clothes and boots by their comrades. Often the bodies were curled into the foetal position as they had hunched for warmth, but I vividly remember one Russian at the end of the line. He was pitifully thin and looked barely more than a teenager. Unlike the others he had died lying straight with his arms outstretched as though he was embracing the cold. His clothes had not been stolen – they were neatly folded at his side as he had left them. It was clear that he had suffered enough and had gone out to deliberately die, naked in the blizzard. Perhaps his fellows had left his possessions alone for superstitious reasons. It was understandable; he looked like a white alabaster sculpture of Christ. What struck me most, though, was that while the faces of the other bodies were contorted into expressions of agony, his features were perfectly at peace.

We set off once more, staying again in the vanguard of the army. I was grateful to be away from the miserable suffering behind. I *almost* felt guilty about my relatively comfortable night. There had been no breakfast and we all surreptitiously started to nibble on the hard, sour black bread we had in our pockets. It was not pleasant, but when your stomach is telling you that there is nothing between your belly and your spine, you find yourself going for more. Wilson demonstrated more willpower than me. He wrapped what he had left in a kerchief and stuffed it at the bottom of his saddlebag, swearing he would not touch it again until the morrow. I kept picking at mine until there was none left.

The day began to follow a familiar pattern: at around eleven in the morning cannon fire resumed from the south. We set off at noon and then by mid-afternoon the vanguard was called to a halt in another sheltered valley, where it would spend the next night.

Some of the Cossacks set out on a patrol and I harboured the hope that they would find another abandoned village for us to shelter in that night. Wilson insisted on joining them and two hours later they were back with three French prisoners. They had found a squadron of French dragoons who had ranged ahead, trying to discern the route of our march. Wilson was full of praise for the way that the Cossacks had ambushed them, killing a dozen, taking the prisoners and chasing the rest off. He waxed lyrical about their horsemanship, fighting ability and comradeship. He proclaimed that they were the best light cavalry he had ever encountered and began writing a note along these lines for Hutchinson, which he read out to us. In it he also claimed that the Cossacks could make the difference in the coming conflict. Given that just days before he had been dismissing these same men as murderous bandits, I found this transformation in his opinion quite tiresome.

I had long since discovered that Wilson was a man of obsessions: he was either passionately in favour of something or violently against it. There was no middle ground. The Cossacks were his new infatuation. More importantly, from my perspective, while they had been chasing the French around the barren countryside, they had not found us anywhere warm to spend the night. As the main army bivouacked in the valley bottom, the Cossacks camped higher up the hill on the treeline. Soon Dmitry had our escort cutting down branches and arranging them over a half-fallen tree trunk to make a rudimentary shelter. We helped in these efforts so that we could get out of the biting wind that blew stronger on the slope than down on the valley floor. We finished the ragged roof just in time as it began to snow heavily, and soon a blizzard blocked our view of the rest of the army. While we would go hungry, we followed the Cossack example of hobbling the horses' rear legs. This left their front hooves free to kick under the snow for fallen pine needles and grass to eat.

With our escort, we squashed ourselves into the shelter, huddling together for warmth. A fire was lit at the entrance and to the surprise of the English contingent, a kettle was soon boiling and strong black tea provided.

"Well, this is very civilised," said Kit as he sipped on the brew. He grinned and added, "I wonder if they will pass around nuts and a cigar next."

"I wish they would pass around some bloody food," I grumbled, "I am famished." A short time later the need for a piss dominated my thoughts. I tried to put it off but knew I would not be able to sleep without going. Securing the fur about my shoulders I crawled outside and gasped in the icy wind. This would necessarily be a quick affair;

there are some places you definitely do not want frostbite. I moved behind the shelter to stand in the lee of a thick tree trunk to piss down wind. As I did so a movement caught my eye. It was a horse shuffling in the snow. From the brass cavalry helmet hanging from the saddle I recognised it as Wilson's. Then my rumbling stomach reminded me what else was secreted on the animal…

"I can't believe it," fumed Wilson indignantly the next morning. "Whatever happened to 'no Cossack would steal from another'. The bloody wretches stole from me."

"You might have to revise that note to Hutchinson," I suggested, suppressing a smile. There had only been two mouthfuls of the black bread wrapped in the cloth, but they had made all the difference to stop my stomach rumbling through the night.

"I will report the theft to Dmitry," insisted Wilson. "He will find the culprit."

"You can't do that," I told him. "You saw what happened to that man who tried to steal from us before. He will probably have our whole escort flogged and we don't even know it was one of them. There are Cossacks camping all along the crest. We will spend the rest of this journey being glared at by men with bloodied backs over a crust of bread."

Wilson conceded that I was right, as I knew he would. He hated such punishments. With typical audacity, a year after he had bought a commission in the cavalry, with no prior military experience, he had published a pamphlet on how the army should be run. In it he had roundly condemned the practice of flogging.

That morning as the troops below us laid out another line of frozen corpses in the snow, we readied to move off. This time we did not travel far. Over the next hill was a small stone bridge crossing a frozen river gulley. It was here we joined the rear of another of the columns of retreating Russians and just two miles further on, we could see the walled medieval town of Landsberg. The thought of walls, roofs and warming fires to protect us from the biting cold – not to mention food – hurried us along the narrow track. By the time we reached the town gates we could see that the streets were full of hobbling soldiery and gun captains trying to push their teams of horses and cannon through the throng. The Cossacks led us round to the northern gate and there we were able to enter. On enquiry, we were directed to Bennigsen's headquarters in a small office above the town hall. The ground floor was packed with Russian wounded, far more carrying injuries from frostbite than enemy action. There were rows of men with blackened feet, which, from their wails, were clearly agony now they were starting to thaw. One Russian officer I met later, estimated that each day of the retreat had resulted in the death of a thousand men from cold and fatigue, on top of any killed by the French.

It was the first time we had seen Bennigsen in four days and I noted immediately that the retreat had taken a toll on him too. He was gaunt, unshaven and hungry, for we swiftly discovered that there was no food to be had at his headquarters. He was, however, still managing the situation from afar, with officers bringing him reports of movements that he marked on a map before sending them away with his orders.

"The French are closing in on us," he explained. He pointed on the chart at the stone bridge we had crossed earlier, "I will need the rear guard to make a stand here, for I will not get the army to march away from these walls tonight.

"Can you not make a stand in the town itself?" asked Kit.

Bennigsen rubbed his stubbly chin and stared out of a window where his soldiers could still be seen toiling towards the walls. "No, we cannot afford to be encircled and there is not enough room to deploy the guns." He pointed at the nearby forest and added, "French skirmishers are trained to fight in loose order among the trees, while my sharpshooter regiments still fight in ranks. They even think that kneeling to shoot is dishonourable. Our outposts would soon be driven towards the town and there is not room for everyone within its walls. We will stop them, but not today. I have ridden ahead; we will fight the French here." At this, his finger stabbed at another settlement just eight miles from Landsberg. We all craned over to look at the place on the map. It was a strange sounding name, and it was to be a cauldron for courage and stubborn resistance. It marked where Napoleon and his army was to lose its reputation for invincibility. The town was called Eylau.

Chapter 8

For much of that day it looked like the army would not survive long enough to see the oddly named town. It was essential that the rear guard held the French at the stone bridge we had passed early that morning. They had to buy time for the army to regroup and for the guns and other wagons to get over more bridges around the town of Landsberg. The first French attacks were repulsed, but then they came on in stronger numbers, with their renowned cuirassier-armoured heavy cavalry throwing back Russian infantry.

From the top of the town hall we could observe the movement of distant columns of men through the cannon smoke. The sight of them came as something of a shock, at least to me. Unlike Wilson, this was the first French army I had seen, and while we could not make out the uniforms on the distant men, it was clear that a battle was underway. We had heard them, of course, over recent days, but seeing them for ourselves brought home the precarious position both the army and *we* were in. I was not sure if my stomach was rumbling through fear or hunger. How had my supposedly safe diplomatic mission left me slap in the path of a rampaging French army?

I wondered what would happen if we were taken prisoner. We were in enemy uniform, but Hutchinson carried diplomatic papers covering our mission. We were supposed to be observers rather than combatants, yet I was not sure that the French would make much distinction. That is if we were not killed in some battle or during the inevitable sacking of Konigsberg, twenty miles to the north, that would follow a Russian defeat. Wilson was sure that if he were captured, he at least would be taken to Paris to answer for his printed slanders. The best the rest of us could hope for was some exchange with French prisoners of equal rank. It was high time that we effected a swift mounted retreat of our own back to the nearest port and then boarded the first ship home. But before I could even suggest this blindingly obvious course of action, Kit ruled it out.

"Well," he said as he studied the distant enemy through his glass. "Now we will get to do what my brother sent us here for: see how well the Russians can resist the French." I bit back my proposal in the nick of time. I could easily imagine Hutchinson's scornful reaction if we turned up having missed the battle. For better or worse, we were with our allies until their army was victorious or broken. As the French continued to advance, it looked very much like it would be the latter.

Bennigsen was obliged to send some of his own elite horseman back down the road to support the defence. Reminded of our mission, Wilson was adamant he was going with them. He was back three hours later and full of his usual fervour. He reported that the Russian cavalry had found the French horsemen disordered from their pursuit of infantry. The resulting charge had pushed Napoleon's men back to the bridge. Yet as the afternoon wore on, the tsar's army was forced slowly back once more. By early evening both armies had endured enough, and the fighting ceased. We could see hundreds of French campfires like stars on the hillside, less than two miles away.

When we had not been watching proceedings from the top of the town hall, we had been in Benningsen's headquarters as he made his preparations. The army was to begin its march that evening as soon as it was too dark for the French to see what was going on. The general thought that Napoleon would expect him to make his stand at Landsberg. If the French thought that the pursuit was over, the Russians could steal a few hours' march on them before the enemy realised that they were wrong. Bennigsen had also finally received messages from the small Prussian army, which was some miles to the north and being pursued by another French marshal. Couriers were despatched to the Prussians, asking them to join with the Russian army the next day.

The distance to Eylau was only nine miles, a comfortable night's march in normal circumstances, but there was nothing normal about this campaign. There were two roads from Landsberg to Eylau. One went around the town; the first mile was a narrow, icy track between two rows of trees with a steep incline . The other went through the twisting narrow medieval streets of Landsberg before emerging onto a similar slope. Neither was ideal to convey hundreds of cannon and wagons as well as thousands of horses and tens of thousands of men.

Particularly as torches and lanterns were forbidden to light the way, as these would reveal our movements to the French. General Bagration and his redoubtable rear guard would remain in the town until well past dawn to give the impression it was still occupied.

Despite not having had any sleep since the night before, we set off on our journey at around seven that evening. An hour later we were still only just leaving Landsberg, having been held up in the streets that were log-jammed with men and vehicles. The hillside was a scene of chaos, with gunners and cart drivers lashing branches to the rims of their wheels to give them some purchase on the ice. Only vehicles used the roads; those on foot or hoof made their way through the drifts on either side. To add to the confusion, it now began to snow again, which with the dark meant we could hardly see anything around us. Ironically, this might have helped those on the road, as the snow covered the ice and gave the wheels more grip. By midnight the blizzard had eased and a passing staff officer told us we were halfway to our destination. Guns and wagons were moving on both roads now the ground was flatter, while columns of grim-faced Russian infantry loomed out of the darkness and marched after the sleds carrying their officers.

By early dawn we had reached the town of Eylau. I had been dozing in the saddle and was awoken by Kit shaking my shoulder. "We're here," he announced. "Let's find somewhere to rest." Having knocked on a couple of doors with no answer or any sign of life within, we realised that the town must have been abandoned. Its citizens had wisely decided that they did not want to be there in the middle of a battle. Heaven knew where they had gone and I was far too tired to care. We forced the lock of a house that had a stable at the back. While Wilson tended to the mounts, I searched in the cupboards for something to eat. Not a scrap was left, but, fortunately, as the former occupants had not been able to take their beds when they left, I was soon snoring on one of them.

Morning revealed that Eylau was a sizeable town with a large church. The laggard units of the Russian army were still marching towards the town from the south-east. The ground there was flat with several frozen lakes surrounded by hedges and trees. There was no sound of gunfire from that direction either, indicating that the French had not started the pursuit. Most of the Russian army was being directed beyond the settlement. To the north-east there were some hills that overlooked the town and the surrounding land. It was open exposed country and it was where Bennigsen had chosen to make his stand. His army had more guns than the French and there was no cover from which enemy skirmishers could shoot at his men. To attack, Napoleon's army would have to march up the snow-covered hillside and into a storm of cannon fire.

It had gone nine in the morning by the time I woke. Having seen we were in no imminent danger my first thought was to light a fire in the hearth of a room from where we could watch the enemy approach. If we were going to be observers, I thought, there was no reason not to do it in comfort. Having broken up some furniture, we soon had a blaze going and were warming ourselves as we watched the last of the cannon being hauled through the town. By ten we could hear gunfire to the south, which got steadily louder as the morning progressed. Then at noon we could see the first of the rear guard on the far side of the frozen lakes. They were pulling back in good order with some artillery offering support. As the French followed them onto the ice, we watched the leading battalion engage in a musketry duel with a Russian regiment.

"Look there!" called Wilson and he pointed at a column of Russian cavalry approaching along the lake shore behind a line of trees. I thought the French would be bound to spot them through the gaps in the foliage, but perhaps the whisps of loose snow that the wind was blowing about the flat surface of the lake obscured them. Oblivious to the danger, the men in blue kept pushing the Russian infantry back, now exposing their flank to the horsemen. They made a target too good to miss. The Russian troop commander knew his business; he arrayed his men for the charge and then signalled it with a slash of his sword rather than by blowing a trumpet. We watched in fascination as a line of mounted death swiftly advanced across the ice towards its prey. Wilson was banging the windowsill and cheering them on even though they were at least half a mile away. I thought that the French would see them or even feel the vibrations of hooves on the ice, but the surface was covered in a foot of whirling snow, which probably muffled the noise.

At last, a cry of alarm must have gone up, for the French line abruptly fell apart. It was far too late to attempt forming square. Some soldiers panicked and ran across the flat, featureless lake surface in a doomed attempt to outrun the mounted men. The rest tried to form small groups with a hedgehog of bayonets to keep the riders at bay. It was not enough. We saw a furious fight around the largest of those clusters before some riders peeled away holding a pole in the air. Elsewhere, sabres rose and fell, leaving blood to soak into the ice. It was near perfect conditions for cavalry, with a broken enemy and no cover to hide them. The horsemen exacted a heavy toll before, belatedly, some French cavalry arrived to support their comrades. As the Russians pulled back, the sight of hundreds of corpses on the ice indicated that, for most, the rescue was far too late.

"I told you the Russian cavalry were a match for anything the French can offer," boasted Wilson. "We will have more cannon here too." He slapped Kit on the shoulder and added, "Soon we will be reporting to your brother a splendid Russian victory and the Corsican tyrant will be scampering back to France, if he has not already been caught by a Russian bayonet."

I was not so sure about that; one swallow does not make a summer. This brief victory did not hide the fact that the Russians had been retreating before the French since we joined their army. But there was no holding back my comrade's enthusiasm as the leading horsemen of what turned out to be the St Petersburg Dragoons rode past us, holding their prize aloft. "That is a French eagle standard," Wilson shouted, before leaning out of the window to yell, "Bravo!" at the bloodied horsemen. I caught a brief glimpse of the gilded carving of the bird atop the gold-painted pole. Rumour had it that regimental eagles were conferred by the emperor in person and were as precious to its soldiers as a colour flag in a British regiment. Even I had to concede that its capture was a good omen for the contest ahead.

Our celebrations were interrupted by the arrival of more Russian soldiers into the house. They were detailed to defend it against the coming French and were soon knocking loopholes to fire from out of the walls. It seemed to me high time we retreated to Bennigsen's headquarters and for once my companions did not disagree. We rode through the town, which was now full of soldiers building barricades and piling furniture in windows, to continue up the slope on the far side to the main Russian position. Batteries of cannon lined the top of the ridge. There must have been at least three hundred guns, and more were stationed in the valley below protecting the rear guard and the town. The artillery was the pride of the Russian army and here it had a commanding view over any approach the French could make. As I tightened the bearskin around me in the biting wind, I reflected that while we had cursed the icy weather it had probably saved the Russian army. A thaw, such as we had experienced when our carriage had sunk in the mud to its axles, would have forced them to abandon many of their cannon.

As we had come to expect, Bennigsen's headquarters was nowhere near his front line. It was a mile back in a large farmhouse that was now packed with generals and senior officers. Our red uniforms stood out in the crowd and on seeing us Bennigsen made room at the table and explained his plans. The village would be the first line of his defence, but he did not expect to hold it. Instead, he hoped that his cannon would inflict casualties and demoralise the attackers before they began their assault on the ridge. That was where he hoped to stop the French and, with luck, the Prussians would join on our right flank to complete the victory.

It sounded a sensible plan, but I will be honest and say that I was more than a little distracted by a plate of poultry bones on the table that suggested we had just missed a meal. I was not the only one thinking along those lines, for Kit's stomach groaned so loudly that we all heard it. Even Bennigsen laughed, before – at last – summoning some food for us. I was salivating at the thought of roast fowl, but instead came three small squares of black bread. Our commander apologised that it was all they had left. The hen had been shared among a dozen of his staff and they had not found more. Several of his officers were looking enviously at us with even this small offering. I smiled gratefully as I bit into my share. I damn nearly lost a tooth, for the thing was as hard as a rock. In the end I had to use a small knife to cut off chunks, which I then had to soften in the corner of my mouth like a plug of tobacco.

A short time later we were joined by General Bagration, the commander of the rear guard and a young ensign who had captured the eagle. The cavalryman was wounded and as he laid the trophy down on the table for inspection, I saw that it too was bloodstained, the shaft half cut through by a blade. The wooden eagle had its wings open but pointing down and was less than a foot tall. It was a strange thing to die for, but as I was to learn later in my career, men and even young boys were to regularly sacrifice themselves for the two yards of cloth that made a British regimental standard. Bennigsen congratulated the ensign and promised him that the eagle would be sent to the tsar with the tale of his valour. At this Bagration said the courier should wait, as there would be a flock of such birds to send on the following day. Wilson translated this remark for us as Bagration did not use English or French, instead speaking in German to his commander.

It turned out he was *Prince* Bagration as well as a general. I never did understand Russian nobility, for as far as I could tell, Bagration was no relation to the tsar, while the tsar's brother, who I met later, was only a grand duke. I was impressed that he had brought the young soldier who had captured the eagle with him, rather than claim the glory for himself. The general must have been exhausted from commanding the rear guard over the last week, yet he was shaved and smartly dressed. He still had a vibrant energy about him as he discussed Bennigsen's plans for the following day. I got the distinct impression that if he had been in command of the army, its headquarters would not have been a mile behind the front line.

It was getting dark as a series of couriers arrived with reports that the French were intensifying their attack on Eylau. The Russian commander in the town was pressing for reinforcements, but instead Bennigsen ordered him to pull his forces back to join the main battle line. "I always planned to give up the buildings," he insisted. "Our cannon cannot defend them against French skirmishers in the dark. We must preserve our forces to fight the enemy on our terms." Bagration did not argue and announced that he must return to his men. Wilson suggested that we should ride back with him to check that the French were not advancing beyond the town. I had no wish to go blundering around at night, but Kit agreed and soon we were on our way back to the ridge.

Wilson chatted to the prince in German – he could never resist toadying to royalty – and the two got on well. It was dark as there was a new moon. Bennigsen had forbidden fires to stop the disposition of troops being revealed to the French. Shadowy groups of men were just visible against the white snow. They sat huddled together for warmth. Judging from the smell of woodsmoke on the wind, the soldiers in blue were more fortunate. I suspected that every hearth in Eylau was now ablaze and the open ground across the valley was dotted with yet more fires.

As we bade farewell to the prince, I looked along the slope. Hidden in the darkness were tens of thousands of men, perhaps fifty or sixty thousand. Opposite was a smaller number, but more were still to arrive. All would know that a battle would take place on the morrow. I wondered how many, like me, felt sick with fear at the thought. There may have been a few serfs who would view death as a blessed relief from the torments of their life, but for most the urge to survive would be strong. They knew as well as I, that by the following evening these hillsides would likely be strewn with dead and injured. Perhaps even then they were praying to be spared. I had to remind myself that we were only observers. Unlike those poor bloody peasants, we were not going to be herded around for slaughter. Yet in any battle there was risk. A cannon ball would not care about who it maimed and there was always confusion in combat. As it turned out, for all of Bennigsen's planning, Eylau hosted more confusion than most.

Chapter 9

If anyone claims they can describe the battle of Eylau to you, they are lying, for I was there and yet still only saw bits of it. Much of the battle was fought in a snowstorm, which added several inches to the two foot of snow that was already on the hillside. I spent most of it bewildered and terrified, as dangers loomed at me from all directions. Yet the start of the day was relatively calm.

We had slept at Bennigsen's headquarters. Well, perhaps 'spent the night' would be a more accurate description, at least for me. While there was no food, vodka had been found from somewhere and on empty stomachs, several of our companions were soon roaring drunk. I took a nip or two myself, but it did little to settle my nerves. I lay half wrapped in my bearskin in the middle of a crowded floor with a moustachioed Russian colonel snoring loudly in my left ear and breathing spirit fumes in my face. I had pushed him away twice, but he kept rolling back and a sharp dig in the ribs had failed to wake him. Before we had retired, most of the officers toasted their imminent victory, loudly insisting that there was no question as to the outcome. I was to see such behaviour in many armies over the coming years, particularly when men had doubts that they would survive the following day. Wilson joined the toasts enthusiastically, but Kit was more circumspect. "I wonder if they did the same before Austerlitz," he murmured to me.

I lay awake for hours, listening for the sound of gunfire in case the French launched a surprise night assault. My eyes had only closed for a moment, it seemed, before I was shaken awake as the eastern sky started to brighten. As we prepared to leave, the men around us were much quieter as the enormity of the day ahead began to sink in. Some checked the loads of pistols, others sharpened blades and I saw at least one poor devil dry retching in the corner. An infantry major near me was hastily writing a letter. He smiled as his pen scratched out the words. It reminded me that I had not written to Louisa for a while, not that I had the means of delivering a note from this godforsaken backwater. My companion used a burning candle to close the now folded note and impressed the wax with the seal on his ring. He kissed the paper briefly and then started to look around the room. He must have been searching for someone he thought stood a better chance of surviving the day than him. When his eyes alighted on me, he murmured, "Ah Britansky, you will not be fighting today. Would you do me the service of holding this letter for me?" His eyes looked sadder as he added, "And, er...deliver it for me should I fall?"

I looked down at the address, half expecting one in St Petersburg. Instead, I read 'Dorothea Benckendorff,' with an address in Konigsberg. "Of course," I agreed. "We are due back in the city soon." He half sagged in relief and on impulse I reached out and gripped his shoulder, adding, "But I am sure that you will be back with your Dorothea yourself by then."

"I pray to God you are right, friend," he smiled wistfully. "If a man has to die, there is no better place than entwined in those limbs. This snowy hillside will make a poor shroud in comparison."

I was sure he was right. As I listened to the man still heaving in the corner, I thanked my lucky stars that we only had to observe the battle. I planned to do so from a *very* safe distance if I could manage it.

This plan did not start well as Bennigsen decided to lead his staff away from his secure headquarters and take them the mile to his front line. He wanted to view the valley between the opposing forces as the dawn light spread across the sky. I have to say that I was mightily heartened. The Russian infantry was being arrayed into a long defensive formation interspersed with cannon. The front battalions were arrayed in line while behind them were reserve battalions in column, ready to move forward and fill any gaps. The hillside they stood on had been chosen not for its height – it was much the same as the hill on the opposite side – but for its lack of cover for any attacking enemy skirmishers. But this also meant that every one of the Russians was exposed to the French, as Wilson put it, from "hat to heels." They made a formation stretching some three miles, these cold, weary men who had all endured that punishing retreat through Prussia.

Also suffering that journey had been the gunners and their artillery. The guns had been a massive burden at the time, but now they would come into their own. In addition to the battalion guns there were several huge batteries. Seventy guns were gathered opposite the town of Eylau, a further sixty on the right and forty on the left with another score of guns on each flank. Bennigsen expected the French attack to focus on his right in order to separate him from the Prussians, who were still expected to join us later in the day. At the time it did not seem to matter, for as we looked under the low brooding clouds into the valley ahead, hardly a Frenchman could be seen.

We knew from prisoners that the Cossacks had captured that in addition to Napoleon, his Imperial Guard and cavalry, there were only two of the six army corps in Prussia with him. He had perhaps half the men we did, although we did not doubt that his other marshals would now be closing in on us. It seemed to me that at that moment the French emperor was vulnerable. I wondered what would happen if we launched an all-out attack then, especially as his army was still in bed.

Bennigsen just laughed when I put the thought to him. "Ah, Captain Flashman, you are not a general. When you make a plan, you must stick to it." He was about to ride away, but then, perhaps wondering what we would report to Hutchinson, he turned back. "If my army were fighting in the town, I could not use my cannon. The gunners would not see friend from foe. The French would hold us at bay until reinforcements arrived and then their skirmishers would use cover to drive us back. No, we fight here, on our terms." He grinned, "I will wager fifty roubles with you, Captain, that we are fighting six French marshals and their emperor by sunset today. With that, he galloped off with his staff. Three officers in red were left mounted in the reserve line, at least one of whom was wondering what on earth they had let themselves in for.

At the time I was not convinced by the strategy. From what little I knew about Napoleon, he won battles precisely because he *did* change his plans, to exploit mistakes made by his enemies. I felt more certain a few minutes later when orders were given to the Russian artillery to open fire. Evidently, the French were used to starting their battles, as the gunfire caught them by surprise. I watched as the streets of Eylau were suddenly filled with running men, some only half dressed, as cannon balls crashed into the buildings around them. They must have thought we were attacking, but gradually they saw the Russian ranks still on the hillside and order was restored. Still, it was at least a quarter of an hour before the first French gun returned fire. By then the main batteries were wreathed in gun smoke and we rode some distance away from them so that we could still watch the enemy. It was a damn good job we did.

The French gunners slowly got into their stride. Judging from the amount of smoke there were fewer of them and they made much better use of cover to protect their cannon. The Russian gunners were all on the open hillside, although I saw that some had piled up snow in front of their batteries, forming deep embrasures that stretched along the slope. I had laughed at the thought of snow stopping a cannon ball, but I should have guessed that no one knows more about snow than a Russian. Later I saw these banks peppered with holes and embedded cannon balls still visible at the end of the tunnels they had created. Yet these ramparts could only be built so high if the Russian guns were to fire over the top of them – which left the gunners still horribly exposed.

While the Russian cannon blazed away at any target they could see, or the general direction of the town if the smoke blocked their view, it was clear that the French artillerymen were carefully targeting the Russian guns. A huge duel developed between the gunners. I was told afterwards that over four hundred guns were firing, the most in any battle ever at that time.

It was deafening. Soon you could no longer tell where the low cloud stopped and the plumes of smoke began. There were screams and clangs as guns were hit and dismounted. Sergeants shouted orders at soldiers to remain in their lines between the battalion guns and I saw several smears of crimson, stark on the white snow, where men had been snatched away by flying iron. Death became an utterly random affair. It was fortunate we had already dismounted for we had to duck as a ball whistled low over our heads. Slowly, we edged even further away from the nearest gun. I cursed Bennigsen now for choosing a hillside completely devoid of cover. I tried to use the saddle of my mount as a rest for my telescope; it gave some comfort to have something between me and those muzzles spitting destruction. Yet the animal was skittish and anyway, I knew that less than a ton of horseflesh would not stop a cannonball coming my way. Columns and lines of men around us stood stock still. Honour demanded that we stand with them and risk our share of the punishment.

Twice I saw men falling as their legs were torn away beneath them. Another ball ploughed through three men at once and left a pile of limbs and offal that was hopelessly mashed together. My mouth was soon dry with terror, and I found myself becoming obsessed with whether I had been born lucky or not. Luck alone, it seemed, would determine if I lived or died. I remember clutching my sword hilt tightly and recalling the outrageous stroke of good fortune that had won me the weapon. Did that mean I was lucky? Or perhaps I had used up any providence I had to obtain it and was now doomed.

I know I was not the only one having these doubts. As a gun was thrown back from its carriage, crushing two gunners underneath, I distinctly heard Kit mutter, "Oh dear God, please spare us." Even the reckless Wilson joined me in adding an "Amen" to that, crossing himself as he did so. One of them must have had far more influence with the Almighty than I do, for in less than a minute our prayers were answered.

"It's snowing!" I called as the first flakes began to fall on my sleeve. Within mere seconds we could no longer see the village of Eylau and then it became so thick that I could barely make out a file of men twenty yards away. Now blinded by the weather, the cannon on both sides of the valley ceased firing. The thundering noise and fear of being in the middle of a pitched battle, was replaced with an eery silence and the sensation of being almost alone in a white world. I will swear that in that valley containing at least a hundred thousand men, in the first minute after the guns stopped, not a single shout could be heard.

The three of us looked sheepishly at each other, none willing to acknowledge that our joint summoning of divine assistance might have brought on this marvel. For even though snow was hardly a rare occurrence that winter, it did indeed seem like a miracle right then.

"We should go closer to those men," I whispered, gesturing at the battalion in the reserve line that we could only now glimpse intermittently. "They might clear off during this storm and leave us alone against the entire French army when it stops."

My companions chuckled at the thought, but we did edge over in the direction I suggested. "Bennigsen does not change his plans, remember," chided Wilson. "The Russian army will stand firm."

"Instead of fretting over the Russians retreating," added Kit, "perhaps we should be more worried about the French advancing."

"But they can't," I protested. "They would never be able to co-ordinate an attack in this blizzard." I was certain I was right and even if I wasn't, the French were bound to attack one of our flanks. We were slap bang in the middle of the Russian defence and we had their largest artillery battery just a hundred yards away. Yet as we stood there, we began to hear distant shouts and orders. I was not sure if sound travelled in snow like it did in fog, but I could not make out whether they were French or Russian.

After what seemed like five minutes of straining our ears, Wilson announced, "Most of the shouting is coming from the left of our line." Then to confirm his words cannon fire started up again from that direction. It had to be some nervous gunners, I thought, firing at the voices or phantoms in the snow. I was even more certain when I heard French guns firing back. Surely they would not do that if their men were in the middle. I was relieved that the fighting was all to our left. The only danger we faced was nearly being run down by a cart bringing more ammunition to the main battery. It was all so damned disorientating. Watching snow in the wind can leave you mesmerised. Sometimes it muffled the sound of gunfire so that it sounded further away, but then it would seem to be closer. After half an hour we were sure that it was intensifying. The main battery was firing now. On the wind we heard distant men screaming as some of the shots must have struck home. Then we were distracted by a movement of the soldiers in the column to our left. They were changing their formation into a hollow square. Instead of having the ends of their ranks facing us, there were now lines of men closer to us with fixed bayonets pointing in our direction. It was an ominous development.

"Perhaps we should pull back?" I suggested.

"We would probably be killed if we tried it," replied Kit. "We are safe from that regiment because they saw us standing here with their general. To other Russians we are in strange uniforms and we don't speak their language. The chances are that they will think we are French."

Wilson volunteered to ask the soldiers if they knew what was happening. I held his horse as he strode over until he was just a few feet in front of their bayonets. The men we could see stared back at him implacably. He called out, enquiring if anyone there spoke English. There was no response and so he tried the same question in German. Finally, after a nervous glance at us over his shoulder, he enquired in French.

To our surprise, when a reply finally did come, it was in heavily accented English. "What you want, Britansky?"

"Do you know what is happening?" asked Wilson. "Why have you changed formation?"

Through a swirl in the snow, I could make out the silhouettes of several men standing behind the nearest rank of soldiers. We could hear Wilson's question being translated and rumbling voices as an answer was debated among them. Eventually, the voice shouted back, "We know nothing, but the French have many horsemen. Our colonel wants to be ready if they come."

"Well, the devils could have offered us shelter inside their square," muttered Kit as Wilson returned. The officers had gone, and the ranks remained solid and decidedly uninviting, their lines of bayonets still pointing at us. I agreed, although privately I thought that if hordes of French horsemen did appear, we would be better off mounted, taking to our heels and yelling "Britansky!" at the tops of our voices. Then as Wilson took back his reins, our world was turned back to front.

There was some shouting from our right and rear and urgent yells of alarm, and as we turned in that direction, we heard several shots.

86

Then, from almost directly behind us, came the last noise we expected to hear, a chorus of "*Vive l'Empereur!*"

"The French are behind us," I gasped in disbelief.

"Christ, we must be surrounded," muttered Wilson. He drew his sword and stared wildly around him, but apart from the nearby Russian ranks, the world was still stubbornly white. In the next moment we heard orders being shouted. Then with a startling roar, the lines of men we could see broke into a run, charging off into the blizzard behind us. Those on the flanks broke around us like a wave, all apart from one hairy peasant, who tried to go through me and knocked me to the ground. Half sprawled in the snow I was gripped by fear as my mind tried to work out what the hell was going on.

"Should we go after them?" asked Kit.

"We have no idea what they are charging towards," I countered. I desperately wanted to ride for safety, but now I had absolutely no idea where that was.

"If the French *have* brought cavalry," warned Wilson, "they will easily cut through a disorganised mass like that." By the time we had finished dithering, we had left it too late as all the Russians had disappeared through the surrounding curtain of snow. We stood there, three men alone in the middle of a pitched battle, listening to screams and yells from just a hundred yards away. We mounted up, ready to move quickly if needed. Wilson still held his sword, but Kit and I kept a hand on the pistol hilts tucked inside our coats to keep dry. Our clothes were coated in snow and when they had been beside us I saw that the Russian coats were pasted white too. The French had to be similarly caked in ice and I resolved to shoot at anything that came charging towards us.

We craned our heads to the sound of fighting nearby, trying to gauge what was happening. There was hardly any musket fire; the snow must have dampened the charges and priming. It was fortunate that the Russian army's main weapon was the bayonet as it was now all they had left. Then, as we squinted towards the fighting, I noticed something else: dark shadows were looming into view.

At first, I thought they were moving towards us, but I was wrong. The snow was stopping as quickly as it had begun and in less than a minute its veil had disappeared entirely. We whirled round to discover the scene of chaos and carnage it revealed.

"My God, they have broken right through the middle of our line!" exclaimed Wilson, pointing. I followed his gaze and saw that several battalions of French infantry were right behind the Russian centre. They seemed as surprised at their location as we were. Orders were shouted as they hurriedly tried to form a square. The nearest one was already engaged with the Russian regiment that had been next us, but trumpets were rallying Russian cavalry to this unexpected incursion. We could see clearly now the path the French had made through the deep snow. One column must have trudged quietly by, little more than a hundred yards from us. Another had routed a reserve column to the west of us and captured their battalion guns.

When I stared into the valley, I could see from their trail that they had started their march in the east on the French right. Yet as they climbed the slope they had veered left – we could see the bodies strewn in the snow as they had crossed in front of the main battery. Perhaps they had lost their bearings in the blizzard, as we could see more French regiments that had stayed further east. There, the French attack was stalling. Now our gunners could see them, the artillery was doing terrible damage and cavalry were gathering to chase them back to their own lines. Yet in the centre the French were already *behind* our guns. I saw some of the artillery men who had been chased off, now rushing back to tend their pieces. It would not take them long to turn them around, although now hundreds of their own soldiers were milling around between their muzzles and their prey.

As we watched, the men in those isolated squares got themselves organised. Their ranks straightened and now that it had stopped snowing they swept the slush from their priming pans, dried them and the muzzles began to spit death again at those around them. The Russian infantry who had charged in an unformed mass now started to fall back, having made little progress against a wall of bayonets. Cossacks and other cavalry wheeled about, but none fancied hurling their horses against that line of steel. I could see the French officers mounted inside their squares calling to each other and staring back to their own lines. The squares began to move, but not to retreat; they were aligning themselves to cover each other.

"They are trapped," concluded Wilson triumphantly. "They cannot retreat, for the guns of our batteries would tear them apart in those slow-moving, densely packed squares. But if they break formation, our cavalry will pour into the gaps." He pointed, "Look, those gunners will soon move their pieces and then if the French do not yield, they will be blasted with canister to breach their ranks." What he said made sense and I saw that some Russian gunners were already calling for teams of horses to pull their guns, while others were industriously digging them out of the snow drift that half covered them. I almost felt sorry for the men in blue; even if they had got lost in the blizzard, they had shown immense courage to get where they were. They were fighting bravely to keep half of the enemy army at bay and yet they were doomed. It was a foolish thought, for as we sat and watched the plans for their imminent demise, we should have realised that we were not the only ones surveying the scene.

"By Satan's beard, would you look at that." Kit was staring at something behind me and when I wheeled my mount around to look, my jaw dropped. Appearing around the edge of Eylau were lines of French horsemen. There were hundreds, no, thousands of them, and they were still coming. There was light cavalry, such as hussars, green-coated dragoons with their brass helmets and carbines and behind them the heavier cuirassiers, with steel breastplates astride their big horses. I frantically began to count them, multiplying an estimate of the number in the first rank by the number of rows behind. One thousand…two thousand…three thousand… I gave up and I was still only halfway down the formation. A clarion of distant bugles began to ring out. While the calls might have been intended to prompt the horsemen it also, at last, spurred the Russian batteries into action for the first guns crashed out.

The roar of cannon brought home another rather more urgent realisation, "They are coming this way!" I shouted above the noise. Of course they were. Napoleon had seen his trapped infantry and was sending his cavalry to rescue them or perhaps to break the rest of the Russian line apart. Regardless, it made where we were standing a damned dangerous place to be.

"I am going to join those Russian hussars," shouted Wilson, pointing his sword towards a group of Russian horsemen circling one of the beleaguered squares. "They will help drive the French cavalry back," he predicted with unbounded optimism. Without waiting for a reply, he galloped off, leaving Kit and I staring at each other in bewilderment.

"Hasn't he seen how many there are?" asked my companion. "There must be at least five thousand of the devils and I doubt the Cossacks will charge formed troops."

The first of the French hussars were already splashing through the stream at the valley bottom and I searched around desperately for a place of safety. A well-formed infantry square was what we needed, but I feared there would be precious few of those. The regiment we had stood beside was still milling around one of the French squares and was oblivious to the danger galloping towards their backs. Most of the men forming the first line of the Russian defence could see what was coming, but made no attempt to change their formation. They just stood and watched impassively as their destruction galloped towards them. Then at last I spotted salvation.

"There!" I shouted, pointing. One of the reserve regiments in the second line was moving its men. It had an advantage as it was already in column formation and so was halfway to a square. The ranks were moving damn smartly, keeping lines straight. There was order and discipline to their movements, which I thought promised a secure defence. It was also a stark contrast to the rest of that Russian hillside. There was pandemonium all about us: some of our cavalry were recklessly advancing to meet the new threat; smoke spreading from the big Russian batteries was obscuring the view of the tightly packed horsemen; and other gunners who had just turned their guns to face the insurgent squares were now desperately pulling them around again. Soldiers ran to and fro, and orders were screamed and shouted, while at least a score of messengers rode towards Bennigsen's headquarters, perhaps seeking orders that were bound to arrive far too late. Yet amid this confusion, T. Flashman Esquire had one simple urgent objective – a safe harbour for the coming storm. I galloped across the slope with Kit close on my heels. As we approached the square, I saw muskets being pointed in our direction and quickly held up my sword arm to show it was empty.

"Britansky, Britansky," we chorused. I looked over my shoulder and was alarmed to see that the first of the French hussars were already through the gap in the Russian lines and chasing off the Russian cavalry. "For God's sake, let us in!" I pleaded as we dismounted and walked up to the bayonets now pointing at our chests. Grim, unyielding faces glared back at us, but there was not a moment to lose. I was just reaching forward to push one of the muzzles aside when an order was shouted. To our relief two files of men quickly stepped back, leaving space for us to run through, pulling our horses after us.

"That was close," exclaimed Kit as we watched the gap seal up again behind us. "Will we be safe here, do you think?"

"We should be. They seem steady enough and I doubt that the French gunners will risk firing at us with so many of their horsemen about." I knew that soldiers in a square were impervious to cavalry as long as they kept the lines of bayonets that protected them solid and uninterrupted. But such a tightly packed mass of humanity was desperately vulnerable to artillery, which could tear open gaps for the horsemen to exploit.

I turned to search out the officer who had allowed us into this haven and found myself looking at a familiar face.

"I must keep you safe for my Dorothea," the Russian major grinned at me.

As Kit stared at me, puzzled, I patted the pocket where I kept his letter, "With stout ranks like these," I gestured to the men about us, "I am sure you will be delivering something entirely different to her yourself in a day or two." He laughed at that but was then distracted by a call from one of the sides and rushed off to keep his lines straight. Left to our own devices, Kit and I swung ourselves back into the saddle so that we could see what was happening outside. The main Russian battery fired a final salvo, producing screams from men and their animals, but then through the smoke charged the horsemen sabring at any gunners they could find. The French were led by an extraordinary peacock of an officer, who hacked down at one artilleryman before waving his sword above his head and urging his men on. He was astride a superb horse with a tiger skin as a saddle blanket, and he wore an ermine-trimmed green uniform. There was enough silver on his boots and saddlery to make a canteen of cutlery and he sported a huge white feather in his hat. He looked ridiculous, but there was no doubting his courage as he spurred on towards the men surrounding the French squares.

To my astonishment, the Russian battalions remaining in their front line managed a volley to fend off the first charge, yet it did them no good. The French cuirassiers just swept through the spaces around the unmanned guns and attacked the poor devils from behind. Few infantry will stand against those armoured men and none when attacked simultaneously from front and rear. The survivors scattered in all directions, leaving an even wider gap now in the Russian line. There was a cheer from the trapped French regiments as their escape route was cleared. They broke ranks and ran back through the newly opened space and past the now silent cannon on either side. If the Peacock had wheeled his men about and ridden back with them then he would have done a fine job, but in my experience, cavalry officers of every nationality are not known for their restraint. He must have looked about and seen that he dominated the centre of the Russian position. Perhaps at first he thought the battle won, as enemy infantry were streaming away from his horsemen in droves. But then he looked east and saw beaten Russian cavalry and Cossacks reforming around Bennigsen's headquarters. It was too tempting a target and sure enough, once more the sword flashed in the air and he led his tired horsemen on.

I confess that at the time I felt little more than relief. Some cuirassiers had swept past us, their horses already blowing hard from the charge up a slope that was covered with over two feet of snow. Half a dozen feigned a charge to test our resolve, clanging their swords against their metal-covered chests and roaring their challenge. They could have spared themselves the theatrics, though, for the Russian line facing them did not even twitch, never mind flinch away. I was surprised that they did not fire as the Frenchmen were well within range, but instead they stood steady and silent like a surrounding rock wall. The horsemen were evidently looking for easier pickings and so moved off to follow the Peacock east.

"Thank God for that," I breathed as I watched them go. Then I turned to Kit and asked, "What the hell do we do now?" A short distance beyond Bennigsen's headquarters was a crossroads, one road heading east back to Russia and one north to Konigsberg. Our general had been determined to protect it. I could not help a wry smile as I imagined him still poring over pins in his map as some surly French hussar kicked his door in. Then I heard the defensive battery, which had been placed around the farmhouse as a last resort, open fire. I thought of trying to make our way cross country to the north, but French horsemen were likely to be rampaging all around the area.

"It does not look like the battle is over yet," Kit said, gesturing to the gap in our lines. A Russian general had arrived and was shouting orders. All around him men who had thrown themselves into the snow to avoid the thrusting sabres were now rising to their feet. Others were marching south from further up the line and in a moment our square had been given orders to move north, right into the middle of the gap.

"What is going on?" I asked the major as he went past. It looked very much as though we were moving from the frying pan into the fire. The Peacock would soon notice that his line of retreat had been blocked and was likely to charge through us again.

"We are going to trap them," he explained, pointing at the riders still milling about Bennigsen's headquarters.

"But that is madness," I protested. "They will just cut the army up again." More importantly, I thought, whereas last time we had been on the edge of the French attack, now we would be right in the centre.

My new companion just laughed. "Britansky, you watch, we make more …" and he drew a square in the air before moving off to give new orders. I was far from convinced. After all, if a lion charged into your house, you would not trap it there, you would open every door and window to let it out. I looked across the plain to see that what he'd gestured to me was correct; soldiers were being pushed and pulled into lines to form new squares. However, they were looking damn shaky. Dismounted hussars were jostled into lines with infantry, picking up muskets from the dead. One formation was more of a triangle than a square, and as for their lines, I have hairs growing on my balls that are straighter. I would not have wagered a farthing on any one of them standing up to a determined charge. My only comfort was that the square we were in was looking by far the safest. I had seen them stand up to the cuirassier and though I looked across the slope for a better place to survive the coming onslaught, I could not find one. The regiment had marched to its new position still in formation and even as they had moved over the dead and a dismounted cannon, the lines had not waivered.

"Where do you think Wilson is?" asked Kit as we led our horses around the smashed gun carriage.

"If he has got any sense, miles from here," I grinned ruefully. "But knowing our friend, he is probably among those bloody Cossacks." We came to a halt in the middle of a line of squares, organised diagonally so that the faces did not fire on each other. I noticed that the surviving gunners of the grand battery had now turned their guns to face east to fire over us, while other battalion guns still able to fire were being arrayed on our flanks.

Further conversation was interrupted by the start of a new barrage from the French. It was soon clear that even the enemy gunners did not think that the new squares would stand as they did not waste their shells on them. Instead, they resumed their duel with the opposing artillery, who would be in a position to flay the retreating horsemen with canister. I was keeping a lookout to the east for any sign of the Peacock's return. I could see that he was pulling back from Bennigsen's farm and regrouping, but his huge command of horsemen had not yet begun to advance on us. I expected distant bugles to signal their return, but when I next heard the horns, they were coming from behind me. I span around in surprise to see more horsemen emerging from the French lines.

There were only five hundred of them this time, but they moved with immaculate precision. Some of the Peacock's troopers had been riding mounts in poor condition but these horses had not been stinted on rations and their glossy coats were testament to their health and vigour. I did not know it then, but these were heavy and light horse squadrons of Napoleon's elite Imperial Guard. The troopers looked huge with their tall bearskin helmets, and I watched in awe as they moved from column to a line facing us, with every horse turning at the exact same time. I was no expert in cavalry like Wilson, but I knew instinctively that these men would not be stopped easily. Certainly, our gunners thought so too, for they hurriedly started to turn their guns yet again to face this new threat. Many would not get the chance, though, for with a new bugle call, the light horsemen, sabres drawn, advanced at the gallop in their direction. Ominously, the heavy cavalry, with their longer, straight blades, were now coming towards us and the other squares.

Perhaps naively, I still thought we would be safe. Our formation was steady, while others were already wavering. I felt sure that the cavalry would focus on them first. The danger to us would come from panicked Russian soldiers trying to break through our ranks for refuge. I would have been right too, but for an appalling mischance: a Russian cannon ball whistled low over my head to strike our square near to where I was standing. Perhaps the gunners had just turned their weapon too far and were anxious to fire before they were overrun; equally, they could have been blind drunk or ham-fisted. It did not matter. I just remember staring appalled at a gap torn apart in the triple line of soldiers facing the charge of the French heavy cavalry. It had been an oblique shot and half a dozen bodies, or parts of them, had been blasted out of the square while several more men staggered away with wounds. There was a gap six men wide and already I could see horsemen changing their approach to charge straight through it. I knew that once they were inside we would be done for, but incredulously, the soldiers on either side of the breach made no effort to fill the space. They just stood staring, one or two looking for officers to give them orders.

For God's sake, close up!" I roared as I dropped down from the saddle. Grabbing one of the soldiers in the third rank by the shoulder, I bodily pushed him into the gap. The horsemen were only two hundred yards off, and there was not a second to spare. I grabbed another man from the same row and pushed him in front of the first, gesturing for him to go down on one knee, like the others in the front line of the square. The rows either side stood to form a triple row of bayonet points. I heard another officer shouting for men on the other side of the gap to close it up as I grabbed two more from the back row and pushed them to form up alongside the first pair. The leading trooper was now only fifty yards off, his blade stretched out in front of him as he roared his challenge. He was aiming where there was still a one-person gap in our line. There was no one else within reach, but I knew that if that space was not filled, we were doomed.

I stared across at the other officer – it was the major. That glance between us could only have taken a second, yet it spoke volumes between us. We were the only other men available and it was obvious what we should do, but I could not bring myself to do it. I started to back away, muttering, "No, no…"

The major lunged forward and grabbed my arm, "Come, we must, or we are both dead," he urged, pulling me back towards the gap. "Go in front and stay low, I will stand behind you." This was no time for niceties; his boot kicked me in the back of the knee and I found myself going down. A musket with its bayonet attached lay at my feet. I automatically picked it up, bracing the butt against the frozen earth just like the men alongside me had done so that the steel point stuck up at forty-five degrees. I remember noticing that the hammer was hanging loose – the spring inside the lock must have rusted through. And then I looked up. I may have emitted a whimper of terror as my vision was filled with charging death, those steel-shod hooves now level with my face and just a few yards off as they kicked up lumps of snow.

"Steady, Britansky." I heard the major speak behind me and felt his hand on my shoulder. His voice was nearly drowned out by the animals in front thundering towards us and the triumphant yells of their riders. My nerve failed me then, and I am only surprised it did not happen sooner. I dropped the gun and started to rise, my only thought to get somewhere, anywhere, else. I have no idea what happened next, for I admit that my eyes were tightly closed in what was literally blind terror. I was sure that I would be crushed by a hoof or that my skull would be split open by a blade. Instead, I heard a flurry of shots and as I tensed, I felt a blow to my chest that sent me flying backwards. I opened my eyes then just in time to see the underside of a horse as it jumped over me. I tried to turn, but fell, and sprawled face down in the snow with something heavy landing across my shoulders. Perhaps I blacked out briefly – certainly all sound was muffled. When I opened my eyes, to my surprise all I could see was red. The snow under me was crimson with blood; I could smell its metallic tang. My first thought was that it was mine. I tried to move my limbs and found no

97

pain, but when I took a breath to try and heave myself up, I felt an ache so sharp I cried out.

"Flashman, you are alive, thank God." I heard Kit's voice and then felt a body being dragged off my back. The noise of battle had grown louder. I looked up in alarm and found myself staring into the face of a dead horse, but over its neck I could see that by some miracle the square around me stood firm. "That was a gallant move," shouted Kit above the rising sound of musketry. "I looked round and there you were in the breach." He helped me into a sitting position, causing me to gasp in agony again as I stared about me. Two dead cavalry men lay nearby, but over the heads of the surrounding soldiers I could see many more riders charging around in all directions. Screams of desperate men rent the air. Slaughter was afoot outside our square, but at that moment I did not care a jot about them. I tore open my coat and felt gingerly inside for any sign of a wound. My coat was wet with blood, yet I quickly concluded that none of it was mine. I had been punched just below the ribs once before and this felt much the same, forcing me to take short, shallow breaths.

"What…is…happening?" I gasped.

"Only two made it into our square," explained Kit, "and they were killed quickly." He held up his pistol and added, "I shot at one myself. The riders wheeled away for easier pickings as other squares have broken." As he spoke, I looked up to see a disturbance in the ranks on our northern side. Desperate soldiers were pushing their way through the ordered lines of men. Their officers should have told them to stand firm as, according to all the tenets of warfare, once the square is broken it is destroyed. Instead, the soldiers were either pushed back or stood aside and a flood of panic-stricken men poured towards us. I could see riders beyond shouting in triumph as they wielded their swords against the Russians around them to force a way through the gap. There would be no escape now. I tried to get to my feet but was knocked to the ground again by a crowd of soldiers surging from a new breach in the ranks behind me.

It was the beginning of a new desperate struggle. I quickly found myself at the bottom of a pile of struggling soldiers, who had fallen either over me or the corpses of men and animals about me. Men snarled and swore at me as they tumbled down. It was probably just as well that I could not understand a word. At first, I tried to curl onto one side to protect my bruised chest, but then I felt some cove trying to pull off my boot and had to lash out at him with the other one to keep him away. Still being trampled by half-booted and frost-blackened feet, I struggled repeatedly to get back upright and I began to wonder if I would ever see the light of day again. However, years of sport at school now paid off. As men screamed, kicked and yelled above me, I grabbed at their legs to bring them down so that I could begin to crawl over the top. As I reached the pinnacle of what was now a massive scrimmage, I discovered that there was a far more lethal affair on its outskirts.

What 'all the tenets of war' fail to consider is that a collapsing square might have nowhere to run to, or that other squares surrounding it might collapse sooner and fill the void within it. The hollow centre that the cavalry was planning to rampage through was now packed with heaving humanity. The riders could not get inside or make any headway at all towards its centre. The precise shape of the square might have been lost, but its perimeter was still manned by those using bayonets to keep the horsemen at bay where they could. I remember the ground vibrating as thousands of hooves thudded into the snow nearby. Looking up, I glimpsed the peacock's tired troopers passing us and heading back to the French lines.

There was a steady crackle of shots, whether from the riders or muskets I could not say, and then I heard more bugles. Kit told me later that some of those were sounded by Russian cavalry who charged to attack the now disordered Frenchmen. Yet others called for Napoleon's men to withdraw. Perhaps the more disciplined Imperial Guard had remembered that their role was to rescue the 'rescuers' and not get drawn into another trap themselves.

As the enemy galloped away, slowly the pressure of men packed tightly around me eased. I had a nosebleed from where I had been kicked in the face, but the ache in my chest had subsided and I could beath more easily. My bloodstained coat was torn and a boot was only half on, but at least it was still there. I rolled over to pull it back over my leg and ignored the groan of the Russian I was sitting on. For all I knew, he was the wretch who had tried to steal them. Then Kit was at my side, reaching down to help me to my feet. While his clothes were undisturbed, his ashen features told me that the same could not be said for his spirit. I knew he had not been in a battle before and this experience had certainly been a rude baptism. By then the French were well on their way to their own lines, while Cossacks hunted down any stragglers.

"I have had enough of this bloody battle," I grumbled, reaching up to wipe my nose. Then I flinched as a cannonball thudded into the snow twenty yards away. With their cavalry out of the way, the French gunners did not waste any time in letting fly again. They would not have an easy time of it, though, as instead of blocks of men to aim at, their prey was scattering all over the hillside.

In their relative safety, the minds of the infantrymen – as is true the world over – now turned to loot. Here, though, it was a little different, for while pockets were still searched for coin, it was boots, coats and other clothes that were most prized. I watched as a squabble broke out around the dead Imperial Guard trooper. His thick coat had already been taken and two soldiers had acquired a boot each and were angrily demanding that the other give up their trophy.

I looked up as fresh flakes of snow began to fall on the scene and shuddered, not entirely due to the cold. I did not want to be on that hillside any longer; heaven knew what fresh horror this next blizzard would reveal. "Perhaps we should ride to Bennigsen's headquarters," I suggested. "We don't even know if he is alive and still in command."

I was not surprised when Kit readily agreed. He turned to retrieve our horses, which were still in the square. I was about to follow him when on impulse I turned to a corpse lying face down on a bloodstained patch of snow. The body had already been relieved of its boots and coat. As I stepped towards him, a soldier, who had just stolen a ring from its finger, hurried away. I gestured for another man, wearing just one French boot, to come and help me and we soon had the corpse on its back. I was certain it was the body that had fallen to lie across my shoulders and it was not hard to see why it had bled so heavily. The chest had been cut open by a sword that had smashed through the ribs and left a torn heart visible through the wound. I looked down at the face staring blindly up at the falling snow. There was still enough warmth in his cheeks to melt the flakes, but soon he would be cold and stiff. The man had been standing right behind me in the square and the lethal blade must have passed just inches over my head. He would not get to enjoy time with his Dorothea again. I felt a pang of sadness as I reached and patted my pocket. If it was still legible despite his soaked gore, I would have to deliver a letter when this day was done.

Chapter 11

It was still only noon when we reached the familiar farmhouse, although it felt like at least a day had passed since the Russian barrage had begun the battle. We watched as couriers rode to and from the building; clearly someone was there giving and receiving orders and duly, our spirits rose. A pile of bodies lay by the artillery battery defending the farm, yet the guns were still manned, and a squadron of Cossacks rested nearby. The arrival of two British officers attracted no great attention. Perhaps they remembered us from earlier in the day, for we were able to walk into the headquarters unchallenged. We found Bennigsen alive and well, still poring over the pins in his map. As we entered the room he looked up and demanded, "Do you have new reports?"

"The French cavalry have pulled back from the centre," I told him. He just tutted in irritation and turned back to his map. I was clearly not the first to bring him this news.

A new courier arrived and delivered some information in Russian that we could not understand. The general grunted in reply, then leaned forward over the map, moved a pin and stood back to admire his handiwork. He adopted the pose of a great artist viewing a masterpiece rather than a nearly captured general pondering a map that appeared badly attacked by woodworm. It was absurd that he was trying to manage affairs a full mile behind his own front line. It would be several minutes before he heard of any move of the enemy and several minutes more before his own men received his orders to react. Particularly in a snowstorm, that was likely to be far too late.

A more diplomatic man might have kept his trap shut, but I was cold, hungry, had nearly been killed and was bloody furious on behalf of his soldiers who had been butchered, while he shuffled papers like some counting house clerk. "Do you not think it would be easier to command your army from within sight of your front line, sir? You would be able to respond much faster to moves by the enemy."

Clearly Kit was feeling irritated by the German too, for he added acidly, "…And see the approach of French cavalry."

Bennigsen put down a fresh pin and pursed his lips. I noticed a couple of his aides step back nervously as though the man were about to erupt with rage. He knew that neither of us had commanded more than a company in battle and yet here we were giving him advice when he had a string of victories to his name. He would have been well within his rights to kick our arses out into the snow and certainly most other generals would have done so. Instead, with admirable self-restraint, he invited the emissaries of his allies around to his side of the map.

"You see, my front line stretches for three miles. There is no place I can see all of it and certainly not when it is snowing. A general must have the complete picture to understand what the enemy is doing and here my couriers know where to find me." He pointed to a collection of pins on the right-hand side of the map. "I thought Bonaparte would advance here to cut us off from Konigsberg, but the ground is boggy there and his forces have not moved. Instead, he launched a holding attack on our centre, but his real assault will come from our left. He has a new marshal arriving there with fresh troops and they will try to outflank us and capture this high ground here." He pointed to another spot on the map. "If they get guns up there, they will pound our own artillery and our centre."

My anger did not diminish as I heard the attack that had nearly killed me and broken his whole line in two, being dismissed as a mere holding action. Kit, though, was clearly more impressed with Bennigsen's detailed assessment of the enemy's plans. "What will you do to counter them?" he enquired.

"I am moving all of my reserves to defend this high ground, but to beat them we will need the Prussians to join us."

"Where are the Prussians?" I demanded, staring down at the charts.

"They are not yet showing on the map," Benningsen conceded. "But we do not think that they are far away. Although when they arrive, they will bring another pursuing French marshal and his army with them."

There are times when you wish you had not asked a question and for me this was one of them. The situation had been precarious before, but now we knew what was in our general's mind, it was truly desperate. He was seeking salvation in the arrival of some nine thousand exhausted Prussian soldiers, who were expected to do what seventy thousand Russians could not: drive the French back. Yet even if they did arrive, the marshal and another corps of enemy soldiers on their tail would surely counter even this advantage. I thought that for all his pins, Bennigsen could not see what was staring him in the face: his fellow Germans could not save him – he was beaten.

Kit and I went outside to discuss our next steps. Behind the farmhouse we could see the crossroads that the Russian army had to hold. For them it comprised a road east back to Russia, while for us the road led north to Konigsberg and hopefully a waiting ship, just nine miles away. As I stared up the northerly track, Kit declared, "Well it seems obvious what we should do now."

"Yes, it is absolutely clear," I agreed, thinking that we could be at the coast before dusk.

"We must observe the key parts of the battle. As you have already shown your courage stepping into that breach," he continued, "I suggest that I ride to watch what happens on the left flank, while you search out the Prussians."

"I do what?" I repeated, appalled.

"Come now, Flashman," countered Kit completely misunderstanding my indignation. "You cannot hog all the glory to impress my brother. Anyway, finding the Prussians will be no easy task. There are bound to be French cavalry patrols between them and the Russians, possibly in strength if they are trying to keep the armies apart." He pulled out his watch and snapped it open. "Shall we try and meet back here at four? It will still be daylight then. If you see Wilson tell him to meet us here then too." With that he swung himself back up into the saddle and turned his horse south, towards the left flank. "Good luck, Flashman," he called over his shoulder, while I stood there speechless, gaping like a codfish.

I was damned if I was going anywhere near the bloody Prussians. Equally, I knew that Hutchinson would not thank me for abandoning his brother in the middle of a battle and riding for the coast. A sudden increase in gunfire coming from the direction of our left flank showed that Bennigsen was right about what was happening there. Then I remembered what he had also predicted about the opposite flank. It was not expected to see any action and so it was the obvious place for me. It was the northern end of the Russian line and so also close to the road to Konigsberg. Should the sausage-eaters finally appear, they would come from that direction too.

A snowstorm started up again as I set off, but I kept the lines of Russian troops on my left until I came to another farmhouse. Its stone walls were still intact although one end of its roof was missing. As the wind and snow whirled about me, I deemed it the perfect place to wait out the blizzard. I found the building full of Russian officers and while I had an excuse for being there ready if challenged, no one asked why a strange British officer was among them. They even edged around to allow me to get closer to a roaring fire made from fallen roof timbers. With most of the heat going up through a hole in the roof, I was not so much warmed, instead just a little less cold.

I had hoped for something to eat roasting in the flames, but I was to be disappointed there. I discovered, though, that while the Russians were often without food, they were rarely bereft of vodka and it was not long before I was passed a flask to warm my insides. They must have been drinking for a while as every so often one of them would start singing. They would all join in, bellowing a rousing refrain that I could not understand. As their officers caroused inside the stone cottage, their men stood outside in silent lines or columns in the snow. There were drifts building around their feet and their coats were now white. Occasionally, formations disappeared entirely in the storm but at length it began to lift and they stood like lines of white statues. There would be mutiny or at least loud complaint in most armies as they listened to their drunken officers in such conditions, but I had become accustomed to the extraordinary resilience of the Russians to harsh treatment. I imagined that they would still be standing there when the French overwhelmed them, which reminded me of the precarious position I was in.

As visibility improved, and fuelled by vodka, I climbed up into the attic space of the cottage and began to make my way across the remaining beams. Twice they moved beneath my feet and once I nearly pitched back into the revellers below. Eventually, though, I reached my goal: the end of the roof with the missing thatch, which gave me a high vantage point to watch proceedings.

It was bitterly cold and the wind was like ice as I wedged myself between a timber and the straw roof. With the naked eye I could see that Bennigsen was undoubtedly right – the battle was now on the Russian left. Heavy cannon fire had been coming from that direction for well over an hour. Now with my glass I could see files of distant men moving around some high ground that had been behind the Russian line. There were still one of our batteries there, but I could see French troops charging to capture it. Every gun in the French and Russian lines seemed to be firing at the same spot, to aid either attackers or defenders. It had to be a maelstrom of hell to be anywhere near it. I hoped to God that Kit was still alive and that he had the sense to stay back. When I looked at the French lines opposite my position on the Russian right, most had taken shelter where they could, and few were visible. They were probably grateful for their placement too.

Craning around I could see no sign of the wretched Prussians and it soon looked like it would be too late for them anyway. At around three o'clock, according to my watch, the French finally captured the battery on the high ground and then brought some of their own guns up to enhance it. They now had a commanding view of the entire Russian line and set about using their artillery to destroy it. Both sides had been fighting for more than six hours. The more recent French arrivals would have marched part way through the night to join the battle, but now they threw forward their final reserves.

A rider approached the farmhouse. It was our rear guard commander, General Bagration, who was furious when he saw the inebriated state of the officers down below me. Within a couple of minutes he had most of the reserve columns and half of the officers following him up along the slope to help stop the French. While he issued orders, I ducked back into my concealed nook under the roof.

The last thing I wanted was to be roped into some desperate, doomed defence.

Bagration's efforts, however, made little difference; by four o'clock Benningsen's farmhouse fell once more to the French and they were threatening the crossroads beyond. Heaven knew where Kit and Wilson were or if they were even still alive. But with the road to Konigsberg threatened, it was time for me to leave. I lowered myself down into the now near empty cottage below and was relieved to find my horse where I had left it, in the lee of the cottage walls. Snow was still falling steadily but I knew where the road was. With most of the army fleeing east, any French pursuit would be in that direction. There would not be many heading north.

I was just trying to work out what I could say to Hutchinson if his brother had indeed been killed, when emerging from the blizzard came a squadron of lancers. I reined up in alarm, thinking at first that the French had worked around our right flank. Then I saw that their uniforms were black: the Prussians had finally arrived on the scene.

Surely it was too late now for them to make a difference, I thought, but as trumpets sounded and they moved from column into line, causing fleeing Russians to scramble out of the way, I decided I would stay a little longer. I would look a prize plum reporting defeat to Hutchinson if they somehow turned the tide after all. Although it was starting to get dark, more columns of horsemen came out of the gloom and followed their fellows. Then I heard shouts and screams from around Bennigsen's farm. The French had made their final assault in loose order, probably intent on loot and shelter as they watched the broken Russians scatter before them. The last thing they expected were well-ordered ranks of lancers and hussars charging them down.

The men in blue had no chance to form any kind of square. I stopped and listened to the sounds of slaughter not far away. I was not the only one; a growing crowd of Russian infantry had also come to a halt nearby, unsure now what to do. We stood there, an audience watching a parade of men in black. Infantry were appearing now as well as a group of officers, led by a starchy old cove with a white moustache. He noticed me sitting on my horse and bellowed a peremptory order. I could not understand a word but with a gesture at the soldiers milling behind me and then in the direction of Bennigsen's farm, the meaning was obvious. He evidently thought that they were my men and was commanding us to join his attack.

As I watched him gallop off to follow his own legions, I thought that there was no chance in hell that the Russians would obey me. I could not give a single order in their language, after all. But when I turned back to look at them, I saw that most were staring at me expectantly. I realised that the majority were serfs, who had been told what to do for generations. Finding themselves in a disordered mass with no leaders must have been an alarming experience. I had nothing to lose and so I drew my sword and yelled, "Men, you will attack the French!" I brought the blade swishing down in the direction of the enemy. The gesture was the same in any language. To my immense gratification, at least half of them gave a throaty roar and charged off, bayonets outstretched before them. I was feeling quite pleased with myself until I noticed that the rest were still watching me expectantly. I had an ominous feeling that they were waiting for their officer to lead the advance, so I kicked my horse onwards. I wanted to see what was happening anyway.

I was anxious not to get too far ahead of my men, who had grown in number now to some two hundred. There was an increasing crackle of musketry, particularly to my left where the first Prussian regiments were engaging. The snow was starting to lift again, and I could make out their black columns pushing forward against the white landscape. I squinted nervously ahead, apprehensive about what might be lying in store for us. Suddenly, as though a curtain had been swept aside, I spotted my soldiers who had charged earlier, bayonet to bayonet with the French. The men in blue were falling back – they must have been caught by surprise – but already an officer beyond them was trying to rally a company into line to mount a new defence.

I knew instinctively that we had to maintain momentum. The French could not be allowed to stand. I waved my sword once more. "Flashman fusiliers, advance!" I bellowed and urged my men on as my horse cantered forward. Charging soldiers surged past on either side and I was careful to let them get ahead. They could see that they outnumbered the French and having taken punishment all day, they were eager to add their own bayonets to the fray. Already the French company was falling back and as Prussian lancers appeared behind them, they took to their heels and ran.

"Flashman!" I looked up as I heard my name to see a tall officer galloping towards me with a handful of Cossacks as escort. "How on earth are you leading your own regiment of Russians?" Wilson enquired, laughing.

"Oh, they are just some strays I picked up while I was looking out for the Prussians," I lied, glibly. "Do you know what is going on? Have you seen Kit?"

"There are more Prussians pushing back the French right flank." He pointed to the high ground the armies had spent most of the afternoon fighting over and added, "We will soon take that back and then we will have them on the run." By now he had ridden alongside me and he reached out and clapped my shoulder. "It is a splendid Russian victory, Flashman, and the first defeat on the battlefield for the Corsican tyrant."

For a while it seemed he was right. The French had overextended their line when they thought the day was won and were pushed back easily. Bennigsen's farm was quickly recaptured, although there was no sign of its former occupant. The Prussian general I had seen earlier, a man called L'Estocq, drove his men on. He worked with some other Russian generals, whose forces remained intact, to try to retake the high ground and push the enemy back to the other side of the valley. Yet for all their efforts, curiously, progress began to stall.

As the light faded, I looked across our hillside to see it littered with men. Many sat wounded, with the snow red all about them. I was to discover that there were hardly any doctors left among the Russian army. Many had been captured at Guttstadt before the retreat began, but even the skills of those who were left were not trusted. When I asked an officer why, he replied, "The best surgeon for a man who has lost his leg to a cannonball, is another to finish him off." Alongside the wounded were several thousand soldiers who did not seem to have a unit. They just milled about, unsure whether to join the fighting around the hill or retreat with the thousands who had run earlier that afternoon. But far more numerous across the slope were the small mounds in the snow that marked the covered dead. Where the cavalry had charged and squares had fought in the morning, on what had once been a featureless hillside, there was not a level yard of ground.

The temperature was dropping sharply now as the sun dipped over the horizon. The warming effects of the vodka had long since worn off. I was freezing and pulled my coat tighter about me as I stared at the fighting still underway on the high ground. Wilson's predictions had proved optimistic as the French had been able to regroup there. Flashes from cannon and musket muzzles showed that they fought tenaciously to hold their hard-won vantage point. Yet as darkness fell, so did the volume of fire. Every man there, on both sides, had been either marching or fighting since dawn. Some of the reinforcements had set off well before sunrise and exhaustion was taking its toll. As sometimes happens, the battle just fizzled to a halt as weary officers and men could no longer summon the energy to continue.

Chapter 12

We gathered back in the farmhouse where candles on the table revealed an L-shaped front line marked out in pins on the map. The vertical section was the line around the bottom of the high ground while the rest was the original Russian line that still stood. Bennigsen had disappeared. Many suspected that he had fled west in panic when his headquarters had been overrun for a second time that day and all looked lost. I did not blame him for that, for I would have done the same. Yet when my hide is at stake, I want a commander who manages a battle directly, rather than sitting safely a mile behind the lines and risking little more than a prick from his pins. So I joined the others in holding him in contempt – at least, that is, until I saw Kit again. Like me his uniform was spattered in blood; a man standing right beside him had been pulverised with a cannon ball. Kit insisted that our general *had* left his headquarters and had been in the thickest of the action earlier that afternoon when the Russians had been trying to defend the high ground.

"Well, where is he now?" I grumbled as L'Estocq and the other generals argued over what forces they had left and how to use them. The Prussian general suggested a night-time assault on the high ground to push the French back. Some of the Russian generals agreed with him, insisting that the French were tired, disorganised and must be short of supplies and ammunition. One artillery officer vowed that a full third of the enemy force had been either killed or wounded in the barrage from his batteries. Yet other colonels insisted that this final assault would have to be made by regiments other than their own. Many had seen their forces halved by casualties and desertions. Moreover, their men were exhausted, cold and hungry and there was still no food to be had. The same could be said for the men around that table and their tiredness soon caused tempers to fray. L'Estocq had just started a furious argument with one of the reluctant colonels, when abruptly the Russian stopped shouting, his jaw dropping in surprise as he noticed a new arrival standing in the doorway.

Bennigsen ignored the astonished muttering as he stepped back inside his headquarters. He must have been aware that more than a few were not pleased to see him, perhaps relishing the opportunity his absence had provided. A colonel standing next to me leaned over and whispered in English, "The whipped dog returns to feed on the scraps of our victory." All very poetic, but I did not need a translator when General Bagration asked the more pertinent question of his commander: "Where the hell have you been while your army has been fighting?"

I had expected the Hanoverian to at least look abashed as he explained his absence, yet he was nothing of the sort. "I have been on our right flank, gentlemen," he said as he began to rearrange the pins on his map. "While you threw all our reserves against the French holding the high ground, you ignored the arrival of a French marshal who had been pursuing our Prussian friends. They are now well established on our side of the valley. If you ride north, you can see hundreds of their campfires." He raised his gaze to look his officers in the eye, perhaps daring them to challenge him, but most were staring down at his map. After the markers had been rearranged, the Russian front line was now U-shaped. The bottom still faced the town of Eylau, with the sides pushed back by the French-held high ground and new arrivals.

"We now face Bonaparte and four of his marshals," Bennigsen continued. "All the enemy forces on our right are yet to engage in battle. Their ammunition pouches will be full while our soldiers are presently short of supplies. We know that there are at least two more French marshals and their corps out there somewhere," he gestured to the west, "almost certainly closing in on our position. If just one of them arrives tomorrow, we risk encirclement and the complete destruction of the tsar's army." Our returned commander took a deep breath before concluding, "I regret, therefore, that we have little alternative but to retreat."

There was a second of shocked silence and then everyone began to shout at once. L'Estocq was apoplectic at the suggestion. He had marched his men for days to join the Russians, turned the battle around and was pushing for another attack. The last thing he wanted was a retreat, and to give up further Prussian territory.

Some of the more aggressive Russian commanders like Bagration were convinced that the French were on the verge of collapse. Come the dawn, he asserted, if we stood with determination and resolve, they would retreat and leave us masters of the field. I thought that the reverse was likely to be the case. Many of Napoleon's men would enjoy the shelter provided by the walls of Eylau during the night while our troops would be on an exposed and icy hillside. The dawn would reveal how many we had lost the previous day. I doubted that the frozen scarecrows left would intimidate an emperor with thousands of fresh soldiers to throw into the fray.

One Russian general contemptuously dismissed the idea that another marshal had arrived. Laying extra fires to fool the enemy was an old ruse that he had once used himself near the Black Sea. Only a timid child would abandon his position to such a trick, he sneered, before demanding to know what other proof Bennigsen had for the existence of these forces. It transpired that prisoners had been taken by the Cossacks and even L'Estocq reluctantly admitted that he had been pursued by at least one marshal and his men for the last week.

The arguments went on and on. Wilson was convinced that we should stay and fight, but Kit was not so sure. Like me he was probably remembering his brother's approval of the Russian retreat after the battle of Pultusk. The situation here was exactly the same. Eventually, Bennigsen turned to his colonels and asked how many of them had sufficient men and supplies to fight for another full day against fresh troops. Several immediately raised their hands, although I doubt one of them had a clue how many men or cartridges they had left. They were the proud Russian aristocrats who clearly hated having a foreigner in charge of their army. The rest were more hesitant, glancing around, clearly hoping that others would volunteer for the front line while their battered forces could stay in reserve. The final decision was made when the artillery commander admitted that they were running low on powder and ball.

The guns had been the backbone of the defence and without them, few were confident of making a stand the next day. That is not to say that Bennigsen convinced everyone; L'Estocq was still furious at the idea of retreat. He was positively incandescent with rage when his army, which had done the least fighting, was detailed as the rear guard. He had his revenge that night, however, when he marched his force off alone, leaving the Russians to fend for themselves.

The ability of the Russian commissary to keep its soldiers supplied had been an object of scorn and mockery for days. Their system had completely collapsed and if the army was to get the provisions and shelter it desperately needed, Konigsberg was the only option. As we stared at the map, we could see that the French would not have to advance far to cut off the road to this now vital link. For once, Wilson then had an excellent idea. "That narrow track will be jammed with men and guns before dawn tomorrow," he whispered to Kit and I. "Our horses have not ridden far today. We could set off tonight and have breakfast in the city tomorrow morning."

He had me at the word 'breakfast', but the more I thought about the idea the better it was. After we left the map room it was soon obvious that we would not get any sleep that night. The rooms we had used before the battle were now chock full of the wounded, many wailing piteously. Anyone tending to the sick would have struggled to make it across the space without treading on them. Agonised screams from a side room attracted our attention and through the door I saw the only surgeon at his grisly work; an officer was being held down on a table while the sawbones cut furiously through his leg. A stone jar of what I presumed was vodka lay nearby on the floor. I thought it was for the ease of the patient, but then saw the surgeon stoop to take a heavy pull from it himself. Watching him stagger back to his task, I did not hold out much hope for the survival of the officer.

That sight was sickening enough, but we quickly discovered worse when we stepped outside. The injured with a roof over their heads were the lucky ones. Huddled against every wall that protected against the biting wind were hundreds more men. Some with their wounds bandaged in rags and others with broken bones or innards still visible through the gashes in their torn uniforms. The vapour from their breath hid their agonised faces, and the lack of it from some revealed they had already expired.

We were all just glad to get away from that place of suffering. I don't recall any of us speaking as we guided our mounts around the clusters of bodies that covered the ground between the farmhouse and the track north. Most of the dead had already been stripped by their comrades in a grisly harvest to aid the living. On our approach to the crossroads a chorus of yells attracted our attention, not least because the calls were in French and begging for mercy.

"Dear God, would you look at that," Kit gasped in horror. We stared after him at a scene illuminated by two burning torches. A score of French prisoners were in the final stages of being stripped entirely naked. Most were huddled together for warmth, their skins already mottled blue in the cold, while their captors argued over their clothes and possessions. As we drew closer, several of the Russians snatched up their muskets. One, wearing a French greatcoat over his own, shouted something to us that we did not understand.

"Britansky," shouted Wilson in case they were thinking of adding us to their haul. I was not convinced that they were entirely deterred, as I noticed several glaring covetously at the thick bearskin I had wrapped around my shoulders.

"What should we do?" asked Kit. "They are leaving those prisoners to freeze to death."

"Nothing," I told him, wheeling my horse away. "Bennigsen has no time to worry about prisoners. If we try to stop them, we are likely to end up joining the poor wretches." Reluctantly, Kit followed Wilson and I onto the trail north, where we found we were not the only ones with the idea to start the journey early. For the next three hours we trotted past a stream of limping and walking wounded. Many left a trail of blood in the snow that was churned by plodding feet and hooves. Some had dropped by the wayside and called for help as we rode past. Others stared silently at us from eyes sunk deep in shivering, ghostly white faces. Many were soaked in gore and I knew they would not survive the night. Having seen what passed for a surgeon, I wondered if the embrace of that cold winter's night would not be a more merciful end.

Helping the wounded were many able-bodied soldiers and we passed more of these as we progressed. They had clearly run from the battle when all seemed lost. There were officers amongst them, one leading a whole company of men. By dawn we had left them all behind. As the sun spread its light from the east, we at last glimpsed the church spires in Konigsberg, showing over the top of the earthworks that surrounded the city.

"Thank God," I cried in relief as we goaded our mounts into one final effort to close the distance. There was ice in the bristles of the beard I had grown since joining the Russians and I felt weak from hunger. Wilson swore he could smell fresh bread, even though we were still a mile from any bakery. No establishment would be open at this hour, but we would raise holy hell at the lodging house we had stayed in before, until they provided some food.

"We should see my brother first," suggested Kit. "We will be one of the first back with news of the battle. He should hear of the affair from us before he learns of any local gossip." Half an hour later found us on the landing outside his lordship's room, hammering loudly on the door panels. There was now grease and crumbs mixed in with the frost on our beards, for we had raided the kitchen larder on our arrival, sharing a few slices of sausage and a small seeded cake.

At first Hutchinson was far from impressed with our diligence. He half opened the door and stood before us in his nightshirt, his features already coloured with rage. "What the devil are you doing waking people at this ungodly hour?"

"Brother, we have news, urgent news," whispered Kit, glancing over his shoulder as a couple of the other lodgers were now peering out of their rooms to see what the ruckus was all about. He went to push the door further open, but Hutchinson already had his foot behind it, blocking his way.

"Unless you are here to tell me that a French dragoon could kick in this door before I have had my breakfast," growled his lordship, "I would be obliged if you would wait with your news until then." He ran his eye over all three of us and mellowing slightly, added, "You look like you could use a rest and some fresh clothes anyway."

Kit was looking quite hurt at the rejection, while Wilson seethed with impatience, yet I had spotted an explanation for Hutchinson's reaction. I nudged his brother and gestured to a patch of the rug we could see in his lordship's room. Unless he was in the habit of wearing ladies' petticoats, it was clear that our chief had company. "Apologies, brother," grinned Kit. "You can tell the lady that no French dragoon will kick their way into your company this morning."

"Ach, let zem in," came a woman's voice from behind the door. "I vant to hear ze news."

With a heavy sigh Hutchinson relaxed his grip on the portal. It swung open to reveal a tousle-haired portly matron arranging the sheet to cover an ample bosom. "I think we can dispense with the introductions," he muttered. "The lady's husband is with the Prussian army."

"Oh, are you vounded?" she demanded on seeing us. Without waiting for an answer, she added, "*Liebling*, bring those chairs over, they look exhausted."

Kit and I were spattered with gore, but we assured her that it was not our own as we settled to tell our tale. The woman was keen to know where the Prussian army had gone and if it was also returning to Konigsberg. Presumably, she wanted to be back home when her other *Liebling* came over the threshold. Hutchinson was much more interested in whether the French would pursue the Russians. It was the crucial question and yet we had to confess we had no idea. Both armies had taken huge numbers of casualties with thousands of wounded to tend to. While the French supply system had to be better than the non-existent Russian one, they were still likely to be short of food for men and animals. Wilson was sure that Napoleon's men had been whipped and repeated his view that if the Russians had stayed, they would now be enjoying the sight of the French quitting the field of battle. Kit merely shrugged his shoulders when asked his opinion and so Hutchinson's gaze moved on to me.

"I doubt that the soldiers who fought the battle yesterday will be in a fit state to advance," I agreed. "They must be short of powder and cartridge. Yet there were two marshals on our right whose men had seen little action and a third in the vicinity. They could spearhead any advance on the city, which would be a very tempting winter refuge."

His lordship began to pace up and down, clearly lost in thought. "If his losses are as bad as you say," he conceded, "Bonaparte will need a day or two to lick his wounds. That should give most of Bennigsen's force time to reach us here. Have they more fight in them, do you think?" he asked before continuing to answer his own question. "The French would block any retreat to Russia, but I doubt the people here would want to risk the city being sacked in winter. It would be certain death for most of them if they were forced into the cold." He shuddered at the thought as the woman gave a little cry of alarm. "Don't worry, m'dear," he said, "although I am damned if I will travel on that shingle track north again."

"Perhaps we should try and get a passage on a ship away from the city," I suggested.

I was rewarded with a withering look. "Have you seen the port?" demanded Hutchinson. "It has been frozen solid since last month. There is no escape that way. If the French advance on the city, gentlemen, then I strongly suspect the war will be over and we will be prisoners."

Chapter 13

After quitting Hutchinson's doom-laden company, we went in search of a proper meal. We were soon tucking into plates of pork, bread and their strange, pickled cabbage. I think we were all too tired to worry about the future then. Once my stomach was comfortably full, I went to my room. I slept for twelve hours straight and woke to a vastly different city.

By then five thousand wounded had reached Konigsberg, many piled high on sledges and carts, undoubtedly emitting groans of pain at every jolt in the road. Yet more were still struggling on foot behind them, and thousands would not complete the journey at all. The tales they brought of battle and slaughter spread fear throughout the city. Already this advance party of injured men made up a tenth of Konigsberg's population. Space had been tight before with other refugees, but now when I looked out of my window, I could see wounded men, with nowhere else to go, huddled in an alley opposite for shelter. Wilson suggested that he and I share a room and soon six wounded Russian officers were filling my old attic chamber. Any sense of noble charity we might have felt diminished that night as we were kept awake listening to their moans and wails through the thin plank walls. A Prussian doctor called the next day and the resulting screams as he carried out the necessary ministrations and surgeries were so loud, we had to go out. We could not bear to listen to those agonies; we both knew the random nature of warfare and how easily we could have been in the same state. Over the next few days I saw three bodies carried out of that room wrapped in blankets, but as any vacancy was immediately filled with a new casualty, it is hard to say how many survived.

The day after we reached the city the rest of the Russian army began to arrive. Bennigsen immediately put them to work improving the defensive earthworks and the artillery was dispersed to strengthen those ramparts. By then the number of Russians outside the city nearly matched the Prussians inside it. Meanwhile, the number of wounded in the city had already doubled from the previous day. The bloody trail of men still arriving from the south showed no end. Worryingly, the tsar's forces still had no supplies. Appeals were made for food from warehouses and even the citizens' own households – anything that could be spared. It looked impossible to meet the needs of the army. Already parties of desperate soldiers had gone out into the countryside raiding farmsteads, stealing anything they could find and burning the rest for warmth.

Feeling refreshed and with Russians filling the city, I thought it was high time I went to find the recipient of the letter in my pocket. The poor woman was probably already searching in vain for her husband. I changed into my best uniform; I could hardly break the news of widowhood in a jacket covered with his blood. Then I set out through the crowded streets. The address was a large town house that was now packed with injured Russian soldiers. An orderly told me that no women were inside and so I knocked on the neighbouring doors. To my surprise I was told that Dorothea Benckendorff was now a guest at the royal palace. Now doubly pleased I was in my best duds, I made my way through the throng outside the royal residence.

Brandishing my letter, I was granted admittance into an icy-cold entrance hall. The space was full of court officials scurrying between old Prussian generals, who were urgently debating the state of the war. The Prussian army had still not returned to the city. I was not sure if L'Estocq was still feeling slighted by Bennigsen's refusal to stand, or if he was wisely seeking food and supplies somewhere else. As I waited, I saw men carrying various chests and trunks up and down the stairs and wondered if the king and queen were planning a return to Memel. Eventually, some bewigged major-domo found me and haughtily demanded to know my business. I showed him the address on the letter and explained that I understood the lady was now in the palace. He tried to take the document, but I snatched it back. "I fought with her husband at Eylau and promised him I would personally deliver this to her hand," I told him. This was not entirely true, but I was keen to see more of the palace, not to mention this mysterious woman who had so enchanted my former comrade.

The courtier looked me up and down with suspicion, as though I was some itinerant snake oil salesman. Then to my amazement he announced, "I will see if the *countess* is willing to see you."

"Countess?" I repeated in surprise, feeling a sudden pang of alarm as I wondered what I had got myself into. Benckendorff sounded German; perhaps my late friend was a member of the German nobility now fighting for the Russians. That would explain why his widow was so welcome in the Prussian royal residence. I was just puzzling this when a flunkey led me up the stairs to a drawing room. I was left alone and began pacing up and down, cursing myself for not coming sooner. Would the countess already know she was a widow? How the hell was I to break the news if not? There was bound to be a hell of a fuss and I would probably get dragged in to tell the king and queen – for all I knew Benckendorff could be related to one of them. Perhaps I would be blamed for not protecting him. I was just starting to imagine myself shackled in some dingy cell, when the far door opened.

In walked a radiant beauty and her maid. To describe the countess does not do her justice. Her neck was a little too long, and she had large ears that she tried to hide with dark ringlets that framed her pale face. I was only twenty-five back then and I guessed she was a few years younger. She wore a loose dress that hid her figure, but it was her dark eyes that grabbed your attention. Those lively black orbs surveyed me as she approached with the casual ease of someone used to power. Despite, or perhaps because of her imperfections, she was quite stunning to behold. I realised that I was staring and hurriedly brought myself to attention.

"I am told you have a message for me that you must deliver personally," she enquired, smiling in amusement at my obvious distraction. That happy face reminded me of the grim tidings I had to impart. It was obvious that she had not already heard, and I had thought of no better way of telling her than to come straight out with it.

"Countess," I started, wishing now I had just handed the letter to the major-domo to deliver. As she looked at me curiously, I took a deep breath and continued, "I very much regret that I have to inform you that your husband has been killed." I had been expecting her to scream or become hysterical, but while her maid gave a gasp of surprise, the countess merely frowned.

"Why would an Englishman bring me such news? If such a thing were true, one of my husband's officers would have told me."

"Well, I am not sure that there were any officers left," I explained. "I came because I was with him the night before the battle and also when he fell."

"Are you telling me my husband died at Eylau?" she enquired, still unconcerned. When I nodded, she offered me a seat and told the maid to fetch me a brandy as though I were the grieving party. As she sat down beside me, she reached out and touched my arm. "I can tell you are sincere, sir, but I must inform you that I had a message from my husband this morning, dated yesterday. He has certainly survived the battle and I am sure is in good health. I fear that you will have to give this news again to someone else."

"But I have this letter," I explained, taking it from my pocket. Her eyes widened at the now brown stains of blood. Then when she saw her name still clearly visible on the front of the note, her delicate hands took it from me as though it was a shard of the thinnest ice. As a brandy was put down beside me, she whispered something in Russian to the maid. The girl hurried from the room. When I turned my gaze back to the countess, I saw those dark eyes now filled with tears.

"Karl was not my husband," she whispered softly. "He was a friend of my brother's and we became close growing up. My husband is away so often in the army."

"I see. Well…er…from what he said, he very much admired you," I concluded lamely. I could see now why Karl was besotted with Dorothea, for I felt more than a little admiration myself. Her obvious grief stirred a deep pang of sympathy in my normally cynical soul. I felt a sudden urge to protect her. "Ma'am, you can rely on my complete discretion in this matter. I give you my word, no one will hear of this from me."

She tucked the letter unread inside her blouse, close to her heart, and wiped away her tears. Summoning a smile that did not hide her infinite sadness, she asked me my name and then to describe how her lover had died. I gave a noble account, explaining how at the last we had decided to step into that breach together to save his regiment. She was suitably impressed and so I told her that he died in my arms, her name the last word from his lips. Of course, it was a load of tosh, but what woman would not want to hear that compared to the brutal truth?

By the time I had finished, the tears were pouring down her cheeks. She got up and rushed from the room. I sat there unsure what to do next: should I leave, or would she return? After a while the maid re-entered. On behalf of her mistress, she thanked me for my time and gave me a small purse of gold coins for my trouble. I was back out in the street a couple of minutes later.

Back then I had no idea how that brief encounter with the countess would change events to come. Why, at that point it seemed that the history of the entire Prussian nation was about to come to an abrupt and humiliating end. Bennigsen was still marshalling the defence of the city, but few put much hope in his demoralised and hungry soldiers succeeding in stopping the French. The Prussian armouries had been able to provide little fresh powder and ball to replenish Russian stores. The tsar's men would have to rely on their bayonets. Even their officers began to lose confidence in their own soldiers. Some of the aristocrats were concerned that if the army were taken prisoner, their serfs would learn more of the revolution in France. The last thing they wanted was such radical ideas being taken back to their own estates to cause unrest. The Russian bishop travelling with the army was summoned. He was instructed to preach that Napoleon Bonaparte was the spawn of Satan and all those that served him were devils.

The next two days were ones of panic and rumour across Konigsberg. Twice it was reported that a French army had been spotted nearby. The streets immediately filled with citizens rushing in all directions. Then we heard that the royal family had left and when that was proved untrue, there were fresh claims that plans were afoot to surrender the city to the French without a fight. As darkness fell men could be seen scurrying around the city with bundles of possessions that they were planning to bury, or perhaps they were the valuables of others that they had just dug up. I even went to the port to see if there was any hope that a vessel might get away. However, I soon discovered that the ice was set solid around the ships in the harbour, while out in the lagoon, where the water was saltier, I was told there was a foot-deep layer of icy slush. One master was doing his best to release his vessel. He had his crew smashing the ice around its hull and lighting a series of fires to melt the ice between the ship and the harbour entrance. I found a British master who, puffing on a pipe and watching proceedings, predicted that the endeavour was doomed to fail. He was right – as soon as the fires on the ice burned through, they disappeared with a hiss into the water below. Minutes later a new film of ice began to form around the floating burnt sticks that remained.

The following day a new rumour circulated that the French were retreating back west. At first we gave it the same credence as all other gossip, but by late afternoon we received reports that Cossacks had ridden to Eylau and found it abandoned by all but the badly injured and the dead. Bells rang out across the city that evening to announce our deliverance.

In just a few hours Konigsberg was transformed. That morning we had anticipated a whole army taken prisoner and the oblivion of the state of Prussia. By nightfall we were all free and safe. It was clear now that the French army had been weakened at Eylau much more than we had thought. The winter marches and the battle itself must have taken a terrible toll, as they could not risk another confrontation with the Russians just twenty miles north. Instead, they had turned around and covered the same ground that two armies had already denuded of supplies for seventy wintry miles, to return to their original winter quarters near the Vistula River.

The two sides had battled each other to exhaustion so that neither was able to continue in the field. They were like two prize fighters who had fought each other to a standstill. In fact, when I heard of the epic thirty-five round Cribb and Molineaux bout, I was immediately reminded of Eylau. Those who had argued that we should have stayed on that hillside and forced the French to withdraw, were not slow to point out that they had been right. Wilson only mentioned it half a dozen times that evening and I was sure that the more aggressive Russian generals were making the same point with Bennigsen.

Despite this good news, by the following morning a 'draw' was not enough; our deliverance had to be proclaimed with calls of *victory*. A procession marched through the city, led by Bennigsen and a hundred Russian and Prussian officers to accept the adulation of the relieved populace. Behind them tramped several thousand Russian soldiers, some with feet still wrapped in rags and many showing the marks of battle. When the procession was marred as a number broke ranks to pillage a bakery, it was clear that they were also still hungry. In front of the palace six captured eagles were displayed, while the king and various generals made speeches, as their men shivered behind them.

This civic backslapping did little to diminish the divisions within the forces. Russian generals now had even more reason to detest their Hanoverian commander. L'Estocq was still fuming and doubtless told his monarch that with more resolve they could have liberated most of his kingdom from the invader. Meanwhile various Prussian generals and courtiers, who had lost nearly everything with their own reckless endeavours, sneered at the Russians as amateurs in the art of war. To keep these conflicting parties united and effective would take a diplomat of exceptional skill, I realised. Unfortunately, we had Lord John Hely Hutchinson.

"Who the devil is Countess Lieven to you?" demanded his lordship a few days later. I told him that I honestly had no idea before he handed me a pasteboard invitation. A celebratory reception had been organised at the palace. As with previous events there, my rank as captain had been insufficient to attend. This time, though, my plans for an evening in an alehouse, attracting the attention of a comely beer maiden, were thwarted. I stared down at the gothic script to see that I had been invited as a guest of the countess.

"I am sure I have never met the lady," I insisted, while wondering if the delectable Dorothea had somehow arranged it. The others stared at me with curiosity, or, in Hutchinson's case, downright suspicion.

"Her husband, the count, is a general in the Russian army. A close friend of the tsar, I am told," he informed me. "If you get caught in the wrong bed, Flashman, I will have you sent home in chains," growled the man who had been sleeping with a Prussian officer's wife.

That evening, in our best uniforms, we arrived at the modest royal residence in the heart of the city. A military band was playing outside to entertain a small crowd that had gathered to watch the attending dignitaries. At the sight of us in our red coats, the musicians struck up *God Save the King* as we walked through a guard of honour made up of alternating Prussian and Russian soldiers. Friedrich Wilhelm III was clearly trying to show appreciation to his allies, although Hutchinson was far from impressed. "That tune," he gestured to the musicians, "is a sign he is after more British gold in subsidies. But what do we get for our money, eh?"

"The combined army has inflicted a major defeat to the French," Wilson answered. "The first the emperor has suffered. That has to be worth something, surely."

"Then explain to me why I have seen a copy of a French *Bulletin* this morning describing the battle as a major French victory," demanded Hutchinson. "That is how it is presented in France. Napoleon is still unbeaten there." He gave a snort of derision and added, "When *I* beat French armies they surrendered, and everyone knew that they had been defeated."

It was a sour start to an evening that was intended to be one of self-congratulation. Glasses of vodka or schnapps were pressed into our hands and various speeches began. Each one finished with a toast and we waited for glasses to be refilled before the next dignitary stepped up. Bennigsen in his oration made a point of congratulating Hutchinson for the gallant conduct of his British officers at Eylau. I confess to a moment of pride at that. Even his lordship gave a brief nod of acknowledgement, which for him was high praise indeed. The king gave an awkward speech in which he praised his Prussian soldiers and L'Estocq for saving the Russian army at the end of the battle and securing victory. It might have pleased his people, but I noticed that markedly fewer glasses were raised for that. "I thought we were here to save *him*," grumbled one elderly Russian officer to me.

By the time the doors were thrown open to a small ballroom, where a gathering of ladies and some food awaited, I was more than a little drunk. I must have consumed half a bottle of vodka on an empty stomach. I was keen to get something to eat and find out who this mysterious Countess Lieven was. Yet as we tried to make our way through, we were intercepted by Major Schmidt, who told us that Bennigsen wanted a private word with us. The Russian commander was pacing alone in a corner of the room, his earlier good humour replaced with a brooding anger.

"Do you know anything about a man called Leclerc who visited the palace this morning?" he demanded as we approached.

"What the devil is this about?" Hutchinson was his irascible self. "Do you think I care about court gossip?"

Bennigsen lowered his voice, "This visitor came in civilian clothes, but with an escort of French cavalry and under a flag of truce." Bennigsen looked up to where Friedrich Wilhelm and his chief minister were locked alone in conversation on the other side of the hall before continuing. "A letter was passed to the palace and Leclerc was then received here by the king. He only left an hour before the reception started."

"I knew nothing of this," Hutchinson grunted as he looked the Russian in the eye. No one spoke for a moment as we considered the implications of this news. The ally we were supposed to be protecting appeared to be in secret negotiations with the enemy.

"The tsar is on his way here. The Russian army has sacrificed thousands of men to save his throne and yet..." Bennigsen's voice choked with fury as he was unable to elaborate on such treachery. By now we were all staring at the king. Perhaps our sudden hostility emanated across the room, for his chief minister looked up and whispered urgently to his monarch. Friedrich Wilhelm started round like a rumbled pickpocket. There was fear on his features, but as he continued to receive whispered counsel he straightened up and a rictus smile forced itself across his features. It was certainly not returned and so, hesitantly, he made his way across the floor to join us.

"Gentlemen, I trust you are enjoying the evening," he began, giving Bennigsen and Hutchinson a formal nod of greeting, snapping his heels together as he did so.

"We would like to know about your visitor today, *Monsieur* Leclerc," snarled the Russian commander, coming straight to the point, an unmistakable note of menace to his tone.

"Of course," the king tried another smile but was betrayed by beads of sweat appearing on his brow. "I was going to tell you tomorrow, but we can discuss it now." He licked his lips as he surveyed a row of stony, impassive faces and went on. "It is no secret. I knew he would be noted as he passed through the pickets. The man was an emissary of Bonaparte – his real name is Marshal Bertrand."

"Bertrand?" interrupted Hutchinson, "I captured that cunning devil in Egypt! What is the rogue up to this time?"

"He wished to conduct secret negotiations to end the war, but I of course refused. I tell you this in a spirit of openness."

"I am sure my tsar will be grateful," said Bennigsen, adopting a sardonic expression as we all wondered precisely how open the king would have been had we not found out about the visitor for ourselves. "What exactly was Bonaparte proposing?"

"It is of no consequence," the king waived his hand airily. "He was suggesting a truce, a peace between us."

"Then why did he not also send a messenger to me, or is he only offering peace to Prussia?" probed Bennigsen.

"The peace was conditional on Prussia breaking its alliance with Russia, which is why I of course refused it."

"And what would you get in return for breaking with your allies and leaving the Russian army that has come to your aid, dangerously exposed to French attack?" demanded Hutchinson.

"That does not matter, for I have turned down the proposal. I will not abandon my alliance, which is why I have told you of the approach. Now, gentlemen, if you will excuse me, I must attend to my other guests."

"Treacherous weasel," muttered Bennigsen as we watched the king stride into the next room. "Bonaparte will not be happy when he learns we know of his approach. It shows how keen he is to end this war."

Hutchinson led the British contingent into the ballroom. As we entered, I looked across the swirling figures and spotted my countess dancing with a Russian general. His lordship led us on to a buffet table that had already been half depleted. We quickly grabbed our fill and moved to one side where he ruminated on feckless monarchs, careless of who might overhear him. I had just finished a small pastry when I felt a hand on my arm.

"Captain Flashman, I think you promised me the next dance." I turned and there was Dorothea standing beside me, looking even more radiant close to. Once again I found myself tongue-tied in the presence of her unusual yet striking beauty.

"Oh…er…of course, Countess, I would be honoured." I turned back to my companions who, without exception, were staring with mouths agape. "If you will excuse me, gentlemen," I murmured, taking no small satisfaction from their expressions.

"I suspect that I have you to thank for my invitation here," I said as we took our places on the dancefloor. "You will have to point out Countess Lieven to me so that I can thank her."

"That is easy to do – you are holding her," Dorothea grinned, "I am Countess Lieven. Benckendorff is my maiden name. Karl used it as he knew me before I was married."

"So, it is *your* husband who is a close friend of the tsar?"

"Christoph's mother was appointed by Empress Catherine as governess to Alexander's younger siblings. They have known each other since childhood. He is here tonight, but keen to leave me and go and welcome Alexander to Prussia. He thinks I do not know he has taken some Prussian sow as a mistress." She was searching around the room, but evidently could not find her errant spouse and I wondered if he had left already.

"Have you been married long?"

"I was married at fifteen. We have two sons who are currently staying with my father." She winced as I trod on her foot for the second time. "Perhaps we should sit out the rest of this dance. Let us go over to that corner, I would like a word with you in private." I thought she was going to ask me more questions about Karl, but instead she sternly demanded, "Tell me, Captain, are you one of those men who think women should not involve themselves in affairs of state?"

"Not at all," I assured her. "A few years back I was in India and there was a begum, a female ruler, who ran rings around all of the maharajahs."

"Good. Has your Lord Hutchinson heard of our French visitor to the palace today?"

"Yes, General Bennigsen told us. We have just confronted the king about it."

"What did he tell you?"

"He said that Napoleon was offering a truce if he abandoned his alliance with Russia, but that he had rejected the proposal."

"I overheard a conversation between the king and his chief minister and can tell you Bonaparte offered rather more than that. He is willing to restore all Prussian territory to the king so that he can return to Berlin. In return the king must break the alliance with Russia and promise never to go to war with France again. Friedrich is worried that this might make Prussia a vassal state of France. He has sent one of his closest aides to Napoleon to explore terms."

"So he has not rejected the offer after all!" I exclaimed. "He might still sell out his allies." I could understand why. For a monarch hanging on to just a few cities, the restoration of the whole of Prussia would be a tempting prospect. It might even be worth having a French minister who ensured he complied with the emperor's wishes.

"Do not worry," she soothed, "He will not accept the deal."

"How can you be so sure?"

"The queen has not heard of it yet, but I will make sure she does. She would never tolerate such acquiescence to a man who accused her of whoring herself to form the alliance with Russia."

It was the common belief that the queen had pushed for the war with France, partly to address this insult. But the war had been a disaster for Prussia and that must have damaged her sway with ministers. Even if the king was reluctant to defy her, there would be many others who would find the offer irresistible.

"I think you overestimate the queen's influence," I whispered, checking again we could not be overheard. "Thousands of Prussians would support the deal if it gave them back their estates and property. Just a few days ago many thought that the state of Prussia would cease to exist. Napoleon could easily win the country peacefully and break the alliance at the same time."

Dorothea was thoughtful for a moment as she saw the strength of my argument. "Then we must do all we can to stop it, for Russia's sake and for Britain. My husband will ensure that the tsar writes to the king in the strongest terms, but that will take some time. It would be helpful if your Lord Hutchinson could add to the pressure on behalf of Britain."

"That will be no problem. He will be furious when he finds out."

"Then he should tell his mistress," Dorothea told me, smiling. When I looked at her questioningly, she added, "She is the wife of the aide sent to negotiate with Napoleon. The chief minister is using her to spy on Lord Hutchinson and tell him what you British really think." I could not help but smile as I anticipated the pleasure of ruining his lordship's evening.

His rage at the news was indeed verging on the volcanic, but once he had calmed down, new opportunities presented themselves. The wily old fox soon saw a way to take his pleasure and wreak his revenge. That evening as our chief was about to bed down with his double-dealing *Frau*, I knocked on his door. As we had arranged, he loudly told me to go away and come back in the morning.

"I have an urgent despatch from our spy in Napoleon's headquarters," I whispered. This fictional agent had been my idea to protect Dorothea's identity as the source. I listened as the bed creaked and I heard his footsteps cross the floor. Hutchinson snarled angrily at me as he took the letter I had written, yet could not resist a conspiratorial wink as he played his part.

"This had better be important," he growled as he tore open the seal. There was little acting required on his part as he read the details, which I had already recounted to him in the carriage back to our lodgings, as well as some embellishments of our own invention. He had been incandescent in the carriage and his cheeks were flushing again in genuine anger as he perused the facts in my letter. "The villain!" he roared.

"Vot is it, my *Liebling*?" asked the woman, her eyes alive with curiosity.

"Here, read it yourself," Hutchinson tossed the incriminating paper in her direction. "Your king is planning to sell out his allies and make a new alliance with France. The pompous pipsqueak has no idea what he is doing. Napoleon is already planning how to take the Prussian army for his other wars. Once the soldiers are away, he can make demands for tax and anything else he wants. Prussia will be ruined and if France does not do it, then Britain and Russia will. Damn that Prussian prig to hell, for we will not forgive this kind of treachery." He threw over a chair as he began to pace the room, planning reprisals. "There will not be another guinea from the British purse and the subsidies we have paid already will now be repayable. We will blockade the coast, seize every Prussian asset we can find and give Russia any support it wants to annex Prussian territory."

"I should leave you. You vill vant to write letters and make plans," the mistress announced. She was reaching for her clothes and suddenly anxious to depart. No doubt she wanted to rush with this intelligence to the palace, but Hutchinson wanted to exact a more personal revenge first.

"No, you should stay," he replied ushering me out of the door. "I need your company to help calm me and work through my frustration."

Judging from the squeals and grunts that emanated through the adjoining wall over the next hour or so, his lordship certainly had a lot of frustration to deal with. Kit, Wilson and I muttered darkly over the report that she would eventually deliver. Letting her read the letter had been a masterstroke, as it also contained an entirely fictitious but derisive opinion of the Prussian king and French plans. Our 'spy' reported that Napoleon considered Friedrich Wilhelm to be a witless fool, who spent far longer admiring his own reflection in his highly polished boots than he did considering strategy. The letter spelt out that the French planned to gain Prussia, a new army and fresh taxes and destroy the alliance, all without spilling another drop of French blood. The despatch described the Prussian king as a gull, who would be controlled like a puppet. For such a proud man, that kind of revelation would be devastating.

The next morning we learned that Hutchinson's *Frau* had taken the letter with her when she finally escaped his lordship's company in the early hours. "She damn well earned it," he grunted, stifling a chuckle. "But I doubt I will see her again now."

Later that morning I received a note from Dorothea. She told us that there had been shouting over the royal breakfast table and crockery had been thrown as the queen vented her fury on learning of the proposed treaty.

We congratulated ourselves on a job well done. I confess I was beginning to enjoy this art of diplomacy. With a little help from us, the Prussian king had painted himself into a corner and we had only to wait. Doubtless Napoleon had his own spies in Prussia who would report that the confidential offer had been shared with the allies. That alone might cause the deal to be withdrawn. It would certainly make discussions harder for the Prussian emissary. Even when Friedrich's man did return, the king would struggle to trust any assurances he carried.

As we waited for events to unfold, Wilson joined a Russian cavalry force which was returning to the battlefield at Eylau. I had no wish to see the place ever again and from Wilson's report when he returned, I had made the right decision. He was there exactly two weeks after the battle and found stables, barns and buildings in the town still stuffed with the dead and dying, suffering in appalling conditions. This time the Russian soldiers did their best to help the survivors of both armies and a steady stream of wounded continued to make its way back to Konigsberg. Cossacks pursued the French army but found little more than a seventy-mile-long cemetery of abandoned corpses of men and animals in devastated countryside.

A week after Wilson returned, on the eighth of March, we were visited by the Prussian foreign minister, an elderly general called Zastrow. He assured us that his king was no longer pursuing an alliance with France. He had evidently heard of our fictional agent in Napoleon's headquarters and was confident that this man would confirm what he said. Hutchinson took him at his word and listened as the minister laid out an appeal for more help from Britain. As well as more gold, they wanted the Royal Navy to land an expeditionary force of ten thousand men further up the coast behind the French lines. This force would then join a coordinated attack with the Prussian and Russian armies. Zastrow was convinced that the presence of British redcoats would encourage other Prussians to show resistance and help drive the invader out of their country. It was a bold and ambitious plan and to my great surprise Hutchinson agreed to it immediately. Zastrow was delighted, as his lordship promised to send a despatch recommending the scheme to London the very next day. The Prussian minister might have been less thrilled had he heard our conversation after he left.

134

"This is excellent news," enthused Wilson. "A British army fighting shoulder to shoulder with our allies to throw the French back. But do you think that Horse Guards will be able to find ten thousand men? The expeditionary force in Buenos Aires must be taking up a lot of troops and transports."

"I am absolutely certain that they will not send a single one," Hutchinson responded, much to Wilson's dismay. "That is why I agreed to their request."

"But why would they not help?" asked Wilson.

"The expedition to Buenos Aires is turning into a disaster according to the despatches we have seen," said Kit, answering for his brother. "The government in London is under pressure from the king and opposition. It cannot afford another military debacle. To have a British force isolated behind enemy lines would be a very risky affair."

"So why have we told the Prussians we will help?" I asked. "Why not just turn them down flat?"

"Because our mission here is to encourage them to fight on," explained Hutchinson. "I will write to London as promised. If they are devious enough to put a woman in my bed, they are certain to read my despatches. Grenville will know to ignore the request."

As March turned into April, it became a very odd time for the alliance. Everyone expected that campaigning would resume in the spring when the weather improved, but no one really trusted each other.

Prussia vehemently insisted to all that it was now ready to fight the French again. Yet when talking to us, Prussian officers would dismiss Russians as ignorant of military strategy, whose success had been achieved by a primitive weight of numbers.

The Russians were even more divided, with many of their officers still detesting Bennigsen, who they blamed for robbing them of a clear victory due to his cautious retreats. Not that we British were any better, as we deceived them both over the prospect of an expeditionary force. Hutchinson was his usual irascible self. When he was shown the captured French eagles by proud Russian officers, he asked how many Russian standards were now on the way to Paris.

Yet despite this disunity, confidence was growing that 1808 would be a time of victory and success for the alliance. The previous year had been a catastrophic disaster for Prussia and most had feared that the poorly trained Russian soldiers would be roundly thrashed too. Instead, they had held their own, fighting the French to a standstill. Cynics like Hutchinson would point out that this was as much due to the weather as fighting ability, but this argument did not stand as both sides had endured the same conditions. Certainly, Russian officers expected more victories, and emphatic ones at that. Their confidence was swelled not only by the imminent arrival of their tsar, but by the Imperial Guard division that he was bringing with him. This new force packed with scions of the gentry and consequently better trained and equipped, was commanded by the tsar's brother, Grand Duke Constantine. The enthusiasm of the common soldiery was tempered, however, as the provision of sufficient supplies had not improved. With the spring thaw, the rains increased, turning roads into quagmires. Russian forces were dispersed over a vast area stretching back into Russia to find the food they needed. We even heard of one regiment who had received a consignment of ox hides that were intended as tent covers. The men had been so hungry, they had boiled and eaten them instead.

Tsar Alexander and the king finally met on the seventh of April in a grand ceremony and military review. We too were invited to the gathering and after Friedrich Wilhelm's recent dalliance with the idea of a French union, I had half expected the greeting to be frosty. However, it was clear that their differences had already been patched up and they greeted each other warmly. It swiftly transpired that these two young monarchs had a common interest: uniforms. They had both arrived with their grandest troops, whose tunics and boots had been brushed and polished to perfection. As a result, they spent the rest of the day reviewing these men; their faces in rapture over braid, frogging and medals. I noted, while I was watching them, that not once did they look at a musket. I wondered if the Russian weapons held by these new troops were any better than the rusty ones I had seen before.

That evening the king hosted a dinner for the tsar at a nearby mansion requisitioned for the purpose. There was no shortage of food or wine that night as Friedrich Wilhelm went all out to impress his fellow ruler. Over the days that followed there were further discussions on military preparations. It was then that I met Dorothea's husband, the Count of Lieven. He was in a group of officers introduced to us while we were with the tsar. He was around ten years older than his wife and tediously dull. He told us he commanded a brigade of two sharpshooter regiments but when I asked how much ammunition they normally carried, he looked almost insulted that he should be expected to know such details. Showing little interest in the military planning then underway, he spent most of his time in the private rooms of Friedrich Wilhelm's mansion. I suspected that Dorothea's suspicions of him having taken a mistress were well founded. A large gathering of Russian nobility, including grand dukes and princes, had attracted the attention of Prussian ladies keen to climb the social ladder. A steady stream of carriages arrived with an array of women folk, including various beauties, their maids and even their mothers – who, frustratingly, guarded their charges from unwanted advances, such as from an untitled Englishman.

When not entertaining, Alexander proved popular with his soldiers. He had created a new medal for the campaign, which exempted its holders from being flogged as a punishment. He spent much of his time pinning it to chests. Most recipients were officers who would not be beaten anyway. To our surprise, we learned that he had not forgotten his new British allies. Wilson, Kit and I were called forward and had the order of St George, third class fixed to our tunics, by the tsar himself, for our action at Eylau.

Alexander was a tall, slightly balding man aged around thirty. He spoke to us in English, asking about our part in the battle and what we thought of his army. Like dutiful toadies, we piled on the praise. He then asked us about the expected British expedition. As Hutchinson was not present, Kit answered that the request had been sent to London and we expected news any day. It was a response we were to give often over the coming weeks.

Winter was firmly behind us now and we watched the trees blossom and horses graze on shoots of new growth in the meadows. They at least had fresh food. I imagined what would be happening in the French lines as the spring rains dried and the roads became passable again. Trains of wagons would be bringing supplies to their army: new boots for marching in the coming campaign; uniforms; replacement men and horses for regiments; ammunition and food. Army bakeries would be transforming sacks of flour into fresh bread with the smell wafting over their barracks. My stomach would rumble at my own imaginings before reality bit and I turned to survey the Russian army.

Their commissary had barely improved since the winter, despite St Petersburg being considerably closer than Paris. Some new boots and ammunition had been sent, but as men had been dispersed in their winter quarters, they had been left to effect their own repairs. The scarecrow army that had fought at Eylau now began to regather, wearing coats and trousers patched in various scraps of homespun cloth. Some black, most brown, but I also saw patches of blue that came from French uniforms. Many resembled troops of harlequin soldiers. The contrast with the immaculate, but untested Guards regiments could not have been greater. Their commander, Grand Duke Constantine, who turned out to be even more of a martinet over uniforms than his brother, was appalled. Instead of pressing for better supplies, he insisted that his men would not stand alongside any officers or men who were improperly dressed.

As the weather improved thoughts turned to the coming campaign. Both the Prussians and Russians were supremely confident of victory, despite the narrow outcomes of the earlier battles. Perhaps no one wanted to contemplate defeat in front of their monarch, and many made bold claims about marching west and driving on to Paris. To our alarm, their imagined victories invariably included a large British force pushing south from the coast and occupying the attention of several marshals. When pressed by one Prussian general to estimate the number of redcoats on their way, Wilson suggested a figure of fifty thousand and confidently asserted that they would arrive within weeks.

"Why the hell did you say that?" I asked when we were alone.

"Because I think his lordship is wrong," he told me. "I have been sending my own reports to ministers in London urging them to seize this opportunity. If we commit fully to this alliance, we could end this war and Bonaparte at the same time." His eyes gleamed with the possibility of victory, but he was to be disappointed. We heard in May that the government of Grenfell had collapsed. All that politicians in London were interested in then was the coming election. So instead of an army, the only British forces to sail into the Baltic were three small naval sloops.

Various councils of war were held with the monarchs and their commanders. In anticipation of our contribution, we were also invited so that we could co-ordinate our force. We watched as aggressive generals laid out before their commanders-in-chief, complex schemes of marching columns that would divide and drive our enemy back. Both monarchs would appear enthusiastic and Bennigsen would make positive noises, yet at the end of the day he did not commit to any of them. He appeared to have no plan of his own other than to form a line in front of the French and wait for them to attack. Personally, I was grateful for his caution and wondered if the Hanoverian had his own contacts in London. Friedrich Wilhelm, though, was hugely frustrated by this strategic void. As the days passed he grew increasingly vehement about the opportunities being missed. His Prussian generals would nod in agreement, and I suspected that many of the Russian officers felt the same. They looked to the tsar for their lead, but he would always put his hand on Bennigsen's shoulder and assure them that his commander would make the decision when the time was right.

Apart from a brief spell at the start of the year when Bennigsen's army had advanced, Danzig had been behind French lines. In March Napoleon's forces had started to encircle the city. At first no one was greatly concerned as it had been well supplied. The expectation was that the besiegers would be forced to pull back when the French retreated from a general allied advance. Then in mid-April came shocking news: the Prussian garrison at Danzig was running out of gunpowder. At first, Friedrich Wilhelm insisted this could not be true. He had personally checked that supplies had been despatched regularly to the city from a gunpowder factory outside Konigsberg. Riders were sent back to the capital to investigate, and I went with them to update Hutchinson on proceedings.

His lordship had stayed away from the tsar, probably because he did not want to be harried over plans for the British force. While time with the British chief was not something I relished, I volunteered to go back to the city for another reason. Ever since I had last seen her, the charms of Dorothea had often been on my mind. Her beguiling beauty was fixed in my memory, as was the calm, calculating mind that belied her youth as she helped us manipulate the Prussians. She was little short of bewitching, and I was fully under her spell. Not that I felt badly about it, for she was to prove to be one of the finest diplomats Russia has ever had.

By the time I reached the city, the mystery of the missing gunpowder had been uncovered. It was one of monumental incompetence. The Prussians prided themselves on their adherence to orders, but, while laudable, often this resulted in a complete lack of common sense. The powder had been sent down the shingle spit to Danzig in carts at which point the officer in command was to leave it north of the Vistula River for the city garrison to transport across. Unfortunately, his instructions did not include telling the garrison that it was there for collection. Even when he delivered subsequent loads and the first had not been gathered, it did not occur to him to make sure plans were in place to take these vital supplies into Danzig. He simply built up a vast stockpile that was now being used by the French to shoot shells into the city.

"I would not trust those fools to run a whelk stand, never mind a siege," Hutchinson fumed as he told me. He was similarly unimpressed with the news I brought of the complete lack of progress in planning the coming campaign. "This bloody shambles will end in disaster, you mark my words," he predicted. "The only thing we can take comfort from is that there will be no poor bloody redcoats stuck in the middle of it." He fixed me with another suspicious glare and then grunted, "You should see your spy in the palace. She may have more information on what is really going on around here."

I did not need asking twice. So it was that an hour later I was presenting myself at the royal residence, this time claiming to have a message from the countess's husband. I was shown into the familiar drawing room and this time as soon as she saw it was me, the maid was dismissed.

"Do you really have a message from my husband?" she asked, "or is he too busy chasing the Prussian strumpets now flocking to the tsar's headquarters?" Sometimes when you have been apart from a woman, your imagination enhances their beauty so that a reunion is something of a disappointment. If anything, the reverse was the case here; I was enraptured, not just by the dark eyes in the flawless skin, but by her sharpness of mind. She clearly had her own spies in Friedrich Wilhelm's mansion and knew far more about what went on inside its walls than I did. I grinned in delight and bent down to kiss the back of the proffered hand.

"No, I come entirely on my own account," I replied. Then I added something that I felt sure would please her. "Although Lord Hutchinson says that he and the British government would greatly value your opinion on current affairs, for your assistance previously was invaluable."

She laughed, "I very much doubt that your Lord Hutchinson is ever that diplomatic." But immediately, she became serious and put her hand on my knee, which almost distracted me entirely from her next words. "You should remember that I serve Russia and not Britain." Then she leaned towards me, filling my nostrils with her sweet scent as she looked me in the eye and innocently enquired, "There is no British army force coming, is there?"

I was lost in those dark staring pools for a moment and then to my horror, I heard myself whisper, "No." Hastily, I tried to recover, "Well, no final decision has been made. Our government might still decide to send a force and we have sent three naval vessels."

She giggled at my confusion and took her hand from my knee to slide it through my arm. "You should not worry, Captain, you have not told me any great secret. General Bennigsen is sure that no British force will come and he has already told the tsar not to expect one."

"Please, Countess, call me Thomas," I interrupted, feeling slightly relieved.

"Then you must call me Dee," she insisted. "Dorothea is too long. But did you not know that your naval force is already reduced to two ships?"

"What, one has been sunk?"

"The captain was brave, although I hear a little reckless. He tried to force his way through to Danzig up the river, but his ship was well within musket range of both banks and under fire from cannon too. I am told that he lost a mast and over half of his crew before having to retreat." I remembered the narrow channel from when we had come up along it. It was barely a hundred yards across. The vessel would have been lashed with shot from stem to stern. If he had tried it in daylight, then the captain was a bloody fool.

So far all I had done was divulge a British secret – not that I would admit it. I thought it was high time I found out some other intelligence, so that I had something to report to Hutchinson. "Does the tsar have confidence in Bennigsen?" I enquired. "He does not seem to have any plan beyond waiting for the French to attack."

Dorothea looked at me carefully before answering, clearly weighing up how much to divulge. "It would be difficult for the tsar to dismiss Bennigsen. The general was one of the conspirators who murdered the old tsar; some say he stabbed and then strangled him with his own hands."

"Good God." I was astonished. "Does the tsar know?"

"Of course. Alexander was brought up by his grandmother, Catherine, who had little time for her son and heir. He was also involved in the plot and had dined with his father that same night. He claimed that he thought his father would be forced to abdicate and did not know he would be killed. He is either lying or a fool to say such a thing, for he would have known that his throne would not be secure while his father was alive." She shrugged, "I do not think Alexander is a fool, do you?"

I gaped at her, still taking this in and reconciling her innocent young beauty with this casual knowledge of palace coups and murder. "No, he does not strike me as a fool either," I admitted. He had given the impression of kind consideration, but it was now clear that there was a streak of utter ruthlessness to him as well. A man prepared to murder his own father would do whatever it took to stay on the throne. "How do you know all this?"

"My mother is one of the old tsarina's closest friends. I too served her as a maid of honour in the palace. When Alexander used to visit his mother, she would put a casket containing the bloodstained shirt of her husband on the table between them as a reproach. She knows what he did."

"Were you in the Russian court for long?" I asked. I was surprised, for she seemed to have packed a lot into her short life. She had mentioned before, for instance, that she had two sons and yet was only in her early twenties.

"When my mother died the old tsarina was my guardian for three years. She would visit every week and she eventually arranged my marriage to Christoph. He thinks I should stay at home in St Petersburg, but I will not be shut away. I can help him; I got him his post in the army and I can help Russia too."

"Well, you certainly helped keep Prussia in the alliance," I told her.

She smiled and I felt my heart skip a beat. "The king never did learn how his wife discovered his plan, but the queen and I are now close friends. Do you want to know what else she tells me? Would that help you with Lord Hutchinson?"

"Well, any information would be gratefully received," I murmured, hardly able to believe my luck.

"The Prussians and the Russians are both negotiating with the Austrians, trying to persuade them to join the alliance too. Yet the Austrians are unlikely to make a decision until they see the outcome of the spring campaign." I was disappointed as we had already heard these rumours, but then she went on. "Austria will claim back territory it lost to Prussia in earlier wars as a price for joining the coalition. Alexander would agree to such a deal but Friedrich Wilhelm will not."

"Now that *is* interesting," I admitted. Until now the two monarchs had seemed as close as brothers, but it was clear that they and their advisors did not entirely trust each other.

"The ministers here talk in front of me over dinner. Perhaps they think that I am some silly young woman who would not be interested in their schemes. They discuss annexing some of the German states captured by the French when the alliance advances. The British territory of Hanover could find itself surrounded by Prussia." She looked me in the eye and then shrugged those delicate shoulders. "I do not think that either Russia or Britain will want Prussia to become too powerful when the war is over."

I had already learned not to underestimate the countess. Her beguiling beauty was a weapon she used in her own diplomatic war and she did not hesitate to meddle in the affairs of states. I did not doubt that my own inadvertent admission would soon be finding its way to the tsar's ear, as would the Prussian plans – if they had not been sent already.

Hutchinson too was impressed with her news of division between our allies. He was less worried about any threat to Hanover. "Let's see them beat the French first," he barked.

"Did you know that Alexander was involved in the plot to kill his father?" I asked him.

"Of course I did. Did you read nothing about Russia before you came here, Flashman?" He gave a weary sigh of despair. "The old tsar was as mad as a March hare, that was why Catherine had him shut away during her reign. She probably convinced Alexander that such an act would be necessary after her death."

"She encouraged her grandson to murder her own son?" I queried, shocked.

"If it would save Russia from chaos, yes," he insisted. "She had a ruthless streak. After all she had her own husband overthrown and murdered to seize the throne herself."

Hutchinson decided to join me on my journey back to Bennigsen's headquarters. I had told him that the allies were having doubts about our contribution of men. He thought he would personally bring news of the latest cash subsidies to remind them that Britain was still a valuable ally.

The journey was not a pleasant one as his normal choleric nature was made worse by a rotten tooth. Eventually, we stopped at a village and with the help of the coachman and acts of mime, we found someone to help him pull out the offending molar. There was no doctor, but the blacksmith was willing to help. First, though, he had to make some smaller tongs for the work, as his other tools were more suited to fitting horseshoes. By nightfall the smith was ready and as I held a candle flame virtually under his lordship's nose, he went to work. In the end it took another man to help hold the head still as the smith tugged and pulled – to growing roars of agony. Eventually, the thing was out. Hutchinson was given more of the local firewater to clean the wound, on top of a pint of the stuff he had already drunk to dull the ache. Needless to say, he slept well.

Free from pain and soothed by spirits, his lordship was in a benign mood when he finally met the two monarchs. He was remarkably sociable as he made small talk, laughed at their jokes and even ignored one or two barbed comments about missing redcoats. He explained that the calling of an election was beyond his control. He reminded them that their ambassadors in London could confirm that a decision to send men would now be made by the new government when appointed by the king.

A council of war was held to agree what to do about Danzig. The decision was made to send a relief column of eight thousand Russians to break the siege and resupply the Prussian garrison. The tsar gave this command to the young general, Kamenski, who was anxious to expunge the disgrace earned by his father's eccentric behaviour. Discussion then turned to how they could divert French attention away from this column and stop the enemy from reinforcing the besiegers.

Bennigsen began to propose a cautious plan to advance a few regiments a short distance, while keeping his defensive line intact. To his surprise, the two rulers interrupted. They must have been frustrated by the caution of Bennigsen's earlier schemes and had clearly agreed their own plan. Now they overruled their general and insisted that their combined eighty thousand strong host would advance up to the French lines. It was by no means clear what they would do when they got there, but the more aggressive generals eagerly supported the idea, no doubt pleased to see Bennigsen humbled. The Hanoverian looked ill as the situation slipped out of his control and I could hardly blame him. To expose this vast force to the enemy in order to protect just a tenth of their number, and with no coherent plan for when they made contact, was madness to me too.

"But will young Kamenski have enough men to lift the siege?" enquired Hutchinson looking at the papers scattered on the table. "This estimate puts the enemy force surrounding Danzig at around twenty-five thousand."

"Less than half of those are French veterans," announced the king, dismissing the report. "Many of the rest are Polish conscripts," he continued, ignoring the fact that Poles also made up much of the Prussian garrison at Danzig.

"They will not be enough to drive the French away," Alexander offered, confirming Hutchinson's suspicion, "but for the next month or two they will stop those men re-joining Bonaparte and that should help us to win some campaign victories."

Friedrich Wilhelm clapped Hutchinson on the shoulder and added, "This will also give your army time to arrive. Then at last the Austrians will make up their mind to join us."

The colour drained from his lordship's features as we realised that, despite everything, at least one of the allies was still looking to the nebulous support of Britannia for their deliverance.

Chapter 16

Kamenski's mission did not go well. The French had prepared defences south of the city in anticipation of an attempt to lift the siege, The Russian commander, unsure he could break through, tried to gain the element of surprise with a new strategy. As the sea and lagoon were thawing, his men piled onto ships and approached the city from the north. Storms and squalls intervened, however, and his seasick soldiers scrambled to the shore piecemeal, giving the French the time to pin them down. Trapped on the flat, exposed coast, they were unable to break out and reach the city. One of the remaining Royal Navy ships tried to help by sailing seventeen tons of gunpowder up the river to resupply Danzig, but even at night the endeavour was near suicidal. The ship was soon spotted and its deck flailed with fire, killing all around the wheel and manning the sails. The vessel ran aground in sight of the city, whose garrison used some of their last charges to try to destroy what remained of it and its cargo with heated shot. Even that failed and the consignment fell into the hands of the French. Danzig eventually surrendered, while Kamenski managed to get his men back onto ships to avoid the same fate.

The fall of the city was a huge blow to the Prussians, who complained bitterly that the Russians should have sent more men to save it. The Russians pointed out that if the garrison had done a better job of monitoring powder supplies, the relief would not have been necessary. Both sides looked reproachfully at us British. We, of course, saw nothing of the action at Danzig, but what we were to witness over the coming weeks would make Kamenski appear a strategic genius in comparison.

After the council of war, we had expected – and feared – that the whole allied army would blunder blindly into the French, spurred on by the zeal of the monarchs. It transpired, however, that we had greatly underestimated the power of Bennigsen to prevaricate and delay. Day after day maps were studied and plans for an advance discussed and argued over. As the news from Danzig worsened, generals began to distrust each other, convinced that their ally was trying to put them in the tightest spot. The royals soon became bored with this tedium and contented themselves with more military reviews and giving out medals while they waited for plans to be finalised.

In mid-May it looked like a decision had finally been reached. Both monarchs advanced with twenty-two thousand infantry and a vast array of cavalry to join General Bagration and his men who were closest to the French lines. These troops had then stood ready since well before dawn, awaiting orders to advance. As we joined them, (reluctantly, in my case) we all expected the day to end if not in battle, then at least with the enemy being driven back. Instead, Bennigsen, Alexander and Friedrich Wilhelm arrived mid-morning and advanced a short distance alone towards the French positions. They claimed they wanted to reconnoitre the intervening ground, yet none of their staff were allowed to accompany them. We stood around for an hour watching as the three men dismounted and talked privately among themselves. Heaven knows what they said, but when they returned all but General Bagration's men were ordered to return to headquarters, which was then in the town of Heilsberg.

For the entire month of May, while a large part of the French army was occupied around Danzig, the allied army made absolutely no attack at all. The Prussians fumed at the Russian reluctance to fight and Russian officers threw the same charge at their despised 'sausage-maker' commander. To my surprise, Hutchinson was far less critical. I found him one morning inspecting the churches in the town. When we had first arrived these had been empty or used as stables. Now they were full of food, ammunition and other supplies for the coming campaign. Horses that had been skeletally thin in March and April, had regained weight, muscle and stamina. The Russian soldiers were also now better fed, benefitting from a steady train of wagons that came west from Russia and parts of Prussia that had not been raided by allied armies. Uniforms had been patched and repaired and even the boots supply had been improved with those taken from French prisoners and the dead. Bennigsen's army was now in a far better condition to fight than it had been in the spring. Unfortunately, the chances were that the state of the French army had improved too.

It was early June before the orders were finally given again to advance. One part of the French line protruded ahead of the rest and Bennigsen planned to 'cut out' that marshal's forces with frontal attacks and assaults down the flanks to cut them off from reinforcement. The hope was that a whole corps could be eliminated before the rest of the French army had time to react.

Bennigsen had fretted over his plan for days and was not helped by a bladder infection that sometimes left him gasping in pain. With the forces around Danzig now released, he was convinced that the enemy army was larger than our own. He must have known that there was growing discontent over his apparent reluctance to fight; a swift victory would help even the odds between the armies as well as boost morale. Determined that the attack would succeed, the Hanoverian organised it in meticulous detail. Commanders were personally briefed on their comprehensive written orders, as it was vital that the various attack columns appeared at the right place and the right time so that they could support each other.

When I saw it, I had to concede that the scheme was very thorough. If everyone moved precisely as planned and the enemy reacted exactly as we expected, it should produce a stunning victory. Yet even with my then limited military experience, I knew that foul-ups were bound to occur. That risk was even higher with allies and commanders who did not trust each other. Hutchinson was even more derisive. "The plan will collapse into chaos. The man is kicking a hornets' nest and he is going to get stung."

With that condemnation ringing in my ears, the salient question was: Where would I be in this coming debacle? Wilson had already volunteered to ride with his beloved Cossacks, while Kit and Hutchinson would stay at Bennigsen's headquarters. That seemed worryingly close to a collapsing front line to me. Fortunately, when I looked at the map for myself, I saw a much better alternative. At the north-western end of the allied line, the Prussian army under L'Estocq was to make a diversionary attack to deter the marshal there from supporting his colleague to the south.

"I will go there," I declared, pointing at the charts. "We should have someone co-ordinating with the Prussians too." Hutchinson gave a grunt of agreement. I doubt that it had escaped his attention that this end of our line was a bare forty miles from Konigsberg and the sea if things went wrong.

The attack was scheduled to begin at dawn on the fourth of June. On the third, Russian units were to advance most of the ten miles between the headquarters at Heilsberg and the unsuspecting French. They were to stay out of sight, while the Cossack screen that regularly patrolled in front of the enemy lines would stop any French scouts from discovering them. With further to travel, I had left Heilsberg on the second and arrived late on the third. When I had last seen L'Estocq he had been a stiff proud Prussian leading his forces to save the Russian army at Eylau. Now, he looked all of his seventy-one years and barely read the despatches I had brought from Bennigsen.

"I pulled that wretch's arse out of the fire," complained the old general bitterly. "He does not like to be reminded of that and so now he sends me to this shitty backwater. He will keep all the glory to himself now."

Having seen the full plans I thought he should be more grateful he was in the backwater, which did not seem that 'shitty' at all.

It was a pleasant summer evening and one of his officers, a general called Rembow, offered to ride with me to show where they would be attacking in the morning. He wanted to have a final look himself as his five thousand men would be carrying out the assault. We passed many of his soldiers as we made our way down a wooded slope to a point where we could overlook the French lines from around half a mile away. The first thing I saw was a big earth rampart with several cannon muzzles poking over the top. In front of this formidable structure was a network of trenches for infantry to fight from. The French had evidently been busy building defences, but there were precious few soldiers manning them. They were clearly unaware that an enemy was close by as I could see a score of them swimming in the river, washing off the sweat of the day. Beyond the earthworks was a small cottage. Rembow pointed to it and whispered, "We will have our breakfast in there tomorrow morning." From what I had seen, I did not doubt he was right.

At four o'clock the next morning I was with his men again as they crept through the trees. There was just enough dawn light spreading across the eastern sky to show our way. Even though we had been given the order for silence, there was a steady crackle of broken twigs as men made their way through the forest, the odd muffled curse at a barked shin on a stump and the jingle of harnesses as cavalry and some horse artillery moved among us. I thought we would do well to surprise the French with that din, but as we reached our previous vantage point all was still and quiet ahead. Rembow waved his arm and a line of infantry now emerged from cover and began to sprint across the last five hundred yards of open meadow to the trenches. Four hundred yards, then three hundred and still no alarm. Then as the first horsemen emerged from the trees a shot rang out, followed by half a dozen more. Heads appeared over the tops of trenches and I saw the flash of more muzzles in the dim morning light, but it was too late; the Prussians were up to the dugouts and firing down into them.

"General Rembow," a voice called out behind me, but I ignored it as I watched more Prussians moving through a small field of French tents, cutting the ropes as they passed. The first most French knew that they were prisoners was when the canvas collapsed around them. A cannon fired from the main earthworks and then a second, yet already you could see men pouring out of the fortification and past the cottage beyond. The day was won – it was one of the finest attacks I had yet seen.

"Goddammit," Rembow cursed beside me, and I turned in surprise.

"What on earth is the matter? That could not have gone any better," I replied.

He held up a paper he had just been given, "L'Estocq has ordered us to cancel the attack."

"But why?" I was astounded.

"He does not say. We have to sound the recall and bring the men back."

151

"But look, they have nearly captured the redoubt. Ignore the order, take the position and then find out what is going on."

Rembow looked at me as though I had suggested some blasphemy. "A Prussian officer does not ignore an order," he told me tartly before ordering his bugler to bring his men back. They did at least return with some two hundred prisoners and then we slowly made our way back up the hill into the trees. When I looked over my shoulder, I could see dozens of French soldiers now milling around the earthworks, clearly confused as to what was happening and probably unable to believe their luck.

When we reached the Prussian headquarters L'Estocq told us that he had received a message from Bennigsen postponing the attack.

"But we had nearly captured our objective," I complained.

"We are a diversion," the old general reminded me stiffly. "We cannot attack if there is nothing to divert from."

I walked away feeling anger and frustration and I was sure I was not alone. It was a feeling that was to get worse. Late that evening we received another sweat-covered courier from Bennigsen galloping into camp on a lathered horse. Breathlessly, he handed the Prussian general a new message: the attack was back on for the following dawn.

There was a grim inevitability to the scene that greeted us as the sun rose the next morning. The trenches that had been empty the day before were now packed with men as was the earthworks redoubt behind them. The river protected their right flank but now several squadrons of cavalry guarded their left. They were observant blighters too, for barely had we poked our heads through the bushes to stare in their direction, than the first cannon crashed out. Rembow swore volubly in German, but there was nothing to be done. A Prussian officer must obey orders. His men were organised into three attack columns with our horsemen ready to protect against theirs. The poor devils did not stand a chance. As they launched themselves across that final five hundred yards, they were met with a hailstorm of shot and shell. Within minutes men were staggering back into the trees. Many were wounded but several hundred lay prostrate among the meadow flowers.

"What do we do now?" I asked.

Rembow gave me a bitter smile. "We have obeyed our orders – we have created a diversion. There is no advantage to sacrificing more men."

We returned once again to the Prussian headquarters. If there was an attack going on to the south, I could not hear it, although the trees would have muffled the sound. L'Estocq listened to our report without expression and then summoned one of Bennigsen's messengers. "Why was the attack delayed?" he demanded. Awkwardly, the rider admitted that it was because the commander of the Russian army had been taken ill.

"Seriously ill?" L'Estocq could not hide the hope in his voice.

"He has an infection of the bladder," I informed him.

"Are you telling me that I have five hundred dead because one man could not take a piss?" Rembow roared. He was furious.

I shrugged my agreement, for it summed up the day rather well.

As that day wore on, we had expected the French to order an attack of their own, but they made no move. While Rembow organised a truce to help his wounded, L'Estocq directed his frustration into a furious despatch to Bennigsen. He wrote in German so the only bit I could understand when I glanced over his shoulder was the number '500,' which had been angrily underlined twice. The headquarters was not a happy place to be, but I was in no rush to leave as it was also relatively safe. Unfortunately, L'Estocq had other ideas.

"Take this to Bennigsen," he demanded, handing me his now sealed letter. "You can tell that fool what you have seen." Then to add insult to injury he added, "I have had enough of this madness. I am taking my men back to Konigsberg."

That was exactly where I wanted to be, preferably in the remaining Royal Navy ship in the harbour, ready to leave if the Russian plans misfired. "Perhaps one of your own couriers would be faster," I suggested. "They will know the country better than I."

"You found us, you can just reverse your route," L'Estocq barked back. The general would not brook objections. "He will listen to you British, while he thinks we are only fit for diversions."

I managed to delay my departure until dawn the next day, but then I was forced to make my way south-east again, into what might be the cauldron of battle. As I rode, I tried to remember the details of Bennigsen's plan and what should now be happening. The attack should have started the day before with various columns marching to isolate and destroy the forces that protruded from the French lines. By then the enemy should have been broken and driven back, but when I reached some high ground away from trees, I could distinctly hear the noise of battle ahead. I could not precisely tell the direction, but I had a nasty feeling that the overly complicated scheme was not going to plan.

I was to learn later that Bennigsen's strategy had hit a number of obstacles. First, one of his columns went missing and did not support the attack when expected. Second, Bennigsen's bladder now had him in agony. He had spent time personally searching for his missing men, which had left him unable to stand. In desperation he had asked Grand Duke Constantine to take over command. This had only caused more confusion as the grand duke had his own ideas on how an attack should be conducted. He had also refused to listen to one courier as the man was 'improperly dressed and clearly not a gentleman.' Last and by no means least was the fact that the men they were attacking were commanded by Marshal Ney. That name meant little to me at the time, but years later I would come to know him well. Ney was not blessed with any great strategic acumen, but for courage and organising a dogged defence there was none better. He knew he had to buy his emperor time to organise a counterstrike and that is exactly what he did. His fifteen thousand men faced close to fifty thousand and while they slowly pulled back, they made the allies fight hard for every yard.

The morning I set off on my journey, Bennigsen had expected to find that Ney had used the cover of darkness to withdraw his men to safety. Instead, he found that the wily marshal had used the time to strengthen defences for another tough day of fighting. That was the battle I could hear as I travelled south as slowly as I dared, and it sounded as though it was not going any better for the Russians than the day before.

Riding at a reasonable pace, I should have been back at the old headquarters at Heilsberg by the end of the day or otherwise at Guttstadt, ten miles south-west, where the new headquarters *should* by then have been. But as the noise of battle did not diminish, the pace of my ride slowed even more. At each rise I would carefully scan the ground ahead – one could not be too careful. When the road forked, I took the more easterly track to Heilsberg. A couple of miles further on I found a small inn, which gave an excellent excuse to stop for the night. I sat outside that evening, drinking beer and eating roast pork, while listening to the continuing cannonade of a far off battle.

Dawn broke the next morning surprisingly quiet. Only the sound of birds and the innkeeper's wife's singing broke the silence. In some ways that was even more disconcerting than the sound of war. Distant gunfire signified that both sides were still able to fight and were doing so some distance from me. But this relative peace opened up other options: had the armies fought each other to a standstill? There was often a lull in a battle as each side recovered. Alternatively, one army might have been victorious and would now be rampaging over the territory of the other. I knew nothing then of the problems Bennigsen had faced and thought it was still possible – if a little unlikely – that the Russians had been triumphant. They could have caught the French unawares and driven them back in disarray. If they had, then I needed to reach Bennigsen so that he knew what the Prussians were up to. On the other hand, if the French had won, the last thing I should do was head south.

I faced a dilemma as to my next move. So I decided that such big decisions were best made after breakfast. Then, after I had slowly mopped up the last crumb, I accepted the offer of a small beer to allow me to prevaricate further. I was just contemplating another when at last I caught the sound of armies on the wind. I heard marching feet and the shouts of men coming through the trees, but from the last direction I expected – the north. At first I thought that the Prussians had changed their mind and were coming back, then I remembered that we had left the French unopposed. Were they now marching to catch the Russians in the flank? I ran to saddle my horse and was just about to mount up when I saw a group of riders silently moving through the trees around me. They were Cossacks, which meant that the new arrivals were friends.

They turned out to be General Kamenski and what was left of the force sent to relieve Danzig, who were under orders to march south and re-join the army. I remembered the general from when he had been briefed on his earlier mission. Back then he had been brash and assured of success. Now he was more hesitant, clearly bruised by his recent experience. I told him what little I knew of what was going on but as my information was days old, there was no alternative but to continue the march south. At least I now had an escort of around five thousand men, including the Cossack scouts, but it did not make me that much more comfortable.

While I felt a sense of unease, I would have been even more nervous had I known what was happening at Guttstadt. There, Bennigsen and the grand duke were staring across the river at bands playing to welcome the French emperor to their opposing forces. With him was the peacock with his huge horde of cavalry and several other marshals to at least even up the size of the two armies. As Hutchinson had predicted, the nest had been kicked and the hornets were indeed emerging.

We were now obliged to go at the pace of Kamenski's infantry, which did not bother me at all. I was more than happy when the general called a halt in the afternoon to allow the stragglers to catch up. Kamenski had sent some Cossack scouts to Guttstadt for orders, but they would not return until the next day. In the meantime, he agreed that we should continue to Heilsberg. Situated ten miles behind Guttstadt it was the safest place to be if circumstances had changed.

We awoke the next morning to a thick mist, which made the forest eery and sinister. Men moved among the trees like ghosts and more than once an unnerved shout of alarm rang out. I knew that the summer sun would burn off the mist and I suggested to the general we wait until it did. He gratefully accepted the proposal and in fact seemed almost as hesitant about advancing as I was.

"The Prussians are furious with me for not saving Danzig," he admitted. "They are probably persuading the tsar to relieve me of my command." Soon, however, the prospect of a demotion was the least of his worries.

We had been underway for an hour when we encountered the Cossacks on their return from Guttstadt. The town, they reported, was now occupied by the French. They had captured some prisoners, who they had brought with them for interrogation. I noticed that nearby Russian soldiers quickly crossed themselves at the sight of them. Sermons about Napoleon being the Antichrist and his devil soldiers had clearly taken a firm hold amongst the uneducated peasants that made up the army. It was then that we learned of the stubborn resistance of Ney and how he had bought time for the French emperor to gather his men. The prisoners told us that there were fifty thousand

157

French soldiers at Guttstadt, but they did not know where the Russian army was. They insisted that it had disappeared during the night. They had been patrolling to find it in the fog that morning when they were captured.

"If Bennigsen is retreating," I warned Kamenski, "we had better get a move on or we might be left behind enemy lines." The Russian general did not need more convincing and soon we were on our way again. By lunchtime we were just an hour away from Heilsberg when riders from our Cossack screen came back with further news. Columns of French troops had been spotted moving through the trees towards the town ahead of us. Leaving the men to rest for a few minutes we went forward to investigate. The Cossack led us to some wooded high ground from where we could look down on the enemy from the cover of thick bushes. Sure enough, two regiments were visible and from distant shouting we could hear, there were more of them further on.

"We should follow them," urged a colonel on Kamenski's staff. "When they start their attack, we can fall upon their rear. We will take them by surprise and rout them, destroying their assault on our lines." It was sensible advice and took full advantage of the unusual position we were in. If I were not among this small army, I would have been in full support. But I had no wish to find myself in the middle of another pitched battle, especially as we did not know what other French forces might be approaching behind us.

"Were your orders not to return to Bennigsen without delay?" I reminded Kamenski. "He might be relying on us to fill a hole in his defences. Also, if we charge through a French attack, we could be fired on by our own side."

Our young commander considered for a moment. To catch an enemy completely by surprise is the kind of manoeuvre that a general dreams about. A month ago this cocksure commander would not have hesitated, but recent events had taken a toll on his confidence. "No," he decided. "We will go further east and move around them to reach Heilsberg."

Half an hour later we heard the first cannons fire, followed by a distant crackle of musketry. A new battle was starting to the south of us in the forest to the west of the town we were aiming for. In a short while we emerged from the trees to see Heilsberg in the distance. The town was built on the northern bank of a curve in the Alle River, which flowed east to west, and was dominated by a castle that rose above the tightly packed streets. This was an old medieval building and not suitable for defence by a large modern army. Instead of defending the town, the bulk of the Russian army was arrayed on the open ground in front of it.

The French had not been the only ones to strengthen their defences over the winter. The Russians were arrayed around several huge earthworks. They had been built by the peasant soldiers to protect against a sudden French assault, but now they would form the backbone of a defence that had become necessary following a Russian attack. They were huge 'U'-shaped structures with the open end pointing back towards the town. At the top of the embankments were gun emplacements that were now being filled with the cannon that the army had brought back from Guttstadt. There they would be protected and have excellent visibility to the trees and open ground that any attacking force would have to cover. The earth bank sides would shield infantry and cavalry from enemy fire, but the open ends would not protect the French should one of the defences fall. It was not hard to imagine those muddy banks being covered in blood in the coming hours and I resolved to go nowhere near them.

As Kamenski led his men to the right of the main Russian line, I went on towards the castle. Bennigsen had used it as his headquarters before and, given his preponderance to stay a healthy distance from the front, I expected to find him there again. To my surprise I learned he was in one of the earthworks, but I did find Hutchinson. He asked me how things had gone with the Prussians and when I told him, he gave a groan of despair.

"Things were little better with the main army," he informed me. "One general, who hates Bennigsen, ignored his instructions and let his regiments rest for much of the morning. They were found enjoying a sunlit glade in the woods, listening to the battle they should have been fighting in."

"What do you think will happen here?" I asked, wondering if we would need fresh horses before nightfall. There was still no sight of any French troops; all the fighting was taking place in the forest in front of the main Russian defences.

"Those mud banks look strong," asserted Hutchinson, "but if Bonaparte has any sense, he will just go around them." We stood on the castle ramparts and watched as the battle unfolded that afternoon. I kept watch over our flanks; we had very few men on the southern bank of the Alle River, yet none came to challenge them. We soon learned that the tenacious General Bagration had once again been allocated rear-guard duties. He was putting up such stiff resistance that he was pulling all available French forces onto the northern bank. Perhaps our Cossack screen had stopped Napoleon discovering the earthworks. If it had then they must have come as a nasty surprise by late afternoon. That was when the last of Bagration's men slipped from the trees and took a well-deserved rest standing behind the main defensive lines. There was then a lull in the battle as the French prepared for the next stage.

At length, the first columns of men in blue began to emerge from the forest. When they did, they got a hot reception. The top of the main earthworks near the river erupted in muzzle flashes and smoke as a hail of metal was sent in their direction. Earlier I had counted the guns mounted on top of the mud rampart – there were forty-five of them, with a further eight down each side. Artillery on the next bastion opened up in support and soon the French were marching through a murderous cross-fire. It was hard to see from such a distance and through the smoke, but we could just make out that they were still advancing, although their lines were now disordered. Then bugles rang out and we saw, emerging from the sides of the embankments, hundreds of Russian cavalry. That was enough to break the first attack and we watched the survivors fleeing for shelter in the trees as horsemen sabred down around them.

Hutchinson looked up at the sky; there were only around three hours of daylight left. He confidently predicted that the French would not waste more men in such futile attacks. They would try to outflank us, he insisted, before leaving the ramparts to find some dinner. I stayed on the battlements, grateful for some relief from his morose company.

As I watched, it soon became apparent that his lordship was wrong. There were three of the big redoubts and over the next few hours the French launched attacks on them all, sometimes attacking more than one simultaneously to stretch our defences. On one occasion they managed to get inside the middle earthworks, slaughtering all they found there, yet their victory was brief. It was only moments before a counter-attack turned them from the hunters to the prey. Once trapped inside those huge mud banks there was no escape from the vengeful fury of the Russians. Watching the flicker of muzzle flashes against the fading dusk light and listening to their distant screams I was damn glad I was not any closer to see the horror in more detail.

As the light faded, so did the French efforts and the noise of fighting dwindled away, leaving just the cries of the injured. I could make out torchlit processions as wounded men either limped or were carried from the field. In the town, makeshift hospitals were being set up, although they looked set to be overwhelmed. Kit appeared and said he had been searching for me. Wilson was still riding around with the Cossacks, but Kit had been near the redoubt when it was retaken. He recounted how bodies had been piled more than waist deep at the bottom of the earthworks and how desperate soldiers had tried to scramble up the mud, only to be shot down to tumble back on their fallen comrades.

We went down into the main hall of the castle to find several Russians loudly proclaiming their victory. From the state of them, they had already been toasting it with vodka for some time. Bennigsen, ashen-faced, was standing by his map table and accepting the congratulations of those around him for this triumph. I noticed he winced when slapped on the back enthusiastically. Kit reported that the general had been in agony with his bladder for most of the day. "I saw him once bent over, holding himself and mewing like a cat."

"Did Grand Duke Constantine take over command again, then?" I asked.

161

"No, I doubt Bennigsen would trust him to run a bath now, never mind a battle," Kit laughed. "His imperial highness was sent to command the forces on the south bank of the river so that he was out of the way." The grand duke was back now, though, standing in his immaculate uniform with several of his Guards officers and glaring with disdain at others whose clothes were stained in mud and gore.

A Cossack came in and whispered something in Bennigsen's ear. The news was evidently not good as the man looked even more pained than before.

"Gentlemen," he called out. The effort must have caused him extreme discomfort, for having attracted the attention of those in the room his next words were barely above a gasp. "We have had a triumph..."

"We have had a bloody marvellous victory," interrupted one of the drunk officers. "We have sent those French devils back to hell where they belong."

"Yes, a splendid victory," agreed Bennigsen, "but now we need—"

"I disagree," interrupted Constantine, who stepped up to the map table and pointed down at the charts. "You kept too many men in reserve," insisted the grand duke, who had never won a battle. "I could see clearly from my side of the river that you should have released all of your reserves to drive the French far back into the forest. I sent you messages about it, yet instead you kept men back to defend those earthworks." He drew his already erect frame up even taller and added, "My Guards regiments are not moles – they should not have to fight in the mud."

There was an awkward silence broken only by Constantine's toadies dutifully murmuring their agreement to their chief. Bennigsen kept his eyes lowered to the map and you could tell he was trying to control his temper. The grand duke was not even thirty, while the general was over sixty and I learned later had fought his first war aged just eighteen. While he would have clearly liked to tell this upstart what he could do with his opinions, the man was brother to the tsar and so considerable self-control was required.

"They are certainly not moles, sir." Bennigsen looked up and forced a smile across his features as he looked at the grand duke. "Many of them fought like tigers today. They earned themselves, and of course you as their commander, great credit." Constantine looked slightly mollified as the general went on, "I regret I did not receive your messages, but the earthworks gave us advantages of defence and clear fields of fire for our guns, which we would have lost if we pursued the enemy into the trees. We also did not know, indeed we still do not know, precisely how many of the enemy we are facing." He waved an arm gesturing to his chart and added, "Which is why we must now decide what to do next."

"Stay here and beat them again!" proposed one of the drunk officers as though it were obvious.

A new voice spoke up. "I very much doubt the French will be as obliging tomorrow." Heads turned towards Hutchinson, who stepped up and looked down at the map. "They will outflank you. I am surprised that they did not do so today."

"You are correct, My Lord," replied Bennigsen and pointed to a place on the chart. "Our scouts report that they are already moving around to the north of us. Soon they will be blocking the road to Konigsberg; they may even be marching on the city itself. The prisoners we have captured indicate that we have today beaten Bonaparte and three of his marshals, but there are still three more marshals who will now be on the march. Perhaps towards us or to take Konigsberg."

"The city must be defended," demanded a Prussian officer. "If Konigsberg falls there will be no Prussia."

I suddenly remembered the letter that was still in my pocket and blurted out, "General L'Estocq has already marched his force back to the city." Hutchinson's eyebrows rose in surprise. He must have realised that I had this information all afternoon and had not delivered it.

"That is not enough," insisted the Prussian. "The whole army must march north to defend the city."

"Nonsense," responded Constantine. "We must maintain lines of communication with Russia, not risk being trapped against the coast."

"But Prussia and Konigsberg have supported this army throughout the winter," called the Prussian indignantly. "You cannot just abandon us to the French."

"Without Russia, Prussia would have already ceased to exist," scoffed Constantine and as another furious Prussian officer looked set to intervene, Bennigsen held up his hand for silence.

"We will send all Prussian regiments along with General Kamenski and his men back to Konigsberg to support the Prussian army. We have given commitments to defend the city, but the rest of the army must maintain its links with Russia." He took a deep breath, and continued hoarsely, "In the circumstances, I think our best course of action is to retreat east."

"Retreat!" exploded Constantine. "Why do all of your so-called victories result in retreat? You cannot win a war going backwards. If you had advanced when I told you, it would be the French who would be retreating now."

"We are where we are," stated Bennigsen wearily. "French marshals will be gathering around us. If we are not already outnumbered, we will be after Kamenski has left. General Hutchinson is right; they will learn from their defeat today and move around us. If we stay, we will be encircled. If we march to Konigsberg, as you say, we risk being trapped against the coast. The only alternative is to retreat."

Constantine twice opened his mouth to say something and then shut it again. I thought for a moment he would insist on advancing the army wildly into the enemy ranks, but even he was not that reckless. "My brother will be furious to hear that his army is retreating again," he warned ominously.

"I will send the tsar a despatch explaining the rationale for the decision," replied Bennigsen. It can go with the news of today's victory and the French eagles we have captured."

"No, I will tell him," insisted the grand duke. "He will not be angry with me." He made it sound like he was doing the general a favour, but

I am sure we were all in no doubt that the tsar would receive a very jaundiced account of the day's proceedings from his brother. Bennigsen simply nodded his acquiescence. There was little he could do to stop Constantine and I imagine he may have been grateful to see the back of him for a few days.

Bennigsen estimated that he lost around five thousand killed or wounded at Heilsberg and that the enemy casualties were double that number. From what I saw that day, I would not disagree. There was bound to be some exaggeration from both sides, but undoubtedly the French losses were higher. Hutchinson was convinced that Napoleon had not been present as their attacks had shown so little imagination. I was struggling to see how the allied army could win the war when after every battle, regardless of the outcome, they were forced to give ground.

"Bonaparte will claim in his *Bulletins* that he won," predicted Hutchinson, "but he will not be able to afford too many victories like that."

The following morning was eerily quiet. A decision had been made to delay the retreat by a day. Some were worried that the French would launch a surprise attack at dawn and so the earthworks were once again packed with men. Outside them were rows of corpses already stripped of their clothes, while beyond them sat or lay the wounded, now mostly French as many Russians had been carried to town. Those who could still walk staggered down to the river for water for themselves and their comrades. There were so few surgeons in the Russian army that none could be spared for these poor devils. Their cries of pain and for calls for help joined the birds' dawn chorus as we watched the line of trees anxiously.

The French did not stir and Cossacks who moved into the edge of the forest reported that they had pulled back a mile. They too were licking their wounds, perhaps while they waited for reinforcements. Men began to unpack supplies from the churches. Some, such as ammunition, was distributed while more was loaded onto carts that now started to make their way over the stone bridge in town. Some of the wounded were laid over the sacks and cried out in pain as the iron-rimmed wheels clattered over uneven cobbles. The first cannon and infantry regiments then began to follow. Bennigsen was sending his army over the river onto the southern bank, so that the Alle was between him and the French. The river flowed north-east before turning due north towards Konigsberg, where it flowed into the sea. It would provide a natural barrier while he gauged what the French might do and decided on a new strategy.

It was a hot summer's day and the air swarmed with insects attracted by the river and the vast numbers of dead soldiers and horses scattered out in the fields. Men exhausted from battle lay and rested wherever they could find shade, lazily waving arms to convince the flies that they were still with the living. A hearty meal was provided for all that evening from supplies that could not be carried. Then, just after midnight, when the temperature dropped, the main army began to follow the carts and some of the guns which had already left. Compared to the retreats we had endured in the winter, this one was easy. The ground was hard and dry and the air was pleasantly cool after the heat of the day. The route was also simple to follow; we just had to keep the Alle River on our left and walk along its bank. At dawn a thick mist appeared over the river, but we trudged on, passing through another small town where we managed to find eggs for breakfast. Hutchinson was with some other Russian generals who were travelling with Bennigsen. I doubt the Hanoverian was much company, for whenever I saw him, he was morosely staring into space and ignoring the salutes of his men. Kit travelled with me and later that morning we were joined by Wilson, who had been with the Cossacks in the rear guard. He announced that the French had marched into Heilsberg that morning but had not begun a pursuit. Instead, the leading regiments had marched on to Eylau. Just the mention of that place gave me a cold chill of trepidation despite the growing heat of the day. Yet when I looked at the map, the French move made some sense. Eylau was roughly a day's march from the Alle River as it curved north and its crossroads gave Bonaparte good road links in all directions, including Konigsberg to the north. He could threaten the city and be well placed to intercept any attempt of the Russian army to rescue it.

We walked on for the rest of that morning, resting the horses for we had no idea where we were going or what we would do when we got

167

there. There was plenty of speculation. Some thought we would go all the way to Konigsberg, with the river to help defend it from the French. Others proposed we would retreat further towards Russia or to Memel, while a few even imagined we might launch a surprise attack on Eylau. That suggestion filled me with horror. Then we were told that we would spend the night at a town called Friedland, just a few miles further along the river. By mid-afternoon the sun was burning down on my left cheek, indicating that we had followed the curve of the river north. It was then that we heard the distant crackle of small arms fire. We mounted up and rode forward to investigate, but the shooting had stopped long before we reached the front of the column. A Cossack officer riding back told us that a French cavalry outpost had been found in Friedland and driven off.

"Bonaparte will know where we are now," I warned, staring across the water.

"He will have probably guessed that we would follow the Alle," asserted Wilson. "Anyway," he added, "look behind, we are hardly difficult to track. We have no Cossacks on their side of the river. I dare say some of their dragoons are keeping an eye on us." When I stared back over our trail, I could see the dust cloud that some fifty thousand men, countless carts and guns threw up. It was like a low, yellowish cloud blowing gently across the fields. I had to agree that the Russian army would not be hard to find.

Friedland was a small town on the western bank of the Alle. The river undulated in several wide 'S'-shaped curves around the town and hill to the south. Even then, in the height of summer, it was too deep to wade across. By the time we reached the place, a few hours later, there was already a queue of men waiting to use the small wooden bridge into the town, while some Russian engineers were starting work on three pontoon bridges. Instead of waiting, we climbed the hill just south of the town on the eastern bank. It provided a commanding view of the surrounding terrain and would make an excellent site for a gun battery.

"Well, we should see any French coming from here," I pointed out, for the country to the west of the town was a plain, stretching at least a couple of miles. In the distance due west, we could see a pond. The late evening sun reflected on a mill stream that flowed from the pond due east to the Alle and which divided the plain into two. The northern half was open, undulating country, ideal for both cavalry and artillery. The southern half had more crops, mostly rye with stems almost as tall as a man. Yet from this high vantage point we would soon spot any approaching force as they flattened the stalks in the fields. I had fought in fields of tall millet in India and vividly recalled the terror of unseen cannonballs crashing through the crop to kill us.

"There may be some in that forest, though," added Kit pointing to an arc of trees beyond the fields. "But I doubt we will be here long." He grinned, "Now, we had better get into town before the Russians commandeer all the rooms."

We made our way back down the slope. Red-faced, sweating Russian soldiers lay in any patch of shade they could find. They looked exhausted; food carried from the stores in Heilsberg had long since been eaten. We had all travelled nearly thirty miles over two hot sunny days and were hungry and weary. The first pontoon bridge had already been constructed from planks lashed to a pair of boats they had found in town. We went across one at a time as they were still adding ropes to keep it steady. Soon we were in the main square with a spired church on one side and what looked like the town hall on the other. A line of French prisoners sat glumly in the shade of the hall; from the horses outside, the building was clearly Bennigsen's headquarters. Almost inevitably, the Hanoverian was inside staring down at his maps with Hutchinson at his side. On seeing us, his lordship came over. "You took your time getting here," he started, grumpily.

"We climbed the hill just south of here to get the lie of the land," said Kit cheerfully, ignoring his brother's tone, while I stared about hoping to find some food.

"Well, if you have any ideas, you better share them with him," Hutchinson gestured over his shoulder at the map table. "The man seems to have no clue what to do next, but as long as he keeps taking us north to the coast that will serve us."

"Are there any French nearby?" asked Wilson.

"The prisoners say Bonaparte and most of his army are still at Eylau," replied his lordship. "One marshal is closer, but most of his men could not be here before dawn tomorrow." Hutchinson looked up at a disturbance at the door and grimaced before adding, "That is just what we need, a royal blockhead throwing his weight around."

I turned then to see Grand Duke Constantine striding purposefully into the hall. Beside him walked another general I had not seen before. He was a senior man, judging from the decorations and braid.

"Perhaps Bennigsen is about to be replaced," whispered Kit. "You can imagine the tale of incompetence that the tsar heard from his brother."

"Constantine is certainly looking very pleased with himself," I added.

The grand duke had the expression of a local squire about to see a troublesome poacher hanged. "Bennigsen," he called out in a peremptory tone across the room. By now all conversation had stilled and a fair few Russian officers could not hide a smirk as they anticipated the downfall of the Hanoverian. "We need a word with you in private." With that the pair of newcomers turned on their heel and strode to one of the side rooms, throwing out several officers they found inside. Bennigsen was left to follow them like some chastened schoolboy. A hush fell across the hall as we all listened for any shouting or protestations. We were to be disappointed, however, for we could only hear the low murmur of voices until the three emerged once more. Bennigsen led his visitors back to the map table and to the surprise of many, still seemed to be in command. As he looked up at a sea of faces watching them, he must have recognised the displeasure in some at his survival, for with a weary sigh, he ordered the room to be cleared.

"He will have been told to be more aggressive," predicted Hutchinson. "One more retreat and he will be replaced for certain. Although quite how he beats the French is beyond me. With the Prussians and Kamenski gone, we are only around fifty thousand, while if Bonaparte and his marshals come together, they will be close to double that number." It was a grim reflection to end the day and,

170

feeling downhearted, we went off together to find some lodgings and a meal.

The arrival of the army had seen virtually every pig in the village slaughtered, butchered and sold on for a very healthy profit by the locals. We found lodgings in a cottage and after provision of coin, our share of the livestock was served with potatoes and pickled cabbage. Some cloudy beer was provided but Hutchinson insisted on a cup of tea. Afterwards we sat outside; it must have been around nine as we enjoyed the cool of the day and watched the sun sink to the western horizon. Most journals do not include such details, but I will confess that I had not taken my boots off in two days and my feet had swollen in the heat. The now redundant pig trough was filled with cold water from the stream. The four of us sat in a line splashing our own bare trotters in it and enjoying the blissful feeling of relief as the swelling subsided. The peace, however, did not last long.

"Gentlemen, you must leave immediately and cross to the other side of the river," a breathless young ensign called from the door of the cottage.

"What the devil are you talking about?" growled Hutchinson, not attempting to move.

"The Cossacks have seen French forces approaching the town," the boy gasped. "The general thinks that they might attack tonight. He has ordered all forces back to the eastern bank of the river." With that the lad disappeared, leaving us struggling to put our boots back on over our wet feet.

"Bloody ridiculous," grumbled his lordship, getting up. "We have not heard a shot fired from the outpost pickets." He paused, looking around at us. "They surely would have set pickets out in those rye fields."

I was not sure if that was a statement or a question, but we decided that it would be prudent to cross back over the river. There were three extra bridges now and in the fading light I saw that an artillery battery had been established on the high hill to the south of the town. We could see a group of officers on it silhouetted against the evening sky, with their glasses pointed west, but I knew they would struggle to see

171

anything in the rapidly fading light. We sat on the grass for nearly an hour as Cossack scouts rode to and fro over the bridges. Still we did not hear a single shot fired. In fact the only thing to disturb the peace was the rasp of grasshoppers and the breaking of wind – pickled cabbage can have a potent effect on the guts.

Eventually, it was decided that the earlier reports were a false alarm. No French forces had been found by the subsequent scouts and we were all allowed to go to bed. Hundreds of tired men filed back over the bridges and were soon tucked up under blankets. Not that we were to have a huge amount of sleep.

The storm started at two o'clock in the morning – flashes of lightning followed by long growls of thunder. It woke us all up and while the others muttered and turned over to try and get back to sleep, I stayed awake, listening to the rain drumming down on the cottage roof. And then I heard a new sound: the tramping of boots outside. I got up and went to the window. Another flicker of lightning illuminated a column of soldiers marching past. The darkness was back in an instant, but I remembered clearly the image revealed. Those expressionless peasant faces that I had become used to, now soaked with rain and being driven like sheep out of town in the direction of the French. It was a grim and forbidding sight and one that I could not forget as I settled back down and tried to sleep again. I was just managing to doze when a new sound brought me back to my senses. At first I thought it was more thunder, but as another salvo was fired my suspicions were confirmed. "That is cannon fire!" I called to the others.

Hutchinson half sat up and cocked his head to listen.

"It is the guns on the hilltop, I think," I told him. "I have not heard any return fire, but perhaps we wouldn't from here."

The battery fired once more and his lordship's head sank back on his pillow. "Confound them," he grumbled. "It will be another false alarm. The bloody fools will be firing at shadows." The rest were content to slumber on too, but, unconvinced, I went to the window again to see if there was any sign of alarm from those outside. It was lighter now, a dim glow appearing in the eastern sky, which did little more than illuminate the dark brooding storm clouds above. It was an ominous start to the day.

His Britannic Majesty's military representatives finally deigned to make an appearance on the fields outside Friedland around seven that morning. The cannon fire had been intermittent, usually firing a few salvoes just as one was about to fall asleep. Hutchinson had refused to rise before six and had insisted on his breakfast first. "Nothing will happen at this ungodly hour," he had pronounced. "This is all show to impress General Popov."

"Who is General Popov?" asked his brother.

"The tsar's military representative, the man who arrived with Constantine. I found out last night that he is empowered to replace Bennigsen if he is not impressed with the prosecution of the campaign." Hutchinson turned to me and added, "Popov is another of the conspirators who murdered the old tsar. So Bennigsen's involvement will not protect him now."

After breakfast, we made our way a short distance out of town to where the Hanoverian stood with some of his staff, staring east through their telescopes. I was surprised at how many Russians were already on the French side of the river; there must have been over twenty thousand even then and more were following us through the town. Some had been deployed on the left of the mill stream and they had pushed forward to the trees on that side, where a distant crackle of musketry could be heard. The rest were being arrayed on the right including most of the cavalry. A road ran through the middle of this quadrant and three miles down it was another small village. Through a glass you could see riders wheeling about it.

"Ah, gentlemen, you are here at last," Bennigsen greeted us cheerfully. "Let me explain what you have missed." He spoke loudly and invited several of his officers to confirm facts as he told us that at dawn several thousand French soldiers had been seen advancing from the trees on the Russian left. "I have put Bagration in charge there and he soon sent them packing. It is his forces you can hear now mopping up any stragglers in the trees."

"What is happening over there?" asked Hutchinson, pointing at the distant village on our right.

"That is the road to Konigsberg," explained the Hanoverian. The French placed cavalry there thinking it would stop our advance, but I have no intention of using that road. Tonight we will cross back over the river and go north, but I do not want the French to know that. Our cavalry is ejecting the French as we speak. As you can see all is in hand – we only face one French marshal. We shall keep him at bay easily and maul his men given the chance. I trust you approve?" he concluded.

The question confirmed my suspicion that this briefing had been more for Popov's benefit. The tsar's representative gave a smile of satisfaction when Hutchinson confirmed that all seemed in order.

If we thought our arrival on the battlefield had been tardy, it was nothing compared to Constantine, who did not arrive until an hour later. He was in his usual petulant mood, indignant that the battle had started before he was ready. "Bennigsen, have you been ordering *my* Guards regiments about?" he demanded.

The commander of the Russian forces was clearly feeling more confident of his position this morning. "They are part of *my* army and yes I have sent two regiments north along the river to guard bridges in case the French try to get behind us." He gestured ahead of him, "The rest are being deployed in our centre."

The grand duke was furious at this response and became positively incandescent when he learned that one of the regiments sent upriver was the Preobrazhensky Guards. "You know what will happen if they are destroyed," he hissed, before turning on his heel and calling for his horse. We did not see him again for the rest of the day and I doubt he was missed by many.

For us, the morning passed relatively peacefully. The fighting in the woods died away as the Russians secured the forest and the artillery had long since stopped firing as there were no targets to aim at. Initially, I was surprised that the Russian general commanding on the right only sent horsemen to capture the village. Cavalry cannot defend buildings; you need to send infantry to fight from inside them and from barricades in the streets. Instead, the conflict drew in more mounted regiments, who wheeled about, charged and counter charged. Horse batteries of artillery would roam the plain and fire their guns in support. The Cossacks were out there too and to Wilson's great annoyance, Hutchinson would not let him join them. He was even more frustrated when a short while later a group of Cossacks galloped up with a captured trophy: another French eagle standard.

On the face of it, things were going well for the Russians and yet I could not shake a growing sense of doom. The hair on the back of my neck prickled, which I had learned by now was a reliable portent of

175

disaster. Perhaps it was the weather, for it remained close with dark storm clouds and occasional crashes of thunder to make you start in alarm.

By midday virtually the entire Russian army was over the river. A third of it was to the left of the mill stream and the rest arrayed out in a long line on the right. Only some artillery on the hill and land south of town remained on the western bank. The main problem Bennigsen faced was from his bladder, which was still causing him considerable pain. In the end he decamped his headquarters back to the town square, sending regular couriers to Bagration and the commander north of the mill stream, a man called Gorchakov. We also received a messenger from Konigsberg who had galloped south down the river. He reported that a French force was approaching the city, which was causing panic among the populace. The queen had already fled again up the shingle strip to Memel and many more were following in her wake. Kamenski and the remaining Prussian army were said to be fortifying the earthworks outside the Prussian capital.

The news that the French army was divided only served to increase Russian confidence. As far as we knew, Bonaparte was still at Eylau, roughly halfway between the marshal who faced us and those he had sent north to Konigsberg. It would take a day for the French to march from Eylau to Friedland and Bennigsen planned to be gone from the town by then. He was less clear on where we would march to next, but if the Prussian capital fell there would no longer be any point going north. We would go east and embark back to Britain from Russian territory.

By early afternoon we were relaxing in the shade of the town square. A cloth had been spread on the ground and an impromptu picnic had begun. There was pickled herring, roast pork pie, black bread and a plentiful supply of white wine that had been chilled in the well bucket. By then the only serious fighting still going on was the skirmishing around the town on the Konigsberg road. Some captured prisoners were sent to Bennigsen. He interrogated them personally and was slightly alarmed when one of them claimed that Marshal Davout was also in the vicinity. If we faced two French corps rather than one, we would still outnumber the enemy by two to one. Yet the Russian front line was now several miles forward of Friedland and extended over a similar distance. After a quick consultation with General Popov, Bennigsen decided that a more cautious approach should be adopted. Bagration was ordered to pull back from the forest and establish a new, more compact front line closer to the town. On the other side of the mill stream, Gorchakov was to abandon the town he had been fighting for all morning and bring his forces further back too. After those instructions had been given, attention turned back to the pickled herring.

The afternoon dragged on, the clouds cleared and the weather grew hotter still. Several of the senior generals, like Popov, were now dozing in the shade of the square, while others had supplemented the wine with vodka. The place had the feel of a garden party instead of a military headquarters. General Bagration had left his men to join Bennigsen. He reported that the French had reoccupied the abandoned forest and were now sniping from its cover at his men. Yet he did not appear unduly concerned as he drank wine and tucked into a slice of pie. Gorchakov had stayed in the field but sent his second in command to explain that he was keeping his line where it was as it made the most use of the natural topography. The deputy too was drinking more than was good for him. However, if most of the occupants of that town square were relaxed and at least partially drunk, there was one who was not.

"It is too bloody quiet," Hutchinson grumbled. "If there are twenty-five thousand Frenchmen out there, they should be doing more to pin us down. Instead, it feels like they are waiting for something."

"You English are never satisfied," responded Bennigsen irritably. "When we are under attack you complain that we might lose. When we are not under attack, you still think we might lose. Has it occurred to you that the prisoner might be lying about Marshal Davout? They will want to spread alarm and confusion in our ranks, but they will not succeed. We have taken prudent precautions and now our army can rest. Once it is dark, we will cross the river and move on." Bagration offered to have some Cossacks beat the truth out of the prisoners, but the Hanoverian dismissed the idea. "They will only tell you what you want to hear to stop the blows."

Hutchinson fumed at the rebuke. He stalked back to the edge of town to stare out across the fields. It was not as quiet as it had been earlier. The French had got some of their guns into the forest that Bagration's men had abandoned and were firing the occasional shot at our guns on the hill south of town. There was a smattering of gunfire to the north too, but nothing more than a light skirmish.

When Hutchinson prowled back into the town square, I was foolish enough to catch his eye. "Come with me," he snarled, leading the way to the church. I followed with a sense of trepidation as he turned through a door at the base of the bell tower and led the way upstairs. It was an obvious lookout point and yet most of the senior Russian officers inside were sitting on the steps. The thick stone walls and no windows made the space surprisingly cool. There was muted grumbling as his lordship pushed them out of his way to ascend. I suspect that any protests were stifled when they saw his face, which was now a mask of fury. When we reached the top platform, we found a bell suspended over the centre of the floor. Around it were large shutters, but they were all closed to keep the sun off the handful of Russians stretched out and dozing on the floor. Hutchinson ignored them, throwing open the screens on the western side. The late afternoon sun blazed back at us and after the gloom inside the tower, it took a moment for my eyes to adjust.

"What do you see?" demanded his lordship.

One of the Russians who spoke English answered for me, "The French had a band out there earlier."

"A band?" Hutchinson repeated, astonished.

"Yes, a band," confirmed the Russian. "You know, men marching with instruments."

"I know what a band is!" exploded Hutchinson. "What does its presence tell you about the enemy?"

We all stared at him blankly. To fill the silence the Russian gamely spoke up again. "I saw them through the slats in the shutters when our cannon open fire. They did not stay in sight long when shot landed amongst them." He paused and then added hopefully, "Perhaps the French wanted to hear some music?"

That officer will never know how close he came to being pitched out of the tower. Hutchinson slammed his fist on the sill of the shutter frame in frustration and then turned to look at us, speaking slowly as though addressing imbeciles. "The last unit you bring to a battle is the band. They have no weapons; their only use is to collect the wounded. If there is a band in those woods, the chances are that there is a whole corps hidden amongst the trees and one that is expecting to fight."

I confess that I was not convinced at this stretch of logic and from their puzzled faces, neither were the Russians. One even asked if Hutchinson could close the shutters again. His lordship ignored the request and called me over to him. "Tell me, Flashman, what do you see?"

I stared down at the Russian lines south of the mill stream. They were roughly halfway between the river and the woods now. Most of the men were resting, sitting or lying on the ground. They were hidden from the enemy by the height of the crops, although great swathes of these had been flattened by their earlier manoeuvring. I looked across to the trees but could see no sign of the vast French force that Hutchinson suspected was there. Staring at the scene it looked benign and I thought that Bennigsen was probably right, but I was not foolish enough to say so. I was just considering what response I could make that would not result in another angry eruption, when his lordship prompted me again. "Look at the land, Flashman, the shape of the land."

I studied the area again. It was bordered by the arc of trees to the west and the river to the east. But the Alle curved around the hills on the eastern bank where we had sited our guns. The Russians at the far end of the line would have to travel some distance towards the trees to get around this bend and to reach Friedland. Looking more closely, I could see that there was a relatively narrow neck of land between the river and the mill stream to reach the town too. Unlike the river, the mill stream was not an insurmountable obstacle for a man who could not swim. Yet scrambling down one bank, splashing and wading

179

across and climbing up the other side would take time. I was beginning to see the danger, "It is like a giant funnel," I murmured.

"Exactly," breathed Hutchinson. "The Russians on this side will not want to be trapped against the river. When they run, they will all be jammed in the space between the Alle and the mill stream. If I can see it then so can Bonaparte. He will attack this southern part of the army and he will destroy it."

"You think Bonaparte is here now…" I was appalled at the thought. "Bennigsen says he cannot bring his army here before tomorrow morning."

"If the survivors of that cavalry outpost we flushed out of here yesterday rode straight to Eylau, the French could have started their march last night. Which would mean that they arrive this afternoon. That would explain why they are so quiet; they do not want to do anything that will alert that poxed whoreson to his own stupidity."

Hutchinson brooded for a while, but then, satisfied that I now understood the danger, he sent me down to make another attempt at warning Bennigsen. I suspected that it would be a futile effort, yet with his lordship watching from the tower, I had little choice but to give it a go.

"General Hutchinson sends his compliments," I began, which was the first barefaced lie as my chief had piled a torrent of abuse on the Hanoverian. "But he believes that it is possible that Bonaparte and most of his army are in the trees opposite."

There was a ripple of laughter from the listening officers at this and even Bennigsen smiled after a wince of pain from his bladder as he sat up. "If that is the case, Captain, then why do none of my Russian officers report such a thing?"

I could have given them Hutchinson's view on his officers – that most of them were inbred dolts who did not know their arses from their elbows – but decided something more diplomatic would serve me better. "Your officers do not have the benefit of the view from the tower. If they did, or if you were to take a look, sir, you would see that the southern part of your army is in an area that could become a

180

dangerous trap if attacked. His lordship urges that you start withdrawing the southern part of your army now."

Bennigsen glanced up at the tower and paled at the thought of climbing it. He had found merely sitting on a horse unbearable that morning. Before he could reply, an immaculately attired colonel from one of the Guards regiments interjected, "Perhaps the English general, who dresses like a beggar, is frightened. That is why they did not send an army to help us – the English chickens are frightened of the French fox. We are Russian wolves; we eat foxes for breakfast."

Kit, who had been sitting in the shade jumped up at that, "How dare you. My brother has beaten two French armies and he did not have to retreat after either battle."

"Enough, gentlemen!" Bennigsen held up his hand to still the argument and then reached for his watch. "No one is doubting the courage of the British general, but it is now…past four o'clock. If the French were going to attack today, they would have done so by now. We have shown aggression by driving the French back on both flanks." He glanced up at General Popov, who gave a nod of approval. "We have pulled back to a more guarded position, but we will not make a precipitate retreat now. We will move back across the river in an orderly manner come nightfall."

I went back with Bennigsen's decision and Kit and Wilson came with me. "Even if he could see the sense in retreating," I explained, "I don't think he would dare do it, in case he was relieved of command."

"After beating the French at Heilsberg," added Kit, "many of their officers have lost their fear of the French. The Guards officers in particular have convinced themselves that their previous encounters were all victories."

"But we know the French have an army marching on Konigsberg," countered Wilson. "They can't be in two places at once. Even if there are more marshals out there, we might still be able to beat them."

However, even the optimistic Wilson backtracked on this argument when Hutchinson showed him the precarious position of the southern regiments from the top of the tower. We stood up there for another hour studying the edge of the forest with our glasses. There were men moving about within the trees wherever we looked and twice we saw horses moving cannon into position. After half an hour Kit decided he would try again to persuade Bennigsen. He spoke to him in private, pointing out that having a river behind your lines that blocked your retreat was against all the principles of warfare. The Hanoverian countered by pointing out that he had stood his men in front of rivers at Pultusk and was against a river at Heilsberg. "These men were Russians," he proclaimed. "They would stand where they were told and die where they were told. The river was irrelevant."

By five o'clock we could make out lines of French soldiers standing at the edge of the trees. Hutchinson called up some of the slumbering Russian officers from lower down in the tower and made them look too. Then he led those officers down the tower to make a final appeal to Bennigsen. By then he was a seething mass of fury and the rest of us wisely decided to stay in the tower.

We should not have been able to hear any of the conversation from a hundred feet up, but evidently someone had again questioned Hutchinson's warning. "You ignorant fool!" he roared. "My shit knows more about beating the French than you do. At any moment now the French are going to tear the southern part of your army apart, while its commanders lounge about here drinking wine and eating those vile pickled fish." He turned to one of the men he had brought down the tower, "You, tell them what you have just seen." A timid captain started to explain to a collection of generals what they had observed. He must have been convincing, for I saw General Bagration get up and start to make his way back to his command. Bennigsen and Popov also had a hurried conversation. For the first time there was a semblance of alarm among the officers in the square, but they had left it too late.

Three double gun cannon salvoes rang out in rapid succession from the forest. It was clearly a pre-arranged signal, for a heartbeat later over fifty guns fired all along the French line, sending balls and mortar shells dropping on Russian soldiers who had been dozing in the crops. The edge of the forest was now lined with smoke and from it emerged columns of French troops advancing quickly towards the already chaotic Russian line.

"There are some Russians not willing to die where they are told to," called Kit, pointing. He had told us of Bennigsen's boast and now he gestured to the far south of the Russian line. Some of Bagration's men had been fortifying an old farmhouse by the river to defend the Russian flank, but now they were abandoning their post and running headlong north towards Friedland. The reason was obvious: there was a deep bend in the river between the farm and the town which threatened to cut them off if the French reached it first. As I watched I saw that behind them French cavalry were already emerging from the trees. They had probably been waiting for their own infantry to clear the farm. Now it was vacant there was nothing to stop them charging the sides of the Russian defences, while artillery and infantry assailed their front. No army was likely to withstand a battering like that and already the southern end of the line was collapsing.

From our position in the tower we had a unique bird's-eye view of the battle and we stared down on it with horrified fascination. The French were still a mile off from the town, so there was no immediate danger to us. Now the more disciplined Guards regiments in the centre of the Russian formation looked set to steady things. Their line stretched across the mill stream and they became a rallying point for some of the running men, who also took confidence from the Guard cavalry nearby. Meanwhile, the French were becoming victims of their own success.

The forces of at least one marshal and possibly two had now emerged from the forest. They had come on in battalion columns, but had faced no serious opposition. Yet as they progressed down the narrow neck of the 'funnel' they got in each other's way. As the Russians pulled back a new danger to the French was revealed. With no Russian troops blocking their line of fire, the guns on the eastern bank now blasted the men in blue with canister shot. With the river between them, there was nothing the French could do to stop the murderous spray of balls that now tore into their flanks. Equally, there was no cover in the fields that they could hide behind. We watched as the attack fell into confusion.

For a brief while it seemed that the Russians might yet save themselves. The Guard cavalry charged south to meet the French flanking horsemen, causing already confused columns to try and form square. We could see Bagration trying to rally his men around the Russian centre, but the French were watching too, particularly their gunners. One French horse battery galloped out to just in front of the Guards and began to blast them with canister at a range of a hundred and fifty yards. Guardsmen were mown down, but their commanders were unsure what to do. Their cavalry support was already engaged elsewhere and the rest of the Russian line was trying to form on them. The French guns, now numbering around thirty, started to move even closer. Finally, the Russians charged their tormenters, but they were shot down in waves. One of the regiments lost eighty percent of its number. Although it was an appalling slaughter, it might have bought the Russians time to regroup were it not for another French battery.

The guns firing from the woods over the battlefield into the town and the river were notably heavier. Perhaps they had guessed that the Russians had built more bridges, or maybe they were lucky, for they struck one of the pontoon bridges and blew it to pieces. At first we did not notice, for we were transfixed watching the battle to the east.

"Christ," called Kit, "it is time we left." I turned to see a warehouse near the bridge on fire, sending plumes of dark smoke up into the air. It must have given the impression that the town was ablaze and when I looked north, I could see that wing of the army also now starting to pull back. A score of Russian cannon had been harnessed to horses and their gunners were desperately whipping the mounts to get them over the bridges before the town fell. Where just a few minutes ago senior officers supped wine, the town square was now packed with soldiery. Some were wounded, others panicked, but they all had just one thought: to get over the river before the French came. With one bridge down, the pressure on the others increased. Before, sentries would only allow so many to cross the flimsier pontoon bridges at a time, but any such guards had long since crossed themselves. The narrowest bridge was only three men across and now it was packed. It swayed dangerously and the boats beneath were pushed down in the water nearly up to their gunnels by the weight above.

A gun limber had become wedged on the sturdier town bridge and while men struggled to free it they were impeded by scores who just scrambled around it to get away. Another gun crew decided to risk the remaining pontoon bridge. It was wider and had taken guns over before, but one at a time. The bridge was already full of men as the horses tried to pull their load across. The mounts were wild-eyed, panicked by the planks moving beneath them, one trying to rear up in its traces. Those in front ran to get away from lashing hooves, but still soldiers kept following on behind.

There was a grim inevitability to what happened next. The bridge swayed dangerously and then a rope holding it together snapped. There were screams of panic as men and animals were tipped into the water. The horses anchored to their guns lashed the water with their hooves in terror, striking many about them. Men, half drowning, were swept by the current where they grabbed the first floating thing they could find, namely the boats holding up the smaller foot bridge. Some of those crossing on the foot bridge even shot at those in the water to get them away, but the bow of one of the craft was pulled under the river and soon the bridge planks followed. I turned away as more screaming heralded the collapse of that bridge as well.

Self-preservation was kicking in now. The crush around the remaining town bridge would be impossible to get through. If the French gunners struck that as well, all would be lost. The French now controlled the river to the south, which left only the north. Some of the Russian line there still stood and if need be, I knew I could swim across the river. One final glance east showed that the Russian centre was also collapsing. Bennigsen's army was lost. Now it was every man for himself.

It had looked so simple from the top of the tower. We could see the clear ground to the north. Wilson even pointed out where a road two miles to the north ran to the river and continued along the opposite bank, which he thought would indicate a ford. Kit was worried about his brother, but we tried to convince him that Hutchinson was likely to have stayed with Bennigsen. The Russian commander had probably been one of the first to cross. "He is probably now watching the battle from that hill with the gun battery on it," I assured him. "Let's just get ourselves over the river too."

Our carefully laid plan dissolved the minute we stepped outside the church: a seething throng was pushing through the square towards the river. "The bridges are down," I yelled. Pointing I added, "Go north!" They clearly did not teach English to Russian serfs, for I was met with a sea of blank or frightened faces. As another cannon ball buzzed overhead, there was no time to lose or any alternative but to plunge into the crowd. I could see that the street I wanted to go down across the square was almost empty. Like swimming across a river, I aimed for the left of it, knowing that the human tide would take me to the right. At first I was pushed and jostled as some thought I was getting in the way of their escape, but when they saw I was trying to move across them I found it easier to make progress. When I looked behind, both Wilson and Kit were also trying to push their way through, although they had tried a direct line and were to the right of me.

It took ten minutes of pushing, shoving, pleading and worming myself between hundreds of burly, onion-breathed peasants to get across that square. An hour before it would have taken twelve paces and as many seconds. By then some of the Russians, realising that they were making little progress, were also trying the side street, which made the last few yards easier going. As I reached the corner, I barked my shin on a stone mounting block and stood up on it briefly for a glimpse of my colleagues. They had both been pushed further towards the bridge. Wilson was ahead and almost out of the square on that side. There was no point in waiting and so I pushed on. I ran past a blazing warehouse that had been set alight either by French cannon or Russians trying to stop the contents reaching the enemy.

The smoke gradually cleared, revealing a scene of pandemonium. Hundreds of Russians who had given up on the bridges were running along the riverbank, while to the north the rest of the Russian army was retreating to join them. Regiments had broken up and were charging in a loose mob. I saw six gunners astride a team of their horses, still in traces together, their gun abandoned behind them. Only far off in the distance was there any semblance of order – columns of soldiers were marching around a bend in the river. Heaven knew why, but the French cavalry were not making the most of the pursuit. Perhaps they were just exhausted from the earlier fighting around the town on the Konigsberg road. I could see squadrons of them far to the left, but the troopers were not even mounted up. Counting my blessings, I ran on, but little did I realise that the dangers were to come from my own side.

The distant ford was now easy to spot. There was a crowd of several hundred soldiers growing around it and more heading in that direction. I did not like the look of the situation. As I could swim, I decided I would cross the Alle alone so I turned and headed for the river. A few moments later I was staring down the steep grass bank in horror. The water was full of bodies, some dead, but it was the living that frightened me. They were flailing wildly, drowning, and desperate to grab on to anything that might save them. I could see four men fighting over a plank from the bridge that would only support one or two at the most. They punched and pulled, even holding their rivals' heads underwater in a desperate effort to save themselves.

A score of men from my side of the riverbank were trying to swim across. One of the soldiers on the plank abandoned it and grabbed a swimmer. The man tried to shake him off, but the soldier hung on with the determination of a dying man. Soon both heads were going under as they were swept on down the middle of the current. Even those that reached the far bank were not safe, for it was steep and hard to climb. As I watched, one man half scramble out by holding on to tufts of grass only to be grabbed at by another desperate swimmer. They both tumbled back in the water. This murderous soup was no place for me, I concluded. I still had to cross, yet I coldly calculated that if I tried a few hundred yards further on, the drowned would far outnumber the living.

I ran on until I was halfway between the town and the ford. As I had foreseen, few moved in the water now. Dozens of bodies drifted by, floating face down next to abandoned timbers that they might have previously fought over. No one else was trying to cross here as they were all running on to the ford, where several thousand including cavalry and gunners were struggling to cross. I could hear distant screams and shouts. The water there would still be deep and the crossing chaotic and dangerous.

I glanced back at the debacle that was the battle of Friedland. The town was now ablaze with several fires. Cannon from the hill south of town were still firing to cover the retreat and the sound of muskets continued to ring out. Thousands of Russian soldiers remained jammed in the streets, which must have been hellish. The fortunate ones might soon be prisoners, but the rest were likely to perish.

Anyone who did make it over the Alle should be safe, for there were only a few hours of daylight left and I doubted the French would risk the crossing. I searched the far side for a place I could climb out and saw a group of trees overhanging the water. Their roots entwined with the bank to provide hand holds I could use to haul myself up. It was time to make my own crossing. I pushed the scabbard up inside my belt so that it would not tangle with my legs. The pistols in my pocket would weigh me down and would be useless until dried, but I did not want to abandon them. My soaked clothes would probably be heavier, but I only had to swim twenty yards to get across; I thought I would make it.

After the hot summer's day, the water felt cold as I slipped in. The bank was steep, and after just one step the water was up to my waist. I pushed a floating corpse out of the way and moved on. As I waded out, I was soon in up to my neck and then I was forced to swim. A half-submerged face glared lifelessly at me as I went past and I had to shove the legs of another body out of my way. I was beyond the halfway point so perhaps it was my imagination, but worryingly, I was getting lower in the water. It was a struggle to stop my water-filled boots from sinking. There was a heavy beam floating by with another body draped over one end and I grabbed it for support, kicking on to push it towards the bank. I was nearly there when I felt a hand grip my ankle.

The shock of it caught me by surprise. My imagination was filled with the desperate struggles I had seen earlier and instinctively I kicked out. I tried to turn, noticing that the body from the end of the beam had gone and realising belatedly that it was not as dead as it had appeared. The Russian, dislodged from his support was now grabbing at anything that he could reach, which turned out to be my boot. He tugged hard, trying to keep his head above the surface, only to pull me under. I came up gasping and panicking as I tried to cough out a mouthful of the Alle and inhale at the same time. The man had grabbed my belt now, I felt his fingers pushing between my coat and the leather to get a good grip. I knew he would not easily let go. He was croaking something to me in Russian as once again my head was forced under. Kicking down with my feet, I was still out of my depth and if I did not act quickly, I would be out of life too. My elbow knocked against my sword hilt and I knew what must be done. With my left hand I pushed the gasping man away from me, while my right reached across for the weapon. It was hard to draw with the scabbard so high on my body, and the Russian saw through the water what I was doing. He must have been desperate, for he used his free hand to grip the razor-sharp blade and disappeared behind a growing cloud of bloody water. I felt him pushing the back of the sword towards my chest; the tip was still in the scabbard and my lungs were starting to burn from lack of air. I used my left hand to tug the scabbard free and then twisted the sword out of his grasp. I watched his mouth open as bubbles escaped in a silent scream. Then I thrust the blade forward in a desperate, stricken stab. I kicked up and briefly managed a gasp of air only to be pulled down once more. The water all around me was red now. I could not see the Russian but felt his grip on my belt dragging me down. Feverishly, my left hand tugged his fingers free, while my right thrust the steel at him again for good measure. Then at last I felt him fall away and I kicked up once more for air.

I reached the bank a few moments later with my sword blade gripped between my teeth like some cutthroat. For at least a minute I hung on to the tree root with the same tenacity as the Russian had used to grip my leg. He and the wooden beam were floating on down the current and I felt a twinge of regret. I was not sorry for killing him – it was either that or we both would have drowned. Yet I wondered if he had just held on to the timber, we might both have made it to the shore. My hands shook so that it took three attempts to get the sword back into its sheath and then I summoned the strength to scramble up the bank. As I emptied the water from my boots, I could see that the distant French cavalry were finally starting to advance, but by now there was only an hour of daylight left. Behind me, in the distance, I could make out small groups of Russians walking dejectedly north-east. Most had lost hats, packs and weapons. They were not an army any more, I suspected that many would lapse into brigandage as they tried to make their way home. The Cossacks were little more than brigands at the best of times.

Seeking the security of numbers, I made my way back towards the ford where crowds now milled on both banks. If anything, the scenes there were even worse than I had witnessed earlier. I realised that the water was too deep for it to have been a ford. There had probably been a ferry here, but the boat must have been seized to help build the pontoon bridges in town. Even horses were having to swim across the middle of the river. Desperate men on foot grabbed at their tails in the hope of being pulled across. Many were kicked for their trouble and sometimes a mount would have three or four men hanging from it and would thrash around to avoid drowning. As if that were not confusing enough, some were trying to pull gun carriages through the water using long ropes and teams of horses on the eastern bank. The approaching French were causing more panic, and men were screaming and shouting as they struggled in the water or ran about in all directions on the shore. I had seen enough and turned north-east to follow the trail of wet survivors wherever it led.

As darkness fell men stopped to rest and some used flints to start fires to dry their clothes and get warm. They sat in groups around the flames, muttering in a language I did not understand, glaring suspiciously at me in my strange uniform. I pressed on, joining a trail of refugees that had come directly from Friedland. Eventually, I saw a group of officers, some with their horses, gathered by the side of the road. They were sitting half naked around fires as their clothes dried before the flames. I recognised one, adorned in just a shirt, sitting by a fire on his own. The light revealed his features as he fastidiously brushed some mud off his jacket. It was the Guards colonel, who had been so dismissive of Hutchinson back in the square.

"I don't suppose you have seen my chief, have you?" I enquired. He looked up and frowned and so I elaborated, "You know, the general you mocked for dressing like a beggar, who turned out to be right about the French planning an attack."

"He crossed the river with Bennigsen," the colonel replied disdainfully. "If they are not there already, they were going for Allenburg – another three miles down this road."

"What about my other colleagues, the general's brother and Major Wilson. Have you seen them on your travels?"

"I have better things to do than to look out for you British chickens. If they were not with the general, they will have been taken by the French or killed by now. Hey! Mind my trousers, you nearly trod on them." I looked down to see the garment suspended by two sticks so that they would dry next to the fire. "I must report to the grand duke tomorrow. He will not view a battle as a reason to be improperly dressed, even if my servant has disappeared." He gave a sniff of disapproval as he took in my appearance. "I doubt your chief maintains such standards."

I bit back an acid retort as some of his comrades called him over, waving a flask of spirits in the air. As the colonel strode off, I leant forward and snapped one of his twigs. The seat of his trousers flapped dangerously low over the flames. With luck the arse would be burned right out of them before the pompous fool noticed.

191

I walked on the last few miles to Allenburg, hoping there would be food and wishing that I had partaken in more of Bennigsen's picnic before the battle. The place turned out to be a small village and if there had been a scrap to eat there, it had long since been consumed. The moonlight revealed that its streets and even surrounding fields were now filled with exhausted soldiery, sleeping wherever they had dropped down. I found a corner of meadow that had not been trampled flat and joined them.

I was awoken the next morning by the strengthening daylight and did not feel at all inclined to move. I was hungry, my clothes were still damp, my joints were stiff and I was thoroughly fed up. I lay back and let the sun slowly warm me, while watching bees industriously visiting the meadow flowers that nodded gently above my head. Perhaps I was the only survivor of the British mission. If I was, where would I go? Konigsberg would fall to the French; Memel was the best option and from there a ship home. I would be the only British witness to the destruction of the Russian army and events that led to the oblivion of Prussia. Ministers would want my views and my diplomatic career would advance. I was just imagining the stories I could tell for maximum credit when my musings were interrupted. A shadow fell over my face as someone stood between me and the sun. "Are you going to lie there all day?" a voice growled.

I opened my eyes and squinted. The sun formed a halo around the head of a person staring down at me, making it hard to see their features. I knew it was no angel, though, unless angels routinely wear a British general's uniform jacket over an untucked and stained shirt.

"Your lordship," I muttered, hastily getting to my feet and watching my daydreams evaporate before me. "I was not sure any of us had survived, I only just made it across the river myself."

"My brother and Wilson have gone on ahead," Hutchinson barked brusquely, showing no interest in any ordeal I might have suffered. "Having lost much of it in battle, Bennigsen is now determined to kill the rest of his army with exhaustion. We are to march another eleven miles to Wehlau today where we can shelter behind the River Pregel. The tsar is in Tilsit, another thirty miles further on, behind the Niemen River. I suspect that is our ultimate destination." He looked around the meadow and pursed his lips, "I take it you have mislaid your horse like the others?"

"It was taken in the rout from Friedland," I admitted with growing irritation. Hutchinson was a callous prig. I had nearly been killed and yet he clearly did not care at all.

"Well, you can fetch mine, it is in that stable over there. Jump to it, man, I want to be at Wehlau before the rest of the ravening hordes arrive."

I strolled off fuming, my earlier thoughts of diplomatic glory now a very bitter taste in my mouth. The mount was saddled and I was just leading it out when a group of horsemen galloped into the town square. The sight of one of them caused me to quickly double back into the stable. It was a group of Guards officers, led by a colonel wearing an old saddle cloth tied around his middle.

"You there!" I heard him call out and wondered for a moment if he had spotted my precipitous retreat.

I peered around the door to see him instead riding up to Hutchinson. "Are you addressing *me,* Colonel?" The British general had clearly heard from his brother about the earlier mockery of his appearance and courage. His voice was icy with disdain.

"My apologies, sir, but I was hoping you could direct me to your aide. Not your brother or that major, but the captain you have on your staff." I cringed, expecting an accusatory finger to be pointed in my direction. Glancing around the stable I saw there was no other way out, but then I realised that Hutchinson was not answering. I risked another glimpse around the edge of the door and saw he was staring at the colonel's curious attire.

"You appear to be improperly dressed this morning, Colonel." His lordship's face was twitching in amusement as he added, "I am surprised that such attire is acceptable in your regiment; your kilt would be scorned at by the poorest crofter."

"That is something I wish to discuss with your aide," snarled the colonel in barely contained fury. "Where is he?"

"Captain Thompson," Hutchinson paused as he took on a doleful expression. "I rather fear that he did not survive the day at Friedland. I think you will find that he is dead."

"I can assure you, sir that he isn't, by God I can do that. But I promise you this, if I catch up with him, he will be." With that the colonel yanked hard on his horse's reins and led his smirking band of companions up the road to Wehlau.

194

"Flashman, you can come out now, they are out of sight," called the general. I emerged from the stable to a rare vision – a smiling Lord Hutchinson. "I suspect our 'friend' will soon find out that Captain Thompson does not exist, but in the meantime why don't you tell me of your journey here. I have a feeling that it will be enlightening."

Hutchinson walked beside me, holding the reins of his horse as I told the tale of my near drowning and then my encounter with the colonel. He chuckled darkly at that and then described how Bennigsen had used the artillery on the hill south of Friedland to cover the retreat of much of his army. Wilson and Kit had finally made it across the town bridge despite parts of it being on fire. "The Hanoverian fool estimates his losses at just ten thousand," Hutchinson remarked. "Even if that were true, from what I have seen he has also lost at least that number to desertion. Morale has been broken; I doubt that they will fight again and certainly not under his command."

"At least a thousand must have drowned in the river," I told him. "But if they are not going to fight, what happens now?"

"Prussia is finished. The tsar has no choice but to seek terms with the French." He grunted in amusement before adding, "That will not go down well with their church. After all the sermons the bishops have given recently, they now have to explain why Alexander is now supping with the devil."

We caught up with Kit and Wilson just outside Wehlau. They had already been interrogated by the Guards' colonel, who was continuing his quest for 'Captain Thompson'. He had flown into a rage when they told him that they had honestly never heard of such an officer. The only thing that had stopped him calling them out for lying to him, was his wish to kill me first. He swore in front of all present that he would demand satisfaction when he finally tracked me down and shoot me like the villainous dog I was.

Kit laughed when he told me. They had guessed who the mysterious captain really was, but wisely decided to keep my real identity to themselves. I did, however, learn that the colonel was called Metchnikoff and was a close aide to Constantine. In contrast to Kit's jollity, Wilson was beside himself with despair at the thought of

French success. He confided to me later that he had written to both the tsar and the Prussian First Minister imploring them to continue the war. I doubt that they would set much store by this appeal. In any event the allies had no choice but to stop the conflict, for they had no army left capable of stopping the invader.

At Wehlau we found around twenty thousand men, and a surprising number of cannon. As several of the Russian batteries were on the eastern bank of the Alle, they had managed to escape, along with a few guns dragged through the river. More men were still coming up on the road behind us and many more were scattered in the surrounding countryside, but few were in a fit state to fight again. This was evident when a French patrol was spotted that evening. A squadron of eighty cavalry was enough to cause panic in the town, a stampede of hundreds crossing over the one bridge, which was then torched. As I squinted at them through the smoke, I could imagine the troopers guffawing with laughter at the reaction they had provoked. They just turned on their heel, not even bothering to round up as prisoners the scores of Russian stragglers now trapped on the western side of the river.

There was at least food in Wehlau and to my relief, no sign of Metchnikoff. We learned that Constantine had joined his brother in Tilsit and guessed that the Guards officers had ridden on to report to him. We marched on the next morning, being joined on the road by some of Kamenski's force that had now abandoned Konigsberg to its fate. It was baking hot and our clothes and throats were soon caked in dust thrown up by the men marching on the dry earth ahead. Yet we could not falter, for we knew that the French would be on our heels. It took two days to reach Tilsit, which was guarded by some extraordinary reinforcements that had just arrived from the depths of Russia. They were the hard-faced men from the Far East, excellent horsemen and expert archers. The town was on the eastern bank of the broad Niemen River, which marked the border between old Prussian and Russian territory. Clearly the Russians did not yet feel secure, for the day after we arrived, the long wooden bridge was put to the torch.

The tsar was not receiving British or Prussian guests. He was staying in the largest house in town and holed up with his leading Russian advisors. We learned that Bennigsen was now talking of an army to defend the Niemen River border, but his goose had long since been cooked. While he had sent his ruler a diplomatically worded description of what had happened at Friedland, General Popov and others had been far more scathing. The Hanoverian was relieved of his command – not that we were there to witness it.

I had removed my distinctive red coat and had been hiding in a camp on the outskirts of town to avoid Metchnikoff. The Russians took their duelling very seriously. We had all heard the story of a duel between a Russian and a Prussian the previous year. The man from St Petersburg had not fancied his chances with either sword or pistol. So he had insisted that they cut a pack of cards to see who should die. The Prussian had lost, but had dismissed the affair as something of a joke – that is until the Russian had killed him with a shotgun when he stepped outside. I was mightily relieved when Hutchinson announced that we were leaving. To avoid a diplomatic incident, I was to stay out of sight in a private carriage.

We were travelling back to Memel, which for now was still in Prussian hands and, with a change of horses, was only a day's ride away. There was an end-of-term feeling as we bounced along the road towards that distant harbour and ships for home. Even our chief was in rare good spirits as he eagerly anticipated reclaiming his mistress from Lord Calderdale's bed.

"Our mission cannot be viewed as a success," he concluded, "but little blame can be attached to us."

"It is a disaster," countered Wilson, who was as usual more dramatic and had still not got over the recent calamitous events. "The whole of Prussia is lost to the Corsican tyrant, her poor queen is homeless and now Russia is at the mercy of the French."

"Pah," our chief grunted his disagreement. "That *poor queen* should not have goaded her buffoon of a husband into starting a war he could not win. I agree Prussia will be lost. It was doomed from the moment the war started. But Bonaparte does not want a war with Russia. He

197

and his army have been away from France for a year; they will want to return in triumph after this victory. He will send emissaries to meet those of the tsar and they will agree a peace. The border will almost certainly be the original one with Prussia along the Niemen River. Then the Russians can go home too, so that they are all back before the next winter."

It seemed Hutchinson was right, for when we arrived in Memel we learned that the French were insisting that the Prussians surrender that port and the few fortified towns that were still holding out before negotiations could begin. Ships in the harbour were preparing to leave and I was just bargaining over berths home for us when more news came in. Napoleon was proposing a personal meeting between himself and the tsar with no preconditions. At first, I did not see the significance. It was well known that the Corsican liked to manage things himself. If he did not trust his own officials to negotiate the treaty, then this made sense. Hutchinson, though, had a far more ominous view.

"It is one thing to agree a peace treaty," he warned, "but what if the French try to inveigle Russia into an alliance with them? That would leave Britain alone and isolated in Europe."

Wilson was scandalised at the very idea. "The tsar is a noble and honourable man. We have all met him. Who among us could say he was capable of such perfidy of…of such treachery? No, I for one will not believe it."

Even Kit looked doubtful. "Many of the Russian aristocracy will be grieving after losses at Friedland and elsewhere. They won't take well to an alliance with the man who killed their loved ones. The church and even the superstitious peasants would certainly object.

His brother nodded and even he began to doubt his own theory. "Well, we need to know for sure. We cannot leave now; London would expect us to find out." He paused, considering. "The Russians would not welcome us back at Tilsit. We need another way." Turning to me he added, "Your countess, she boasted of her connections. Could she be persuaded to help?"

198

It is not often I have been ordered into a lady's boudoir on government business, but it was certainly not a hardship to track down the delightful Dorothea. I swiftly discovered that she was not in the little town hall in Memel, which was being used again as a palace by the king and queen. She had been forced to take some rooms in another house nearby. She had the same maid, though, who smirked at the sight of me and rushed off to tell her mistress.

I was kept waiting a few minutes but could hear whispering and giggling from the other side of the door as well as the sound of trunks being opened and closed. It was mid-morning. Surely the countess was up? I wondered if I should have called in the afternoon but just as I was considering returning later, the door was thrown open and there was Dorothea, still smoothing down some folds in a low-cut silk dress.

"Captain Flashman, what a pleasant surprise." The radiant beauty had not diminished one jot from my memory and I struggled not to ogle at the vision before me. The dress matched her eyes and only provided her breasts with the barest restraint. I thought she would offer her hand to kiss as before, but this time she leaned up to kiss me on the cheek pressing her body briefly against me. In a cloud of her scent, I allowed her to lead me through the door.

"You will have to sit close beside me on this sofa, for as you can see, we are sorely pressed for space and furniture." She gestured around the room, which was half filled with trunks and packing cases, along with a small table and one chair, on which I guessed she had her meals.

"I suppose the king and queen are just as squashed in that tiny town hall," I consoled, as I sat down so close that our thighs were touching.

She grinned conspiratorially, "I am quite happy to be away from them. They have both been very bitter, blaming poor General Kamenski for the fall of Danzig, when the real fault lay with their army delivering ammunition to the city. The king has been very stiff with me. I think he suspects that I told his wife about his negotiations with France."

"You certainly helped to cook that little plan," I flattered.

"But what good has it done?" She reached out and put her hand on my arm. "So many good men died at Friedland and now we are forced to sue for peace."

"I hear that the tsar is even thinking of meeting the French emperor—" I began, only for her to snatch her hand away.

"So that is why you are here. You have heard that my husband is one of the tsar's advisors and you have come for news." She looked hurt as she added, "I thought we were friends and you cared for me."

"Oh, I do, and we are... friends, I mean. I swear to you by all that is holy that I had no idea that your husband was advising the tsar on this matter." I was speaking the truth and I think she saw it, but it was a struggle to hide the excitement at her news. To have a source so close to Alexander would be invaluable, yet I knew I would have to play things carefully. She had warned me before that she would not be disloyal to her tsar, but I also remembered her delight in political intrigues.

"Do not worry," I started. "I know you will not betray Russia to Britain. You will always do what you think is right and I am sure your husband is the same." She nodded, her back stiffening a little in pride before I went on. "But between us, do *you* think it is a good idea for the tsar to meet Napoleon?"

She paused for a moment and I thought she would not answer. Then those kissable lips pursed in irritation and she blurted out, "The French want them to meet as equals. The tsar of all the Russias and the son of a Corsican nobody. Christoph thinks that the French want the meeting to add legitimacy to the Bonaparte dynasty, as the Austrian emperor refused to meet Napoleon after Austerlitz."

Now we are getting somewhere, I thought, and it gave me an angle to play: snobbery. "Did you hear that Marshal Lefebvre was made Duke of Danzig after he captured the city? His wife, a former fish gutter from Boulogne, is now a duchess. She would doubtless expect you to curtsy to her at any formal gathering." As I had hoped, Dorothea shuddered deliciously at the thought. In truth I had no idea what the marshal's wife had been, although we had heard from deserters that Lefebvre was as tough as nails and did not disguise his origins as a common soldier.

"Hell will freeze over before I bow to a fishwife," she muttered. "My family have been providing governors and generals to Russia for generations. The Lievens can trace their line back to a bishop in the thirteenth century."

"But what if Alexander agrees an alliance with the French," I said, airing our greatest fear. "Then your noble houses will be mixing with former fishwives, whores and chambermaids as equals, not to mention men that your church has declared devils. It will only be a matter of time before their revolutionary ideas start to take a hold in Russia. Then, who knows. There might be a guillotine set up in St Petersburg. Surely you don't think that is right for Russia."

"Of course not," she snapped. "Christoph does not think it necessary for them to come together at all. He wants emissaries to agree the peace as the Austrians did. Yet Alexander wants to meet his rival and he is probably being encouraged by his brother. The French have sent Constantine flattering notes, claiming that his Guard regiments were the bravest men they have fought."

"Is there anything we can do to stop them meeting?" I mused.

"I doubt it. The tsar is angry with the British for not giving him men and support, when you have found men for your armies in South America and elsewhere. He would not receive General Hutchinson at Tilsit and nothing has changed. Alexander is simply curious about Bonaparte and wants to get the measure of the man."

"But the rest of the army cannot be happy about an alliance with the French. Thousands were killed by them just a week ago."

"No one is talking about an alliance, only a peace. The army will be pleased to go home, as will I. No one apart from the Prussians will want to be here again next winter. You worry too much, Thomas. The tsar would never agree an alliance with the French. The bishops would be appalled and certainly the nobles will not want their serfs getting ideas from the republicans."

"Some of our aristocracy has worried about revolution too," I admitted. "That is why we want to remain friends with Russia." I reached forward and took back her hand, "I would certainly like to remain your friend," I looked her in the eye and added, "I think we could be very helpful for each other."

"I will tell Christoph of the ardent desire of Britain's officers to stay close to the bosom of Russia." She giggled and added, "Perhaps it will make him jealous enough to leave his Prussian mistress. Now you must tell me what really happened at Friedland. I want to know if Bennigsen was foolish, or just unlucky as he claimed."

I spent a very pleasant hour in that room, describing the battle. I learned that Dorothea was well informed by officers who were not admirers of the Hanoverian and I flirted as much as I dared.

I left just before noon as she was meeting a Prussian duchess for lunch, and I have to admit to feeling quite pleased with myself. Dorothea and I were getting on splendidly and I sensed that there was more than a spark of mutual interest between us. Yet more important was the intelligence on the Russians that she had provided. I felt sure that Hutchinson would be impressed to learn that she believed that the tsar was unlikely to conclude an alliance. Once again, though, I was destined to be disappointed.

"We cannot advise the government based on the opinions of some chit of a girl who has heard some parlour gossip," he scorned.

"She is hardly a chit of a girl," I protested. "She has served the tsar's mother in court and knows his character well. On top of that her husband is one of the tsar's advisors and it is his letters that form her opinion. The Tsar is only meeting Napoleon out of curiosity; he has no intention of forming an alliance."

"It is not *his* intentions I care about," growled Hutchinson. "Alexander is young and naïve. The only other ruler he has met is that fool Friedrich Wilhelm. Bonaparte has schemed his way to power. The fact that he is already manipulating Constantine shows that he is determined to exploit this opportunity. We need someone we trust at Tilsit to tell us what is really going on."

"Well, I don't see how," I countered. "Alexander has made it very clear that the British are not welcome there."

"There is always a way, Flashman," his lordship half smiled to himself. "Yes, there is always a way."

I should have been more suspicious that evening when Kit asked why his brother had gone to meet Dorothea. I had no idea of the reason, but felt the first pang of disquiet. I told him of my visit and could only guess that Hutchinson had gone to hear her assurances first hand, or ask further questions. Wilson came to join us, and we were just tucking into supper together, discussing when we might get a ship to Britain, when the door to our room opened. To our astonishment, instead of the maid, in walked the countess. As we leapt to our feet, she was followed into the room by Hutchinson, a broad smile of satisfaction on his face.

"The countess has decided to pay a visit to her husband at Tilsit," he announced. Then he fixed his gaze on me and his grin broadened, "You, Flashman, will be part of her escort." My jaw must have gaped as the prospect of a homeward voyage receded. Then other thoughts began to whirl in my head.

Dorothea must have seen the consternation cross my features and raised a mocking eyebrow, "Why, Captain, men are not normally so reluctant to spend time in my company."

"Well, obviously I would like to come," I started, "but I thought we were not welcome in Tilsit."

"That is why you will be disguised as a sergeant in my husband's regiment," she replied.

"But what about Colonel Metchnikoff?" I protested. "If he sees me back in Tilsit he is bound to call me out and cause as much trouble as he can."

"You will be a sergeant," she repeated happily. "Metchnikoff will take no notice of common soldiers. But you should wear your Order of St George medal to ensure you are not beaten."

That brought me up sharp, for I would now be among those poor devils who were treated as little more than dumb beasts of burden by their officers. I had a sudden vision of being robbed of my boots and marched off into the wilderness in a column of serfs who could not understand my protests. "We will never get away with it," I wailed. "I don't even speak Russian."

"I could give it a go, sir," volunteered Wilson, "I speak good German and know a little of the Cossack tongue now too."

"No," grunted Hutchinson, who shook his head at Wilson. "I know you too well, you will struggle to remain inconspicuous. It must be Flashman. He has been in disguise before and the countess promises me she will look after him." He turned his gaze to me, "Keep your eyes and ears open and report back as soon as you have news on what they have signed."

So early the next morning I found myself one of six troopers riding out of Memel alongside the countess's carriage. She had claimed that she was travelling with the barest of essentials, but there was still her maid and another servant riding on the postillion seats at the rear of the vehicle and three large trunks lashed to the roof. I was adorned with the green coat of the count's regiment instead of my usual red. My gold-hilted sword had been replaced by a utilitarian one of steel and my medal was pinned prominently on my left tit. The escort was commanded by a Lieutenant Lvov, who alone knew my real identity. He was to keep me out of trouble when Dorothea was with her husband. He had been impressed to learn that the order of St George had been genuinely earned. We were just comparing our experiences at Eylau when the coach was ordered to a stop. Now we were away from prying eyes, I was invited inside.

"Are you not pleased to come on our adventure?" Dorothea asked, with a gleam of excitement in her eyes. "I was so bored in Memel. We should be where history is being made." It was the first time we had been alone since I had been shanghaied into the scheme. She looked at me and perhaps sensed that my enthusiasm for this trip did not match her own, "Your Lord Hutchinson thought it was an excellent idea."

"I am sure he did," I agreed, feeling once more that his lordship saw me as the most expendable member of the party. Perhaps my father-in-law would have his wish granted even yet. "Of course, I am happy for your company, but I would not want to embroil you in any scandal. If I am discovered, will things not go badly for you and your husband?"

"My husband will never know about you. If you are discovered, I alone will take the blame. I will be seen as a silly woman tricked by a wily English officer."

That did not bode well for the 'wily English officer' I thought. "So the count will not tell us what is being discussed with the French, then?" I asked.

"He will tell me and if it is in the interests of Russia, I will tell you," she replied primly. "Christoph is very loyal. Before I met him, he spent a year in England and likes your country, yet he would not do anything that might displease Alexander."

"Will Alexander share all the details with him? Are they still close?"

"Christoph joined the army at fifteen and later served as minister of war for Tsar Paul. That was a bad time. The old tsar was mad and would introduce new laws, for example on the height of collars. Then the very next day he would order Christoph to imprison officers or send them to Siberia for being improperly dressed. It was hard for all of us and in the end Christoph feigned illness to be relieved of his duties."

"Was he involved in the plot to kill Paul?"

"No, but one of our closest friends was. He did not tell Christoph in advance as he knew he would be too conflicted." That was worrying, I thought, if even his closest friends did not trust him. Perhaps his nerve had been broken by Paul. I resolved to keep out of his way. I just had to trust that Dorothea's confidence in Alexander spilling the beans to her husband, and him then divulging to her, was justified.

We changed horses halfway and then rode on so that by evening we were approaching the large town of Tilsit. I was back on my mount by then, as a countess could not be seen sharing a carriage with a common sergeant. As we rounded the final bend, instead of the settlement I had seen before, there was now a temporary city spread across both banks of the river. It was vast. The whole French army was on the far bank with tents visible through the trees as far as the eye could see. On the eastern shore the cleared fields around the town would produce few crops this year as they were covered with a harvest of humanity. There were canvas structures added to the buildings to increase their size and many men were camping out in the open, enjoying the warm summer nights. On both sides of the river men were splashing and washing off the dirt of the day. The Niemen was wide and the current slow. It could easily be swum, yet none attempted it. The bridge I had seen burnt before had not been rebuilt, but now, lashed to the pilings in the middle, was a large raft. There were several boats tied to it and craftsmen were putting the finishing touches to two tented pavilions, one on the Russian side and one on the French. Clearly the leaders could not agree on whose shore the meeting should take place and so a neutral zone had been created.

We rode through the town until we reached what must have been the tsar's residence, judging from the guards outside. Our arrival caused quite a stir as there were hardly any other women to be seen. A crowd of officers appeared to view the new arrival. As Lieutenant Lvov handed Dorothea down from the carriage, a thin, careworn general stepped forward. I recognised Christoph from our earlier meeting and from his expression, he was not greatly pleased to have his wife join him. Perhaps his aides were hurriedly removing his Prussian mistress from his quarters. I discreetly studied the other officers now standing in the porch. Several of them wore uniforms of the Guards regiments. Constantine was among them. A couple of paces behind in the crowd, I spotted Metchnikoff. The last thing I needed now was to be recognised and so I hurriedly dismounted and hid my face behind my horse's neck.

"Come this way," called Lvov. With our charge delivered and the coachman unloading the luggage for the servants, we made our way back out of town. The lieutenant would usually have reported back to his regiment, but that would have generated too many questions about the mysterious new sergeant who did not speak Russian. Instead, he took our party to a spot overlooking the remains of the bridge. The other troopers did not mind, for the countess had provided a generous allowance for food and drink. They too wanted to see the encounter on the river. Lvov spoke good English. I learned that his grandfather had been a shipwright born in Bristol. This forebear had travelled to St

207

Petersburg back when the first Tsar Peter was building the city and Russia's first navy.

We watched less skilled craftsmen put the finishing touches to the raft and discovered that we had timed our arrival to perfection. The tsar and Bonaparte were to meet for the first time the following day. Hundreds had already reserved their places and the atmosphere along the bank was one of a county fair. Locals strolled along the shore hawking small pancakes flavoured with herbs, along with glasses of their homemade vodka. I tried both and they were very welcome.

It had been another warm day. As the light faded some of the men around me began to sing. Deep, baleful voices joined in all along the riverbank. Lvov told me it was a song about missing home. It was certainly not a cheery ditty and in response, some of the French on the far bank struck up a tune of their own. I could not make out the words, but from the pace of it, suspected it was a marching song. Darkness brought an end to these 'revels' and it was not a hardship to sleep out under the stars that night. I lay back and wondered what those who would meet in that tent the next day were thinking and what their decisions would mean for me. I did not sleep well.

I was awoken just after dawn by the smell of cooking fires. Soon there was a cup of well-brewed black tea and a boiled egg in my hands for breakfast. Apart from men strolling down to piss in the river, little was happening. A couple of boats containing Russian and French officials shuttled across as they made the final arrangements. Clearly, emperors of any hue do not want to be seen too early. It was noon before there was any sign of the coming encounter. We could hear distant cheering on the far shore and some of the men on that bank ran back through the trees, waving their hats in the air. For them this was a celebration of victory, their enemies either humbled or destroyed.

The mood was quite different on our shore. The only sound to break a sullen silence was a ripple of sycophantic applause marking the arrival of the tsar's party. We did not have a clear view as hundreds of soldiers were standing in the way. A single cannon fired up-river, which prompted both parties to set off. I craned to see who was in Alexander's boat. The tsar was seated in the stern, his brother

208

Constantine beside him. Next came a bank of six oarsmen, and in the bows I could see Bennigsen, two men I did not recognise and to my relief, the count of Lieven.

While the tsar's oarsmen made a stately progress across the water, Bonaparte clearly had other ideas. He was standing in his craft and urging his crew on so that he would reach the raft first. He was in good spirits, turning to wave an acknowledgment to his soldiers still cheering him on from the bank behind. The French boat reached the wooden platform when the Russian vessel was little more than halfway in its short journey. Napoleon was impatient to get proceedings underway. Leaving his companions in his boat, he leapt up onto the raft and rushed across to the Russian end. As Alexander's oarsmen hooked a rope around a bollard on the raft to hold it steady, Bonaparte held a hand down to the tsar to help him up onto the platform. It was impossible to hear anything being said on the raft with the continued cheering from the far shore, but I could see that the French emperor was smiling as he half hauled the tsar up from his boat. The tsar looked awkward, more so as Napoleon turned the helping hand into a double-armed embrace of his fellow ruler, who was obliged to respond in kind. Alexander must have been all too aware of the stony glares of his own army, as he accepted the enthusiastic greeting of a man widely believed to be a devil.

Constantine stood in the boat, arm half raised, clearly expecting to be welcomed up on to the raft next, but Napoleon ignored him. The rest of the French party were still in their craft and perhaps the Russians saw this as Alexander was guided into the tent. The French ruler had engineered a situation where the two emperors would meet alone.

We sat watching the canvas walls on that raft for over two hours, speculating on what was being discussed behind them. Top of the agenda was surely the future of Prussia and yet the Prussian king was nowhere to be seen. Lvov had heard that Friedrich Wilhelm was in Tilsit, yet the royal muff had not even qualified for the boat party, never mind the discussions in the tent. The future of the Prussian throne now lay in the hands of two other men. Alexander had inherited power, although he had been trained by the ruthless empress, Catherine. His opponent was a man who had fought, plotted and schemed his way to an empire and was used to getting what he wanted. The French were also in a far stronger negotiating position. We had heard that upstream they had been building pontoon rafts to make a bridge should they need to march across the Niemen River.

I could not imagine things going well for the Russian side, a feeling that grew stronger as time passed. Yet when the monarchs finally reappeared, the tsar was beaming in delight. Now he introduced the rest of his party in the boat. We could see the two rulers laughing as they joked with others in the now bemused Russian contingent. Alexander's parting embrace looked far more genuine as he took his leave and climbed back into his launch.

I was in a fever to learn what had been decided, but I knew that it would take a while for the news to leak out. The tsar would share what he chose to with his advisors, and then with luck the good count would succumb to his wife's questioning. In the crowded headquarters, I thought that she would have to wait until she got him into bed before extracting his news. To my surprise we received information before nightfall. It had started with the sound of cheering near the town. Then we saw men running towards us, shouting. What they yelled caused the celebrations to spread, some men even firing their muskets in the air. Lvov grabbed a messenger by the arm and made him repeat what he knew and confirm where it had come from. Then he turned to me, and translated, "The tsar has announced that he has secured Bonaparte's agreement to a peace and the continuation of a Prussian state."

The rest of the escort cheered at the thought of going home. I had been expecting a peace treaty, but was amazed that Friedrich Wilhelm had also kept his kingdom. It was surprisingly generous. I could not help but wonder what Bonaparte was hoping for in return. We were told that negotiations would continue the following day, when the new borders of Prussia would be agreed – and at that point its king would finally be allowed to join the discussions.

That evening barrels of vodka were distributed by order of the tsar. Water was hastily tipped out of canteens that were then refilled with the spirit. Soldiers were enthusiastically celebrating the thought of shaking Prussian mud off their boots and whatever delights awaited a peasant soldier in Russia. The vodka was a lethal brew; I had drunk half a bottle and found that the river was swaying like a seesaw. By nightfall there were great circles of men dancing and singing all down the riverbank. Many had gulped down far more than me and I wondered if the way they linked arms as they danced was to keep each other upright.

Dawn brought a raging thirst and a sore head. The pancake sellers did a roaring trade as the army staggered blearily back to life. It was mid-morning before I noticed that while we had been carousing, someone had been busy on the raft. Above the door on the Russian side a large laurel leaf circle had been painted in green and in the middle a large 'A.' I suspected that it was as much to flatter Alexander as it was to snub Friedrich Wilhelm.

The meeting gun sounded again at noon. This time there were rousing cheers from both banks as the monarchs set off. Napoleon raced ahead again to welcome Alexander and help him up onto the raft. Their embraces and smiles were now far more genuine, with the tsar happily waving back to his army. The Prussians must have insisted on their own boat. They had to wait as the Russian one cleared away from the mooring point. By the time Friedrich Wilhelm's craft was tied up, the other two rulers were already inside the tent and the Prussian king had to scramble up alone. He stood outside for a moment, stiff and awkward as he straightened his uniform, an expression on his face as though he was enduring a bad smell. Then, finally accepting that no one would be welcoming him, he cautiously stepped inside the canvas portal.

I suspected that the neglect at his arrival did not bode well for the Prussian king. My suspicions were confirmed by his reappearance two hours later. He staggered out, ashen-faced and gesturing for his boat, as though anxious to leave that floating island as soon as possible. The tsar and emperor emerged a short while later, still embracing as they departed. This time we had to wait longer for news. Lvov had left one of his troopers outside the palace and just before nightfall, Dorothea's maid brought out a note. It was no great betrayal of her tsar, for the news would soon be public knowledge. Prussia was to lose the western half of its territory. Some went to the kingdom of Westphalia, ruled by Napoleon's brother Jerome. The new Grand Duchy of Warsaw took another chunk, the French would remain in Danzig and in what the king would see as an act of betrayal, Alexander claimed one province for Russia.

I thought that the gathering would break up after that, but it was to last for almost two weeks. The atmosphere became that of a festival, although most of the celebrations took place on the French side of the river. The next morning both Alexander and the Prussian king were rowed over to the far shore, where a much larger tented pavilion had been constructed. Cannon salutes were fired – with notably fewer guns for the Prussians – honour guards inspected, marching displays performed and gifts exchanged. To ensure Russian representation, Alexander had the entire Preobrazhensky Guards regiment rowed across too so that they could demonstrate the precision of his army. They were the only Guards unit that had escaped decimation at Friedland, as Bennigsen had sent them to guard a crossing further down the river. I remembered Constantine being furious at this. Lvov had to explain that they were the senior regiment in the army. They had been used by Empress Catherine to seize power and had provided more than one of her lovers. Consequently, its ranks were filled with the sons of the most senior noble houses. Had they been slaughtered too, Alexander might have faced revolt in St Petersburg.

On another occasion the mounted archers from the Far East went across to give a display. They scorned the offer of boats and simply swam their mounts across. I heard that they then bested some French dragoons in a contest of firing at targets at the gallop.

As the great and the good crossed to the French bank, I was happy to stay on my side of the river. I had already had one unexpected encounter with the man who wanted me dead. While walking down the main street of Tilsit with Lvov, I saw Metchnikoff leading some other officers straight towards me. He was just a few yards away. There was no time to hide and so I hurriedly joined the end of a file of soldiers who were presenting arms in salute. I kept my eyes subserviently down, glad that I had not shaved for a week, which added to my rough soldierly appearance. I was certain he would recognise me and braced myself for a cry of triumph as he passed within a couple of feet. I dared not look up, but to my astonishment I saw his highly polished boots move past without hesitation. Lvov told me later that the colonel had barely glanced at the saluting men. "They take it as their right," he assured me. "They will only look at the face of a soldier when inspecting their own regiments and even then, they will not trouble to know their names. He will only notice you if you step on his toe."

My plan to stay on the Russian bank changed when I saw an extraordinary character striding down it towards me. The fellow was six inches taller than most, wearing a Cossack tunic and had stuck to his face the most luxuriant false moustache. "What ho, Flashman," he shouted cheerily to me in English.

"Wilson, what the devil are you doing here? For God's sake keep your voice down, there are not supposed to be any English people here, remember."

He beamed carelessly back and proudly twirled the end of what resembled two dead mice stuck to his face. Then he added in a lower tone, "Hutchinson agreed I could come now. He has received your note on the peace treaty, but he wants to know if you are sure there is not more to discover."

"Dorothea has not sent any new messages," I told him. "Lvov has a trooper outside the palace every evening, but her maid has not come out."

"I hope Alexander has seen sense and stopped talking to the Corsican tyrant."

"They are certainly still meeting, I keep hearing the gun salutes, but it is all happening on the other side of the river so that I cannot see what is going on. He and boatloads of his officers go across every day."

"Then we must cross too," Wilson declared.

"Are you mad? We cannot just row uninvited into the enemy camp and especially with you figged up like some pantomime villain."

"Nonsense, there are hundreds of yards of riverbank. They can't be guarding it all. I have brought some Cossack friends with me. You watch, we will get across all right."

As it turned out the task was easier than I thought. Wilson had made the acquaintance of a Russian general called Worontzow, who we learned was now stationed with some men on the French side. There was a steady stream of boats coming and going across the river and no one checked who was boarding at the Russian bank. On the French side a sentry asked us our business and Lvov, in halting French, announced that we were to see the general. Both Wilson and I were fluent in the language, but we knew that a peasant soldier speaking French would raise suspicion. We wanted as few people as possible studying Wilson. His two Cossack friends were at least dressed in similar costumes to him, but being shorter could do little to hide his ridiculous 'mouse-tache'.

Whether to be helpful or to ensure that we did not stray, the sentry escorted us to Worontzow's quarters. The general grinned in delight at the sight of us and dismissed the sentry before inviting us inside his tent. The obligatory welcome vodka was poured and Lvov, who had stood back in the presence of such a senior officer was invited forward. "Come, Lieutenant," called Worontzow, "sit beside me, for you are the most senior officer amongst this group of reprobates." He laughed and added, "Constantine would be appalled to see a general drinking with a common sergeant. While he is embracing the French, he has not yet adopted the principles of their revolution."

"That is why we have come," I explained. "We wanted to see how discussions are proceeding. We rarely see the tsar now on our side of the river."

"Yes, I guessed that," said the general becoming serious. "Alexander meets Bonaparte every day. They spend hours discussing things in a grand pavilion, but don't ask me what they talk about. I have no idea and they keep the place well guarded." He turned to Wilson, "You should be careful, you are not unknown amongst the

French with your writing. They would be sure to arrest you if they saw through that…er…disguise."

Worontzow thought that there was far too much fraternisation between the French and the Russians. Memories of the men he had lost at Friedland were still raw and he was particularly critical of Constantine. The grand duke had ordered banquets where his Preobrazhensky Guards had hosted a similar number of the Old Guard. There were even rumours he had accepted an honorary colonelcy in a French regiment. The general was interrupted by the distant sound of regular cannon fire. "Another salute," he groaned. "Come, you had better see how things are for yourselves."

We marched through the camp and in the company of a Russian general, nobody bothered us. The clearing, now used as a parade ground, was easy to find by following the sound of guns, and there we joined a large crowd watching the display. The Preobrazhensky Guards were marching and counter marching with perfect precision in front of a dais where the two emperors sat taking their salute. Constantine stood beside them, like a proud father watching his offspring perform. This was clearly what he thought soldiering was all about. A group of French marshals sat on their horses on the other side of the square. They seemed far less impressed, in fact most looked bored as they talked among themselves.

"Look at them," scorned Wilson, "all that braid and decoration, they look like iced gingerbread men. And as for that marshal," he pointed to the one I called the peacock, "he could be a May Day chimney sweep in the carnival."

The man was resplendent with his tiger-skin saddle cloth, silver fitments polished to a gleam and a three-foot white egret feather in his hat. "That is Marshal Murat, commander of their cavalry," explained Worontzow.

"A dandified fop," dismissed Wilson. I was not so sure. The marshal certainly took huge care in his appearance, yet I remembered that when I had seen him at Eylau, that white feather was usually waving above where the fighting was toughest. We saw a regiment of the French Imperial Guard readying to give their own performance and so decided to move on. On our way back towards the river we passed a large, tented pavilion. It would not have looked out of place at a wedding, especially as on either side of the main entrance there was an intertwined '*N&A*' motif painted on the cloth. We did not need Worontzow to tell us that this was where the emperors met.

"We need to get inside there," urged Wilson.

"I don't see how," I replied, "look at those guardsmen standing at the entrance. I doubt that they would let a French marshal in without the emperor's express permission, never mind a Cossack with a dodgy moustache." Despite the mixed initials, I noticed that all the men standing around the pavilion were French. The first Russians we saw were when we walked around the structure. There we found a score of soldiers carrying wooden crates into a side entrance. Worontzow led us up to the officer in charge to find out what was happening. Just as he was about to ask, a soldier staring at the tent instead of looking where he was going, knocked heavily into his officer. The lieutenant was clearly embarrassed at being nearly floored by one of his own men in front of a general. He lashed out at the unfortunate soldier with a riding crop, shouting at him in Russian as he struck the fellow. The cringing man fell to the ground, pushing his crate out of harm's way. He must have thought that its contents were more valuable than his own miserable existence.

"Grab that box and take it in," hissed Wilson. Then he shoved me forward bodily, so that I only just avoided barging into the angry officer myself. The lieutenant whirled round and the riding crop rose once more, but fell again as its owner saw the medal on my chest. Worontzow asked a question, which distracted him. The general moved slightly so that the officer now had his back to me and began to engage him in conversation. Wilson silently urged me on with his eyes. I noticed that his shove had dislodged half of his moustache, which now drooped over his lip. Poor Lvov looked horrified at being involved in this affair and I knew precisely how he felt. The last thing I wanted to do was risk discovery in that tent, yet as the crate still lay abandoned on the ground, I could think of no good excuse not to make use of it. I bent down and picked it up. Glass clinked inside and from the weight it must have contained full bottles of something. I slipped between two other soldiers carrying identical burdens and followed them through the side flap in the tent.

I found myself in a storage area. There were boxes of cherries, some other berries I did not recognise and sacks of potatoes, with two chamberlains guarding the produce from pilfering Russians. They directed us to put down our crates to join a row of the boxes stacked three high. I went and stood around the back of the line as I placed my crate on the end. Another Russian stumbled against one of the guy ropes as he entered the tent and I used the distraction to duck down out of sight.

"Careful, you fool," shouted one of the chamberlains in French.

"Don't worry," soothed the other. "One less case of this revolting muck will be a blessing. It is pitiful that these fools think that they can produce wine as good as the French."

"Are we really going to serve this to the emperor and his staff tonight?"

"Of course not, we will empty one of the bottles and refill it with Chambertin." He laughed and added, "If the tsar drinks it by mistake, he will probably weep at what he has been missing!"

They were still chuckling at the thought of the rest of the French staff being forced to drink Russian wine when I found another flap in the canvas wall behind the crates. I peered under it to see an empty room with a table and two chairs. Staying low, I wriggled through. I had to be quick, as I had no idea how many more crates of Chateau Volga were being delivered. If I didn't re-join the last of the Russian men my intrusion would be discovered, so I jumped up decisively and strode over to the table. I had hoped to find drafts of an agreement or notes that I could stuff inside my jacket, but there was just a map of a region that made no sense at all. Instead of Prussia, I was looking down on what was unmistakeably the coastline of Greece and the Adriatic. The town names were in Russian, but many were still recognisable. Someone had inked a circle around three areas. There was another larger map pinned to a board on an easel; this one covered the whole of Europe. It was clear that the imperial discussions were very wide ranging indeed.

I dared not stay any longer and rushed back to wriggle through the flap. I was halfway under the canvas when I realised that there were no more Russians left in the tent. The doorway was empty and I could hear the chamberlains discussing the menu for the evening. Someone called Dupont was expected with some lamb carcasses, but I doubted I could wait until then or remain unnoticed if I joined his group. I crawled to the end of the line of crates but there was still a distance of several yards to the door. I was bound to be spotted. Then there would be interrogations and they would swiftly learn I did not speak Russian. I looked at the damn boxes of wine and cursed myself for a fool and Wilson too for getting me in this mess. Then I had an idea: if they thought me guilty of a smaller crime, then they may not suspect me of a larger one. Carefully, I pulled my knife from my pocket and inserted the point between two of the slats of wood that made up the bottom crate. I took a deep breath and then pushed the handle down. There was the sound of splintering wood and in no time two chamberlains came exclaiming and rushing in my direction.

"You thieving swine, what do you think you are doing?" demanded the first.

Cowering like I had seen the much-beaten Russian peasant do, I mumbled, "Vodka." Then I muttered some gibberish that I thought sounded Russian and reached my hand into the crate for a bottle.

"Get away from that, it is not for the likes of you." The second chamberlain had come up behind me and now kicked me hard in the back. "Go on, get away, you filthy scum." I got up and staggered to the door, collecting another kick from the first chamberlain on the way.

"Vodka!" he scoffed. "What can you say about a people that drink the juice from fermented potato peelings. Go on, clear off."

I emerged running from the tent. Two French sentries were already moving towards the doorway, alerted by the commotion inside, but I saw Wilson and the others where I had left them and hurtled in their direction. Worontzow shouted to the guards in French that I was one of his men and he would ensure that I was severely dealt with. Then he yelled furiously at me in Russian before ordering Lvov to grab me by the scruff of the neck. In a moment I was being frogmarched back to his tent with Wilson whispering urgently in my ear, asking what I had discovered.

"Can you remember where in Greece was marked on the map?" asked Worontzow when we were safely under cover.

"There were some islands south of Greece and the coastline south of Venice. There was also a ring around Turkey," I recalled.

"The Dalmatian coast south of Venice is a Russian possession, but it borders France's Italian territories." Worontzow looked thoughtful, "If Napoleon has persuaded Alexander to give it up, I wonder what we get in return?"

"There was a map of the whole of Europe on an easel," I recounted. "One thing is for sure, they are talking about a lot more than Prussia." I glanced at Wilson, "Which means that they are certain to be discussing Britain too."

"It is bound to be kept secret," agreed the Russian general. "There are many grieving families in St Petersburg. They will not be happy about Alexander becoming friendly with the French. Many of the generals here, including me, think he has got far too close to Napoleon. If they learn he has given up territories to the French as well, then things could turn ugly for the tsar."

He was undoubtedly right. We needed to know more about what was being agreed and there was only one likely source for that information: Dorothea. We had to get back across the river and speak to her urgently, but before that there was one more thing I wanted to do.

"Ouch, what did you do that for?" yelped Wilson as I tore the ridiculous moustache off his face. One side had been hanging at near ninety degrees to the rest.

"You looked absurd," I told him as I tore the thing in half. I re-stuck one piece, which was still as long as his upper lip, back under his nose. "There, that is better, now we can leave without being arrested."

Seeing Dorothea was far easier said than done. As we were crossing back over the river, we encountered her travelling in the opposite direction. She had been invited to the reception in the pavilion and would soon be enjoying the delights of Russian wine. She was to stay for most of the following day, which was when the treaty between Napoleon and Alexander was signed.

A great crowd witnessed the monarchs putting ink to paper, but few if any knew what the documents contained. Then Alexander conferred on Napoleon the Cross of St Andrew, which was Russia's highest order of chivalry. Not to be outdone, Bonaparte bestowed on the tsar the Grand Cross of the Legion of Honour. Then he gave Constantine, Bennigsen and all the other Russian generals present lesser awards in the Legion. In a typical theatrical gesture, he also removed his personal Legion of Honour cross and awarded it to a Russian guardsman, to recognise the gallantry of his former enemy.

We heard all about that later, but from our side of the riverbank we could see the French Imperial Guard and the Russian Preobrazhensky Guards lining either side of the route back down to the river. Napoleon escorted Alexander to his boat. At one point they were walking arm in arm and there were hugs and embraces when the two monarchs finally parted. The resultant cheering was noticeably louder on the French side of the river.

Many Russians had been waiting two weeks now to start the journey home. They had tired of seeing their tsar in the thrall of the French emperor who had defeated them. I saw Count Lieven and his wife in the third boat to follow the tsar over the Nieman River. Neither looked particularly happy; they sat stiffly ignoring each other. I had planned to try and catch Dorothea's eye, but noticed just in time that another of the passengers was Colonel Metchnikoff. I had seen him several times in Tilsit by now and Lvov had been right – he always ignored common soldiers. Yet trying to attract the attention of one of his fellow passengers might be pushing my luck. I was about to turn away when I saw the next boat coming. It was full of servants and there among them was Dorothea's maid.

Wilson returned to Memel that afternoon to give Hutchinson the information we had gathered. I was still hopeful of discovering more. That evening I stood with Lvov and the rest of the escort outside Alexander's residence. The countess had passed word she wanted some fresh air and we were to accompany her for a walk. It was early July; there was still an hour or two of daylight and in the cool of the evening, this was the best part of the day.

"How was the dinner last night?" I asked as we walked out of earshot of those around us.

"It was frightful," she snapped. She was clearly still in a temper and the maid walking behind looked cowed as though she had recently felt the brunt of it. "I was sat opposite a general's wife who spent most of the evening picking at her teeth. A vile, uncouth character."

"Has your husband told you much of the discussions?" I asked, deciding to come straight to the business in hand.

She stopped and took a deep breath to calm herself. "We have talked of little else," she admitted. "He told me that Bonaparte might soon be looking for a new wife as his empress is too old to bear him children. He wants a son to continue his dynasty and had the audacity to ask about the grand duchesses. He has set his sights on poor Katya. Instead of turning him down flat, Alexander agreed to consider it, even though he is particularly close to her. Can you imagine it?" she exclaimed, throwing her arms up in the air, "my friend forced to marry that corpulent rogue, yet Christoph will not counsel against it."

It was an alarming indication of just how well the two emperors had got on. The price of being a royal offspring was often a dynastic marriage and Empress of France was a good title. Yet many amongst the proud nobility of Russia would be similarly appalled at the idea of a blood link between the houses of Bonaparte and Romanov. It might start a worrying trend that could see their own precious offspring married to the child of a fish gutter.

Christoph, the former minister, had to be looking at the political angle. Such a union could bring Russia and France closer for

221

generations. All the countries in between such as Austria and Prussia could not risk upsetting both formidable neighbours. Russia and France would dominate Europe, leaving Britain weaker and isolated.

"Such an alliance would be powerful," I admitted, "but I think we both know who the dominant party would be. Russia might end up a vassal state to France."

My intention was to stir up her patriotism and I was not disappointed. "Alexander would never allow that to happen," she protested. "He will always defend the interests of Russia."

"Really?" I queried. "You don't think he and his brother have been swayed by the French charm offensive, the exchange of medals, the parades, the compliments on each other's troops?" She opened her mouth to reply but then closed it without saying a word. She had to be having doubts and so I pressed on. "It is not just his sister he is thinking of offering to the French. They are after the coastal area of Dalmatia and possibly territories in Greece too. Maybe he has already given them up. Before you are so quick to defend him, perhaps you should speak to your husband to find out what was really in that treaty."

"You just want to know what is in the treaty for Britain," she accused.

"Of course I do," I admitted. "But I know you will not betray Russia. All I ask is you find out what is in the treaty. Once you know the terms, if you think that the future of your country is best served being tied to France, then tell me nothing." I paused to let that sink in and then continued quietly, "But if you do not want to see the grand duchess become an unhappy empress of France or French dukes picking their teeth in the Winter Palace, there is only one nation that can help Russia resist, and that is Britain. You have already helped thwart Bonaparte's plans once. You can have a major role in the future of your country; you have far more sway than your husband, and he will not even know what you have done."

We turned back after that. Dorothea was quiet, lost in thought, which I hoped boded well. The following morning the tsar announced he was returning to Russia and the army prepared to march back with him. The count would accompany Alexander. Dorothea was to travel first back to Memel and then home via Riga to visit her father and collect her children. I wondered if the separation indicated another row between the couple and if so, whether she had managed to gather the information we wanted. I should not have worried, for we were barely out of Tilsit when she ordered the coach stopped so that I could climb inside.

"Alexander has given the French the Dalmatian coast and the Ionian islands," she spat out before I had even sat down. "In return we get French *permission* to attack Turkey and Sweden, as if we ever needed that before." She thumped her fist down on the seat beside her and gave a wail of frustration. "It is a humiliation for Russia and yet we act like grateful dogs being thrown a bone."

"I am sorry," I consoled, hoping desperately that she had discovered more, for we had guessed most of this already.

She paused, looking out of the window, and I sensed that there was indeed further news. Once the words were spoken, they could not be taken back. It was a momentous decision to betray both her husband and her ruler. It could only be justified if she believed her understanding of the situation was better than theirs. But Dorothea did not lack self-confidence. "There are secret clauses," she spoke in almost a whisper. "Russia is to broker peace talks between Britain and France." She held up a hand to stall any interruptions. "I know they will not succeed; no one expects them too. When they fail, Russia will join the continental blockade against trade with Britain. Finally, when the time is right…" she paused again and then said slowly, "…Russia will join an alliance with France to fight the British."

Our worst fears were confirmed. Even though I had more than half expected it, hearing the words was a blow. Our diplomatic mission had been a disaster. Rather than helping to protect Prussia, we had driven our most powerful ally into the camp of our enemy. Not that I thought Hutchinson could take much blame for that. The Russian army had been doomed to defeat from the outset. It was perhaps a miracle Bennigsen's cautious retreats had kept it in the field so long. Others would claim that if Britain had sent an army to help, we would have made a difference, but I doubt it. We would simply have had dead men and prisoners in red to go with the ones in Prussian black and Russian green. While our navy was the best in the world, back then we simply did not have a large and experienced army that could take on the French. At that time, the one force we might have used was getting its arse kicked in Argentina by the Spanish.

Yet while I sat in a slough of despair, Dorothea raised her chin. She had been considering the news for longer than I and she was not ready to give up. "We are not beaten yet," she declared. "The dowager empress will never agree to Katya's marriage. If Alexander does not tell her, I will make sure she hears about it. That is the least I can do for my friend."

I confess that the fate of the grand duchess was not uppermost in my thoughts, but Dorothea went on, "The alliance is secret for now and they would deny it. We must not mention it to protect Christoph, but the whole army has seen what happened at Tilsit. Many generals and officers were disgusted at how Bonaparte was feted. They have watched for months as priests and bishops have taught the men that he is the Antichrist. Landowners have been ensuring that their serfs get the same sermons, as all are fearful of a revolution. We can stir up the court so that Alexander will have to reconsider."

"I doubt Napoleon will let him off the hook that easily," I grumbled. "He will find some way to hold Alexander's feet to the fire, so that he does what he is told."

"No, you are wrong," she countered. She was suddenly animated and jumped across the carriage to sit beside me and slide her arm through mine. "You can campaign openly while I will work behind the scenes, but together we will save Alexander and Russia." She gave a heavy sigh, while her eyes blazed with a new passion. "I have always thought it was my destiny to be more than a courtier or wife. I will be a diplomat in all but name. Those who underestimate me will do so at their peril."

"I think the Prussian king has already learned that to his cost," I agreed, grinning. Of course, I thought she was being hopelessly naïve, but I don't object when beautiful women hang on to my arm and work themselves into a fervour. I was hoping now that there would be an opportunity to cement our alliance on a more personal level, but there was little chance of that with Lvov and five other troopers riding alongside the carriage.

When she insisted on us meeting privately with Hutchinson on our return to Memel, I thought he would be similarly dismissive. Instead, his lordship listened to her carefully, his eyes narrowed in concentration.

"What you have said is most interesting," he told her. "I think you are right; the day is not lost yet. With your considerable influence and that of the British government, we will make a formidable alliance." Dorothea beamed with pride at this flattery and his lordship turned to me raising one eyebrow, "I trust I can rely on you to act as our…er…liaison with the countess?"

"Absolutely, sir," I agreed and grinned in delight. I was not sure, but I think I had just been ordered to try and seduce the pretty woman at my side to British influence, which was a considerable contrast to the orders he had given me in the past.

"We do have one other weapon, of course," continued Hutchinson. "Wilson." I had never considered the gregarious major as a diplomatic weapon, but his lordship went on, "He is the life and soul of any gathering and all will know him to be a passionate supporter of Russia. I will order him straight away on to St Petersburg to begin to extol the benefits of friendship with Britain."

"Is he not likely to get a little carried away?" I cautioned. "He took it upon himself to write to the tsar warning against meeting at Tilsit. When he learns of the secret clauses, he is bound to rail against them and then our actions will be seen very much as fuelled by self-interest."

Hutchinson considered this for a moment. "We will not tell him of the secret clauses. I agree he would struggle to keep them to himself, but his energy and commitment to both Britain and Russia will be invaluable. I have some despatches to write and then Kit and I will follow on to St Petersburg too and join this diplomatic crusade." His face broke into a broad grin, which did not seem at all at home on the face of the normally dour peer. He came over and took Dorothea's hand, raising it to his lips before adding, "With you at our side, my dear, we will drive back the infidels and secure the promised land."

I went away slightly disturbed by this strange change in Hutchinson's demeanour. He had picked up on Dorothea's optimism far too easily and I wondered what other schemes were whirling around in that mercurial mind. Not that I fretted over this for long, for the journey to St Petersburg would take around three weeks and promised to be a delight.

I thought we would start first thing the following morning, but countesses do not travel lightly. It was noon when I was invited to join her. As well as the coach, Lvov and the escort troopers, there was also a wagon containing half a dozen large trunks. Her maid sat up beside the waggoneer. Dorothea must have spoken to the lieutenant, for he did not look the slightest bit surprised when she invited me to join her straight away in the carriage. I was now a British captain again and thus it was not so out of place. Wordlessly, he took the reins of my mount, his expression wooden. He knew things were afoot from what he had witnessed in Tilsit, but was keeping his head down. His rank would not protect him, whereas the nobility and foreign diplomats looked after themselves.

"I suspect that my husband will be in St Petersburg," announced Dorothea, making room for me beside her on the forward-facing seat. She was wearing her blue silk low-cut gown again and smiled when she saw me admiring, if not the dress, the décolletage it revealed.

"I am not so sure," I told her. "I think I saw his mistress watching us when we left Tilsit. She is probably back warming his bed already." I was lying, I had not seen her at all, although she could well be back in favour, particularly as the Lievens had parted on bad terms. I thought that a reminder of her husband's infidelity might make Dorothea more amenable to my advances, but she looked me in the eye and grinned as though she had seen right through the ruse.

"I think," she announced, "that as we are representing our nations, we should have our own treaty, as the emperors agreed on their raft."

"A treaty for peace or for war?" I enquired.

"I was thinking of a treaty for mutual cooperation," she replied, dropping her hand to my thigh as we were jolted by a particularly deep rut in the road.

"Perhaps with our own secret clauses," I suggested, very conscious that the hand had not returned to her lap.

"Almost certainly. With march pasts and inspections of each other's forces." She giggled and added, "We might even have to give medals for exceptional service."

There was no doubt as to her meaning now and my voice became hoarse as I raised my hand and ran a finger around the neckline of her gown. "We should certainly include shared territories."

"And possibly special…accommodations," she replied.

"Will we be firing salutes for each other?

"Undoubtedly."

"And how many guns should be fired for a countess?"

Her hand moved up my trousers, "Oh, I think one should be sufficient."

Heaven knows what Lvov thought when he saw the leather screens dropping on the carriage windows, but we certainly did not waste the springs on that carriage. With Dorothea astride, I blessed every rut in the road as we bounced around in delicious ecstasy.

It took us a week to cover the one hundred and eighty miles to Riga. I was not in any hurry, for it was a delightful way to travel. The coachman was familiar with the route and the best places to stop as Dorothea had visited her father while I was away campaigning. Her two infant sons as well as a wet nurse and another maid were staying at the castle owned by the children's grandparents. The countess was recognised at every lodging house and we decided that for form's sake we would stay apart. While the countess was tended to by her maid, I would eat and drink with Lvov, who tactfully never mentioned what he must have suspected was going on in the carriage.

Riga was another old medieval town dominated by a castle that was the residence of its governor, General Benckendorff, Dorothea's father. He gave us a warm welcome, especially after his daughter shared with him news of the negotiations at Tilsit. He did not seem surprised at her ambitions to influence the court against the French. Both of her brothers were generals in the Russian army, currently serving in the south of the country. I had the distinct impression that he thought his son-in-law should have shown more backbone himself in opposing the alliance. I was treated as an honoured guest.

Welcoming though he was, I doubt the old general would have approved of Dorothea showing me a secret passage that led from my part of the castle to hers. It emerged in an alcove behind an old suit of armour just outside her room. For a jape, I thought I would wear the helmet when I knocked on her door. I removed it from the wooden stand, but the supporting frame was rotten or precariously balanced, for the whole bloody lot came crashing down. In a silent dark castle, the sound of twenty pieces of steel plate and chain mail falling from height on to a stone floor was enough to wake the dead. I scurried back down the tunnel like a rat down its burrow and remained in my room for over half an hour. I was sure all in the castle would know about the passage and I half expected a knock at the door from a suspicious father or guards now patrolling the corridors armed with shotguns. Yet to my surprise all remained quiet.

Eventually, lust overcame caution and gingerly I stepped out of my room once more. Holding a candle, I moved behind a tapestry at my end of the passage and carefully advanced. To my horror I spotted a figure waiting at the other end and hastily blew out the flame. I stood frozen in the darkness for a full minute before I realised that the other shadowy silhouette was not moving. I pressed warily on only to discover that the shadowy figure was merely the armour restored to its frame. This time I left it undisturbed; it was to be a 'knight' to remember in every sense.

Chapter 24

From Riga there were another three hundred and thirty miles to St Petersburg. It was a well-travelled road with plenty of places to stop and change or rest horses. Wilson was already well ahead of us. He was travelling in a low un-sprung *britska* carriage and claimed he did not stop between Riga and the Russian capital. It took him sixty-five hours. He arrived exhausted despite dozing at the reins. We took a far more leisurely two weeks.

Our little caravan had expanded now. Instead of one coach, one wagon and the escort, we now had an additional coach and cart for the children and their attendants. Dorothea's sons were young, just one and two years old, and showed little interest in travelling beyond wanting to pat the horses. She spent some time with them each day, playing silly games to make them laugh, but equally did not seem too upset when the maid came to take them away.

"My first child was a daughter," she explained. "I spent every day with her, but she died before she had even learned to walk. The loss nearly destroyed me. I know children often die, but it is hard when it is your first. I am lucky that my boys are healthy but to protect myself, I do not allow myself to become as attached as I was to little Marie."

We stopped at various large houses along the way, which were often half full of strangers. To avoid any hint of scandal, I would stay in my own rooms and dine with Lvov. In my British uniform, as far as anyone was concerned, I was travelling with the countess and her escort for company and protection. Yet once we were out on the open road, if her children were not with her, I would be invited into the leading carriage. Frequently, we would drop the leather screens. I once asked if she was worried that the servants looking after her children would reveal this dalliance to her husband.

"They would not dare interfere in the affairs of their betters," she replied, dismissing the notion out of hand. In this respect she had the typical arrogance of all Russian nobility, yet these people were not cowed serfs. There was a fashion for English ladies' maids then, led by the dowager empress, and I knew all too well that British servants could wreak a revenge when wronged. I well remembered being embroiled in the vengeance of my brother's maid, which had resulted in sparks where he least wanted them. Yet Dorothea had lived in grand houses and palaces nearly all her life and took the attendance of staff for granted. This was not likely to end any time soon, either, for as we approached the capital she announced that she was not returning to the apartments she shared with her husband opposite the Winter Palace. She was still annoyed with him over the Tilsit treaty and had decided that she would reside at the imperial palace at Tsarskoye Selo instead. Such was her status that she fully expected to be accepted as a royal guest without question, as indeed she was.

Tsarskoye Selo was fifteen miles south of the city and when we arrived, I saw that it consisted of several palaces in a huge park. Dorothea stayed in the one built for the Empress Catherine, and there was another constructed for Alexander nearby. I bid farewell to her there as I was keen to go on and see the Russian capital, as well as find out what Wilson had been up to.

I found my friend at the British embassy and discovered that he had already embarked on what could best be described as a diplomatic war, which was to last for the next three months. I may have been critical of Wilson's judgement earlier in this account, but his gushing praise of all things Russian stood him in good stead now. He was seen by all as a champion of Russo–British friendship and received a warm welcome from generals, princes and nearly all other influential people in the capital. Many of these were shocked by the published concessions in the treaty and the accounts they had heard of their emperor's fawning towards their erstwhile enemy.

Wilson had been far better than me at cultivating contacts within the Russian high command while we had been campaigning, and he was soon using these to open yet more doors within the city. I could see all too clearly now why Hutchinson had included Wilson on his staff. Elegantly dressed in his cavalry rig, exuding charm and a passionate appreciation for Russia, the major cut a swathe through St Petersburg society that his lordship could never emulate. Not that Hutchinson had been idle. As soon as he had learned of the secret clauses in Memel, he had sent off urgent despatches to London and for once the government had listened and acted quickly.

We had arrived in the capital in August and we had only been there a week when news came in that more British forces had arrived in the Baltic. A Royal Navy fleet and an army of thirty thousand men were anchored off Copenhagen. With the knowledge that France and Russia would soon pressure the Danes to join their alliance and use their fleet to attack Britain's navy, London had decided to strike first. The Danes had a small army, which would not be able to resist the might of either France or Russia. Their navy, however, was powerful. London could not afford for it to fall into the hands of the French. Demands were made of the Danish government to 'lend' their navy to Britain for the duration of Britain's war with France.

Cynical souls might have suggested that if Britain had shown the same resolve and provided the same forces a few months earlier to fight the French, then Friedland and Tilsit might have been avoided entirely, but it was too late for that. A few weeks later after the Danes refused all ultimatums in an attempt to preserve their neutrality, the British Navy launched a bombardment of Copenhagen. Over three hundred rockets were used, which set fires that destroyed over a thousand buildings. Fortunately, most of the civilians had already left the city. The army, commanded by Arthur Wellesley, was landed to quell any resistance and force a truce. Within days of the bombardment, the Danish fleet was in British hands. Significantly, the British fleet and army stayed on in the Baltic, just a week's sail from St Petersburg. I often wondered if it played a part in our early victories in the 'drawing room war' of late 1807, for against the odds, the British contingent was certainly winning.

One of our first triumphs was engineered by Dorothea. She had stood in the palace eavesdropping on a meeting she had arranged between the dowager empress and the tsar. "Her majesty was incandescent with fury when I told her about the planned marriage of Katya," the countess told me gleefully. "I knew she would put a stop to it and so she did." Alexander often visited his forceful mother, who had insisted on court precedence over even the tsarina. That morning he must have swiftly seen that things would not go well, for there on the table between them was the familiar silver casket, containing his father's blood-soaked shirt. "The dowager empress came straight to the point, demanding to know if Alexander had agreed to a marriage between his sister and 'that French ogre'. The tsar insisted nothing had been agreed and that the idea had merely been floated between them." Dorothea laughed, "I am sure he wondered how she had found out, but she would not let it rest. The empress made him put his hand on the casket as though it were a holy relic and swear on his own life that he would never permit such a union."

If the tsar was unaware who had revealed details of the Tilsit discussions, the Count of Lieven had more than a few suspicions. He sent his wife a furious letter accusing her of betraying his confidence and demanding that she return to their apartments. She refused, insisting that the dowager empress needed her at the palace. I was a frequent visitor at the palace myself, although I never saw the empress. I would call to see Dorothea, waiting half an hour while flunkeys found her and checked she could receive me. Then I would be led on a walk that felt like half a mile, over polished marble floors, huge, fabulously decorated staterooms and up and down stairs until, finally, she was found, usually in a small apartment on one of the upper floors. Well, when I say small, there were at least six rooms with ample space around the furniture, it just felt tiny compared to the cavernous grandeur below.

I diligently carried out my diplomatic duty of staying close to the countess – rarely have orders been obeyed with such enthusiasm. We would 'liaise' at least twice a week and it was not all work beneath the sheets. For her part, Dorothea played on the empress's hatred of Bonaparte to gain her full support for the British cause. Her palace became the second hub alongside the British embassy for anti-French sentiment.

Napoleon must have anticipated this opposition, for he sent his own agent to St Petersburg to ensure that there was no backsliding on the treaty by the tsar. This man, General Savary, was a poor choice. While Wilson used charm and gallantry to promote British interests, Savary was a dour fellow, who would preach about revolutionary principles to landowners whose wealth depended on thousands of serfs. Grand Duke Constantine, who still made a point of wearing his Legion of Honour cross, was one of the few who would receive him and even he found the general tiresome.

General Savary certainly had a thick skin I will say that for him, for he was not deterred by rejection. We hired Russian boys to follow him. They reported that time and time again he would visit members of the nobility, only to have his calling card returned to him on the doorstep and the door slammed in his face. If anyone did waver and receive him, their details would be sent to the dowager empress, who would soon summon them to point out their error. At the British embassy we had a chart listing all the leading nobles and how many times Savary had attempted to visit. We learned that he did not give up at the first attempt, but would try again a second or third time.

Even the tsar himself seemed to be succumbing to our efforts. Wilson was invited to sit beside him at a palace dinner where they spent the evening chatting gaily together. Hutchinson, who had arrived in St Petersburg at the same time Copenhagen was shelled, decided to increase the pressure. Officially we knew nothing about the secret clauses and the imminence of war between our two countries. Now was the time to remind Russia of the monetary value of an alliance with Britain. While France issued veiled threats and ultimatums, Hutchinson and the ambassador spoke secretly to the tsar's ministers about the availability of another subsidy of British gold. I knew nothing of the offer at the time, but it was well received. A Russian frigate was despatched to collect the bullion.

By the end of September, we had convinced ourselves that we were winning the diplomatic war. Wilson proudly asserted that the treaty of Tilsit was now sunk or cast adrift, much like the raft it had been discussed on. We had just returned from a ball where the tsar's sister no less had asked to dance the polonaise with him – probably in gratitude for her escape from unhappy matrimony. Dorothea had danced with both Wilson and myself too, much to her husband's annoyance. We had all played our part. Wilson's ceaseless charm and enthusiasm over the previous two months across the city had kept the nobility on side. Hutchinson's despatches had resulted in the capture of the Danish fleet and he had also helped authorise the 'carrot' of the gold shipment. My efforts were more behind the scenes and unknown to most. Through Dorothea, I had uncovered the secret clauses and scotched the marriage alliance. I suspect that I had used just as much energy as my colleagues, although much of mine had been spent in a horizontal position rather than the vertical.

Yet for all our endeavours, come October, momentum began to slip back towards the French. The first setback was a personal one, for Dorothea announced that she had been persuaded to re-join her husband in their apartment in the city. Perhaps the empress had heard of a certain British officer's regular visits to Tsarskoye Selo. She was not going to have her palace used as a knocking shop. Yet on my final visit to Tsarskoye Selo came more bad news: the tsar was now asking his courtiers to receive General Savary. Count Lieven had already entertained him, although the countess assured me that he would not be welcome when she was back. More worryingly, the tsar's mistress, Madame Narishkin, was set to welcome the French envoy into her home the following day. She was not political, she did it to please her tsar, but she was a leading socialite and where she led others followed.

Over the coming weeks the chart showing which nobles had rejected Savary gradually changed to record those who were now meeting him; although many insisted, at least to us, that they did so under duress. Then towards the end of the month a letter Wilson had sent to the tsar seeking an audience was returned unopened. The explanation given was that it appeared to be concerned with public business and so should be directed to the newly appointed and pro-French foreign minister.

"I don't understand it," complained Wilson. "Just two weeks ago we sat together over dinner and were as close as brothers."

"It is the weather," grunted Hutchinson and when Wilson still looked puzzled, he went on. "We have put our success down to our own efforts, but the Russians have also been swayed by the force at Copenhagen. They knew it could be here in a week and shelling their

234

own palaces. I hear that they have put extra men in the fortress on Kronstadt, on Kotlin Island, to guard the city. Next week will be the start of November and the Baltic will soon start to freeze up. Our forces in Denmark will head home to avoid being trapped there. They will certainly not contemplate sailing further north now."

"But Alexander cannot think we would attack him," scoffed Wilson. "I know he was disappointed that we did not help more in the summer, but we are allies. He would never expect such treachery from us."

There was a heartbeat of silence following that remark as we were all reminded that the victim of duplicity here was Wilson himself. He alone in the room was still ignorant of the secret clauses. "I think, Robert," Hutchinson spoke in a kindly tone, "we have to accept that there might have been things agreed between the emperors at Tilsit that are not in Britain's interests. Bonaparte may be using these to pressure the tsar against us."

Poor Wilson was still far from convinced of Russian mendacity when I left. I strolled over to the Neva River. The wind was bitingly cold and I pulled the fur hat I was wearing down over my ears. I had been contemplating growing a beard to keep my cheeks warm, but they had been made illegal in Russia by Peter the Great over a hundred years before. The law had been repealed, but even now beards were seen as a fashion for serfs and peasants rather than the gentry. Thank heavens I stayed clean-shaven, for it was to save me a few days later.

I walked back across the great courtyard in front of the Winter Palace to a cluster of old ministry buildings and small palaces that have now all been demolished for a new edifice built by Alexander. While the Lievens had a grand house elsewhere, I knew that they spent most of their time in St Petersburg in the apartment above the war ministry. They had managed to retain it even after Christoph lost the post of minister. Various officials were bustling backwards and forwards, coated in furs, while uniformed sentries had their hands wrapped in rags and stamped up and down to keep warm. There was a frostiness about the place now and it was not just due to the weather. I wondered how much longer we would be able to stay in the city; we

235

were certainly not as welcome as we once were. That was certainly the case when I called on Dorothea. I had hoped she would receive me and perhaps give some insight into how things were changing in court. I handed in my calling card and waited.

Half an hour came and went and then an hour. It was obvious by then that they were not even going to bother to reply, never mind admit me. Massaging my buttocks that had chilled on the stone bench I had been sitting on as I waited, I made my way back out into the cold. I was crossing a bridge over one of the canals back into the city when someone tugged on my arm. It was Dorothea's maid, who grinned conspiratorially at me and whispered, "You come with me." I thought she was taking me to her mistress, but instead she led me to a small dressmaker's workshop above a chandler's store. There she pointed me out to a rather short-sighted seamstress. The pair of them babbled away in Russian for several minutes, repeatedly looking at me. I had no idea what was happening until the maid reached into her pocket and handed me a note. It was from the countess and explained that her husband had forbidden her from meeting with any of the British delegation. She knew little of what was happening but explained that both Grand Duke Constantine and General Savary had spent a lot of time with Alexander. The note ended with an explanation of why I was there. If I needed to contact her again, I could do so via the dressmaker. Clearly the wives of St Petersburg had their own systems to get messages past their husbands. I went away with what little I had gleaned, oblivious of the fact that within the week I would be visiting the dressmaker again, and in far more urgent circumstances.

Chapter 25

Declarations of war are usually made by diplomats or by kings and princes, sometimes by armies appearing unexpectedly at the gates, but rarely in the thoughtless question of a fourteen-year-old boy. Not that we should be ungrateful, for he did Britain a great service and more importantly, gave me the chance to settle a score.

To our surprise we had been invited to take tea with Madame Narishkin. She was a kindly lady who felt responsible for our recent ostracisation from the St Petersburg social scene. "It all happened since I was persuaded to receive that foul man," she said bitterly of General Savary. "He lectured me on a woman's role in society and implied that I was some sort of courtesan," she complained. "If it were not for Alexander, I would have had my coachman box his ears."

Savary may have been deceived by the opulent palace that Madame Narishkin lived in and perhaps thought it was a gift from the tsar. In fact, she had been born a princess and she and her husband were fabulously wealthy in their own right. She might not have a title now, but she lived better than most European royalty and, unlike the tsarina, she slept with the tsar. I thought perhaps all was not yet lost. If the Frenchman had been that tedious, he might be doing our work for us. Wilson was looking pleased with himself too and just larding on some more criticism of Savary when Prince Gustav, Madame Narishkin's fourteen-year-old half-brother bowled in. I knew the lad was obsessed with joining the cavalry. He had been riding with Wilson and insisted on hearing all his tales of fighting in Austria, Egypt and even with the Cossacks. He beamed with delight at seeing his new hero and sat down beside him.

"It is my birthday in two weeks," he announced. Then he looked at Wilson and added, "Will you sell me your stallion when you leave? It will make a splendid present."

There was a split second of silence, a moment frozen in time that I recall even to this day. The boy looking expectantly up for an answer, Wilson's brow furrowing in puzzlement, but it was Madame Narishkin's stricken face that was the most revealing. Her eyes darted around the room and she positively shrank back a little when she met Hutchinson's suspicious scowl.

"Gustav, you should not ask such things," she gasped weakly.

"But you said I could have it," said the lad, looking puzzled and staring around, sensing that something was going on that he did not understand.

"Why would I be leaving in two weeks?" Wilson asked the more pertinent question, although several of us were already speculating on that.

Gustav looked like he was about to answer, but his sister held up a hand to stop him. "No. We cannot say, we *must* not say." She had gone pink with embarrassment and turned to us. "You know my position; I cannot get involved with politics. I invited you as a gesture of friendship, but I can do nothing more."

Hutchinson got to his feet, "Madame, your bond with us is most valued. We will say nothing of what happened here to implicate you." He held out his arms to incorporate his officers, "If this is to be a farewell gathering then it is for us a sad occasion, but now we should take our leave."

We stood and embraced our hosts while poor Gustav apologised, though he was still not sure what he had done wrong. Once we were alone in the hallway, Hutchinson gathered us around him. "It seems that a declaration of war is imminent," he declared.

"No, I can't believe that," whispered Wilson. "For all their friendship, the tsar would never go so far as to join with that Corsican devil."

His lordship ignored him and went on, "The young Narishkin lion has clearly overheard discussions by the tsar and his ministers. A decision has been made and we will be leaving within the next two weeks. But why the delay? Diplomats are usually expelled as soon as a decision is made." He turned to me, "Flashman, could you speak to the countess? Her husband may have kept her in the dark too, but she might have discerned something. In the meantime, the rest of us should behave normally so that no suspicion should fall on our host here."

I knew exactly where to go, yet returned to my lodgings first to change into civilian clothes. If espionage was afoot, then the scarlet jacket was far too conspicuous. Wearing a brown coat and with a fur cap pulled down low over my eyes, I emerged from the back entrance of the building and was soon scurrying away down an alley, checking behind me to ensure that I was not being followed. There was no one on my tail and so I made my way cautiously towards the dressmaker's workshop. The old woman nodded warily as I came through the door. She clearly remembered me from the week before, although we soon encountered a problem: she spoke no English and my Russian was not up to the circumstances. I was shown to a counter where there was a pen, ink and paper and invited to write a note. Without giving away Madame Narishkin, I explained that we had recently come into intelligence that we would soon be expected to leave St Petersburg. I then asked if she had heard any more. I passed the letter to the seamstress who tucked it into a pocket. Then she pulled one of her gowns into a large sleeve made of canvas to protect it from rain and mud and walked out of her workshop. It was a clever ruse, for if the count was watching his wife, he would not be alarmed if she tried on a new dress, which could be returned as if it did not fit. Most society women probably had several such visits a month.

I strolled aimlessly around the shop waiting for her return, with what I hoped would be a reply from Dorothea. I was intrigued by a box of furs including royal ermine and several pelts I could not identify. Then idly I tried the door – it was locked. With a slight chill I realised that I was trapped there. Of course the seamstress had locked the door; I tried to justify the act to myself. She would not want me wandering off and leaving her valuable stock unprotected. But what if she was in the pay of someone else? The tsar had his own secret police force who hunted down troublemakers amongst the workers. Perhaps they also used the seamstress as a spy.

I was pacing anxiously up and down the shop half fearing arrest when the seamstress returned and to my surprise she was not alone. Instead of a reply there was Dorothea's maid, who grinned and gestured for me to follow her. I soon realised that we were heading

239

back to the war ministry, although this time we were going around the back. I cursed under my breath, for the war ministry was high up the list of the places I did not want to be in at that moment. If I was found there, they were bound to suspect that we had discovered their secret. Perhaps I would be held until they were ready to expel us. Maybe they would keep me a prisoner, charged with espionage. I was damn certain that the count would not allow his wife to be used as an alibi. We passed down a narrow alley between two small mansions and emerged in a stable yard with the ministry looming in front of us. Then the maid led the way down some stairs into the basement. We passed coal stores and then the kitchens before emerging at the bottom of a narrow staircase that went up several floors. I was puffing with exertion by the time I reached the top, but there the maid held open the first room in the passage and I found Dorothea grinning at me in delight.

"Thank God you came!" She jumped up, wrapped her arms around me and stopped any reply with her lips. "Christoph has been an absolute beast," she complained and then she started to pull off my jacket, adding ardently, "I have wanted you for days."

Now, I had been missing my carnal muttons myself and I have never been a great believer in the adage 'business before pleasure'. In this case it was business *and* pleasure and so I reached behind her to undo the back of her dress. The maid had gone, yet, glancing around, I saw that this was probably her room as there was a narrow wooden bed in the corner. The mattress looked thin, but it would have to serve.

The diplomatic can be a tough life. After some frenetic disrobing, I presented my 'ambassador' to her Court of St James, or perhaps it was St Andrew of Russia. Regardless, it was well received and we were soon undertaking the art of international relations.

"Ooh yes," she gasped before continuing, "Christoph is sure war is imminent… Can you get higher…but he won't tell me anything in case I speak to you."

"We think that too…move your leg a little…ah that's it…but for some reason they are trying to keep it secret."

"I overheard them talking…go harder… It has something to do with a Russian ship at a place called Port-mouth…ah, even harder…

240

Constantine is involved...that's perfect... He has sent a man to England with a message for the ship."

"When did this man leave...? Ahhh...here, let me hold your other leg."

"Yesterday...no not too high...he is travelling through Sweden... Ooh yes..."

"So when will they declare war...? God I love it when you do that."

She giggled, "Not until next week... Will you miss me when you are gone?"

Ten minutes later and negotiations were concluded. We were wrapped together naked under the maid's coarse blanket. I certainly would miss Dorothea, yet already my thoughts were turning elsewhere. What the hell was in Portsmouth that was so important to Constantine?

"You know, you really ought to get your maid a better bed, this one is bloody uncomfortable. She could do with a thicker blanket too, I am getting chilly. There is an icy draught coming from somewhere."

"You are too soft, Olga never complains... Oh, that sounds like her coming along the passage." I slipped out from under the rough covering and pulled on my trousers. The girl would doubtless know what we were up to, but her footsteps sounded urgent, half running now. I suspected that our romantic interlude was over.

The girl knocked briefly but did not wait for an answer before she pushed the door open. You did not have to speak Russian to know that something had gone wrong. She looked worried, frightened even, and pointed out of the little window. Dorothea sat up and muttered something in Russian, which I thought was a curse and then she turned to me. "Christoph suspects you are here. They have a spy watching Lord Hutchinson's staff and they have seen you are missing. When he could not find me, he guessed we are together."

There was the sound of shouting outside and she jumped out of bed and ran to the window. Even my sudden sense of urgency to leave was slightly tempered by the sight of that lithe, beautiful body. I slid a hand around her waist as we both stared down at the scene below. A

241

company of soldiers was gathered in the courtyard. Count Lieven was standing before them and giving orders. Groups of half a dozen were being sent off in all directions, I guessed to guard bridges between his apartment and my lodgings and perhaps anywhere else he thought we might be meeting. Then he glanced up at the war ministry. Instinctively, I shrank back from the windowpane, although I doubt he would have seen me in an unlit room on the fourth floor. When I glanced back a score of men were marching towards the building's entrance.

"They will search every floor," Dorothea announced unnecessarily, "we must get you away." I was already ahead of her there. I had pulled one boot on and was reaching down for the other. "Wait," she called, and I looked up. She still stood brazenly stark naked in front of us and even at that moment, leaving such a prime piece seemed a criminal waste of an afternoon. She reached down and picked up her abandoned dress, but instead of handing it to her maid, she held it out to me. "Put this on," she commanded. "They will be questioning any men trying to leave, but not the women."

"Are you mad? I will never fit into that, I am several stone heavier than you and, well… look at me, I will never pass for a woman."

Olga the maid might not have understood English well, but she could certainly see the flaws in her mistress's plan. She turned and took from a hook on the back of the door a thick winter cloak with a fur-trimmed hood and then pushed me to one side so that she could rummage in a trunk of her possessions. Two minutes later and I was standing in a burgundy dress that gaped open at the back. They had been forced to cut part of it to get the gown on me and only some lacing stopped it from falling off my shoulders. Fortunately, this impromptu dressmaking was hidden by the cloak, which was fastened under my chin. Olga grinned as she applied some rouge to my lips and cheeks, so that I probably resembled a pantomime dame, while Dorothea urged her to hurry.

"You will have to leave by yourself," she told me. "Do you remember the way?" I nodded, earning a curse from the maid, who nearly rouged my left eye. "Olga will need to fetch me some new clothes before the search party gets here." She smiled, "I will tell Christoph I was inspecting the servant's quarters and saw that they need thicker blankets for the winter. If you get away, he will be none the wiser."

My escape looked long odds at that moment, even after the hood had been pulled over my head down to my eyebrows and I had been given a rabbit fur muff to cover my hands. But there was nothing for it but to make my way out into the passage. I headed towards the stairs while Olga ran in the other direction to reclothe her mistress, who looked rather fetching dressed in just my overcoat. Already I could hear men shouting on the floors below and the sound of hobnailed boots on the floorboards. I scurried down the narrow staircase, at one point almost falling when I stood on the hem of my dress. Holding it up with one hand, I paused on the next landing and peered through the half-open doorway. Six soldiers were working their way down a corridor towards me, opening every door and searching the rooms inside. There was not a moment to lose and so I hurried on, hoping that they would not hear my boots on the stone steps.

What would happen if I was caught? I wondered. The count must know I was sleeping with his wife. She had been living apart from him for several months, while he enjoyed the company of his mistress. He would not want her infidelity dragged into the open, but I suspected that he was more concerned about her betraying the secrets of Alexander. A former minister who had survived under the mad tsar, Christoph was a political animal, who would be aware of the rising ascendancy of the French faction at court. Dorothea had made no secret of her support of friendship with the British. Now he had to make sure they were seen as being on the 'right' side. He could certainly do that by turning over a British spy to the foreign ministry. There would be formal complaints to London and I would probably be expelled with the rest. It might be the end of my diplomatic career, but I doubted it would be any worse than that. On the other hand, men could get damn jealous over their wives. More than a few duels have been fought in such circumstances and lovers horse-whipped.

243

There was certainly no reason to dally, and I scampered down the remaining flights of stairs. These were the ministry floors and the doors to a servants' stairway, mercifully, were shut. I emerged back in the kitchen where a man was scrubbing a pile of pots. He looked up and started in surprise. I was fairly sure that he had been there when I arrived and wondered if he recognised the eccentrically made up 'woman', as the man in the brown coat earlier. He stared, mouth agape for a moment. I worried that he might raise the alarm to the other kitchen staff I could hear talking beyond some tall cupboards, but abruptly he dropped his eyes and meekly returned to his pots. To use one of Dorothea's expressions, he had decided not to interfere in the affairs of his betters. Voices sounded from above me on the stairs; soldiers would be working their way down the building and I could not afford to delay. I rushed on past the coal stores towards the back entrance to the ministry.

Four soldiers stood in the courtyard, looking bored and talking among themselves. It was just what I had been afraid of – they were hardly likely to leave the back gate unguarded. Yet how the hell was I to get past them in my poor disguise and speaking little Russian? Shouting from the direction of the kitchen indicated that I had no choice but to try. I pushed the door wide open and ran up the steps to the courtyard. Those peasants must have some strange women in their villages, for they did not seem surprised or unduly alarmed by my wildly rouged appearance. They were on the lookout for an Englishman, not an eccentrically dressed trollop. They did not even move to block my path to the street, instead they just chuckled amongst themselves and then called out an enquiry. I stopped and turned; they were watching me expectantly. Of course, I had no idea what they had said, but to not answer might raise suspicion even amongst these lax sentries. Then I realised that the world over, there was really only one question that bored soldiers asked women. I drew myself up in what I hoped was an expression of outrage and in my highest voice barked, "*Niet!*" before striding off into the street.

That was not the last proposition I received. As I hurried through the streets of St Petersburg, I am quite sure I had offers of amorous attention from two sailors and a drunk. I ignored them all while I worked out where to go. Our lodgings were clearly being watched and I was sure that by now they would have people outside the British embassy too. Had Dorothea got dressed in time? Was she even now convincing her husband that this was all a false alarm?

I could think of nowhere else to go and found myself moving back towards our lodgings anyway. We were all staying in a large, terraced house with a Mrs Lazimir, our housekeeper, who had an apartment in the basement. When I turned the corner at the end of the street my worst fears were confirmed. Another half dozen soldiers stood right outside the property, making no attempt to hide the object of their interest. I wracked my brains for a way of getting in without them noticing. Then I remembered the one time I had needed to speak to Mrs Lazimir in her part of the building. It gave me an idea.

It was not hard to look weary at the cat calls and propositions called to me as I approached the soldiers. They looked disappointed when, instead of going past them, I turned into the house next door to ours and went down the steps to the basement. I turned the door handle, preparing to put my shoulder against it if it was locked, but it opened easily. An old couple looked up curiously as I stepped into what was their parlour. They sat close to a fire where, judging from an appetising smell, their dinner was cooking in a cauldron above. I gave them a friendly smile to indicate I meant no harm and wished them a "good afternoon" in English before pressing on to the back of their property. There, as I expected was another door, leading to a yard that was separated from ours by a low fence. By the time the old couple had followed me to stare curiously after their strange visitor, I was already running up the back steps to our lodging.

"I was not expecting you here again this afternoon," growled Lord Hutchinson as he came up behind me. I paid him no heed as I was staring from behind curtains out of the front window, where a new soldier had joined the group outside. I wondered if he carried a description of an eccentrically dressed woman and was half expecting the soldiers to point to the house next door. Instead, they were turning to leave. "I will have to delay our reunion until later," continued his lordship. Then as he squeezed my right buttock through the cloak he added, "That damn fool Flashman has got himself in trouble."

"He would be in less trouble if you unhanded his rump," I muttered.

"Holy hell…" Hutchinson snatched his hand away and then his jaw dropped in astonishment as I turned to face him. "Tell me you did not walk the streets of St Petersburg looking like that? Even a dockyard pimp would set the dogs on you." I glanced in the mirror hanging on the wall and had to agree he had a point.

"When you have finished admiring my feminine charms, I have some information from Dorothea," I replied gruffly. "Then I am going to wash and get changed."

"Does she know if Alexander will declare war?"

"She is sure that war is coming," I told Hutchinson, "but Constantine is up to something. He wants to get a message to Britain before war is declared. Dorothea overheard two officers talking and thinks it has something to do with Portsmouth."

"Portsmouth!" Hutchinson repeated, looking as confused as I. "What the devil could there be in Portsmouth that would… Damn me, they are after the gold."

"Gold, what gold?" Now it was my turn to repeat his words and look confused.

"Some weeks back we offered a gold subsidy to support the Russians in their fight against the French. As far as I know it has not yet been paid, but I will wager my own weight in bullion that it is soon to sail from Portsmouth. Constantine will be trying to get their ship to sail with our coin before we hear that we are now at war. The treacherous double-dealing swine. It will reflect badly on us as I was the one to recommend the shipment. A few weeks back it seemed a good idea as Savary was being cold-shouldered by all who mattered."

I could easily imagine how annoyed the Treasury would be when they discovered that they had just funded our new enemies.

Hutchinson interrupted my thoughts. "Are those soldiers outside anything to do with you? Do the Russians know that we have learned about Portsmouth?"

"I am not sure. The soldiers have just left, but Count Lieven certainly suspects that I have tried to meet his wife. She may have convinced him that we have not spoken."

"When did Constantine's courier leave?" enquired his lordship thoughtfully.

"Yesterday. He was travelling through Sweden."

"Well then," declared Hutchinson, "it seems that there is only one thing to do. We must catch him and stop him."

"But the man has a day's head start and we have no idea which route he will take." I did not like the 'we' in his lordship's statement. I strongly doubted he would be the one risking his neck galloping through snowstorms in the night over unfamiliar terrain.

"He will have taken the coast road as it is the shortest. Wilson is good at covering long distances quickly. We will send him." I breathed a sigh of relief before he added, "If Lieven suspects you have spoken to his wife, you had better go too. It will stop him asking awkward questions."

Chapter 26

We left St Petersburg at three o'clock the following morning, when the dark streets were near deserted. Late the previous afternoon Kit had visited the British embassy to bring them up to date on developments and to arrange a carriage for our journey. They had a coachman who knew the route well. We would have to travel three hundred miles across Russia and Sweden before catching a series of ships that would take us across the Gulf of Bothnia and then down the Baltic and across the North Sea for home. I very much doubted it would be a comfortable journey.

Hutchinson had spent our final hours together stressing the importance of stopping the Russian messenger and making sure that the gold did not leave our shores. Wilson was in a fever to leave and convinced that Alexander could have no part in such diplomatic treachery. "It will be his brother," he predicted. "I dare say the villain plans to keep most of the specie for himself."

Dressed in our warmest clothes, with bundles of spare garments and possessions wrapped inside our bearskins, we made our way out of the back door of the lodgings. Kit had already checked that the path behind the terrace was not being watched and we emerged on a dingy side street. Ten minutes later we found an open-top lightweight carriage waiting outside a theatre. I cursed at the lack of roof, for it was already a cold night, but at least it was well sprung. A man stepped out of the shadows and then, to confirm he was our driver, Wilson asked him in German if he was the man from Saxony. He replied in the same language and so in haste we climbed aboard.

We had to travel north of the city through a neck of land just thirty miles wide between the end of the Baltic and a vast lake. The coachman told us that there was now a checkpoint on the main road on the outskirts of the city, but he knew side roads that would avoid it. He wanted to be past the narrowest part of the neck by dawn as in daylight there were frequent cavalry patrols. We were soon setting off at a fair clip, the sound of shod hooves on stone ringing out in the silent streets. There was a leather hood on the back of the carriage, but we kept it down so that we could keep an eye out for anyone following us. I was relieved to see that as we left the city, the road behind remained clear.

After half an hour we put out the lanterns on the coach and turned off the road onto a much smaller track. What little moonlight there was illuminated huge rocks on either side of our trail that were easily big enough to break a wheel, throw us out of the carriage and bring our venture to a premature halt. The coachman and his horses must have travelled this route before, though, for we kept up a good trot while bouncing around over numerous ruts and potholes.

Dawn found us resting the horses on a small rise that overlooked the main road. Wilson studied it through his glass and declared it clear in both directions. The coachman was satisfied with the distance we had covered. The checkpoint and narrowest stretch of land was behind us, but we still had another fifty miles to travel north before we could turn west for home. We made better progress on the main road, which was still well rutted but much wider and began to pass vehicles heading towards St Petersburg. Wilson had calculated that we might be back in England in just three weeks, which, given the time we had taken to come the other way seemed wildly optimistic. He offered to take a turn at the reins to give the coachman a rest, but the driver shook his head. "I know how hard I can work these horses," he told us. Given the impatience of his passenger, he probably suspected that Wilson would push them to lathered exhaustion.

"We don't need to go at breakneck speed," I reminded my friend. "We just need to catch up a day on the Russian. Finding the devil and then waylaying him will be the tricky part."

"But that gold could sail even without the courier's arrival," he replied. "We have no idea what arrangements are keeping it in Portsmouth."

There were several roads and they all largely followed the coast. On the second day we finally turned west and the following afternoon the driver announced that we were in Sweden. We felt a small relief at that, for we no longer had to study the road behind for signs of pursuing cavalry.

The countryside was covered in dark pine forests, lakes and scrubby countryside where little grew. The few peasants we saw must have been hard as nails and I guessed that they got much of their food from the sea. They knew that even that would soon freeze over and to that end, beside all the cottages were racks of drying fish. We had taken to asking at all the major settlements we stopped at to see if they had seen a Russian courier. Given the distance to travel, he would have been in a carriage like ours, for a riding horse would be exhausted covering forty miles a day for a week. There were few places to exchange mounts and none of quality, just some shaggy ponies. Even hurrying, he would have had to stop for the night to rest his animals. We hoped he might have had a broken axle or suffered some accident to slow him down, while fearing the same fate might befall us.

Few could understand Wilson and I when we asked, and they were wary of strangers. The coach driver had more luck as he was a familiar sight on the road. In several places they swore they had seen no such vehicle, but there were other roads the man might have taken. Yet other places confirmed that there was a Russian on the road ahead of us. He was remembered for being surly and rude as well as for being in a rush to get on his way. When we stopped at one inn for the night, we were told that our quarry had slept there the previous day. The landlord had been impressed with the thick wool coat of his earlier guest and told us that when he removed it to eat, he was wearing an army officer's uniform underneath.

It was a further four days before we reached Turku, the biggest city in the western part of Sweden, which a year or two later was to become the Grand Duchy of Finland. There was an impressive castle and a cathedral, but we had no time to explore them. It was the docks we were interested in, for it was here that we were to catch a vessel for the next stage of our journey. Having studied a map, this seemed our best chance of catching our quarry. The crossing of the Gulf of Bothnia was usually done in two stages. The first was to a harbour on the Aland Islands in the middle of the Gulf. Then a second boat was taken from there to Stockholm. At first, we thought we would find a captain to take us direct, but the locals poured scorn on that idea.

There were only two masters in the region who would attempt such a journey, and neither happened to be in port. Indeed, with a storm in the offing, we struggled to find any boat willing to set off that day at all.

Instead of gaining on our prey, it was looking like we would slip further behind, but then we met a captain called Korhonen. For thirty thalers he would take us as far as the Aland Islands, but ominously he warned that by the time we reached our destination we would probably wish he hadn't. We had no thaler coins but instead offered him silver roubles of the same weight, which he took, and only then did he show us his craft. It was a broad-beamed barge, designed for a shallow draught, such as you might see used on rivers in England. It looked a precarious vessel for the open sea, especially with a promised storm incoming. I was reluctant to board at all, but Wilson insisted.

"Come on, Flash, we have no choice," he called stepping down the gangplank. "Britain is depending on us." He was right; if we got to Britain first and stopped the shipment, we would be hailed as heroes. On the other hand, if we failed, we would be blighted as the fools who recommended gold for our enemies. With a strong feeling of misgiving, I followed him aboard.

In a straight line the distance between Turku and the Aland Island harbour was just over seventy miles. In reality it was well over eighty as there was an archipelago of rocks, islands, shallows and reefs between the two. I soon saw why the boat had such a shallow draught – the water was crystal clear and the seabed looked close enough to touch. We helped to haul up a huge gaff-rigged sail and as the icy wind came from the east, we were soon making good progress. Korhonen pointed to long poles that had been secured by cairns under the water which marked out lethal rock ledges that were hidden at high tide. He explained that it took years for masters to learn all the safe channels. With no keels and strong winds in the region, boats could easily be blown far from their planned course and had to be able to navigate around the hazards in poor weather. That was why few captains were confident to sail all the way from Turku to Stockholm. "And you would be well advised to avoid the fools that are," he

251

growled. He had a point; twice I spotted on the seabed the broken timbers of boats that had been torn apart on the rocks.

We explained that we were trying to catch up with a man ahead of us, although we did not say why. Korhonen told us that the breeze had been light the day before and so the courier might not have made much progress. The growing blow was making up for that now, though, and the boat was scudding across the waves. Our master stayed hunched over the tiller staring out for surf breaking over rocks so that he could keep his bearings. He told us that if we were past a certain rock by nightfall then we would be able to sail safely partway through the night, but if not, it would be too dangerous. Wilson urged the wind to carry us on and watched the great billowing sail. I shivered in the cold, for it was truly an icy blast. The shallow hold was only waist deep and so we were forced to remain on deck. We had soon unpacked the bearskins for warmth and huddled down against the bulwark for shelter. The shallow water we were crossing did not create big rollers, but now and then the bows would bite into a wave and freezing spray would add to our discomfort.

The captain spotted the rock he had been looking for at dusk and announced we could press on for a few more hours. By then I was so cold I had lost feeling in my feet and our fur coverings were glistening with ice. I sat there thinking that the Russians were welcome to any bloody gold they could find, just as long as I could get in front of a nice warm fire.

It was midnight when we finally heaved to. Korhonen had been forced to stop as he knew we were getting close to more rock shoals, and now flurries of snow were further hampering visibility. The white flakes moved horizontally in the wind and swirls of them whipped around the little craft like angry sprites. Our weary commander kicked us awake as we had both dozed off, and made us help him wrestle down the main sail. The canvas was frozen stiff as a board. We had to punch it to get it to fold, which made our fingers painfully numb. We dropped two anchors over the side and only a small stay sail was left to keep us before the gale. We tied another scrap of canvas over the long tiller bar and to the sides of the ship to make a rudimentary shelter and then we crawled inside. The planks were still covered in ice but it was a haven compared to the windswept deck outside.

"You look like the white bears of the north," Korhonen managed to laugh at us as he undid a small cupboard in the compass housing. I looked down to see that our fur coverings were now caked in snow, hiding the colour of the pelts beneath.

"You don't get Arctic bears this far south, do you?" asked Wilson through chattering teeth. We had heard of the great predators, and I had even seen one, albeit stuffed. It was exhibited by a man in London, who claimed to have been a seal hunter and that the bear had killed two of his companions.

"No, not here," he assured us. "Now take a swig of this to warm you and there is some dried fish if you want it." I took the spirit, but was not hungry. Korhonen spread another piece of old sailcloth over the three of us as we huddled together, letting bone-chilling tiredness consume us.

I have no idea when we woke as it was still far too cold to burrow into my clothing for my watch. The canvas roof over my head sagged from the weight of snow and there was at least six inches of the stuff all over the deck. It was daylight but visibility was not much more than a hundred yards, for it was still snowing heavily. Wilson and our captain were still fast asleep and so I slithered out from under our coverings until I was standing on the deck. The sea all around us was white. The wind had dropped from the night before, but it was still strong enough to swirl clouds of snow over the frozen surface surrounding us. I reached down with an oar to find that the sea was covered in several inches of snow and slush rather than solid ice; at least we would still be able to move through it. This explained why they used tall poles as their markers instead of buoys.

We had to wait a couple of hours for the snow to stop before we could move. Even landlubbers like us could see that we would barely survive a few minutes in that water if we were to run into a rock looming out of the blizzard. Wilson and I used the time and a couple of brooms kept for the purpose, to push the snow on the deck overboard as it was weighing down the little ship. The activity warmed us up. By the time we had finished there were hints of blue in the sky above and Korhonen called us to help pull up the anchors.

We made slower progress now, partly as we had to force our way through the floating sleet but also because the winds were lighter. We were soon picking our way through more islands. There were hundreds of them, some large enough for small settlements, others just offered grazing for some hardy goats and yet more were merely piles of unforgiving rock. By mid-afternoon, one island considerably larger than the rest appeared through the archipelago and our captain announced that we would soon be at our destination.

We were in a fever of impatience when we finally tied up on the quay and the locals stared at us with suspicion. Korhonen went ashore and swiftly discovered that the Russian courier had set sail for Stockholm earlier that morning. We were catching up on the devil! Our joy, however, was short-lived. We approached a new captain that Korhonen had recommended for the onward journey and Wilson offered him thirty thalers of silver if he set sail straight away.

"I would not set off now for a hundred thalers," he told us. "There is only an hour of daylight left and we would be surrounded by jagged rocks when it failed." Wilson dashed his hat to the ground in frustration, but the fellow just laughed at him. "You will catch your quarry tomorrow," he assured us. "His boat will have to anchor in the strait tonight and you will sleep a lot more comfortably than he will. We will leave at first light and if I am a judge," he sniffed at the air, "the winds will be stronger then too."

Thoughts of a warm comfortable bed, a roaring fire and a full belly were a persuasive argument after a night on a cold hard deck and only dried salt fish to eat. We found an inn and after we had consumed a tasty dish of lamb and a flagon of the local cider, even my companion conceded that a night ashore was not a bad idea.

Chapter 27

We were back at the harbour at first light where our new boat was waiting for us, along with a freshening breeze. The sail was soon up and once more we were on our way. Our helmsman clearly knew the route well, for we were soon weaving between the islands and then across a stretch of open sea before the coast of Sweden appeared before us. Stockholm was not on the coast directly, but behind another archipelago of islands. We must have sailed for thirty miles between them. It was dark by then but there were lights on the coast for navigation. Finally, at ten o'clock that night, we were tying up in the harbour.

It was only then that we began to seriously consider how we would waylay the courier. Hutchinson had warned us that we could not kill or seriously harm him. He did not want to create a diplomatic incident when we still hoped that Russia would break with France at some point in the future. First, though, we had to find him. We only had one night to do that, as he would probably leave again in the morning, if he had not already. It was not a big city. I reasoned that he would not be far from the docks if he wanted to travel on the next day. Our captain had pointed out the best hotel near the harbour, which he had assumed would suit our needs, and so we headed there first.

"Perhaps we can try to befriend him," suggested Wilson. "Get him drunk and leave him gagged and tied up in his room, while we get a fast ship in the morning." As he was saying this, we were momentarily distracted by an enormous blonde tart plying her trade along the harbourfront.

"Or we could pay her to sit on him until noon tomorrow," I chuckled.

We both expected that finding the courier would be our biggest challenge. He was just one man in a city. We had no idea what he looked like. He may even have been keeping a low profile, wary of being followed. All we had to go on was that he was probably Russian and had arrived earlier that day. I thought it would take all night, especially as neither of us spoke Swedish and few locals understood

English, although we had more luck with Wilson's German. In the event, it took us less than five minutes. Five thalers in silver got us into the best hotel, rooms for the night and the intelligence that six other single guests had sought rooms that day. For an extra coin the clerk was most informative. Two of the guests were known to him and having affairs out of sight of their wives. Three of the other four were at that moment in the hotel dining room. We made our way there and stood just outside the door studying those inside. Almost at once I spotted a familiar face and swore softly under my breath.

"What is it?" asked Wilson, peering in the direction I was looking.

"Over there, the chap in the brown suit, that is one of Constantine's officers. He has to be the courier."

"Are you sure?"

"Yes, and he knows me. In fact, he would dearly like to kill me given the chance."

As we watched, the man turned away the approach of one of the 'hostesses' in the hotel, who would keep a single customer company for a consideration. I also noticed that on his table there was a carafe of water to go with the one of wine. It did not look like we would be able to exploit any vices to waylay him. Colonel Metchnikoff must have sensed our inspection, for he suddenly turned in our direction. I ducked out of sight just in time, while Wilson concentrated his attention on a notice detailing the evening's menu.

"Let's get out of here," I whispered. "We don't want him to recognise us before we have a plan." We made our way to a tavern a few doors down the street. A rougher establishment where the 'hostesses' were far more explicit about the transactions involved.

"We are not allowed to kill him, he is not getting drunk and he is turning away women. The man is clearly on his guard, perhaps expecting someone to stop him, and to cap everything he both knows and hates you. How the hell are we supposed to stop him?" Wilson poured us both a drink from the bottle just placed on the table and gave a heavy sigh. "I suppose we could try to bribe the master of the next boat he takes, but we have no way of knowing which one that will be."

256

We sat drinking in silence for a while as we pondered our dilemma. I found myself watching a pretty young girl who was sharing a table with a huge fellow the size of a bear. She was matching him drink for drink and while his eyes were becoming glassy from the liquor, the girl seemed unaffected. A man with a fiddle had started a tune and the hostess stood up and held out her arms as though she wanted to dance. Her companion stared at her, frowning in confusion, and then struggled up onto his feet. He swayed like a tree in a gale for a moment before crashing down to measure his length on the planking. It was clearly a common occurrence as two barmen dragged the fellow into the back of the establishment, where doubtless he would be stripped of his valuables and then left somewhere else to recover. Wilson looked around at the disturbance and then exclaimed, "Damn, we have come so far but there are so many obstacles."

Suddenly I grinned. "To misquote an old friend," I told him, "we have to turn those obstacles into advantages. I think I know how to nobble our friend, but first I need to have a word with that girl over there."

A few minutes later I was strolling back into the hotel, a bottle in my hand and a little unsteady on my feet. I winked at the porter to show all was well and staggered off into the dining room. "Colonel Metchnikoff, is that you?" I called loudly from the door. "What on earth are you doing here?"

The colonel looked up in surprise and then his eyes narrowed in suspicion. "More to the point, what are *you* doing here? I thought I caught a glimpse of you earlier, and a man looking very much like Major Wilson."

"Oh yes he is here too," I waved a hand airily over my shoulder and continued to walk to his table. "Between you and me," I confided, as I pulled out a chair to sit uninvited at his table, "things aren't going well for the British now in St Petersburg. We thought we would leave before we were kicked out anyway."

"I did not ask you to join me, Captain, and I have no wish for your company. I have sworn to seek satisfaction after our earlier encounter.

It is only the fact that I am currently on duty that prevents me from shooting you now."

"Oh, you mean when I left you bare-arsed," I laughed, deliberately goading him. "And what duty are you on, checking out the best knocking shops in Sweden?"

His lips tightened in fury. "One day, sir, we will meet when I am not under the obligations of duty and then I will make you pay for that remark."

I chuckled again. "You know full well we are unlikely to cross paths again. You are probably counting on it with this 'duty' excuse."

"What are you suggesting, sir?" Metchnikoff's face had flushed red with fury now as he understood I was questioning his courage.

"We can settle this now if you want, and with no great jeopardy to your precious duty." I pointed to the half full carafes on the table, "You have been drinking vodka and wine this evening and I have a fair bit on board too." I held up my bottle. "The tavern down the road sold me this local firewater. They say it is the strongest brew you can buy. I say we share it and whoever is standing at the end is the victor. You can carry on with your duty – if you have one then – albeit with a sore head."

"I am not drinking with the likes of you," Metchnikoff spat. He gave me a look of utter scorn and I just grinned back.

"I thought so. You are either a coward or scared of being out drunk by an Englishman." I got up then and deliberately contrived to hook my leg between those of the chair, knocking it over.

"Wait," I heard him hiss in suppressed rage. I knew I had him then and half turned, unsteadily, pulling the chair back upright as he signalled for two clean glasses. "Know this," he whispered as they were put before us. "When I win, I will have you dragged out into the street and I will shoot a ball through your head myself."

"That don't seem very sporting," I told him, "but each to their own. In that case, when I win, I am going to set fire to your trousers again, perhaps this time with you in them." I carefully filled the glasses and raised my own to my lips. "Cheers, old chap," I called before taking a swig.

I messed up slightly pouring that first glass, for the bottle was full. The spirit burned my throat and I gasped with surprise, but I knew it was nothing to the shock coming for Metchnikoff. It was the bottle I had seen being used at the inn. There are several names for it but the one I know is the Portsmouth pottle. Essentially, it is two glass bottles blown into the one mould, usually with the label hiding the join. Hundreds of landsmen have shared a companionable drink from a Portsmouth Pottle only to find themselves at sea the next morning with a sore head. My half was filled with water but some of the spirit from the other half had splashed into my glass. Even diluted it was enough to make you shudder. I shook my head as though I could not believe what it was doing to me. Then I took a deep breath and downed the rest of my goblet. "Your turn," I croaked.

Metchnikoff smiled with contempt. He picked up his glass and downed it in one. I watched him in astonishment. For a second I thought I had been gulled and the innkeeper had filled both sides with a dilution. Then I noticed that his knuckles around the glass were turning white and his eyes were watering. He hurriedly put down the goblet and wiped away a tear that was starting to form.

"It is strong stuff, isn't it," I muttered as I carefully filled both of our glasses again, this time making sure that I only got the water. "Now watch how an Englishman drinks." I pretended to try and down mine in one too but deliberately failed and spat some back. I paused, breathing heavily for a moment, and then gulped the rest down. I remembered to clench my own knuckles as I looked expectantly at the Russian.

Metchnikoff looked down at his glass with the same anticipation that Socrates must have felt for his hemlock. But he was committed now and could not back down. Even though he knew what was coming, to my surprise he once more emptied his glass in one attempt. This time, though, he swayed in his chair and gulped slightly as though some of the spirit was trying to come back up. His hand was shaking as he put his glass back down on the table. Beads of sweat broke out on his brow as he watched me refill both of our goblets again. As far as he was concerned this was a fight to the death and his confidence of

259

an easy victory had now evaporated. I picked up my glass and looked him squarely in the eye before giving a nod and then gulping all of it back. "It is getting easier now," I gasped, "Or perhaps I am more used to it."

Now Metchnikoff had to hold the glass in both hands and I wondered if he would be able to drink at all. Several people on the next table were now watching us. I saw some coins get passed across the table as they wagered on the outcome. The colonel, however, was oblivious, his attention fixed only on the liquid before him. He took two swallows this time in quick succession and then let out a small wail as though his insides were being burned.

I wanted to bring things to a conclusion and so this time after I had poured again, I staggered up to my feet. I deliberately swayed a little and held on to the table as I reached forward for the glass. "We do this one standing up," I announced, adding, "if you can." Then I swallowed my water down, to a round of applause from the table next door. All eyes were on the colonel now, and the whole dining room had gone quiet. Wilson and the hotel clerk stood in the doorway as Metchnikoff stared at that glass before him. His chair scraped the floor as he pushed it back. He leaned on the table to pull himself up, forcing me to push down on my side to stop it toppling. He was upright, frowning in concentration as he reached forward for his drink. There were titters of amusement from the diners as he missed at his first attempt – God knows how many glasses he saw swimming before his eyes. Then he grabbed it and in one smooth movement, tipped the contents down his throat. There was the briefest of pauses and then his eyes rolled up in his head. Like a falling tree, he toppled backwards, making no effort to break his fall.

"Quickly," I called to Wilson, "get him up to his room." My companion and the clerk rushed forward and hauled Metchnikoff up between them. I was going to help before I remembered I was supposed to be intoxicated too. I picked up the bottle – it would not do for that to fall into the wrong hands – and staggered after them. There was more applause as I left, pretending to grip the stair banister like a long-lost friend.

We gave the clerk another thaler of silver and told him not to wake Metchnikoff until late the following afternoon. As soon as we were alone, I told Wilson to remove the colonel's trousers while I searched his luggage for his uniform trousers and another pair he carried.

"Why are we taking his clothes?" asked Wilson.

"Come with me and you will see," I told him, leading the way down the back stairs and into the street. I still had my bottle with me and holding my thumb over the half with the water I tipped the spirit over the garments now piled on the snow. A moment with my tinderbox and some burning wadding was added to the mound. We both stepped back as a blue flame leapt up into the air. It danced over the clothes like a ghost, giving off a fierce heat. "I doubt friend Metchnikoff will be in a fit state to travel tomorrow," I crowed, "but if he is, he will need to buy some new kit first." I could not help grinning at the thought of the colonel waking the next day. I could not imagine the scale of the hangover, but on top of that was the thought of being outdrunk by an Englishman and then the indignities done again to his wardrobe. I was still laughing as I hurled my Portsmouth pottle far out into the darkness, hearing it splash into the harbour.

Chapter 28

We had a choice for the next stage of our journey. The local Royal Navy squadron was no longer welcome in Denmark. To avoid getting caught in the ice, it had moved its anchorage to Gothenburg, where it could still patrol the entrance to the Baltic Sea. We could reach Gothenburg by road from Stockholm, cutting across the southern part of western Sweden. It was a journey of two hundred and fifty miles over some rough roads. The alternative was a sea voyage of three times that distance, including the narrow straights between Sweden and Denmark that we had nearly foundered in before. One glance at the frozen and choppy harbour and we were heading for the stables where we could hire a carriage and driver for our onward travels.

"How bad was that drink?" asked Wilson. We sat huddled under bearskins as the carriage rattled out of the city. It was already bouncing wildly on the frozen ruts in the road, causing us to hang on to the sides.

"I only tasted a diluted version, but it was enough to make you gasp," I admitted. "That huge timberman in the inn only managed three glasses. I was astonished that Metchnikoff swallowed four. I was not pouring small measures."

"Perhaps we are lucky he is still alive," suggested Wilson, who had checked on the Russian before we had left that morning and reported back that the colonel was still snoring loudly. I doubted he would be in a fit state to consider a wildly pitching carriage until tomorrow at the earliest and even then, there was no guarantee of a ship for him in Gothenburg. He might prefer a voyage to Elsinore, whose normally crowded harbour would offer more chance of a ship willing to take a Russian passenger to England.

To this day I have no idea how or even if Metchnikoff made the next stage of his journey, but I do know he could not have done it quicker than us. The road between two of Sweden's biggest cities was well travelled if not well maintained. There were coaching inns along its length and several offered replacement horses. Our bones were so jolted by the penultimate day that we abandoned the carriage and rode the last thirty miles on horseback. As we galloped down the final hill into the town, we were rewarded with a glimpse of the anchorage there and three Royal Naval ships swinging from mooring cables in the middle of it. After all the miles we had covered from St Petersburg, it felt like we were almost home.

Captain Ellis was pleased to receive us aboard his ship the next morning, and even more delighted with our news. While to us the imminent war was a disappointment, to him it offered the enticing prospect of more prizes and wealth. "If you are certain they will declare against us," he announced, "we can take Russian ships completely by surprise. The first they will see of their own country's announcement is when they are back here under our flag of capture. Two fat Russian merchants sailed past here yesterday." He grinned wolfishly and I'm sure was already calculating their value to him in his head. I brought him back to the matter at hand by reminding him of our requirements. "I can let you have the *Snipe*," he told us. "She is only a gun brig, but she is fast. I will impress on Lieutenant Champion, her commander, the need to get you to London without delay.

Wilson, who was apprehensive about going to sea again, was even more nervous when he saw HMS *Snipe*. She was half the size of the ship that had brought us from England, having only twelve guns, although I reassured him that she was bigger than the ship I had sailed aboard in the Mediterranean. Still, there was a grim inevitability to what happened next as Wilson's curse struck again. As soon as we were past the southern tip of Norway, a south-westerly started to build. Lieutenant Champion had the sails harness as much of the wind as he dared and we fair scudded across the sea towards England. But it was carrying us north and he soon admitted that unless we waited to ride out the storm, we would not make landfall in London. Wilson just wanted to be ashore as soon as possible and so we urged him to continue to run before the wind. I just hoped we would not end up in the Orkneys.

Champion looked nervous as we approached the coast. We were not entirely sure where we were as he had not been able to use the sextant since we had been off Norway. He confided that back in February that

263

year the *Snipe* had run aground and sixty-seven passengers and crew had drowned. I decided not to share this intelligence with Wilson…

We made landfall and put ashore at the town of Scarborough on the thirtieth of November 1807, having set off from St Petersburg on the eighth of that month. You would think after such an ordeal a man would be entitled to some rest, but no. A post-chaise carriage was hired and in a matter of minutes we were on our way again on the London road. Wilson was in a fever to get to Canning, the Foreign Secretary, and would allow no rest until we arrived in the capital. I had tried to persuade him to drop me off in Leicestershire, but he insisted that we arrive together as I could corroborate what I had learned from Dorothea.

It was three o'clock in the morning on the second of December when we finally drew up outside the foreign ministry. Of course, Canning was not there, but Wilson demanded his home address, announcing that it was a matter of international importance. Off we went again arriving at half past three outside a sizeable town house. I had given up trying to convince him that we should return at a more civilised hour.

"We cannot afford to waste a second," he claimed. "For all we know Metchnikoff might have docked in London already." He hammered at the door, bawling up for someone to answer, yet the windows remained stubbornly dark and shut. Others didn't, though, and one shot open on the other side of the street. An apoplectic old codger leaned out to warn Wilson that if he did not desist that instant, he would have a pack of dogs set on him. I had stayed in the chaise, in part because I was exhausted and just wanted to sleep and now to also avoid any canine visitors. Eventually, someone in the Canning household decided to act to prevent a riot among their neighbours. "Come on, Flashman," my companion called, "I can hear them unbolting the door."

I stepped down just in time to come face to face with an angry old man as the portal was thrown open. "What the devil are you about, sir?" he demanded. It was not Canning, as the man had a full head of hair, and realising this, Wilson pushed past him.

"I do not have time to explain," he shouted over his shoulder as he made for the stairs, "I must see the minister at once." I went after him, reassuring the old retainer as I went past that we were both British army officers on urgent business.

There was a scream as I reached the top of the stairs and Wilson emerged flustered back on the landing muttering, "Wrong room."

"What the deuce is going on?" The voice came from beyond Wilson and I saw the light from a wall candle reflect off a bald pate.

"Sir, we apologise for the intrusion, but we bring urgent news from Russia," I started to explain. As Canning stepped towards us, I noticed that he had a lit candlestick in his left hand and a loaded pistol in his right.

"I am Major Robert Wilson," my fellow intruder introduced himself.

Canning looked over his shoulder at a woman now standing in the doorway from which Wilson had previously emerged. "I will deal with this," he said sternly. The minister turned his gaze back to me, "I know you, don't I?"

"We had dinner a few years ago at Castlereagh's," I admitted.

"And you did some work for Wickham," he finished, lowering the pistol. "Well, you had better come with me," he muttered, leading the way back down the passage to his room. "And this had better be worth getting me out of bed, disturbing my family and half the street."

He listened to our tale without interruption, sitting on his bed, his pistol discarded on the coverlet. "But the last I heard from Hutchinson, you were being received by the tsar and all seemed to be going well, despite those clauses in the treaty at Tilsit."

"I am sure that Alexander is not behind this, sir," stated Wilson emphatically. "This will be his brother Constantine's work. He has been suborned by the French and is now completely under their influence. We overtook one of his couriers on the way here, who wanted to get the news to their people before it reached ours."

Canning's large brow furrowed at this and he looked first at Wilson and then at me. I shook my head almost imperceptibly to indicate that my companion was unaware of the secret clauses. I had thought of

265

telling him on our journey, but I knew that he would struggle to believe that his saintly Alexander would be capable of such treachery. It would have soured the rest of our trip with arguments and recriminations.

Wilson continued hopefully, "Do we still have the gold, sir?"

"Yes, it is at the docks in Portsmouth, as is a Russian frigate waiting to take it away. Their ambassador has been pressing urgently for its release for a while now. He wanted their ship to sail before the Baltic froze, the route via the Black Sea being considerably longer." Canning smiled, "I confess, Major, that I do not entirely share your faith in Alexander. I was waiting to see if their mood changed once they knew that our fleet, which had bombarded Copenhagen, could no longer reach St Petersburg."

"So our gold is safe," I concluded, feeling a sense of relief. Our diplomatic mission had not turned into an embarrassing shambles after all. Hutchinson and our ambassador could return home without being scorned for funding our new enemies.

"Not only that," added Canning, grinning, and reaching out for a bell pull. "I can now send a courier to Portsmouth to seize a Russian frigate for our navy."

Historical Notes

Many of the place names have changed since the time the book was set. Both Flashman and Wilson used contemporary names in their accounts and to help you follow the progress of the tale on a map, the following information may prove useful:

- Danzig is now Gdańsk
- Eylau is now Bagrationovsk, named for General Bagration
- Friedland is now Pravdinsk
- Konigsberg is now Kaliningrad
- Memel is now Klaipeda
- Pillau is now Baltiysk
- Tilsit is now Sovetsk

I am indebted to a range of sources for confirming the information in Flashman's accounts. In this case the detailed books *Crisis in the Snows* and *Napoleon's Triumph* by James R Arnold and Ralph R Reinertsen were invaluable, bringing together various contemporary sources. In addition, there are the published works of Wilson himself, which give a colourful picture of his personality and the life endured in Russia. These feature his calamitous luck with sea travel including the near shipwreck which opens this account. His views on the general military and political situation were, however, heavily biased in favour of the Russians, possibly with a view to having his work endorsed by Tsar Alexander. Other biographies on Wilson by Michael Glover and Ian Samuel were also helpful. The biography of Dorothea Lieven by Judith Lissauer Cromwell was also vital in detailing the early career of this extraordinary lady.

Prussian War 1807/8

The causes, principal events and outcome of this campaign were all as described by Flashman. Prussia had been reckless in going to war with France and relying on outdated tactics. Its resulting catastrophic defeats at Jena and Auerstedt left the Prussians relying on support from Russia for their very survival. The winter campaign of 1807/8 was a test of endurance for all armies involved. As Flashman

267

describes, thousands of men were lost to frostbite or exhaustion on top of those lost in combat. The battle at Eylau was a brutal affair, much of it fought at close range and in the snow. Casualty estimates vary wildly, but there is little doubt that it was one of the bloodiest battles ever to that point. Many of the wounded, who might have otherwise survived, also perished due to the weather and lack of medical attention.

Marshal Bertrand really did visit Friedrich Wilhelm in disguise after the battle to sound the Prussians out on a separate peace. Following this approach, the Prussians sent an officer to Bonaparte's headquarters to explore what terms were available. However, news of these negotiations leaked, which angered both the French and the Russians.

Flashman also gives an accurate account of affairs around Danzig and the Spring campaign that culminated in the battle of Friedland. General Hutchinson really was in the Friedland church tower and warned Bennigsen of the danger his army was in. The Hanoverian dared not risk another premature retreat with his command on the line and no decisions were made until it was too late. This spectacular victory broke the Russian army and left the Prussians and Russians with little alternative but to sue for peace.

Treaty of Tilsit
The initial meetings of Tsar Alexander and Napoleon took place as described on a raft in the middle of the Niemen River. The French emperor set out to charm his fellow monarch. He apparently succeeded in converting an erstwhile enemy into a new ally to assist in isolating Britain. However, Alexander's commitment to the alliance is debatable. He was certainly capable of dissembling. This was, after all, the man who had dined with his father while fully aware that Tsar Paul was to be deposed and probably killed later that evening. Convincing Napoleon of his friendship would be no great difficulty, but Alexander had to be aware of how great a challenge it would be to sell this new alliance to his court. While territorial concessions were made, little other assistance was offered to France. Within two years Russian

merchants were ignoring the continental blockade and trading with Britain again. This led to the disastrous French invasion of Russia in 1812 that fatally weakened France's ability to defend itself from its enemies.

There were secret clauses in the treaty as described. While Wilson's memoirs make it clear he was unaware of them, there is considerable evidence to indicate that Britain's foreign secretary, George Canning, did know of their existence a short while after the treaty was signed. There has been much debate amongst historians on how this information leaked, some speculating that there was a spy hidden on the raft and a few even suggesting it was Wilson himself. It is highly unlikely that there was a spy on the raft and there is evidence that most of the detailed negotiations took place on the French riverbank later. Certainly, the spy was not Wilson, for he would undoubtedly have boasted of such an achievement in his memoirs, rather than feigning ignorance.

The 'drawing room war' in St Petersburg largely took place as described. Young Prince Narishkin inadvertently let slip that diplomatic relations were about to be broken off in a prelude to war. It was then learned that a Russian courier was on his way to Britain with advance news of hostilities. Wilson was despatched to overtake and delay him, which he did in Stockholm. The timings of the journey quoted by Flashman match those in Wilson's account, as does the description of arriving at Canning's home in the early hours of the morning and briefing the minister in his bedroom. As a result of this intelligence, a Russian ship was indeed later seized in Portsmouth.

Sir Robert Wilson

While an enthusiastic self-publicist, Wilson is not a well-known historical figure despite an extraordinary career. After the activities described in this book, he was given the command of the Loyal Lusitanian Legion, a force of Portuguese émigrés and British officers that he took back to fight in the Peninsular War. (See *Flashman in the Peninsula* where Flashman and Wilson's paths cross again.) He was given the rank of Brigadier General in the Portuguese service and

269

much to Wellington's irritation, saw himself as an equal. Wilson was convinced that a small force skilfully commanded could do as much damage to the enemy as a large one.

In 1809 while the British army was being driven out of Spain at Corunna, Wilson deceived both his Spanish allies and the French as to his real strength (approximately one thousand men). As a result, the Spanish were persuaded to defend one fort while his Legion held another. Consequently, an army of nine thousand French soldiers were stopped in their tracks. The Legion later stopped a similar sized force commanded by Marshal Victor at the Alcántara Bridge.

When Wellington beat the French at Talavera, Wilson exceeded his instructions and came close to liberating Madrid, although such freedom would have been short lived, as he was almost trapped by approaching French forces. Wellington did not appreciate his officers exceeding their instructions and animosity grew between the two officers, leading to Wilson returning home.

He spent time writing memoirs and then in 1812 was offered the role of military attaché in Constantinople. Turkey was then at war with Russia and Wilson worked to help secure a truce so that Russian forces could be released to face the invading French. He then, without orders, made his way to St Petersburg (fighting alongside old comrades such as Bennigsen and Bagration at Smolensk on the way) to renew his friendship with the tsar. When the French army was forced to retreat after its capture of Moscow, Wilson joined the Russians in their pursuit of the invader. He remained with them throughout the fighting in Russia and Prussia, where he won more acclaim from allied governments for his counsel and courage on the battlefield.

His habit of sharing intelligence both with members of the British government and with his friends in the opposition, did not, however, earn him credit at home. In 1814 he was given a new and less important posting in Italy, before returning to England after Napoleon's abdication. He became a military adviser to the Whigs but after Waterloo Wellington and the Tories were in the ascendancy and he could see that no new opportunities would be forthcoming. He moved to Paris with his wife and family. What happened there is covered in the following short story: *Flashman's Christmas.*

Following those events, Wilson was no longer welcome in France and returned to London and eventually became a Member of Parliament. He was a radical, championing various unpopular causes. Yet he got in the most trouble by attending the funeral of Queen Caroline, the estranged wife of George IV. A riot had broken out as the cortege went through the streets and Wilson was instrumental in stopping the escort of soldiers firing at the crowd. He was accused of interfering with the soldiers in the execution of their duty and was summarily dismissed from the army.

A civil war broke out in Spain in 1823 when France sent a force into the country to support the king against those who wanted a more liberal constitutional monarchy. Britain remained neutral, but Wilson went to Spain and was soon appointed an officer in a local constitutional militia. He was shot in the leg and while recovering became involved in an ugly dispute with the local British envoy, making promises to the Spanish government that he had no right to make. Returning to Britain he gradually became less radical and was even reconciled with Wellington. He was readmitted into the army and in 1842 was appointed Governor of Gibraltar. He died in London in 1849 and is buried at Westminster Abbey.

Dorothea, Countess (later Princess) Lieven

Flashman is the only source to place her at Memel during the signing of the Treaty of Tilsit. She was, however, known to be deeply opposed to the treaty and took her children to live at the palace at Tsarskoye Selo to avoid any of the festivities arranged to celebrate the treaty in the capital. Later that year her husband resigned his commission in the army and joined the ministry of foreign affairs. Initially appointed back to Prussia, the count was rather dull and lacked any diplomatic flair. Fortunately, Dorothea more than made up for these shortcomings. She was soon drafting his despatches and reports. Her lively, if snobbish, personality made her a centre of the social scene where she expertly extracted useful information. In 1812 the count was appointed Russia's ambassador to Britain, a post he held until 1834. It was soon evident in London that the countess had at least as much influence as her husband and many referred to them as the 'two ambassadors'. Certainly the tsar thought so as he once wrote to his foreign minister Nesselrode stating, "It is a pity Countess Lieven wears skirts, she would have made an excellent diplomat." Little did he realise that she was already an excellent diplomat and used her skirts to good effect. It is likely that she took several influential lovers while in London, although claims that she replaced them after every cabinet reshuffle are an exaggeration. She also had a very close friendship with Metternich, the Austrian chancellor.

She did not want to return to Russia when her husband was recalled and it was there that they met tragedy in the death of their two youngest sons from scarlet fever. She left Russia and settled in Paris where she continued to influence international affairs, particularly during the Crimean War. She died in Paris in 1857.

John Hely-Hutchinson, second Earl of Donoughmore
Hutchinson was born into a wealthy Irish family in 1757 and joined the army in 1774. While he travelled the continent and studied at the Strasbourg Military Academy, he does not seem to have been a particularly inspiring commander. This is probably because he was generally irascible to all those about him and was notoriously untidy in his appearance. Several of his fellow senior officers attempted to block his command in Egypt. While Hutchinson certainly lacked an engaging demeanour, he made up for it with his strategic understanding and common sense. Consequently, he forced the French to surrender at both Cairo and Alexandria.

Hutchinson met Wilson in Egypt and their strange friendship continued after their adventures in Prussia. Their surviving correspondence shows that while his lordship occasionally sent heartfelt notes of congratulation, he rarely missed an opportunity to scathingly criticise Wilson's optimism. Clearly, Wilson knew him well enough not to take offence and valued his sage advice. After their adventures in Prussia, Hutchinson retired back to Ireland and died there in 1832 aged seventy-five.

Flashman's Christmas

Chapter 1

Our worst fears were confirmed when we saw a company of soldiers forming up on the wet cobbles, stamping their feet against the early morning chill. They stood outside the Luxembourg Palace, which despite its name was in the centre of Paris. It had over the previous few days served as a courtroom and a prison. The guilty verdict had only been announced at midnight and the sentence of death had come as no surprise. The whole thing had been a sham, rigged from the start, and the prisoner did not stand a chance. I had been one of those to speak for the defence. I had helped to destroy the false testimony of the chief witness for the prosecution, a man even the Prussian, Marshal Blücher had dismissed as a 'shit'. It did no good, for the main legal defence was ruled out as a technicality. When the defence lawyer, in desperation, tried to declare that the prisoner could not be tried for the charges as by birth he was not French, his own client overruled him. "I fought as a Frenchman and I will die as a Frenchman," he growled, proving that he at least had little doubt as to the outcome.

It was the seventh of December, 1815, nearly six months after Waterloo. The royalists were wreaking their revenge on those who had supported Bonaparte. Ironically, their initial efforts had been led by Joseph Fouché, a man who had signed the old king's death warrant and who had for years been minister of police under Napoleon. But as those who have read my earlier memoirs on the Waterloo campaign will know, that wily devil was a master of playing both sides. He had seized control of the country after the battle and blackmailed some royalists to secure his old job under the returning king. Then to prove his loyalty to the new regime, he had launched a persecution of his old comrades. Top of his wanted list was the prisoner.

I had only met the man that March, although I had faced him in battle several times. He had even ridden past me once in Spain when I had been disguised as a Polish lancer. Heaven knows how we formed a bond, for we are complete opposites. I am a craven coward with little sense of honour and a passion for self-preservation. Marshal Ney on the other hand was the most courageous man I know, with an immense sense of pride to serve France and, to his cost, very little understanding of the strategies and schemes of others.

Some Bonapartists blamed him for the defeat at Waterloo, although he was not alone in that responsibility. The royalists blamed him for changing sides when he was sent to arrest Napoleon. They had been shocked at how easily the country had abandoned the king and were determined that such a thing would not happen again. This meant making an example of the traitors. Several had been executed already and many others had fled the country. Ney had also made plans to leave, but had delayed too long. He had been forced to go into hiding as a wanted man and some rogue had betrayed him. He had been a dead man ever since he had been caught; it was only the timing and manner of his death that was in doubt. Now even that was known: he was to be shot. While he might have hoped for a few days to finalise his affairs, the royalists wanted the matter over and done with quickly.

"The princess has gone to the palace to make a final appeal for clemency," Colonel de Briqueville confided, glancing up at the sky. "By the time the king rises to see her, it is likely to be far too late."

Ney had accrued an array of titles under his emperor, the most senior of which was Prince of Moscow. They seemed a hollow mockery now and most royalists ignored them, but my companion always gave his marshal due honour. Ney had saved his life, crawling over brittle ice to pull him from a river. In return de Briqueville would be loyal to the end.

The colonel had nearly lost his life again recently. His dragoon regiment had been mauled by the Prussians after Waterloo, and he had taken sabre cuts to the head and right wrist. Even then, months later, he wore a leather cap to protect his skull and had wooden splints on his arm. We had served the marshal together earlier that year. It was de Briqueville who had begged me to return to France to be a witness in the trial. I had known it would be a waste of time and had sworn after the battle in June never to leave the shores of Britain again. Yet for all that, it was an appeal I could not ignore. Ney had saved my life too;

this was the least I owed him. We had given evidence, watched the trial and tried to comfort the princess. Yet as a black carriage emerged from the palace and the soldiers formed around it, we knew it had always been leading up to this moment.

There were not many spectators for this final act, maybe a score of men, including a Russian general who rode his horse alongside the procession. Perhaps more were waiting at the Plaine de Grenelle where the executions normally took place, but the carriage headed in the opposite direction across the Luxembourg gardens. We fell silently in step at the back of the crowd, listening with disgust to the excited chatter of several royalists about us. They crowed about the death of a traitor when they were not fit to lick his boots. At least they ignored us and left us alone – perhaps some remembered our participation at the trial.

In no time at all the carriage was coming to a stop in front of a large wall at the edge of the park. The final journey was already over. Ney emerged wearing a long dark overcoat and a top hat. He must have been refused permission to die in uniform. A priest stepped out of the carriage next, which surprised me as the marshal had never struck me as a religious man. Yet the condemned prisoner stood with his head bowed as the cleric gave him a final blessing. As Ney raised his head again, he reached into his pocket, took out his purse and handed it to the priest. Then, almost as an afterthought, he smiled and unhooked his watch and passed that over too. Stripped of all valuables, he strolled calmly to stand in front of the wall.

"Come," called de Briqueville, "we should stand near the front so that he sees he has some friends here." Most of the soldiers were forming up to make three sides of a square with the wall as its final face. Inside with Ney were a dozen men of the firing squad, two officers and the priest, who had now fallen to his knees where the marshal could see him. We stood between the soldiers forming the perimeter and I saw the marshal run his eyes along the watching crowd. When his gaze met ours, he gave a brief nod of recognition. I felt absurdly relieved that he knew he was not surrounded by enemies. He could take comfort that at least some witnesses would report he had died with courage. There was not a hint of fear on his features, but then he was not known as the 'bravest of the brave' for nothing. An officer stepped forward with a blindfold, gesturing that the prisoner should kneel to meet his end. I heard Ney growl that he would stare death in the eye and remain standing on his feet.

I found myself wishing that he had died at Waterloo. Heaven knows he gave the Grim Reaper enough chances to carry him off. Five horses had been killed under him that day and yet he emerged without a scratch. I have often scorned those who talk of a noble death – it is rarely any such thing. There is nothing noble about screaming in blood-soaked agony on some foreign field. Yet given his career, meeting his end in combat would have been far more fitting than this squalid affair.

The remaining officer began to give the orders for the firing squad to prepare and take aim. Ney interrupted, his voice ringing out loud and clear across the square. "Soldiers, when I give the command to fire, shoot straight at my heart. Wait for the order, it will be my last to you. I protest against my condemnation. I have fought a hundred battles for France and not one against her…"

The senior officer who had looked nervously about as Ney began to give his speech, now gestured to his junior to give the final order. He must have been under instructions to ensure that there were no last statements from the prisoner, but the Marshal realised that his time was up. Before the junior officer could even open his mouth, Ney gave his final command: "Soldiers, fire!"

The volley crashed out, Ney staggered back slightly at the impact of the balls and then tumbled forward to lie face down in the mud, his hat rolling away to one side. There was a silence that lasted several seconds as we all stared down at the scene. The man who had cheated death so many times was finally meeting his maker. Even the crowing royalists were stunned and quiet. They knew that not one of us present could have commanded our own execution with the same calm dignity that the marshal had shown.

The escort commander, feeling that he was losing the moment, called out, "*Vive le roi!*" The answering echo, even among the supporters of the king, was at best desultory. The officer looked almost embarrassed at what he had just ordered done. He was now clearly in haste to be away from the scene. Shouting orders for the firing party and escort to form up, he looked awkwardly down at the body. It seemed that only now was he thinking of how it could be removed. I watched him glance at the carriage and dismiss the idea of propping a bleeding corpse up inside it. In the end he just gave a very Gallic shrug and left it where it lay. As they marched off, Ney's body was abandoned where it had fallen, with only a praying priest and a few gawping spectators for company.

Eventually, we had to interrupt the cleric. Someone had already tried to steal Ney's hat. Others had dipped handkerchiefs in the bloody puddles for a gory memento of the morning's work. Helped back to his feet, the clergyman sent a boy with a message for a cart to a nearby church. He assured us that the body would be treated with respect and prepared for burial. We learned that he was the Abbé de St Pierre. He had stayed in Paris throughout the Revolution, even when priests were being persecuted and killed. He had blessed those on the way to the guillotine and seen more than his fair share of death, yet even he had been impressed with the courage displayed by Ney. He told us that he had been with the marshal for his last few hours and had heard his final confession.

"I can call on his widow and assure her that he was at peace at the end, if you think that would be helpful," he offered.

"I am sure that would be welcome," I told him before exchanging a glance with de Briqueville. At that moment the 'widow' was still at the palace waiting to plead for her husband's life. Someone would have to break the news to her. At that moment a cart rumbled towards us.

"Flashman," whispered my companion. "I am not sure I could face the princess. Could you tell her, while I accompany the body to the church?" It looked like I had drawn the short straw. I nodded reluctantly in agreement, having no idea where this random choice would lead.

Chapter 2

Mercifully, someone had already broken the grim tidings by the time I reached the palace. Ney's wife was being helped into a carriage, where she wept inconsolably. Her Paris townhouse had been ransacked by a royalist mob and so we headed to the home of her sister. She insisted I recount her husband's final moments, but interrupted every sentence with a fresh howl of grief. I felt I was making the situation even worse rather than providing comfort. Back at the house, the news was broken to Ney's sons and all but the youngest took it stoically. They had seen their father for the last time the day before.

It was a miserable scene and a part of me felt guilty. I knew better than anyone how finely balanced the Waterloo campaign had been. I had some responsibility for the French defeat. Without me, Napoleon might have won and Ney would have still been alive and a foremost marshal of France once more. Of course, in that scenario, there would doubtless have been more such scenes of despair on the other side of the English Channel.

Just when I thought things could not get any worse, a Madame Lavalette arrived to share in the grief. She was even more distraught than the new widow and was soon renting her clothes and screeching in a fit of demented fury. I decided it was high time to leave and slipped out of the front door.

I could have gone back to de Briqueville, but I had no wish to linger over a corpse. I had seen enough of death that day and the morning was still young. I wanted some relief from the gloom and almost without thinking, I found myself walking up the hill towards Montmartre. Soon I was strolling along a street I had last visited six months before. It was a modest row of terraced cottages and if you have read my previous memoirs about Waterloo, you will know that in one of them I had seduced the dim-witted daughter of a courier who lived there. Meeting that pretty blonde piece again was just the sport I needed to lift me from my current melancholy. I knocked hopefully on the door and silently prayed that the father was not at home.

"Monsieur 'obhouse, you have come back!" There was still a naïve innocence in those cornflower-blue eyes. I smiled at the memory of our last meeting. Suspecting she might be tracked down by the authorities, I had told her my name was Cam Hobhouse; the real Hobhouse had been sitting in a Paris square at the time. She had clearly never discovered the truth and there was no reason to disabuse her now.

"Of course I have," I beamed at her and then leaned forward and kissed her on the lips. She jumped back in surprise and I laughed. "Come now, you were not so bashful the last time we were together."

"That…that was just to fool those men watching from across the street," she stammered.

"That might serve as an excuse for the first time," I leered, "but not the second or third. Is your father at home?"

She blushed scarlet at the memory and so she should, for once she had got into the swing of things, she had been a very enthusiastic lover. "No, he is at the market." She was already looking confused as I guided her back into the house.

"I told you before that if your father delivered my message, we would beat Napoleon and so we did." I hung my hat on a peg and turned to kiss her again, and this time she did not back away. "The king himself has asked me to pass on his appreciation," I whispered in her ear, "especially when I told him what an ardent royalist you were."

As I spoke, I reached a hand up to cup a breast and heard her gasp over my shoulder, "The king truly knows what we did?"

"He does and he is very grateful. He asked me to think of a suitable reward. Now, why don't we go upstairs and I can start to pass on his appreciation."

She pushed me away angrily, "What kind of girl do you think I am? Do you think that you can turn up on my doorstep and I will just go to bed with you?"

"Come now, we both know you are not a coy virgin. Anyway, the last time I was here you mentioned a desire to be Mrs Hobhouse. In the eyes of God, if not in the eyes of the church, we might already be married after that visit."

"Swear to me that you do not already have a wife," she demanded.

"I give you my word that there is not a Mrs Cam Hobhouse," I assured her, leading the way up the stairs.

I doubt she had been with a man since my last visit. She soon set to with enthusiasm but had the annoying habit of prattling on while engaged in the capital act. First she asked if she would get a medal, and what reward her father would receive and then she put me completely off my stroke by mentioning Fouché. His rodent-like features were the last thing I wanted to be reminded of. "That devil's men will not interrupt this time," she giggled. "The duke de Richelieu has sent him packing once and for all. He will never bother France again."

The minister for police had indeed been dismissed just before I embarked for France – to my great relief. "I heard that they shot the traitor Ney this morning," she went on and another unwelcome memory filled my mind. I could have stopped her mouth in the French manner, but instead I hauled her up horse artillery style. After that she was too busy squealing to distract me again.

I was just enjoying a post coital slumber with her finally peaceful in my arms, when we heard the door slam below. "It is Papa!" She leapt out of bed and pulled her shift on over her head. "Quickly, get up, he will want to meet you." With that she strolled to the door and called down the stairs, "Papa, I have wonderful news."

I had my trousers on before she was out of the room. Long experience had taught me that fathers do not react well when they learn strange men have been dallying with their daughters. I could not catch what the girl said, but I heard a booming voice repeat, "Married?" as I pulled my boots on. There was more female chatter as I tugged my shirt on over my head and then I heard him demand, "Are you telling me he is still here now?"

That was undoubtedly my cue to leave and I had the window open in a flash. Throwing my coat into the street, I swung a leg over the sill as I heard shoes thumping up the stairs. As I dropped down to dangle from the sill by my fingertips, I caught a glimpse of an angry bearded man entering the room and then I let myself fall into the street. There was no point in reasoned debate. I just grabbed my coat and ran off down the road as the enraged *père* leant out and demanded that I return.

As I turned the first corner I realised I had left behind my hat, but that was a small price to pay. I knew that the fellow would be after me in a moment, but I had no intention of running. I paused, put on my coat and strolled into a nearby barber's shop. The bored attendant got to his feet and I held up a ten-franc coin, worth far more than a shave. "For your silence, monsieur," I said quietly as I settled into his chair. The man grinned as he wrapped the cloth around my shoulders and then started to lather my face. I had discovered when escaping from another angry father in Portugal, that hiding served better than running. We both watched through the mirror as the old courier, red-faced and panting emerged onto the street. He looked in both directions and then charged off to the right. He did not even glance in the shop, but even if he had, I doubt he would have recognised me under the suds.

The barber chuckled a moment later as the daughter appeared, still dressed in only her shift. She looked quite fetching as she ran off after her dear papa, still shouting to him that I would marry her. I had planned to wipe the soap off, but the man was skilled and had me shaved in just over a minute.

I emerged back on the now quiet road and turned in the direction my pursuers would least expect: back down their street. When I got to the cottage, I found their front door still wide open and so reached inside to recover my hat from the peg. Then under the gaze of several curious neighbours, I strolled away.

Chapter 3

"How is the princess?" asked de Briqueville when I returned to his house. The day had taken its toll on him as he was lying on a couch, his leather cap removed and a wet cloth resting over his head wound. "You were there a long time."

"I had to check she was settled," I explained, deciding not to mention my detour to Montmartre. "She was fine until a woman called Lavalette called. A crazy old biddy who made more noise than the rest of the family put together."

"Ah, that poor woman." De Briqueville winced in pain before continuing, "Her husband is another Bonapartist sentenced to death. She blames herself for his fate."

"How is it her fault? Surely that is down to the royalists."

"You will have seen she is not young. They have a daughter who is fifteen, but she always wanted to give her husband a son to carry on his name. She was with child after Waterloo and Lavalette would not leave her or risk her health with a long journey. So he stayed in Paris, thinking he would escape prosecution. Now he is condemned and while she gave birth to a son a month ago, it died after just a few hours."

I could understand now why she was hysterical, but then I frowned. I knew the name of most senior French officers from my time spying on their war ministry, but I did not recall a Lavalette. "Where did her husband serve?" I asked.

"He was a general years ago and his wife is a niece of the Empress Josephine, but more recently he has been the minister for the postal service under the king and the emperor."

"The postal service?" I repeated. "Why on earth do the royalists want to execute a glorified postman?"

De Briqueville sighed, "Because they refuse to accept that people willingly abandoned the king and returned to Napoleon back in March. They insist that there must have been a great plot and that this was conducted through the post. I know Lavalette, I have visited him in prison. His wife is determined to save him, yet he will die like the marshal. Sadly, in his case, his death will only serve to support a royal fiction."

With an effort the colonel sat up and removed the towel. Though his skull had been cracked by a Prussian sabre and he had been suffering intense headaches, he now summoned a smile. "Come, we must get ready. We are going to the private room above the *Gilded Trotter* inn for a secret meeting of Bonapartists."

"You can go if you like. I want no part in any more conspiracies. It is time I started to think about going back home."

"But we must go, they want to hear how Ney died. Already royalists are spreading rumours that he was weeping and begging for his life."

I laughed, "No one who knows him will believe that for a second. I doubt your friends will want me there anyway. While I fought with the French in the morning at Waterloo, as you know, I was with the British in the afternoon."

"You are wrong, in fact a British general is attending the meeting and what's more, he is welcome."

"A British general?" I repeated, astonished. "If Wellington finds out, the fellow will be cashiered."

In the end I allowed myself to be persuaded to come, in part to see who this errant British officer was. We set off after dark. The *Gilded Trotter* was in a dingy part of town and as we drew close, I noticed several men with the bearing of old soldiers loitering near the entrance to the street; they were clearly there to deter any royalist agents. They nodded in greeting to de Briqueville. We climbed a wooden staircase on the outside of the building, passing two more unofficial sentries on the way and then entered a large hall. The British general was not hard to spot, even though he had his back to me. I was astonished to see that he had come in uniform. I strolled over and if his presence here had been unusual, it was nothing to his identity.

"Hello Flashman, they told me you might be coming."

I stood gaping at the fellow. If I had been asked to list the officers I would *never* expect to see at a Bonapartist meeting then General Sir Robert Wilson would be right at the top of the list. When I had served with him in Russia, he had hated Napoleon with a passion. He had even published a book slandering him. Yet now here he was with the emperor's most fervent admirers. My first thought was that he must be a royalist spy. I knew he had returned to Russia while I had been in Canada in 1812. He had been close to the tsar, had fawned over the queen of Prussia and rarely missed a chance to ingratiate himself with a royal. The new royalist chief minister, Richelieu, was also tight with the Russians. He must have persuaded Wilson into this act of lunacy.

As I recovered myself, I grabbed his arm, getting him to stand, and then guided him to a corner of the room where we could talk in private. "What the hell are you playing at?" I whispered urgently. "Don't think your uniform will save you from a knife in the ribs when they find out you are a royalist."

"But I am not a royalist," Wilson insisted, looking puzzled. "Far from it, I thought the execution of Ney was disgraceful. I wanted to thank you for trying to defend him in court."

"But you have always hated Napoleon," I hissed at him.

"So I have, but you cannot deny that he was better for France than this cabal of nobles trying to drive the country back to feudal servitude. Hundreds of men, particularly in the south, have been lynched simply for doing their duty. The allies should be ashamed of themselves for allowing it to happen."

I shook my head in bewilderment. Wilson had always been a man of extremes. There was no considered middle ground with him, he was either passionately in favour of something or vehemently against. Even so, this conversion from the man I had known in the past, made St Paul's revelation on the road to Damascus seem like dithering. But it was not all altruistic intent as I was soon to discover. "Is that why you are in Paris? To help the Bonapartists?"

He shifted uncomfortably and finally admitted, "Well I had been a military adviser for the Whigs before Waterloo. You know how Wellington hates me. Now he is triumphantly back with his Tory friends, he was bound to make my life difficult. There would certainly be no further postings, so I thought I would take some leave and come to Paris. Jem and some of the brats have come too." I knew his wife

285

Jemima was blind. He had told me in the past that they had eloped together and she had given him thirteen 'brats'. Despite the casual tone, he doted on his wife and children. I had seen him reject the enthusiastic advances of several Russian beauties while we were in St Petersburg. "When we have finished here, you must come back and meet her," he insisted. "Lord Hutchinson has regaled her with many tales of our adventures."

De Briqueville and I gave an account of Ney's death, resulting in many wails and vows of vengeance from our audience. Then I introduced my two old friends to each other, which turned out to be a mistake as they were both cavalrymen. Soon I was bored to death with comparisons of units, horse breeds and even the best kind of saddle soap.

To escape the tedium of their debate, I looked out over the rest of the gathering. My eyes were soon drawn to one of the few females in the room. I had not noticed her before, perhaps she had just arrived, but she was not short of admirers now. She wore a long peach-coloured dress and had her back to me, but was surrounded by half a dozen young blades making sure her glass was never less than half full. Just as I was settling in to enjoy the spectacle, Wilson distracted me by asking whether I would back a Polish lancer or a Cossack in a fight. "Neither would fight on their own," I reminded them. "They fight in packs and if groups of an equal size met, I would back the lancers – they have more discipline."

"I told you!" crowed de Briqueville.

When I looked back up the girl had disappeared into the crowd.

It was as we were leaving that I saw her again. I was just getting up when I heard a female voice behind me say, "Why, Colonel Moreau, what a pleasure to see you again." It was the name and rank I had been using in the French army. When I turned around, there she was. The peach gown did little to disguise her slender frame or curves, but it was her face that made me gasp in surprise. I knew it well; damn, I had tried and failed to get her into bed – twice. It was my pursuit of her that had resulted in me standing on that bloody hillside south of Waterloo.

"Pauline Leclerc, the pleasure is all mine." I glanced back into the crowd, "Is your uncle here too?"

She laughed, "I doubt Pascal here would have been quite so attentive if the fearsome Marshal Davout was glaring at him, do you?" She was undoubtedly right as the young hussar at her elbow had gone pale at the mention of the name. He had clearly not known who she was. "Thank you for what you tried to do for poor Ney," she continued and then she leaned forward to kiss me on the cheek. Deliberately pressing her breast up against my arm, she whispered in my ear, "I hope you are going to be here next week. I still have that scar to look at." At that she whirled away, grabbing the fortunate Pascal's arm and leaving me thinking that perhaps I should not rush home after all.

The next week passed slowly with a succession of depressing encounters. De Briqueville and I helped the princess arrange the marshal's funeral. We also had to help fend off a stream of visitors who were ostensibly paying their respects. In reality many barely knew Ney – one or two were even royalists. They were just looking to obtain new gossip to spread across the salons of Paris. One frequent visitor we did have to let in was Madame Lavalette, who was growing increasingly desperate as her husband's final appeal looked set to be rejected.

I began to look forward to what became regular dinners with Wilson and his wife. They were high-spirited affairs with lots of laughter, for Wilson's mood was rarely down for long. They would soon cheer me up. Then we would entertain Jemima with tales of our encounter with the mad king of Denmark, or the elderly Prussian general who had forgotten who he was fighting.

I would return to my lodgings much happier after such evenings. On impulse I had taken the same rooms that I had used for three months earlier that year. The landlord had not wanted to let them to members of the occupying forces and told me no one had been living there since my last stay. It was a comfort to have the familiar walls around me, for little else in Paris was the same. Whereas before the streets had teemed with French troops, now there were few to be seen. The city was still home to regiments of British, Prussian and Russian soldiers and the king at least was in no rush for them to return. He was relying on them for his own protection. His own army was largely banished from the city; they had risen en masse for their emperor and were not to be trusted. The only French soldiers around were the National Guard, a sort of local militia under direct control from the monarch. When de Briqueville and I strolled the streets together in uniform, they would often salute me, a British major, and ignore my companion, who was a French colonel.

The evening I was due to attend the next Bonapartist meeting I headed back to my rooms to change out of my uniform with a feeling of carefree anticipation. That all changed as I stepped on to my upper-floor landing. The room to my door was ajar and when I stepped closer, I could distinctly smell roast chicken. That brought me up sharp with a strong sense of déjà vu: the last time I had returned in those circumstances Joseph Fouché and one of his aides had been waiting for me on the other side of the door. The thought of meeting that Machiavellian devil again chilled my blood. At least this time I had a pistol in my pocket. I drew it and cocked the weapon before slowly pushing the door further open.

At first it seemed that my worst fears were confirmed, for there before me was the same smiling aide as before. And just like last time there was a half-eaten roast chicken and wine glasses on the table. Keeping the pistol levelled at my guest, I pushed the door round to reveal the end chair where the minister for police had sat before. I could not hide my relief when I saw it was empty.

"My master is not here," said my intruder, "although I am here at his request." He stood up and held out his hand in greeting, "We were not introduced before. My name is Marcel Dubois."

I ignored the hand and kept the pistol on him as I replied, "What the hell are you doing here?"

Dubois smiled and sat back down, gesturing for me to take a seat in my own apartment. I remained standing, as he continued, "My master sent me to offer you his assistance."

I laughed bitterly at that. "I have had enough of your master's assistance. It would have been more useful two weeks ago when we were trying to save Ney from the firing squad, but then it was your master who had started the purge against his old comrades. So it is timely of you to visit now when it is too late. Anyway," I added with spite, "I doubt your master could offer much help anyway, now that Richelieu has kicked him out of the country."

The servant gave a weary shrug as though he had anticipated my objections. "We both know that Ney was dead the moment he was caught. There was nothing that anyone could do to save him then. My minister knew this back in June, which is why he gave the marshal a passport in a false name and urged him to leave the country. You can

289

shake your head in disbelief, but ask the princess, she knows it is true. She was encouraging him to use it."

"Even if that is true, how far would he have got? Your master was encouraging Bonaparte to leave too on some French frigates, while at the same time telling the British exactly where to find him."

Dubois laughed. "My master's methods were well known among many. Michel Ney had known Joseph Fouché for far too long to trust him to make travel arrangements. But the marshal could easily have gone over the border into Spain on his own and from there got a ship to the new world, where his family could have followed. You know that as well as I."

I had to concede that he was right. I had been incredulous to find that Ney had tried to hide in France, and that was before I knew that he had a false passport. "So what help are you offering?" I asked at last.

"My master was not able to save the marshal, but he has saved the princess from arrest. Did you know that she offered his jailer a huge amount in gold if he could engineer Ney's escape? The man should have reported it and the princess would have joined her husband in the cells. Fortunately, the jailer is our man who only told my master, which brings me to the purpose of my visit." Dubois sipped from his wine glass and gestured to the one poured for me on the table and the rest of the roasted fowl. "Please do sit down, Colonel, I mean you no harm, quite the reverse." This time I complied, putting my weapon down, but within easy reach.

"I came to warn you that Madame Lavalette is making the same mistake. Once again the jailer is keeping her confidence. She blames herself for his capture and has even been discussing with some breaking him out by force. You must talk to her. The scheme cannot succeed and will only result in them both going to the guillotine."

"Why don't you speak to her directly? You seem to know everything that is going on."

My uninvited guest smiled and shook his head. "The Lavalettes know I work for Fouché, who they blame for their plight. She would sooner stab me as I crossed her threshold, than listen to anything I have to say. No, the warning must come from a more trusted source."

290

"But I certainly do not trust you," I countered. "You may just want Lavalette dead as he was originally condemned by your master."

Dubois did not answer at once. He sat staring down for a while at the planks of the table and then spoke quietly. "When you met the minister at this table before, you understood him a little, I think. His experiences during the Revolution taught him never to fix himself to just one faction. He cares little for ostentation or glory, but he relishes power, the ability to manage events and control his own destiny. As you know he has er…leverage on most people, but not Richelieu, who left France before his eleven years as Minister of Police began. Fouché did not expect to remain long in the service of the king, the other ministers all hated him, but Richelieu treated him with contempt." Dubois smiled again and added, "As you can imagine, that is a very dangerous thing to do. I can give you my word that my master will do nothing to strengthen Richelieu's position. Quite the reverse."

"Yet you do not want Lavalette to escape."

"On the contrary, I would be delighted if he escaped, as would Fouché. The king's ministers and the prosecution have portrayed him as the master plotter of the emperor's return. If he were able to flee justice, there would be panic in the court at more imagined intrigues. Yet for that reason I fear escape would be impossible; the royalists would be determined to recapture their prisoner. The city would be sealed, cavalry would patrol the approaches and the National Guard would search house to house until he was found." Dubois paused again as an idea occurred to him. "Mr Flashman, I did not come here tonight to help with the Lavalette escape as I still think it highly unlikely. But if by some miracle it does succeed, I will give you the address of one of the few safe places in Paris that will not be searched. I will speak to the family living there so that they are prepared. Do you have a pen and paper?" He scrawled down an address and then passed it across to me. It was an apartment on the third floor of a building on the Rue de Grenelle. "You will find a green door just inside the courtyard entrance. Use it and climb to the top of the stairs. Consider this a Christmas present from my master. I do sincerely hope that you are able to use it."

I was glad when Dubois left. The encounter had unsettled me; it had reminded me far too much of our earlier meeting including Fouché, which had left me shaking in fear. I hurriedly changed into civilian clothes and then made my way to the Bonapartist gathering.

The sentries guarding the approach nodded in recognition. Even thoughts of escapes and conspiracies could not distract me from the prospect of once again getting my lustful hands on the very willing Paulette. I pushed into the hall and saw almost immediately that I was to be thwarted again. The delectable Miss Leclerc was not surrounded by admirers this time – they would not have dared. Instead, she was hemmed in and given unwanted protection by several matronly women. At the mere sight of me, one of them stepped in front of my prey as though she expected me to ravish her niece on the spot. Then she gave her husband a piercing glare. He must have sensed it from long years of marriage and looked up to see the cause. The man did not have a military bearing. His bald head and spectacles made him look more like a clerk, yet he was the most feared soldier in the room. I knew from experience that his resolve was implacable. To his wife's obvious approval, he stepped forward and grabbed me by the arm, steering us to a corner of the room, so that we could talk in private.

"Colonel Moreau," he growled, "if indeed you are still using that name here, instead of your English one."

"Marshal Davout, it is a pleasure to see you again." I tried to smile, but charm was not going to work here. This was the only marshal who had not pledged loyalty to the king at the emperor's first abdication. He had worked me tirelessly on his staff for nearly three months and, impressed with my efforts, had hung the Legion of Honour around my neck.

"I would have had you shot if I had known you were an English spy," he announced without preamble. "Did you betray our plans to the enemy?"

"I had no chance, sir. If you recall, you only told me of them when you despatched me to escort Ney." I knew he would despise traitors and added, "The marshal knew I had English connections."

292

"Yes, he told me when I visited him in prison. I am grateful to you for coming back to defend him in court. It is more than many French officers did. You showed Bourmont's testimony to be a pack of lies and I gather from de Briqueville that you were with my friend at his end." After a moment's pause, he held out his hand and I shook it. The last time he had done that was when he had given me that small white enamel cross of the Legion. I doubted many Englishmen had earned the respect of this extraordinary man and it was something I valued.

"In the spirit of comradeship, I should warn you," he added quietly, "that my wife is now aware that Major Flashman has a wife in England. You will recall that she was not an admirer of Colonel Moreau. She now dislikes the major even more. If you persist in pursuing my niece, you may end up wishing I had shot you after all."

It took only another glance at his beloved to confirm the veracity of his words. Indeed she looked furious that her husband had not executed me on sight. She was still standing between me and her niece, beating her folded fan into the palm of her hand as though it were a cudgel that she would dearly like to use on my skull.

Reluctantly, I concluded that I was not destined to enjoy the delights of Pauline, at least that evening. I turned my attention to the rest of the room. Like a crow surrounded by lesser birds, the princess sat in her widow's black as a flock of sympathisers approached to console her and decry the injustice she had suffered. It reminded me that I had some questions of my own to ask.

Fouché had given Ney a passport in a false name, the princess conceded tearfully on the journey back to her sister's home. "I begged Michel to use it," she declared. "He swore he would, but I don't think he could bear the thought of leaving France." I did not admit that I had met Fouché's man as she still blamed the former minister for her husband's death. Instead, I claimed that I had been left an anonymous note warning that Madame Lavalette risked arrest for bribing guards and suggesting that the princess had only just escaped the same fate.

"I was desperate," she admitted. "The jailer was kind, but he refused to take my money and insisted that any escape would fail even if he did." She gave a heavy sigh and added, "I will speak to poor Emilie. Antoine would be distraught to have his wife in prison with him and they have their daughter to consider."

For the next few days Madame Lavalette placed her faith in the Duke of Ragusa, another of Napoleon's old generals, who was also known as Marshal Marmont. He had stayed loyal to the king during his emperor's return and had access to the court. He had promised to bring Madame Lavalette before her monarch so that she could appeal for his mercy on her husband's behalf. The lawyers felt sure that an act of clemency after Ney's execution would be granted. Ragusa was good to his word and delivered the tearful woman at the king's feet, but to everyone's surprise, the corpulent monarch treated her with disdain. It looked certain then that the wheels of justice would grind to their grim conclusion.

I confess that I thought the postmaster doomed when de Briqueville came to see me early one morning. "Madame de Lavalette has come up with a plan to break her husband out of prison," he whispered having checked we were alone.

I was surprised that my friend was giving the scheme any credence at all. "What on earth would she know about organising a jail break? Anyway, she has left it too late. I hear he is due to be guillotined tomorrow." I shook my head in dismay, "Some jailer will have accepted a bribe, but I promise you that nothing will come of it."

"You are wrong, Flashman. Just a trusted few are involved and it is something that only she can carry off." I have been involved in a few hairbrained enterprises in my time – virtually anything involving Cochrane for a start – the Alamo, stopping the Ashanti at Nsamankow or the bridge defence at Alcantara. Yet for ventures that put blind faith in success above every practical consideration, the escape of Lavalette was the maddest of the lot.

The whole plot was absurd. At first, I thought they were only discussing it to ease the strained wits of its creator. Emilie Lavalette was close to hysteria as she refused to accept any objection. She was due to visit her husband that evening so that they could share a final meal together before he went under the 'national razor' in the morning. Her plan was simply for her husband to leave the infamous Conciergerie prison disguised in her clothes.

Those that knew the couple tried to point out that she was taller than her husband. She had barely eaten for weeks and had lost any pregnancy weight. Her slim waist was one I doubted any man could match. She had long dark hair and her husband was bald. Their only hope would be for her husband to wear a very thick veil, but she dismissed that idea as she had not been in the habit of using such an item.

"It would raise suspicion," she announced as though a shrunken, stouter and bald version of herself would not. The deception would not fool a child, never mind a score of jailers, guards and sentries who would be on heightened alert.

"I will wear a cloak to hide my figure and a straw bonnet to cover my hair," she insisted. "Antoine can wear my gloves and hold a handkerchief to his face as though weeping."

We were at Ney's sister-in-law's house where Emilie was revealing this so-called masterpiece of cunning. The princess was looking appalled at the risk, but others, including de Briqueville were all for it. "If it fails," he whispered to me privately, "even the royalists would not punish a woman severely for trying to save her husband. But if it succeeds," he stifled a laugh, "what a victory it would be over those who persecuted the marshal."

Only one of Lavalette's old friends, a man called Baudus, tried to inject a note of reason. "Antoine would never want you to be left at the mercy of angry jailers when they discover the escape." Then he added more quietly, "How could he maintain any dignity or peace of mind at his end if you were both caught?"

I wondered if the poor devil would be dragged to the scaffold still wearing his wife's dress, for the vindictive royalists would delight in so humiliating one of their enemies. I think most of us were thinking the same, for a silence fell over the gathering as we imagined such a wretched end, but our instigator was not to be deterred.

"I discussed it with Antoine yesterday and made him promise that he will obey this final request. He will take this last chance as he knows that if he dies, I die. I will hear no more objections. I know it will succeed. I feel that God supports me."

No one could sway her after that and so discussion turned to the details. Emilie would arrive at the prison, as she usually did, in a sedan chair. Her daughter and an old maid would come with her and help shield her husband from prying eyes. If by some miracle Lavalette did get out, he would leave in the chair until he was out of sight on the street, where he would take a waiting carriage. The nurse would then take the daughter to a safe house.

The next question was where to take Lavalette. To everyone's surprise I announced I had an address. I had picked up the piece of paper that Dubois had written on when de Briqueville called at my rooms with news of the plan. "The person at this address will look after him," I announced, "and I am told that it is one of the few addresses in Paris that is not likely to be searched."

Baudus took the paper from my hand and I noticed his eyebrows rise as he read it. He was a canny devil, for he did not say the address aloud. He just tucked the note in his pocket. "Are you sure this person can be trusted?" he asked quietly.

I hesitated only a moment before categorically stating that they could. I felt confident largely because I did not think for a moment that this hare-brained caper would ever proceed far enough for the address to be used. But even if it did, strangely, I did trust Dubois on this. Yes,

I know that Fouché's name is a byword for treachery and betrayal – and by association that goes for those who work for him too. Yet having met the former minister, I thought I had an idea of what motivated him. He was loyal only to himself and was a vindictive man with no scruples. He had been humiliated by the duke de Richelieu and now he would want his revenge. The man who had started the prosecution of Lavalette would now use his escape to punish another enemy. There was a certain symmetry to the scheme that I thought would bring a smile of satisfaction to Fouché's rat-like features.

What I did not immediately appreciate as I handed over that slip of parchment, was that I was now inexorably drawn into this group of plotters. Men called Bonneville and Rouchard were deputed to carry the sedan chair. Another old family friend called Chassenon volunteered to obtain and drive the carriage that would speed Lavalette to safety, while Baudus and I would ride alongside. As provider of the safe house, it was apparent that I was expected to be there to ensure that Lavalette could gain entry. De Briqueville insisted on a role too, despite his injuries. He would enter the prison as a visitor to see Lavalette half an hour before they were to depart to check all was well. Emilie was worried that other friends might try to comfort her husband in his final hours and my old comrade was to ensure that they left with him, to give them time to effect the switch.

I'll admit that it was better thought out than I first imagined, but I was still not concerned that I would be in any danger. There was no way the guards would let a man masquerading as some pantomime dame escape their clutches. Even if the alarm was raised and a search for other conspirators made, I had a fast horse to hand; I would be away before the guards were out of the prison yard. As a last resort, I had the protection of the British embassy behind me. The French king and his officials could not afford to offend the allies that kept him safe on his throne.

So it was that a surprisingly relaxed Thomas Flashman gathered with the others that evening. Madame Lavalette, her daughter and the maid were due to visit the prison at five in the afternoon and leave at seven. She travelled most of the way in the carriage, switching to the sedan chair near the prison. We dutifully gathered around to wish her well as Bonneville and Rouchard lifted their burden and staggered off down the street. As we watched them turn into the Conciergerie yard, Baudus beside me muttered a prayer.

"A brave woman," I whispered to him, "but I doubt we will see her or her husband again tonight." He did not disagree. I looked around and added, "Well we have two hours to wait before they try to come out. I could do with a brandy to keep warm."

Along with the rest of our intrepid band, we found a small inn nearby and sat in the corner where we could not be overheard. We watched as evening light turned to a dark night and a light rain gave a sheen to the cobbles. At a quarter past six de Briqueville left us to begin his own visit to the condemned cell, while the rest of us counted down the minutes to seven. De Briqueville returned half an hour later to report that everything was set to proceed. At five to seven we rose and stepped outside. It was still raining, and the weather matched my mood. I had hoped that common sense would eventually prevail, but instead it looked as though this farce would be run to its inevitable conclusion. I imagined the scene inside the cell as Lavalette tried to fit inside his wife's dress. Would Emilie finally accept that the scheme would not work, or would they press on regardless?

I was just checking the girth on my saddle now the leather was wet when I heard de Briqueville urgently calling my name. "Moreau, come quickly." He was standing with one of the sedan chair men on the corner. I ran over to him, wondering what had gone wrong. "They are there," he whispered urgently.

I turned to Bonneville, "So go and get them," I hissed back. It was then that I realised that the other chair man was missing.

"Rouchard's nerve has failed him," explained de Briqueville. "I would go myself but my hand…" he held up his wounded arm. "You will have to go in his place."

"What?" I was aghast at the idea. "If they have been caught, this will be a trap to catch the other conspirators."

"Come on," yelled Bonneville. Grabbing my arm, he dragged me from the corner so that the courtyard of the Conciergerie was in view. I

298

looked up to see the sentry by the door look curiously in my direction. He must have heard my companion's shout. In front of the guard was the chair. I could make out a dark figure within and beside it, illuminated by two burning torches on either side of the door, was young Josephine Lavalette, holding on to her maid's hand. "Quickly," urged Bonneville and I had no choice but to comply. To back away now would only raise suspicion. "I will take the front, you take the back," my companion whispered as we splashed our way over the cobbles.

I tried to see who was inside the chair as I walked past it, but all I could make out was a dark cloak, a straw bonnet and handkerchief. Yet as I hauled up the poles, the weight of the occupant felt heavier than I would have expected from the slender Emilie. I nearly dropped one of the poles again in surprise as I realised that the condemned man might be just a yard in front of my face. I glanced at the sentry as we moved off, half expecting him to be poised to call out the guard to close off the courtyard and trap us. Instead he appeared wet and miserable, rather than tense and about to spring an ambush. If the switch had been made, I knew we only had minutes before the deception was discovered, but fortunately Bonneville was of the same mind. We set off at a brisk pace, young Josephine almost running to keep up. I still could not quite believe it had worked as we rounded the corner and almost broke into a jog towards the carriage waiting further along the boulevard. At any second I expected to hear shouts of alarm, but only the sound of our footsteps broke the silence.

As soon as the base of the chair hit the ground, its occupant was out and running for the next vehicle. From the way the figure moved it was undoubtedly a man. As soon as he was inside, the coachman whipped the horses into a trot. I was running then for my own mount held by Baudus. Swinging myself up into the saddle, we heard the first urgent clanging of bells from the prison. Steel-shod hooves and wheel rims rang out over the rough cobbles as we galloped down the road. The Conciergerie prison is on an island in the River Seine in the heart of Paris, so we had to get over one of the bridges quickly to disappear into the city. The coachman took the corner too fast and damn nearly turned the coach over as he steered it over the water. I heard its occupant yell in alarm but, then all four wheels were back on the bridge and we were on our way.

"Slow down!" called Baudus, who had ridden alongside the driver, for he was going so fast through the evening traffic that he was attracting attention. Passers-by were staring and they would no doubt remember us when the authorities came looking for witnesses. We turned into a side street and slowed to a more sedate trot. We had already decided to take a circuitous route to our destination to throw off any pursuit and search.

The prison bells were still ringing out across the city, signalling that something was amiss. Several people had stepped out of their houses to discover the cause. One even asked me as I rode past, but I merely shrugged in reply. Fortunately, the wet weather kept all but the most curious inside. We changed directions several times over the next quarter of an hour, and I had thoroughly lost my bearings when we emerged into a small quiet square. I took the opportunity to ride up to the carriage window and found a pale face in a straw bonnet staring back at me.

"Who…who are you?" asked Lavalette. He looked terrified and no wonder as a church bell had now started ringing nearby to add to the cacophony of alarm spreading across Paris.

"A friend of Marshal Ney," I told him. Then I grinned as I saw that he had only managed to pull the dress halfway up his chest, where it had become stuck. "Do you need help with that?" I asked in amusement.

"Please, I could not bear to be caught in it." Perhaps he too had imagined facing the guillotine in a frock. I dismounted and stepped up into the carriage. Normally, I have little difficulty in removing a dress, but Emilie had taken precautions to ensure the garment fitted her husband. Beneath the cloak it had been cut at the back to enable him to get in it. Then she had laced the gap tightly to ensure it stayed on. It took a couple of minutes of sawing at the strings with my fruit knife before the garment was free. As I worked, I saw that a set of men's clothes were ready on the seat, including a wide-brimmed hat.

"Where are we going?" asked Lavalette as I worked.

"We have a safe house ready for you," I assured him. Not for the first time since I had picked up that sedan chair, I wondered just how safe it really was if Fouché was involved. I had not cared when I thought the escape was doomed but now, without knowing it, all of the plotters were in the hands of their most hated enemy.

As soon as Lavalette was out of his dress, it and the bonnet were handed to me and I dropped them over a basement railing. A minute later and he looked a respectable gentleman about town sitting in his carriage on his way to the theatre. We set off once more, this time at a sedate pace, heading towards the Rue de Grenelle, Baudus and I riding along behind.

Over the next five minutes we were passed by two troops of gendarmes galloping in the opposite direction, heading towards the clarion call from the prison. At the next crossroads we found a company of National Guardsmen forming up. "They will have roadblocks soon blocking routes out of the city," warned my companion. "We are not far now; we should finish the journey through the back streets on foot."

We tied our horses to the back of the carriage and the driver, Chassenon, whispered "*Bonne chance*," to us as he led them away. As the sound of hooves receded Baudus led Lavalette and I into a rain-soaked, muddy alley. We hardly saw another living soul after that and certainly none in uniform. A couple of curtains twitched as we went past, but this was an area where people knew to mind their own business. All the same, I kept one hand on the butt of a pistol in my coat pocket. We emerged onto one of the main thoroughfares of the city and hurried across and round a corner. A few hundred yards on, Baudus came to a halt in front of a large government building and looked at me expectantly.

"Why have we stopped here?" I asked, puzzled.

"This is the Rue de Grenelle, the address you gave me. Did you not know it?" There was suspicion in his eyes now.

I took in the flag at its top and a uniformed doorman sitting in a shelter near the entrance to the courtyard. "But this looks like a government ministry," I said hesitantly.

"It is a building owned by the Ministry of Foreign Affairs," Lavalette informed me, before adding helpfully, "The duke de Richelieu's ministry."

"Who gave you this address?" added Baudus sharply.

A great many thoughts passed through my head in the next couple of seconds. I remembered Dubois boasting that the safe house would be one of the last searched. As the ministry of the kings favoured courtier and minister, he was not wrong there. Richelieu was likely to be organising the efforts to recover Lavalette. The last thing he would expect would be to find the fugitive under his own roof. But could Dubois be trusted? Perhaps he had followed his master's example and changed sides? Was I about to deliver Lavalette to a search party that had not even set out yet to find him?

After a moment's reflection, I decided that this was unlikely. Fouché had calmly told me how he had someone murdered just six months before; he would never forgive such treachery. He might be out of office, but he still had a myriad of contacts, spies and agents to do his bidding. Dubois knew better than anyone that it would be fatal to betray his master. Fouché wanted to damage Richelieu and Lavalette's escape would do that. Hiding the fugitive in his enemy's ministry was the kind of twist that I imagined would amuse the old schemer.

"I cannot tell you who gave me the address," I stated, knowing that they would both have been aghast if I had. "But I do trust him. He has his own reasons to help and the best place to hide is the last place anyone will look."

"You take him in, then," insisted Baudus grimly. "I will distract the porter."

He went across the street and started to argue with the doorman about a package he was to collect. I took a final glance up and down the street. I could see no sign of people waiting to pounce and so led Lavalette over the road too. Perhaps it was my imagination, but I could feel eyes burning into my back. Was Dubois watching our approach from a nearby window? I wondered what else his master might be plotting. Baudus had the doorman leafing through papers in his shelter, so that he did not notice us as we went through the courtyard entrance. Then to my immense relief, I saw a green door beyond the archway, just as Dubois had described. "Quickly," I whispered as I led Lavalette through it. As I had hoped there was a staircase behind it. I led the way right to the top.

We found a corridor, but it was pitch black. I was just reaching for my tinder box when a door opened ten feet away. A glow from candles inside lit the passage before the silhouette of a woman stepped into the gap. "Come this way, monsieur," she called quietly. "You will be quite safe now."

Lavalette gave a little sob of relief and then grabbed me in a tight embrace. "Thank you, my new friend. I do not even know your name, but you have done me the greatest service." He pulled himself a way and then added urgently, "If you can get word of what punishment for my escape they inflict on my poor Emilie, I would be most grateful." With that he turned and disappeared into the room, the woman closing the door behind them. I was left again in the dark with a feeling of disquiet. Getting our fly into Fouché's web had been easy enough, but just how hard would it be to get it out again?

Chapter 6

Over the next few days I spent time with Wilson, Jemima and their family as we celebrated Christmas together. While we exchanged gifts, nothing gave me greater pleasure than watching the court and its officials react to events. You cannot begin to imagine the chaos one man's escape created in Paris. To convict him, the royalists had described a vast network of Bonapartist agents plotting the emperor's return, with Lavalette at its centre. That this 'mastermind' had escaped on the eve of his execution only served to prove their propaganda. Many were convinced that another coup was imminent, which could only be stopped by recovering the prisoner.

The ambitious Duke of Richelieu took the lead. He ordered that thousands of posters with Lavalette's image and offers of reward be displayed all over the city, along with dire warning of prosecution for anyone who assisted him. For those who could not read, news sheet vendors down every boulevard yelled of the escape, as well as of the bounty and punishments. Lavalette told me later that he could hear them from his hiding place. As a result, hundreds of bald men were seized and arrested until their identities could be confirmed. All roads out of Paris were blocked and every vehicle was searched for the fugitive. Dozens of wild rumours spread across the city. Some even claimed that Ney had not been executed and a criminal shot in his place. Others insisted that the Royal Navy was sending its Mediterranean fleet to St Helena, to stop a Bonapartist flotilla determined to spring the emperor from his new home.

No one would believe it was simply the act of a desperate wife. Emilie Lavalette found herself trapped in her husband's cell, undergoing endless interrogations. The jailors, having learned from their previous mistake, did not allow any visitors, even her daughter, and so we knew very little of her fragile state of mind. Yet every day she was questioned must have brought a small smile to her lips, for it confirmed that her husband was still at large.

The Lavalette home was ransacked in a search for its owner. The Ney residence was searched again as was the one owned by the sister of the princess, where she was staying. Anyone with even the slightest association with the Bonapartists was now under suspicion. I was not surprised, then, when a few days after the escape, I found four policemen at my door. They were polite but insistent that they search my rooms as I had been a witness for the defence at Ney's trial. De Briqueville, Baudus and all the conspirators had their properties searched, but of course they found nothing.

After a week had passed with no sign of the fugitive, the authorities became even more desperate. Richelieu had vowed that Lavalette must be taken alive and that he would personally witness the treacherous villain's execution. Companies of the National Guard began street searches, going from house to house, disturbing the festive celebrations. If anything, all they succeeded in doing was generating more resentment of the royalists. Of course, government ministries were excluded from such inspections and so Lavalette was one of the few not to be disturbed.

Of the conspirators, only Baudus and I knew precisely where the wanted man was. His wife had insisted that she not be told in case she was tortured and gave her husband away. I went nowhere near the Rue de Grenelle, but after around ten days Baudus returned there. Ostensibly this was to bring Lavalette up to date on what was happening, but I suspect he wanted to see who our mysterious benefactors were. It was the family of one of the junior ministry officials who had an apartment on the top floor of the building. Heaven knew what leverage Fouché had on them, but they seemed genuinely keen to help. Like many people, they knew that the prisoner had been framed for a crime he had not committed.

Lavalette was desperate for news of his wife, insisting that he would not leave the city until he knew she was safe. Baudus wisely told him that she had been released from the Conciergerie and lodged comfortably in the apartments of the Prefect of Police; he did not think it prudent to tell the man that she was still in solitary confinement. After our early hopes that search efforts would wind down after a few days proved unfounded, attention had turned to how we could get this now notorious fugitive out of the city. He could not stay in the ministry indefinitely. He had told Baudus that the whole family he was staying with had been brought in on the secret as had some of their servants. The quiet attic room he was using was supposed to be empty, but the floorboards creaked alarmingly, so they had to be told. It was only a matter of time before some unguarded remark put him in danger.

A Bavarian regiment was due to leave the city and our first thought was that he could be disguised among their ranks, but the National Guard was far ahead of us. They warned all its officers that they faced arrest for helping Lavalette. Then at the city barrier all soldiers were forced to remove their headwear. Bald soldiers would then be sent for inspection by a jailer from the Conciergerie to check for an imposter.

Chassenon knew of a Russian general returning to St Petersburg, who, for eight thousand francs in gold was willing to conceal a man under the seat of his carriage. That is until he discovered who the stranger was and then he refused. He insisted that if the tsar learnt of his involvement, he would be sent to Siberia. At least the Russian's staff would not be humiliated with searches, however, which gave me an idea.

"I know of a British major general who might be willing to help," I told Baudus, "although his wife will probably kill me for getting him involved." I left it a couple of days to see if any other options presented themselves and then, reluctantly, went to visit my old friend. I was not concerned that he would refuse, it was exactly the madcap type of scheme that he would relish. My worry was that he would be too reckless, endangering us all. To my astonishment he told me that another Englishman in Paris, Michael Bruce, had already suggested his involvement.

"But Bruce does not have the first idea where Lavalette is," I protested in annoyance. I was irritated beyond measure that Bruce was interfering at all. He was a friend of Cam Hobhouse, and if you have read my previous memoirs that information should be damning enough. The man was an oily parasite, living off others, particularly his father, who owned a bank. The last time I had visited the princess, I had been disgusted to see that he was buttering her up like a royal crumpet. The marshal's corpse was barely cold and he was clearly trying to get his knees under the table.

"Do *you* know where Lavalette is?" asked Wilson, his eyes suddenly alive with excitement.

"Of course I do. I was one of the bloody fools who carried him from the prison in his sedan chair."

My friend laughed with delight. "My God, Flash, you are a dark horse. I had no idea you were involved."

"That was the idea," I said coolly. "But seriously, Robert, not a word to that pompous idiot Bruce and think carefully about this. The French would not dare harm a British officer, but Wellington could use this to end your career if we are caught. I do not want Jemima coming at me with her cane the next time we meet."

"Oh, I have thought about it," he assured me. "It will be revenge for Ney and if we are going to do it, we must do it properly. I will persuade the embassy to give us a genuine passport for a fictitious officer so that his papers are in order. Hutchinson will also help us."

"Hutchinson!" I repeated, appalled. "Don't tell me his lordship is in Paris. He won't help; he will have our balls on a roasting spit for getting involved." We had both served under Lord Hutchinson in Russia and were all too familiar with his scathing criticism.

"Not Lord Hutchinson, his nephew, John Hely-Hutchinson. He is a captain in the Guards here and will add to our cover. Mind you, if Lavalette is to pose as a Guards officer, he will need a properly tailored uniform to look the part. Can you get his clothes measurements?"

The next few days were filled with preparations. Wilson brazenly lied to the British ambassador about a friend in need of a passport. I visited several wig shops for the most realistic grey hairpiece I could find. Meanwhile Baudus returned to the ministry to take Lavalette's measurements. The military outfitter was less than impressed with the results. "Whoever took these is clearly not a tailor," he sniffed, but he set to work regardless and the garments were ready in a day.

On the eve of the escape, Chassenon's carriage pulled up outside the Ministry of Foreign Affairs. While the porter was called to collect his dinner, Lavalette appeared in workmen's clothes and hurried across the street. In a moment the most wanted man in Paris was out of sight and on his way to the apartment owned by Baudus. It was a risk as the rooms had been searched by the National Guard twice in the previous fortnight, but I felt happier with the fugitive away from Fouché's clutches. In any event we could not set off from the Rue de Grenelle: people were bound to notice a British colonel emerging from the attic of the foreign ministry.

The fugitive was pale and decidedly jumpy when he arrived. Wilson was there with me and, much to my annoyance, he had brought the odious Bruce with him. This louche lothario insisted on giving a grandiose speech of welcome as though he had personally organised the entire escape. Deceived by this bombast, Lavalette muttered a few words of thanks and insisted he would forever be in our debt. Then he asked for a pistol to keep on his person. Shuddering with emotion, he swore to us all that he would not allow himself to be taken alive. Determined not to incriminate us in his escape, he also could not bear the thought of returning to the Conciergerie and the gruesome death that awaited. Then, in a bitter irony, he turned to Bruce and begged him to reassure his poor Emilie should such circumstances arise. "She must be told how much I have valued the extra life she has given me, even if our endeavours fail."

Clearly the poor fool had not heard how Bruce was trying to comfort Ney's grieving spouse. The Englishman insisted he would do all in his power to give her succour, then as evidence of his devotion, announced he had to leave. "The Princess of Moscow is relying on me to help her through this evening," he intoned as though he were a surgeon caring for the grievously ill.

Maliciously, I took Bruce to one side as he was putting on his coat. "Have you heard these rumours that a convict was executed instead of Ney?" I asked quietly with a look of concern.

"Yes," he scoffed, "but they are nonsense. Do you not think the princess would know if her husband were still alive?" Anyway," he frowned, "were you not there to witness the marshal's execution?"

"I was," I confirmed trying to keep a straight face. "And that is what disquiets me. The troops kept us well back and so I am not certain, but the man they shot had the shadow of several days' beard growth, while I am certain the marshal had been clean shaven when I saw him the day before."

"Surely you are mistaken. You said yourself you could not see clearly." Bruce was not smiling now, and the first furrow of anxiety appeared on his brow.

"I am sure you are right, and he would tell his wife if he could...unless...well, the marshal is, I mean *was* of course, *very* protective of his wife. He might be trying to shield her from any conspiracy." I shrugged, "It is probably rumour as you say and with you looking after the princess, I am sure there is nothing to fear."

"Yes indeed," muttered Bruce picking up his hat. I suspected that his imagination was now filling with images of what the notoriously hot-headed marshal would do to anyone caught taking advantage of his 'grieving' widow. I held the door open for him and was satisfied that the princess would be spared his company for the next day or two.

By the time I returned to the main room, Lavalette had been persuaded to try on his new military rig. Heaven knows what measurements Baudus had taken, but the coat was cut for a lopsided hunchback.

"Well, it will not look so bad when you are sitting down in a carriage," insisted Wilson optimistically. "The buttons and other marks of rank are all correct."

Lavalette clearly did not find this reassurance of great comfort, for I noticed his hand brushed against the coat pocket that now contained his pistol.

We all left him with Baudus then, so that he could have a good night's sleep before the start of his journey the next day. His aim was to travel through Belgium and on to Bavaria, whose king would offer him refuge. Wilson was sure he would succeed and relished coming back to Paris when Lavalette was safely out of France. He was off to ensure that Hutchinson would be ready on time. I was to meet them in my British major's uniform the next morning.

When I was halfway up the stairs I saw that the door to my lodgings was ajar. I had half expected it as Dubois was bound to have heard by now that Lavalette had left the ministry. As before he was sitting at my table, but for once he had not brought me food.

"Did you think you could leave without saying goodbye?" he asked impassively.

"I have no means to contact you," I replied coolly, "although I doubt you would appreciate it if I kept turning up in your lodgings uninvited."

"How are you intending to leave the city?" Well, he was coming straight to the point and no error.

"I am not privy to the details," I insisted. "I have not asked as I do not want to be under any suspicion if the scheme miscarries."

"Really, and I thought we trusted each other." There was a mixture of disappointment and menace in his tone now, which was most disconcerting. "Did I not provide you with a refuge that has kept Lavalette safe this past two weeks? Do you think I would have done that if I planned to betray you? My master will be most disappointed at your ingratitude."

"I am certainly grateful, as is the fugitive. I am sure he will express his appreciation to your master when he is safely out of the country. But you must have known that he could not stay in the ministry indefinitely."

"Of course, but I also expected you to share with me plans for his departure. You might still need my help." Perhaps it was my imagination, but he seemed anxious as he talked. Until now he had been in control. Knowing where Lavalette was, he and his master could choose to do what they wanted. But now their bird had flown, they had no way of managing the situation.

"Well, I'm sorry, I do not know how he is leaving. Now if I—"

"Do you seriously imagine that your friend Mr Bruce is discrete?" he sneered. "Let us stop this charade. We both know that Lavalette intends to leave the city tomorrow disguised as a British officer, and that you and your friend Wilson will be travelling with him."

310

"The goddamned blabbermouth!" I fumed at Wilson for inviting that notorious gossip to the evening's gathering. It would only be a matter of time before half the city knew.

Dubois clearly agreed, "It is possible that you will get through the city checkpoints in the morning, but with the semaphore towers, the news is certain to outrun you to the border. If you want to stand any chance of reaching Belgium, you will need my help." He shrugged, "I think I have already proven my loyalty to you, but if you doubt me, you are welcome to attempt the crossing regardless."

Nothing was ever simple when Fouché and his cronies were involved, but even I had to concede that there was a cold logic to what he claimed. "So, how can we get him across?" I grudgingly asked.

Dubois gave a small smile of triumph as he sat back in his chair, "Now you are being sensible," he soothed. "Get Lavalette to take a room for the night at the largest coaching inn at Valenciennes, just before the border. One of our people will meet him the following morning with a fresh disguise. He knows the border area like the back of his hand, as well as which officials there can be bribed to look the other way. If the rest of you cross the border as planned and wait at Mons, our friend Lavalette will arrive in time to join you for lunch."

I grudgingly admitted that the idea was sensible. Even in the depths of winter, I knew that there was enough woodland around the border to provide cover to smuggle a man across. I still had a nagging worry, though; I did not like putting our fate into the hands of Fouché and his accomplices again. Yet he already knew more than enough to betray us if he chose and so reluctantly, I nodded my agreement. "I just hope your man at the border knows his business," I grumbled.

"Oh, he does," Dubois beamed. "My master has used him many times before. He will be delighted to play his part in thwarting the Duke of Richelieu's ambitions." He gave a self-satisfied little chuckle and added, "It is a shame I am so busy here. I would dearly like to ride to Mons to congratulate our former postmaster on his escape."

Chapter 7

At five to eight the next morning I rode up the street where Baudus lived. Looking up side roads and alleys, I could see no sign of National Guardsmen waiting to pounce, just a few people going to work and shops opening for the day. I found young Hutchinson by a trough watering his horse. He was as different to his uncle as night is to day. Laughing gaily, he told me how much he was looking forward to the trip and showed not the slightest sign of nerves. Of course, he had not yet met Bruce. That fool put self-aggrandisement far above any need for secrecy. All his acquaintances in town probably now believed that he alone had organised the escape. I thought we should be grateful if he did not lead a marching band down the street to see us off.

As we chatted and waited, I carefully watched the windows that overlooked us. I caught a glimpse of a grey-haired head peering down from Baudus' rooms and knew that our man was ready. I wondered if Dubois was looking too, hidden in the shadows. What would be going through that mercurial mind, or that of his master? I sensed they had been worried when Lavalette disappeared from their control. Why would that be if they were genuinely trying to help him? We were missing something, I was sure of it, but my musings were interrupted by the rattle of wheels approaching.

Wilson was sitting in an open gig with room for just him and his passenger. I cursed him silently for not bringing a closed carriage, but it was too late now. It had barely come to a halt before Lavalette appeared, looking as tense as a man striding to the scaffold. His right hand was in his coat pocket where I was sure it was gripping his pistol. Hutchinson threw up a smart salute as a captain would to a colonel in his own regiment and the Frenchman stopped in some alarm. Hesitantly, he released his weapon and returned the gesture, but not in the manner that would be used by a senior Guards officer to a subordinate. Wilson had to coach him there and then, for such an error at the checkpoint would be fatal. It was not a promising start.

In the bright morning sunshine the horses trotted on towards the city barrier on the Rue de Clichy. We had chosen this checkpoint as it was half manned by British soldiers, who would not want to see a British major general and his colonel companion delayed, not to mention a major and captain riding as escort. We were all resplendent in our red uniforms, with Wilson wearing, as usual, some of his decorations.

I had hoped that the streets would be busy with other traffic entering or leaving the city, but to my frustration the road was clear as we approached. Half a dozen bored National Guardsmen turned out of one guardhouse and I nudged my horse forward to block their view of the 'colonel'. Over their shoulders my eye was drawn to a noticeboard. There, prominently in the middle of it, was a poster featuring a drawing of the man the whole city was still searching for – now sitting just a few feet away. The presence of senior officers meant that there was a rather more active response from the second guardhouse manned by the British. Commands were shouted, a squad of soldiers appeared and within moments they were presenting arms. Wilson called out in greeting to a captain and lieutenant who were in charge, while Lavalette rather hesitantly returned their salute in the manner he had been taught. I noticed that the captain was frowning as he looked at the Frenchman, clearly wondering how there was a colonel in his regiment that he did not know. Hutchinson must have seen this too and rode forward to explain that it was an honorary colonelcy for some friend of the king. Perhaps the captain knew that Hutchinson's uncle was another favoured friend of our monarch, for the explanation served. More commands were shouted and to our immense relief, the barrier was raised.

As the gig rattled out into the countryside, I saw Lavalette shaking Wilson by the hand and patting him on the back as though the pair of them had won some great victory. There were even tears, briefly, on the Frenchman's cheeks, for he must have doubted that he would ever be free of Paris again. With a genuine British passport in his pocket, he seemed to have no concerns over the border crossing. Only I knew that the greatest challenge might still lie ahead.

We passed several gendarmes going about their business that morning, but none showed any interest in us. Lavalette took to sitting back in his seat at the sight of them and letting his chin rest on his chest, as though dozing. It hid his features, although I noticed that he still had one hand in his coat pocket. At the village of La Chappelle we changed the horse on the gig and set off for Compiègne, where Wilson had arranged for a new carriage and four horses to be waiting. It was getting dark by the time we pulled into the town. Wilson's orderly had arrived the day before to make preparations and was waiting with a lantern to take us to a secluded house on the outskirts.

A casserole of stewed fowl and potatoes appeared as did some good red wine. We were soon tucking in after a long and tiring day. There was an air of celebration around the table, but I struggled to share it. "What is the matter, Flashman?" asked Wilson. "You have had a face longer than my horse all day."

I knew he would not understand and so I turned instead to Lavalette and asked, "What would you say if you knew that the safe house you were in for the last two weeks was arranged by Fouché?"

The Frenchman was incapable of saying anything, for at the mention of the minister's name, he inhaled half a mouthful of wine in surprise and was reduced to coughing and spluttering. As Hutchinson pounded him on the back, Wilson asked, puzzled, "But didn't Fouché start the proscription of Ney, our friend here and all the other leading Bonapartists? Why on earth would he help one escape?"

"How could you trust that devil?" croaked Lavalette, recovering the power of speech.

"I had some dealings with him and his agent Dubois before," I admitted. "Dubois sounded convincing when he assured me that Fouché was willing to help as it would damage the reputation of the Duke of Richelieu. Fouché hates the duke for humiliating him when forcing him out of government."

"Perhaps this Fouché has a conscience," suggested Hutchinson, totally misjudging the man. "He might be feeling guilty now that several such as Ney have been executed and wants to even things up."

"Not a chance," I scoffed. "He is the most unscrupulous man I have ever met. But what puzzles me is why he chose Richelieu's ministry

314

for the safe house. It was not by chance. There must have been other hidden chambers across the city they could have offered."

"Fouché has only one loyalty – to himself," confirmed Lavalette. "Whatever he does it is for his benefit alone."

"But this escape will embarrass Richelieu," Wilson suggested. "Fouché will see his enemy humbled and so this will benefit him."

"No, there must be more to it than that…" I paused, remembering the look of concern on Dubois's features when he learned that Lavalette had left the ministry. Then the penny finally dropped. Now everything made sense. "By Christ!" I exclaimed, "he is not helping us at all." I turned to Lavalette, "He wants you captured and taken back to Paris alive."

"Surely not," protested Hutchinson. "Why would he allow us to get this far?"

"You must be wrong, Flashman," agreed Wilson. Only the fugitive did not seem surprised. Lavalette simply nodded as though he had expected as much since Fouché's name had been mentioned.

"If you are recaptured with the assistance of Fouché and his agents," I explained, "then it will remind the royalists of his value and influence. He will have succeeded where they have failed. But he also knows that when you are taken back to Paris, there will be an inquiry into your escape. Before you are taken to the scaffold, they will want to find out how you stayed hidden. They would stoop to torture if necessary, but Dubois would make sure that your safe house was revealed. While Richelieu boasted of turning the city upside down to find you, people would learn that you were hiding under his roof the whole time. Richelieu would become a laughing stock and his position as minister untenable. That is the kind of revenge that Fouché wants. He will not care that you go to the guillotine, only that *his* enemy is ruined."

"So what are we going to do?" asked Wilson.

"That is easy," I replied, grinning. "We are going to beat them at their own game."

We set off the next morning with Wilson and Lavalette now in the covered carriage and Hutchinson and I still riding alongside. We were bound for Valenciennes, as arranged with Dubois. Now that I had finally appreciated the scale of their scheme, I did not doubt that there would be spies monitoring our progress at every town and village we passed. Once we had left, they would head back down the road to Paris until they reached the troop of soldiers that must be following carefully in our wake. I was certain that they would wait until Valenciennes to make their move, for it was vital that they take Lavalette alive. Perhaps Bruce had told them about the pistol, or they had seen how their prey kept one hand in his coat pocket whenever strangers were nearby. They would hold back until he was at the inn that Dubois had suggested, then they would pounce when his guard was down, perhaps even when he was asleep.

We started at first light, for it was a long day's ride and fresh horses were waiting for all of us at the halfway point. Wilson had arranged these too and I wondered if our pursuers had organised remounts as well. Perhaps they would just commandeer whatever they needed in the name of the king. Two days of hard riding had left me stiff and more than a little saddle sore. It was dark when we made our penultimate stop and I could finally get some relief.

A short while later the carriage wheels finally rattled over the cobbles in Valenciennes. We found the largest inn with ease. It was in a central square illuminated by a number of burning torches. The coach came to a stop and a grey-haired British colonel got out. His travelling companions dismounted too and made a point of embracing the colonel, slapping him on the back and wishing him well. They were in no rush to depart, but eventually the colonel turned away and walked towards the inn. An observant witness might have noticed that the colonel walked slightly bowlegged as though he had spent a day in the saddle. Yet in the dim light the man would have needed the eyes of a hawk and watched us throughout the journey to see the other differences in our party.

If our descriptions had been semaphored ahead, they would still have matched. The British captain had dark hair, literally soot-black, with a matching moustache. Meanwhile the previously moustachioed Hutchinson was now wearing my uniform and was clean shaven. I watched them go and silently prayed that the next stage of our plan would work. Fouché's agents must have seen Lavalette arrive by now and so would not alert the border guards. They would be keen for the British contingent to be out of the way before an arrest was made, so as to avoid any diplomatic incident. Wilson had been sure that arrival at the border post after midnight would give the best chance of success. If, in the small hours, it happened to be well manned with alert sentries, then Hutchinson would take our French friend back out into the countryside and try to cross the border there under cover of darkness. Otherwise, they would go through as planned. Few travelled at that time of night and the officer in charge rarely rose from his bed to inspect the passport holders. He would simply have the documents brought to him and, if they were in order, they would be stamped and their owners allowed to proceed. Ominously, Lavalette assured me that if they were taken, I would hear at least one pistol fired.

Forewarned of his visitor, the hotel manager was at least out of his bed as I walked into his establishment. "You are expecting me?" I asked in French and the man nodded.

He looked nervous and his eyes darted briefly to another guest sitting in shadow. "Room six, monsieur," he muttered. Then as he handed me the key, he momentarily gripped my wrist and fixed me with what he must have hoped was a meaningful stare. His eyes flicked again to the dark corner before he added, "I hope you have a pleasant night with us, sir." Clearly not everyone here was one of Fouché's agents. Perhaps the manager was a Bonapartist who had deduced that things would not end well for his new guest.

"You are kind, sir," I replied before giving him a wink and adding, "But don't worry, I am sure I will sleep very well." I turned to go up the stairs and find my room. It overlooked the back of the building and had a small balcony that would be pleasant to sit on in the summer, facing east to meet the sunrise. I undid the door and stepped out. Anyone watching might have assumed that Lavalette was staring towards Belgium and wondering how long it would be before he was walking its streets. In reality, I was listening for any sound of a pistol shot.

317

Half an hour after my arrival the night was still silent save for the hoot of an owl and a barking fox. I breathed a sigh of relief, for one way or another, Lavalette had to be on his way to Belgium by now. All that remained was to play the game and as it was essential that the fugitive be taken alive, I knew I would be safe. I was exhausted, and so fell into bed.

After such a long ride the previous day, I would have been surprised if our pursuers were able to spring their trap before dawn. However, I awoke the next morning and stared at my watch in surprise. It was gone eight: I was astonished to be still at liberty. I hurriedly used the jakes and got dressed, checking that the pistol was still in my right-hand coat pocket. A glance out of the window showed nothing unusual and so I peered out of my room into the corridor. At the end was another window that overlooked the town square and so I cautiously approached it for another view. I was just in time to see a coach pulling up outside. It was covered in dust, but a golden livery was visible on the door. Behind it were at least a score of mounted National Guardsmen. Riding alongside the officer in charge was another familiar figure: Dubois. I shrank back from the glass and hurried back to my room, closing the door silently behind me. The show was about to begin.

My room had a dressing mirror for ladies, and I arranged it so that I could sit unseen in my chair, but still view outside through its reflection. Sure enough, I saw half a dozen of the National Guardsmen closing in on the back of the hotel to cut off any escape. Five minutes later there was a light knock at the door. "Who is it?" I called.

"It is your guide, monsieur," came a hoarse reply. "Quickly, there is not a moment to lose." I cautiously opened the door, half expecting to be pulled across the threshold and set upon there and then, but the man was alone. He was a grizzled old countryman in his fifties, who looked me clearly in the eye and urged, "We must go down the back stairs, there is a patrol of the National Guard in the square at the front." I followed as bidden. It was strangely nerve-wracking knowing that you are about to be jumped on, but not sure where. I started as a door opened, but my guide must have put this down to the anxiety of a genuine fugitive. "Do not worry, monsieur, you will soon be safe." As he spoke, he turned at the bottom of the stairs and led the way to the back of the hotel. As I followed, I looked up just in time to see the hotel manager looking aghast at me from the kitchen door. They must have been waiting in the space beneath the stairs to pounce, for suddenly a lot happened at once. To a shout of "Now!" both of my arms were grabbed and held away from my sides as I was knocked from my feet and fell to my knees. I just had a chance to glimpse my 'guide' smiling in satisfaction before a sack was pulled over my head. Then hands were rifling through my clothes until the pistol was found and removed.

"We have him!" My captors shouted in triumph as I felt myself being dragged through the hotel. I stayed silent; there was no point in protesting my innocence now as they would find out soon enough. The light through the rough hessian sack increased as I was dragged out into the morning sunshine. I felt my boots dragging over the cobbles until I was dropped unceremoniously on my knees, to shouts of delight from various unseen witnesses.

"Your grace," I heard Dubois' formally announce, "May I have the honour of re-acquainting you with Count Lavalette." He must have gestured to one of my captors to remove the sack; I felt fingers grip it, as well as the wig on my head. There was a gasp of surprise as both were removed. That tableaux of shocked faces will remain long in the memory. The duke's sneering joy turning to confusion and then anger. There was anger too in Dubois' face as he found me kneeling in the dirt before him, but then to my immense surprise he shook his head and grinned.

"Were you looking for a late Christmas present, gentlemen?" I enquired politely. "Your bird has flown and is now well out of your reach."

"Who the devil are you, sir?" demanded the duke furiously.

"I am a British officer," I replied in English. "Now are you going to release me, or is the king going to hear about one of his allies being ambushed?

The duke waved his hand to dismiss my guards. Then he turned to Fouché's man and snarled, "Two days bouncing around in that carriage for this? I should have known you could not be trusted." With that, he turned back to the vehicle and the National Guard escort began to form up around him. Only Dubois and I were left outside the hotel. He had ignored the duke's threat and was still watching me with a smile on his face. "Bravo, Monsieur Flashman, bravo. My master warned me not to underestimate you."

"Well, I should have realised what you were about sooner," I admitted. Fouché had been running treacherous rings around everyone for over a decade, as my past dealings with him had proved. Such experience should have taught me that there would be no simple act of charity from that quarter. Nodding towards the duke shouting at a footman to get his carriage door open, I added, "He has no idea how close you came to ruining him."

"He was our Christmas goose," Dubois chuckled as he stared at the nobleman. "We were looking forward to having him stuffed. The amusement left his eyes as he added coldly, "But we will get him sooner or later." His gaze turned back to me and he asked, "And am I *your* goose? You have, as you say in English, humbugged me and left me with a powerful enemy."

"Powerful but foolish," I corrected. "I have no doubt you will get him eventually." I paused, considering, "No, I don't see you as an enemy," I answered honestly. "We would not have kept Lavalette safe without your help. If I have a goose to stuff it would be that fool, Bruce."

"The...what was it you called him... blabbermouth?" He laughed, "You will have too many enemies if you hate them for being fools."

"I dislike that one for trying to seduce an old comrade's wife. Christ knows I have seduced the odd widow in my time, but I wait for their husbands to go cold first."

We parted then and I wished Dubois and his master well – whether that had any bearing on what followed I cannot say. All I know is that when the prosecutions began and Wilson and Hutchinson were hauled

320

into the dock in a Paris courtroom for high treason, it was Bruce who was standing beside them and I was not mentioned at all.

Historical notes

Flashman's account of Lavalette's escape from the Conciergerie largely matches the two detailed accounts written by others who took part. Lavalette's memoirs were published after his death, describing the conversations with his wife prior to the escape and the act itself. He also confirms that, incredibly, he was hidden away in Richelieu's ministry before he made his break from the city with Wilson's help. He even mentions incidental details, such as de Briqueville's visit on the evening of the escape, although he stops short of implicating his friend in the plot.

Robert Wilson was rather less discrete. On his return to Paris, he proudly wrote his own detailed account of his involvement in the escape and sent it to a friend in London. Unfortunately for him, the servant he trusted to deliver the letter to the embassy for onward transmission to England, was a police spy. His incriminating confession was instead delivered straight to the French authorities and he was arrested, as were Hutchinson and Bruce. Initially, they faced charges including attempting to overthrow the government. Lavalette's escape was still seen as only part of a wider Bonapartist plot to replace the king. This would have seen them face the death penalty if convicted, but after lobbying from the British government this capital charge was dropped. They were ultimately only accused of aiding in the escape of a convicted prisoner. The trial was a high-profile affair in both London and Paris. Wilson defended himself in court and claimed humanitarian motives, but all were found guilty and sentenced to the minimum of three months in prison.

Lavalette reached Bavaria where he was given sanctuary. He was allowed to return to France six years later. Unfortunately, his wife's already fragile mental state was further disturbed by her six-week spell in prison after the escape. She was committed to a sanitorium for several years but was eventually restored to her home and husband. Lavalette lived another fifteen years and died in 1830, his younger wife died in 1855.

Thank you for reading this book and I hoped you enjoyed it. If so I would be grateful for any positive reviews on websites that you use to choose books. As there is no major publisher promoting this book, any recommendations to friends and family that you think would enjoy it would also be appreciated.

There is now a Thomas Flashman Books Facebook page and the www.robertbrightwell.com website to keep you updated on future books in the series. They also include portraits, pictures and further information on characters and events featured in the books.

Flashman and the Seawolf

This first book in the Thomas
Flashman series covers his adventures
with Thomas Cochrane, one of the
most extraordinary naval commanders
of all time.

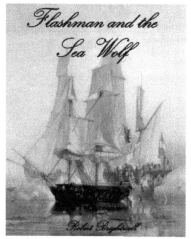

From the brothels and gambling dens
of London, through political intrigues
and espionage, the action moves to the
Mediterranean and the real life
character of Thomas Cochrane. This
book covers the start of Cochrane's career including the most
astounding single ship action of the Napoleonic war.

Thomas Flashman provides a unique insight as danger stalks him like
a persistent bailiff through a series of adventures that prove history
really is stranger than fiction.

Flashman and the Cobra

This book takes Thomas to territory familiar to readers of his nephew's adventures, India, during the second Mahratta war. It also includes an illuminating visit to Paris during the Peace of Amiens in 1802.

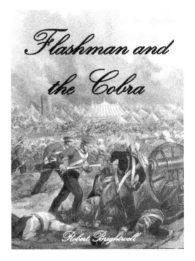

As you might expect Flashman is embroiled in treachery and scandal from the outset and, despite his very best endeavours, is often in the thick of the action. He intrigues with generals, warlords, fearless warriors, nomadic bandit tribes, highland soldiers and not least a four-foot-tall former nautch dancer, who led the only Mahratta troops to leave the battlefield of Assaye in good order.

Flashman gives an illuminating account with a unique perspective. It details feats of incredible courage (not his, obviously) reckless folly and sheer good luck that were to change the future of India and the career of a general who would later win a war in Europe.

Flashman in the Peninsula

While many people have written books and novels on the Peninsular War, Flashman's memoirs offer a unique perspective. They include new accounts of famous battles, but also incredible incidents and characters almost forgotten by history.

Flashman is revealed as the catalyst to one of the greatest royal scandals of the nineteenth century which disgraced a prince and ultimately produced one of our greatest novelists. In Spain and Portugal he witnesses catastrophic incompetence and incredible courage in equal measure. He is present at an extraordinary action where a small group of men stopped the army of a French marshal in its tracks. His flatulent horse may well have routed a Spanish regiment, while his cowardice and poltroonery certainly saved the British army from a French trap.

Accompanied by Lord Byron's dog, Flashman faces death from Polish lancers and a vengeful Spanish midget, not to mention finding time to perform a blasphemous act with the famous Maid of Zaragoza. This is an account made more astonishing as the key facts are confirmed by various historical sources.

Flashman's Escape

This book covers the second half of Thomas Flashman's experiences in the Peninsular War and follows on from *Flashman in the Peninsula*.

Having lost his role as a staff officer, Flashman finds himself commanding a company in an infantry battalion. In between cuckolding his soldiers and annoying his superiors, he finds himself at the heart of the two bloodiest actions of the war. With drama and disaster in equal measure, he provides a first-hand account of not only the horror of battle but also the bloody aftermath.

Hopes for a quieter life backfire horribly when he is sent behind enemy lines to help recover an important British prisoner, who also happens to be a hated rival. His adventures take him the length of Spain and all the way to Paris on one of the most audacious wartime journeys ever undertaken.

With the future of the French empire briefly placed in his quaking hands, Flashman dodges lovers, angry fathers, conspirators and ministers of state in a desperate effort to keep his cowardly carcass in one piece. It is a historical roller-coaster ride that brings together various extraordinary events, while also giving a disturbing insight into the creation of a French literary classic!

Flashman and Madison's War

This book finds Thomas, a British army officer, landing on the shores of the United States at the worst possible moment – just when the United States has declared war with Britain! Having already endured enough with his earlier adventures, he desperately wants to go home but finds himself drawn inexorably into this new conflict. He is soon dodging musket balls, arrows and tomahawks as he desperately tries to keep his scalp intact and on his head.

It is an extraordinary tale of an almost forgotten war, with inspiring leaders, incompetent commanders, a future American president, terrifying warriors (and their equally intimidating women), brave sailors, trigger-happy madams and a girl in a wet dress who could have brought a city to a standstill. Flashman plays a central role and reveals that he was responsible for the disgrace of one British general, the capture of another and for one of the biggest debacles in British military history.

Flashman's Waterloo

The first six months of 1815 were a pivotal time in European history. As a result, countless books have been written by men who were there and by those who studied it afterwards. But despite this wealth of material there are still many unanswered questions including:

-Why did the man who promised to bring Napoleon back in an iron cage, instead join his old commander?
-Why was Wellington so convinced that the French would not attack when they did?
-Why was the French emperor ill during the height of the battle, leaving its management to the hot-headed Marshal Ney?
-What possessed Ney to launch a huge and disastrous cavalry charge in the middle of the battle?
-Why did the British Head of Intelligence always walk with a limp after the conflict?

The answer to all these questions in full or in part can be summed up in one word: Flashman.

This extraordinary tale is aligned with other historical accounts of the Waterloo campaign and reveals how Flashman's attempt to embrace the quiet diplomatic life backfires spectacularly. The memoir provides a unique insight into how Napoleon returned to power, the treachery and intrigues around his hundred-day rule and how ultimately he was robbed of victory. It includes the return of old friends and enemies from both sides of the conflict and is a fitting climax to Thomas Flashman's Napoleonic adventures.

Flashman and the Emperor

This seventh instalment in the memoirs of the Georgian rogue Thomas Flashman reveals that, despite his suffering through the Napoleonic Wars, he did not get to enjoy a quiet retirement. Indeed, middle age finds him acting just as disgracefully as in his youth, as old friends pull him unwittingly back into the fray.

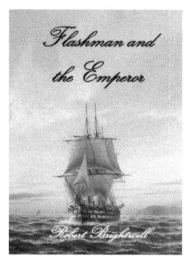

He re-joins his former comrade in arms, Thomas Cochrane, in what is intended to be a peaceful and profitable sojourn in South America. Instead, he finds himself enjoying drug-fuelled orgies in Rio, trying his hand at silver smuggling and escaping earthquakes in Chile before being reluctantly shanghaied into the Brazilian navy.

Sailing with Cochrane again, he joins the admiral in what must be one of the most extraordinary periods of his already legendary career. With a crew more interested in fighting each other than the enemy, they use Cochrane's courage, Flashman's cunning and an outrageous bluff to carve out nothing less than an empire which will stand the test of time.

Flashman and the Golden Sword

Of all the enemies that our hero has shrunk away from, there was one he feared above them all. By his own admission they gave him nightmares into his dotage. It was not the French, the Spanish, the Americans or the Mexicans. It was not even the more exotic adversaries such as the Iroquois, Mahratta or Zulus. While they could all make his guts churn anxiously, the foe that really put him off his lunch were the Ashanti.

"You could not see them coming," he complained. "They were well armed, fought with cunning and above all, there were bloody thousands of the bastards."

This eighth packet in the Thomas Flashman memoirs details his misadventures on the Gold Coast in Africa. It was a time when the British lion discovered that instead of being the king of the jungle, it was in fact a crumb on the lip of a far more ferocious beast. Our 'hero' is at the heart of this revelation after he is shipwrecked on that hostile shore. While waiting for passage home, he is soon embroiled in the plans of a naïve British governor who has hopelessly underestimated his foe. When he is not impersonating a missionary or chasing the local women, Flashman finds himself being trapped by enemy armies, risking execution and the worst kind of 'dismemberment,' not to mention escaping prisons, spies, snakes, water horses (hippopotamus) and crocodiles.

It is another rip-roaring Thomas Flashman adventure, which tells the true story of an extraordinary time in Africa that is now almost entirely forgotten.

Flashman at the Alamo

When other men might be looking forward to a well-earned retirement to enjoy their ill-gotten gains, Flashman finds himself once more facing overwhelming odds and ruthless enemies, while standing (reluctantly) shoulder to shoulder with some of America's greatest heroes.

A trip abroad to avoid a scandal at home leaves him bored and restless. They say 'the devil makes work for idle hands' and Lucifer surpassed himself this time as Thomas is persuaded to visit the newly independent country of Texas. Little does he realise that this fledgling state is about to face its biggest challenge – one that will threaten its very existence.

Flashman joins the desperate fight of a new nation against a pitiless tyrant, who gives no quarter to those who stand against him. Drunkards, hunters, farmers, lawyers, adventurers and one English coward all come together to fight and win their liberty.

Flashman and the Zulus

While many people have heard of the battle at Rorke's Drift, (featured in the film *Zulu*) and the one at Isandlwana that preceded it, few outside of South Africa know of an earlier and equally bloody conflict. Under a tyrannical king, the Zulu nation defended its territory with ruthless efficiency against white settlers. Only a naïve English vicar, with his family and some translators are permitted to live in the king's capital. It is into this cleric's household that Thomas Flashman finds himself, as a most reluctant guest.

Listening to sermons of peace and tolerance against a background of executions and slaughter, Thomas is soon fleeing for his life, barely a spearpoint ahead of regiments of fearsome warriors. He is soon to learn that there is a fate even worse than his own death. He is pitched in with Boers and British settlers as they fight a cunning and relentless foe. Thomas strives for his own salvation, before discovering that chance has not finished with him yet.